To the Sargasso Sea

A NOVEL BY

William McPherson

Simon and Schuster
NEW YORK

Published by Simon and Schuster
A Division of Simon & Schuster, Inc.
Simon & Schuster Building
Rockefeller Center
1230 Avenue of the Americas
New York, New York 10020
SIMON AND SCHUSTER and colophon are registered trademarks of Simon & Schuster, Inc.

Designed by Levavi & Levavi
Manufactured in the United States of America

10   9   8   7   6   5   4   3   2   1

Library of Congress Cataloging-in-Publication Data
McPherson, William.
To the Sargasso Sea.

I. Title.
PS3563.C395T6   1987   813'.54   86-33904
ISBN 0-671-55207-4

Grateful acknowledgment is made for permission to reprint excerpts from the following poems:

"Song for St. Cecilia's Day" by W. H. Auden.
From *W. H. AUDEN: Collected Poems*, edited by Edward Mendelson. Copyright 1945 by W. H. Auden. Reprinted by permission of Random House, Inc.
"The Love Song of J. Alfred Prufrock" by T. S. Eliot.
From "The Love Song of J. Alfred Prufrock" in *Collected Poems 1909–1962* by T. S. Eliot. Copyright 1936 by Harcourt Brace Jovanovich, Inc.; copyright © 1963, 1964 by T. S. Eliot. Reprinted by permission of the publisher.
"Me and Julio Down by the Schoolyard" by Paul Simon.
Copyright © 1971, Paul Simon. Used by permission.
"Peter Quince at the Klavier" by Wallace Stevens.
From *The Collected Poems of Wallace Stevens*. Copyright 1923 and renewed 1951 by Wallace Stevens. Reprinted by permission of Alfred A. Knopf, Inc.

This book is for
Judith Nowak

Though ye suppose all jeopardies are past,
And all is done ye looked for before,
Ware yet, I rede you, of Fortune's double cast,
For one false point she is wont to keep in store,
And under the fell oft festered is the sore:
That when ye think all danger for to pass
Ware of the lizard lieth lurking in the grass.

—John Skelton

one

Although they had been married nearly a dozen years, when Andrew and his wife went to Bermuda in early May it was almost as if they had embarked on another honeymoon—a honeymoon in Bermuda, of all places. They didn't fancy themselves the Bermuda type. For their first honeymoon, which took place in July because Andrew had refused to get married in June like everyone else, they went to a primitive camp in the north woods and on their last day there climbed the mountain that lay reflected in the lake. The Waiski Pond Camp was not exactly a popular resort, lying, as it did, beyond the end of the public road and off a former logging road that was now scarcely more than a trail through the woods. When Andrew had called to make the reservation—a difficult connection because the only line to the camp went through the fire service—and requested a cabin with a shower, there was such a long silence on the other end of the line that he thought he'd been disconnected. All he could hear was static. Finally the proprietor's voice, a rough, weathered woman's voice, came back, a little dumbfounded. "We've got two cabins with a flush," she said, "and if you want a bath you can use the lake."

They didn't get a flush, but they did bathe in the lake. It was a lovely lake—several lakes, actually, connected to one another by little waterways or easy portages, and surrounded by a seemingly endless wilderness whose trails they would sometimes follow in the mornings, before the heat of the day set in, if the spirit moved them and the flesh was satisfied. Easy with love, they explored the lakes in the afternoon, paddling wherever their fancy took them. Andrew knew he had never been so happy, so filled with pleasure, a pleasure he felt he had done nothing to deserve but which came, like God's grace, gratuitous and unearned. Each night, before falling asleep in that rustic cabin overlooking the lake, listening to the lapping of the water and, occasionally, the haunting cry of a loon, and again as the sun's warm rays broke in each morning to fall across their bed, they would tap their wedding rings together and the clicking sound they made filled them with laughter and delight. Those rings, so fresh and gleaming, were their talismans, and the tiny clicking sounds became a private signal between them. Andrew congratulated himself on their incredible good fortune in finding one another, in so utterly loving one another. He thought they were unique. If Andrew fell in love, he had no reservations. It was a dangerous business.

In the pride and ignorance of their youth, they assumed that none of the ten or so other guests at the camp, including a strangely eager, somewhat older Swedish couple, suspected they had been married just the week before. They both believed they were behaving publicly as if they'd been married for some time, two or three years, perhaps. Idly they wondered how the Swedes had ever gotten to that remote edge of the world, but they had no real interest in pursuing their story. They were engrossed in themselves, in their discovery of one another, luxuriating in the pleasure they gave and received. They saw the other guests only in the central lodge where they ate their dinners; they usually missed breakfast.

One day when they were canoeing—never having felt very confident of his athletic skills, Andrew was foolishly proud of his ability to handle a paddle—they pulled up to a tiny island, little more than a smooth granite rock washed in sunlight, with a few pines and spruce growing from its crevices, and Andrew wanted to make love right there, on that bed of pine needles, in the sunlight, on the warm rock near the slowly moving water. But Ann was nervous. Someone might see them, she said.

"Like a moose," Andrew replied, coaxing her downward.

"Like those two Swedes," she said, and refused to be coaxed.

In the midst of all that refulgent, splendid wildness, it seemed impossible to Andrew that they might be observed. To his dazzled eyes there could be no intruders. Certainly they were the only people on the lake, and there was not another camp for miles. But the matter was of no great importance; there would be days and days for love, years of sunlit afternoons.

Andrew had always wanted to make love in the sunlight, but so far he had never managed to persuade anyone else, though he almost succeeded one summer day in the midst of a tree-rimmed field buzzing with bees and scattered with daisies and brown-eyed Susans. The hollow was behind but secluded from their house in Maine, and within the muffled sound of the sea. It was another honeymoon—a renewal, maybe a reprieve—some twelve years after they'd been married and three months after their Bermuda holiday, and it seemed to Andrew as lush with love as the first, though even richer, as if their marriage had aged like a good wine that had at last reached its fullness, a fullness enhanced by the imperfections it contained. Julia, their child, was at the beach for the day, their weekend guests had left that morning, and they were alone—or so Andrew thought, until he heard voices calling their names from the terrace, the voices of the guests they had sent on their way an hour or two before.

Oddly enough, the guests were the same Swedish couple they had avoided on that first honeymoon in the north woods. Ann had met him in her work, or rather, in her search for work. She was just beginning to pursue more vigorously a career of her own, having decided not only that political campaigns didn't pay but that the results were invariably disappointing, and liberation on the larger scale, the great movements that swept their privileged world—of women, of blacks, the protests to end the endless war in Viet-Nam—were, if not a delusion, largely exercises in anger and frustration: it had been almost six years now since they'd gone to Washington on their first march, just after Thanksgiving in 1965, and little had changed but the name of the President. However, the occasional consulting she picked up as a sometimes professional fund-raiser was not enough, though she was very good at it and it had, in fact, made their life more comfortable, given it that margin of safety for which Andrew was grateful. The system would not fall—an alarming goal, in any event—but perhaps it could still be altered. She had thought about law school and rejected it, although Andrew said he'd look forward to having a lawyer in the family and her mother had agreed to pay for it. Jung? What could she do with Jung? "Dream a lot, maybe," Andrew had suggested, but she wasn't amused. She meant for money, of course. She had thought about becoming a psycho-therapist and rejected that, although she felt she had a gift for it; counseling the dying turned out to be too depressing, though she was good at that too. But peace—well, she was all for peace, of course; she'd been working toward it for some time, raising money as a volunteer, marching for McCarthy, against Johnson, against Nixon—and there was an embryonic but promising new field called conflict resolution that this man from Harvard had told her about at a dinner party in New York, and that interested her a lot. One winter day she had gone to a meeting about it, and later she'd signed up for a conference in Miami in April. "You don't mind my going, do you?" she had asked. "I mean I know it'll cost some money . . ." Of course Andrew didn't mind. He urged her to go, in fact, and wondered why she seemed to be asking his permission. It wasn't her habit to ask for things as if they were favors he might grant. Anyway, he was anxious that she should find something to interest her, where she might use her real talents, which Andrew thought lay more on the analytical side than the intuitive. Conflict resolution would probably be perfect. "You learn to separate the people from the problem," she'd said when she got back from the meeting in town. "But the people *are* the problem," Andrew said. He was confused. When she returned from Miami, she said the idea was to negotiate agree-ment without giving in. "Sounds to me like bludgeoning the op-position into submission," Andrew said, more confused. "Oh, it's not like that at all!" Ann exclaimed, exasperated, and Andrew supposed she was right, that it wasn't like that at all, that he simply wasn't hearing her. The next day she'd made another attempt to explain: "It uses a lot of the techniques of transactional analysis," she said. Andrew didn't understand that either, but it turned out that Peter, the male half of the Swedish couple, did. He, in fact, was a transactional analyst, and he had turned up at the conference in Miami where Ann had, incredibly, recognized him. "Is he still myopic?" Andrew asked. He had just opened the windows—the night was almost balmy, unusual for the last week in April—and gotten into bed. Ann was still moving about the room.

"Was he ever myopic?" she asked. "I don't remember that."

"That's about the only thing I do remember," Andrew said. "He was myopic, and you thought he'd see us making love. Maybe he's gotten contacts. How did you manage to recognize him?"

"Oh, he looked familiar, vaguely familiar, you know, in that way people have. By the way, he's not Swedish, he's Swiss." She had come around to her side of the bed and was getting in. "I knew I'd seen him someplace, and I kept wondering where. Suddenly it just came to me. At the camp in Maine. Our wedding trip. Would you pass me the hand lotion, please?"

"Yes, our wedding trip," Andrew said. It was the phrase she liked to use. "Our honeymoon. It was a nice honeymoon."

"Yes," she said, squeezing some lotion into the cup of her palm, "it was. I thought it would never end." She leaned across the space and quickly kissed him while she rubbed the lotion into her hands.

"A man is not a boy forever," Andrew replied, putting his arm around her waist and drawing her toward him. He loved the way her waist felt, slippery under the cool silk of her nightgown. "We set enough records; I had to leave the field to someone else."

"That wasn't what I meant," Ann said.

"No, it wasn't what I meant either." He kissed her again. "You always did kiss better than anyone."

"You weren't supposed to kiss anyone else."

"I know. But I didn't really. I just forgot." He felt, for a moment, the welling of sadness. "You know how it is? Sometimes you just forget?" He reached for the lamp to turn it off. "Like I forgot the Swede."

"I wish you'd stop calling him the Swede. He's Swiss. Only his wife is Swedish. She's a baroness."

"Fancy," Andrew said. "I wouldn't know him if he walked in the door."

"Well, he might," Ann said. "He's only a state away. He lives in New Jersey."

"Where?"

"Camden."

"Camden? The poor fellow. A Swedish transactional analyst in Camden! Why, for God's sake, Camden?"

"Well, I don't know," Ann replied. "Why do we live in New York? I like him. He's nice. He's a good dancer. I'm going to sleep. And he's *not* Swedish, for God's sake, he's Swiss."

"He's a good dancer? How do you know?"

"I mean we danced—at the conference." She was irritated. "One evening seven or eight of us went to Key Biscayne and we all danced and he was very good."

"When you're hot, you're hot," Andrew said. "And the countess? Is she a good dancer too?"

"Baroness. She wasn't there." Ann sounded tired.

"I hope that's all he's good at."

"Don't be disgusting," Ann said. She turned her head toward him in the dark. "I think you're jealous!"

"Why do you sound so amazed?"

"Oh, but he's not nearly so good-looking as you." Her voice had softened, and she shifted the rest of her body toward him, propping herself up with her elbow, her chin in her hand. In the dim light Andrew could see her eyes looking into his face. "Really he's not. He's not so handsome. He's not so sophisticated. He's not like you at all. And I love you." She laughed—"But he *is* a good dancer"—then she kissed him. "You don't have anything to worry about. You'll see. They may come to Maine."

"They?"

"His wife and children. I told him to drop by the house if they happened to be in the area when we were there."

That August they did happen to be in the area, and they did drop in—for a weekend. Ann had seen him again, at another conference, this one on an island not far from their house. The Swedes were agreeable enough, Andrew thought, though rather bland, and Peter still retained that eagerness to please which Andrew had somehow found both irritating and mildly pathetic on their first meeting all those years before. They had returned

for an object left behind—a toilet case or something. "Nice people don't travel in August," Andrew grumbled to his wife as they
adjusted their clothes and made their way up from the field to the
house. "They're already there." By the time the toilet case was
found and the Swedes had once again departed in their van—a
van with a large yellow sun pasted on the back bearing the in-
junction "SMILE"—the sky was overcast, and anyway the moment
for love had passed.

The MacAllisters didn't think of themselves as very conven-
tional people, though of course they were, not very different from
the lawyers and accountants and people in business they were
slightly if secretly contemptuous of—not very different, in fact,
from their own parents, whose quotidian lives had seemed on the
surface so traditional, so unlike their own. Andrew was a playwright, or tried to be. His first play had been an Off Broadway
success a decade before, and won several prizes. It was still produced occasionally at small theaters here and there. With the
early fruits of that unexpected stroke of fortune they had bought
their house near the ocean in Maine, an old house of Euclidean
proportions that made Andrew think of Montaigne and the Age
of Reason, for which he had an indefinable yearning. For a long
time he had kept a line from Montaigne on his office wall: "The
most beautiful human lives, in my opinion, are those which con-
form to the common and human model, with order, but without
miracle and without extravagant behavior." It served as a sort of
admonition, a reminder of a goal yet to be achieved, for he still
clung nervously to a secret childhood belief in the miraculous,
the salvific and the redemptive. That first play had also been
optioned for a film, and although the movie was never made, the
producer had so far kept renewing the option; it was the magical
renewal of the Hollywood money, augmented by the royalties
that continued to flow sporadically from those gratifying regional
productions of *Riverhead*, which kept them going, more or less,
not the insufficient funds his more recent plays and other pieces
of work brought in.

They lived, of course, beyond their means, in what Andrew
sometimes thought of as a forest of mahogany and walnut, the
very mahogany and walnut he and Ann had grown up with and
that had been given to them by one family member or another.

The family's generosity was tempered by the fact that their plethora of possessions proved more than they could handle, but all motives are mixed. There were times when he actually longed for plastic, for something disposable, all surface and no patina, without connections or depth. The only furnishings they had ever had to buy were a couch and two chairs because they needed something comfortable to sit on; those unyielding relics from someone else's distant past never seemed very inviting. Perhaps not so oddly, the few things they bought that they didn't actually need turned out to be much like the things they already had: a walnut desk of some vaguely identifiable period, an old rug from Turkestan, a pair of delicately painted French cache-pots that Andrew had filled with yellow tulips and given to his wife on a birthday. And they bought the mattress for the bed they slept in. The bed itself, a massive mahogany structure that looked as if it would survive the Flood and had indeed survived the lives and deaths and entanglements of several generations, had been Ann's as a girl. All this was housed in a spacious apartment that caught both the morning and the afternoon light on the top floor of a distinguished old building on the West Side of Manhattan, separated by great iron gates and a phalanx of doormen from the junkies and hookers, hustlers and shopping-bag ladies who wandered the street below. Behind their gate, behind the doormen and the elevator men, they felt very protected, secure in their domain if, sometimes, a little uneasy with it, and far indeed above the noise and confusion of the world.

It had been an article of faith in Andrew's family—and in Ann's as well—that capital did not exist to be spent. In the generations they knew, it was an article kept more in the breach than in the observance because the truth was there was not enough capital to support the style in which they found themselves living. In one way or another, all of them—the entire family—lived beyond their means. Ann's mother's trust was regularly invaded for summer and winter holidays and for gifts. Andrew's mother had sold her house in the South a couple of years after his father died; later the piece of land next to his childhood home which, to Andrew, had always seemed inseparable from it; finally the old house on Bellevue Avenue itself, the house the family had lived in since his grandparents' day. The places were too big, she'd said, and cost too much to maintain; she'd rather have the money.

She would enjoy living in an apartment, and somehow she managed to keep two of them, one in the North and one in the South. When Andrew thought about it, he admired her ability—was rather awed by it, really—not to walk away from the past or to wallow in it but to move on from it, with enthusiasm, even. When his father had died he supposed she'd thought her income would be comfortable enough—certainly everyone believed his father had had plenty of money, and probably most people in Grande Rivière still did; they would never have known otherwise from her—but when that turned out not to be the case, well, she would do what she had to do. If that meant selling the house, then she would sell the house. If that meant cashing a certificate of deposit, she would cash it. Even before her sister Clara died and her income was suddenly, fortuitously augmented, she would, if he needed it, cash one in order to lend Andrew money, to provide some means to maintain his own fragile shelter. She was more generous than he sometimes gave her credit for. Only his father's shares in the bank on whose board he had served and in the company to which he had devoted his life were sacred, despite the miserable return they provided on the capital. Somehow the prospectors Andrew's father had supported, those grizzled men with knapsacks and Geiger counters who went off into Canada for months at a time and whose discoveries were to make them all rich, never did strike a lode, except at his father's door. And his brother John? John was dead, and his widow lived in Key West on genteel dreams and whatever blend the liquor store was selling cheapest that week. His brother David? . . . well, it was all the same story. He could call it "Capital Losses," Andrew thought, or "Something Squandered, Nothing Gained." His own, very small inheritance—courtesy of a long-dead grandmother whom he always remembered wearing lavender and pearls and carrying a cane—was long since gone, and so was Ann's, most of hers dissipated in Andrew's vain attempts to master the financial markets, having concluded as a young husband and putative provider that a man's appropriate role was to handle abstractions, to learn the secrets of money and numbers, a role to which he was singularly ill suited. Figures never seemed real to him until they became negative, which was why his own inheritance was gone. They were a little more concrete to Ann, who had pointed out one day not long after they were married that they would soon be penniless unless he stopped placing his bets on the fluctuations of the market and turned to something he could understand. Though he was sure it was a bad time to sell, he did, and they put the last of the money into the apartment in New York and Andrew transferred his energies into his real work, the germ of *Riverhead* he was struggling to realize in the quiet hours of the night or morning. Both decisions proved sensible.

Those properties—the apartment in New York, the house in Maine—turned out to be felicitous investments. They were tangible and real and, in fact, the only investments they had—that and the furniture, oppressive in its weight, which Andrew sometimes thought was why they had had to buy the properties in the first place. Although it was not particularly distinguished furniture—Parke-Bernet would have referred them elsewhere—it seemed impossible for Andrew to part with. It came, after all, with the family, and gained its value for that reason.

two

Like any other marriage, the MacAllisters' had had its lean years and its fat, but it seemed capable of recurring refreshment, a spring that sometimes trickled and sometimes gushed but that had thus far proved inexhaustible. It seemed to Andrew at least as good as any other marriage he knew of, and better than most. They were, he always thought, each other's best friend, and the friendship was important. They had a lovely child, a child they both took great delight in; they were certainly not rich though not poor either; and they often had a lot of fun together. As a promising young playwright—though having just turned forty he was no longer exactly young, and he was beginning to feel perennially promising—Andrew had recently gotten a Rockefeller grant, which was very generous and came with a certain amount for expenses. It made it seem, for a time, as if there were more capital to draw on than there in fact was.

With the help of the grant, the three of them—Andrew, Ann, and Julia—had gone to England in March on a combination holiday and business trip, where they behaved like any other tourists, or almost. Ann had the conference in Miami scheduled on their return, and Andrew was going to Minneapolis because the Guthrie was interested in his newest play. They were expecting a visit from his mother afterward; then he and Ann were flying to Bermuda for a few days—Sam Walcott, the producer, had invited them. Sam wanted to discuss Andrew's career, the career he was struggling for, a career which seemed as if it might again be about to take off. The play, still in previews, was being produced in London, with the hope that it would go to New York later. He was not yet the toast of the West End that in his greedier, more devious moments he would rather have liked to be, but at least the play was being staged—at the Royal Court, in Chelsea —and he was continuing to work on it. Michael Aldrich, his director and friend from childhood, was hopeful. It had also gotten him onto the "People" page of *The Sunday Times*, and that notice had gotten them an invitation to a house on a fashionable square for lunch with a countess, who remembered she'd once met him in New York. The note inviting him—and reminding him of their earlier meeting—was written in a stylish hand on blue-bordered notepaper engraved with a heraldic lozenge. It had not arrived through the ordinary mail but was dropped at the theater—by a servant, Andrew imagined, and the idea appealed to him. Very fancy, he thought, feeling the paper; very swell. Though his memory of her was dim at best, the prospect of lunch with a countess piqued his curiosity and seized his daughter's imagination as well, even though Ann believed and Andrew soon realized that the title the countess had acquired concealed a less-than-subtle opportunist who thought, mistakenly, that his connections in the States would be useful to her.

"My dears," she trilled when the three of them were shown into her drawing room, "it's the next generation's Tennessee Williams!" Andrew thought they must have heard her on the square.

"Don't be ridiculous," he replied, a little more brusquely than he'd intended. "There's no connection between us."

"That's what it said in our own *Sunday Times*, young man," she said, introducing them to the group. "I read it myself! I'm sure all of you've seen it." She picked up the paper which had been opened to the page and waved it about. There was a general murmur of assent.

"You'd think, Lady Rysdale, that he'd be flattered," Ann said, laughing, trying to redeem him. "Instead, it seems to annoy him." Andrew knew who was annoyed. "I don't think he sees much connection in the subject matter." She laughed again, a little apologetically.

"Well"—Andrew laughed, trying to explain, beginning to recover, to make some kind of amends for his rudeness—"the column said 'arguably,' and I guess I'd argue with it, though of course I'm flattered—ridiculously flattered. It would be nice if it were true," he said, managing a smile. "In the sense of accomplishment, of course. But that's preposterous." He couldn't seem to end it, and he didn't mean any of it. Mercifully, the countess's son Patrick broke into his stammering to ask what he'd like to drink, and her attention was momentarily diverted.

"What a charming little girl," she said to Julia, patting her on the shoulder. "Are you enjoying London? Have you seen the jewels in the Tower? How old are you, my dear?"

"She's eight," Andrew replied for her, instantly wishing that he hadn't.

"Eight and a half, Daddy," Julia said. And then she repeated to the countess, "I'm eight and a half." Andrew could see she was struggling to get her tongue around the title, but gave up.

"You must coax your father into taking you to the Ritz for tea. All the young débutantes go there. Such pretty frocks!" She laughed gaily, without waiting for a response. "I'm so pleased, Mr. MacAllister, that you asked if Julia could come. It's wonderfully American," she said to the group, "to include the children." The butler brought Andrew a whisky. Someone, maybe Patrick, had even seen that there was ice in it. Andrew took it with relief and turned his attention to his hostess, making at last an attempt to be a proper guest, to be civilized, to charm. He soon found himself genuinely interested in her; he almost always did, in the most unlikely people, even hustlers like Lady Rysdale.

The countess gave lectures on gardens, as it turned out, to rich American ladies, or on India under the Raj, where she had spent her childhood. In fact, she would talk about anything, if there was money involved. She would even talk about Andrew's play, for a couple of tickets in the stalls on opening night. The only thing she wouldn't talk about was her husband, and lunch congealed quickly when Ann, over the pudding, asked about the earl—who had been involved, Andrew suddenly, sickeningly re-called, just as he now recalled the circumstances of their earlier meeting, in one of those squalid English affairs that the Lords do so well: weekends in the country with girls, and boys, and toys of a sort not found in the ordinary nursery. When the scandal broke, its increasingly lurid and titillating details had filled the London tabloids for weeks, and the earl had taken a very long holiday which hadn't yet ended, though it had all happened a couple of years before. Patrick, an amiable type who also had some deal cooking in New York, or wanted to, said quite cheer-fully, "Oh, we haven't seen Dad for a bit, you know?" and the titled Cotswold nitwits who'd spent most of the lunch talking about horses and dogs and related country matters suddenly began talking louder—about the quality of oats, it seemed, and feed; at any moment the condition of their manure pile, Andrew expected. The other guest, an aging Anglo-Irish spinster with a wacky kind of charm, began talking at the same time about her niece's fortunate marriage to a rich New Yorker, and very soon they were all at the door, all of them still mindlessly chattering at once.

"For Christ's sake," Andrew said when they'd left, "how could you bring him up? Didn't you know they had a picture of him, bare-assed in the grass, with two hookers and a boy in drag, or what was left of it?"

"How would I know that?" Ann asked. "I don't see the En-glish papers." She was annoyed.

"It was in *The New York Times*," Andrew replied dryly. He was annoyed too.

"Not the picture, surely."

"Just the description, my dear. Very prim, very proper, very *New York Times*."

"I thought they were a nice Catholic family," Ann said.

"They are," Andrew said. "One of England's oldest, if no longer stateliest. But who's perfect?"

"We're a Catholic family," Julia said brightly, pleased with her observation.

"Daddy's not," Ann said, and then to Andrew she said, "Well, I think it's disgusting."

"It was. It's too early for a drink, though God knows I could use one. Let's take a look at the British Museum." They hailed a cab and went to the museum, where they spent an hour or two looking around, mostly at the Elgin Marbles, pausing at the Rosetta Stone which Andrew tried to explain, and buying postcards in the shop. Afterward Julia asked if they could please have tea —she loved the English tea, all those pastries and Devonshire cream: her favorite meal—and they got another cab and went to the Ritz. It seemed an agreeable thing to do, the sort of thing any tourist might do. Andrew wished the countess hadn't suggested it; he'd wanted it to be his own idea.

The Palm Court was filled with pink: pink cloths on the tables, pink shades on the lamps—the color of old ladies' underwear, like his grandmother's, Andrew thought, and the thought made him smile—festoons of pink roses borne by pink cherubs, a pink Pan piping in the niche; even the people looked pink. And yes, there were the countess's pink débutantes, expensively dressed and chirping away like well-bred ninnies. By the time they'd gotten settled it was five o'clock and the British were once again serving liquor, which seemed to Andrew and Ann a little more appealing at that moment than tea. They had a drink, and then another, and after a time they began to laugh about the whole matter of Ann's gaffe at lunch and of the countess's arch surprise.

"What's so funny?" Julia asked. "Why is it so funny that the countess's husband got his picture in the paper?"

"Because he's a funny-looking man," Andrew said. "He's got this weird wart on his nose, and besides they caught him by surprise and he didn't like it. Now tell me three things you saw at the museum today. I'll bet you thought the Elgin Marbles were something you play with in the park."

"They didn't have any clothes on," Julia said.

"Who didn't?" Andrew asked, startled.

"Those men in the Elgin Marbles. Why are they all naked?"

"Because it's hot in the museum," Ann said.

"It looks funny," Julia said.

"So did the earl," Ann muttered out of the side of her mouth.

"I think we might switch to tea." Andrew beckoned the waiter, then turned to Julia. "Because it's warm in Greece, I guess, and when the Greeks made statues they liked to make them naked. They believed in the beauty of the human body—"

"I won't mention him again," Ann said.

"—and the human mind, too."

"I think he was more interested in bodies," Ann said. "Oops! Sorry."

"They believed in perfection of form," Andrew continued, his gaze drifting slowly off into the rosy distance of the Palm Court, "in the idea of beauty, the existence somewhere of perfection and truth." He paused. "In their sculpture the Greeks brought the two together, or tried to—naturalism and ideal form." He turned back to Julia. "Does that make sense to you?" he asked.

"I think so, Daddy," Julia said.

"I was afraid we'd lost you," Ann said.

"They were idealists, the Greeks," Andrew said, reluctant to break his spell, "and those magnificent figures embodied their ideals."

"Well, it sounds good," Ann said, finishing her drink. "Whether it makes any sense or not is the question."

"It was a thought, anyway," Andrew said. "Let's talk about the Rosetta Stone. Annie, you're not drinking your tea. And you're not eating your sandwiches like a good mommy. Good mommies always drink their tea and eat their sandwiches, just like good little girls—right, Julie?"

Julia giggled, and the subject was changed. They turned their attention not to the Rosetta Stone but to the chicken sandwiches and the pastry cart. It cost something to change it, though; tea at the Ritz was lavish but expensive. "But worth every penny—I mean pound," Andrew said. "Maybe the Rockefellers will pick up the tab."

"That's all right, Daddy," Julia said. "You're going to be famous. Isn't he, Mommy?"

Andrew leaned over and kissed her on her silky head so she would not see the tears that suddenly filled his eyes. His darling, his only child, could display a touchingly protective pride in him, a pride so freely given, so ingenuous and innocent, and so vulnerable, that it did sometimes bring tears to his eyes, tears of love and pity that the world and its attendant sorrows must someday leave her bereft, and free of innocence and illusion, the innocence and illusion that as a playwright were his stock in trade.

Instead of going to the theater the next morning, Andrew went back to the museum, alone. He wanted to see the Parthenon sculptures again: that mighty horse sinking exhausted—terrified? he wondered—into the sea after his daylong flight across the sky, the figure of Dionysus, of the headless river god, of the woman rushing from the startling, unseen scene, and that whole marvelous procession on the frieze sweating and heaving toward the indifferent gods. It never failed to give him a little thrill, and he never quite knew why it stirred him so. The Rosetta Stone always took him by surprise too, when he came upon it, and gave him a small shock—but of a different kind. He supposed that that broken chunk of basalt so otherwise unprepossessing moved him for what it signified, not for how it looked. Egypt had fascinated him since he'd been nine or ten, and the Rosetta Stone, which he'd imagined as something quite different from—and surely more grand than—that ordinary slab in the British Museum, contained the key to the ancient secrets of the hieroglyphs that no one had been able to know before because no one could read the priestly language. Now people could. He imagined a man or two or three, bent over desks in dry and dusty cubicles, laboring for years to break the code. Scholarship, Andrew thought, was a magnificent and scrupulous endeavor, done in the dark, but the musty secrets it usually bared, like most secrets, didn't turn out to be shattering. No one could know that, of course, until the secrets were revealed. Andrew couldn't even remember what they were—recipes for preserving the dead, probably, and seven ways to wrap a mummy, along with the usual heroic deeds and arcane lore of the birdlike gods and the ancient godlike kings; strange how they always seemed to him to suggest birds or snakes. It was altogether possible, Andrew thought, even likely, that he'd never known those Egyptian secrets.

The marbles moved him in another way: for what they were. "Well, that's art," as Michael Aldrich would have said, with a kind of insouciant shrug. Andrew wondered if that was the essential difference between science and art, that science unlocked the truth from without—forged the key to a lost culture, for example—and art probed the truth from within. Description versus depiction. Eventually they both arrived at the same slippery point, the sought-after, longed-for microsecond of clarity, of revelation—if the synapses worked. Everything was an incredible vast

Möbius strip, Andrew thought, with some dismay: science was art; art, science. . . . It didn't have the ring of Keats: Andrew wasn't confident his synapses were working. But when the hieroglyphs were finally translated, there was still the mystery at the core. Science was not really a question of truth at all but of belief—a highly convincing, functional belief but belief nonetheless, belief and the acceptance of it, which had to be critical. You believed in that system, maybe just believed that system, accepted it the way Catholics accepted the Pope, or used to, the way people now accepted Freud, or were supposed to. Without thought or question. Total submission to the master of your choice, to the rule, as the Jesuits used to say, to the discipline. Dire mastery. Andrew began to feel for the first time that the Marquis de Sade might have been on to something. The art— science?—of bondage and discipline. But Freud, what was he on to? Was he a scientist or an artist?—or simply a nut like that analyst Andrew had gone to for a time, when Ann had issued an ultimatum that she would leave him if he didn't get his head fixed, and sounded as if she'd meant it, too. So Andrew had found Dr. Karnov who, when Andrew had told him at the last possible moment—it was being announced later that day—that he was about to win a prize for his first play, blurted out, "You *what?*" Dr. Karnov couldn't have sounded any more surprised, Andrew thought, than if he'd just told him he'd open his newspaper the next morning and read that he'd hacked up his wife and child and put the pieces in the mail to him, C.O.D. He didn't want a psychiatrist who sounded *that* surprised when somebody said something he'd done was good. It was all right if Andrew was surprised, but he'd rather wanted his psychiatrist to be pleased. Shortly after that he'd ended his sessions with Dr. Karnov, whom Ann had taken to calling Dr. Rip-off, but he continued to wonder about Dr. Freud and his system.

Andrew could get quite involved in such ruminations, and he never seemed to get anywhere with them. He didn't think he knew enough, and yet sometimes he was afraid to know too much. Now why did he think that? he wondered, checking his watch: a person could never know too much. He was having lunch with his London agent, and he didn't want to be late. He wanted to impress her, though he knew that however much agents may like you, may encourage you, may even flatter you outrageously, what really impressed them was the bottom line. He'd have to try to convince her he was trying to do something about that, writing a new play about sex, violence, money, power, beauty, fame—all the old familiar tunes: the tunes, in fact, he'd always played but that no one seemed to recognize. Well, he wanted to do more than elicit a response in the gonads. Dimly, in the distance, he heard the clicking of heels moving across the gallery. Yes, he thought, looking at the heifer in the frieze trying to break away from the procession, and the upturned face of the heifer next to it—such an innocent, sweet, dumb bovine face, forever on its way to the sacrifice. It made him want to laugh or cry, he wasn't sure which. The clicking grew louder, sounded purposeful.

"Tommy MacAllister, I'd recognize you anywhere." The voice was coming from behind him, echoing in the great hall. He recognized it immediately. It was funny about voices, Andrew thought, how they stayed in the mind. He could hear his brother John's voice as clearly as if he'd heard it yesterday, even though his brother John had been dead for a decade. He could hear him speaking on the telephone, and then he began to see him, and he didn't like that, how frail and sick he looked at the end. "I love you, Johnny," Andrew had said then, his very last words to him as he went out the door back there in that terrible Chicago suburb. Stop the movie, Andrew thought, *ordered*, but the movie only switched reels. He could hear his father's voice, though his father was dead too. He could hear it clearly, and see his face. Even his grandmother's voice, and she had died when he was a little boy. He could hear her singing, "*Let me call you sweetheart, I'm in love with you*," and he could smell her powdery smell. The sounds and smells and taste of the past came flowing back to him strong as a river, catching him up, tumbling him in the current and sweeping him along with its force. Sometimes, Andrew thought, he could re-create every last detail of his entire life, if he concentrated on it, and the thought irritated him. Why couldn't he forget things, the way everyone else did? Why did he have not just to remember but to *see* where the lamp stood on the desk in New York right now and where the desk stood on the floor just so between the windows, and where the shade, the silk shade they'd had made by an old Chinese woman when Julia was a baby, where that shade was now frayed; and where that same lamp had stood on a different table in Grande Rivière that day when he was nine or ten when he'd knocked it to the floor but failed to break it. He could furnish every place he'd ever lived, if he tried, and probably remember every telephone number, too. And so he recognized the voice of Daisy Meyer before he'd even turned to see who was calling to him.

Daisy Meyer. When had he last seen her? Not in years and years. Actually, Andrew realized at once, it hadn't been any-where near that long; he'd seen her in New York a couple of years before. It must have been 1969. That was when he'd met the countess, at a cocktail party at the height of her travails, which everyone naturally chose to overlook. Lady Rysdale was chatter-ing on about the gardens at Sissinghurst and some amiable dunce, an American in a Guards mustache, had asked her how they compared with Camden Court's, where the earl had recently and, as it happened, so publicly disported. "A lovely garden," she'd said with what Andrew thought was considerable aplomb under the circumstances; "lovely—in the Italian style, of course," and she'd passed smoothly on to another house, another garden. A couple of years before that, when he'd gone to Washington for the march against the Pentagon and stayed over a few days to do some business with Arena Stage, Mrs. Steer had taken him to Daisy's house—a beautiful, deceptively simple house, full of flowers and light and the blue-and-white Canton ware from her husband's family—and that must have been the first time he'd seen her since he'd been a little boy in Grande Rivière, which was how he'd always remembered her. Daisy had said the same thing then, both times, using his boyhood name: "Tommy MacAllister, I'd recognize you anywhere." Andrew turned to-ward her.

"Even," she added, "if I hadn't just seen your picture here in *The Sunday Times*."

"Well, Daisy," Andrew said, "I'd recognize you anywhere too. Daisy Addington. Daisy Meyer."

"Curtis," she said. "Daisy Curtis."

"Yes, Curtis," Andrew said. "I know. It's been Curtis for years. But it was Daisy Meyer then, the woman on the golf course." He laughed. No matter how many times he had seen her since, that was his vision of her: in a white dress in her backswing, teeing off for the short sixth hole at the country club in Grande Rivière, across the river from the Island where they'd all summered. He'd been eight that summer. It was the summer of his golf lessons. Although she had seemed old to him then, an old married lady and very grown-up, and all married ladies were old to him at eight, Andrew guessed that she couldn't have been more than twenty-three, maybe even twenty-two, scarcely more than a girl, scarcely older than his brother John. A very long time ago, several wars away. He remembered how beautiful and cool and elegant she had looked. "Our Lady of the Fairways. The most beautiful woman in the club," he said. "And still the most beautiful woman in the room." Thirty years and more after that summer she seemed scarcely different from the way he remembered her—the yellow hair, the bright and lively face, the laughter— except that his memory always included sunlight and the white dress, and now she was wearing black and the sun did not light this room. She looked terrific, though. In contrast to the pallor of most Londoners in April, her skin was lightly tanned, and in her stylish black suit and pearls, with her yellow hair and glowing, smiling face, she stood out triumphant against the glorious, ancient marbles like some living figure in a Greek drama. She looks great, Andrew thought, and she knows it: a real actress even if she's never set foot on stage.

"But Tommy, I no longer play golf," she said.

"Yes, Daisy," he repeated, lost in his memory. "I'd recognize you anywhere."

"A kiss, Tommy, a kiss." She offered a cheek.

"You took me by surprise. I'm forgetting myself," and he took her hands in his and kissed her, first on one cheek, then the other, in the Continental manner. Sometimes he surprised himself: how grown-up and civilized he could act. Suddenly he looked at her again. "You no longer play golf?"

"Not since I left Grande Rivière. I moved on to other things."

"To London? What are you doing in London? Where are you staying?"

"With the Huntingtons," she said. "He used to be the Number Two at the embassy in Paris years ago when Curtis and I were there. Now they've retired to Cheyne Walk. It beats a bed-and-breakfast spot in Soho, I can tell you, and they're very generous hosts. Really, it's *quite* grand, considerably more sumptuous than I'm used to. And now that you know where to find me, let's leave dear Lord Elgin's marbles and have lunch."

"I'd love to," Andrew said, and then, suddenly remembering, "Oh, but I'm supposed to be having lunch with Pamela Stickney. She's my agent," he explained. He was dismayed. "Wait. Let me call her. I can talk to her about sex and violence and how they will enhance my new career anytime." He laughed. "I'd much rather have lunch with you."

"To talk about sex and violence?" Daisy asked, her laughter ricocheting in the silent hall.

"Who, me? With a lady?" Andrew asked, playing along. "Well, it's a thought," he said, wondering if he was feeling up to this level of smart conversation, this sophisticated banter. "One of the perennial themes, really, and my agent's very favorite."

"Isn't Pamela Stickney a lady?"

"That's a matter of debate. She's a female. But let's talk about you. I want to know"—he looked at her and laughed—"what happened to your golf game. Really, it's lovely to see you. It makes me feel wildly cosmopolitan, running into someone I know —someone as glamourous as you, someone from Grande Rivière, yet!—in the British Museum. The room must be seething with jealousy. But wait. Let me just find a telephone for a word with Pamela."

In a few minutes they were in a taxi on their way to the Ritz, where they sat down to lunch in the room overlooking Green Park.

"Well, now, tell me about yourself, Tommy. I want to know *everything*," Daisy said.

He laughed. "Only if you'll call me Andrew. I don't go by Tommy anymore." He was looking about the room. "This is rather splendid."

"I know you don't, but I forgot. It's hard for me to think of you as anything but Tommy—and yes, isn't it a beautiful room? I wanted to come here for the view, which beats the food by a long shot. You've never seen it?"

"No, not this room."

"I'm glad. I like introducing people to new experiences."

"But I'm becoming a regular at the Ritz," Andrew said. "Ann

and Julie and I had tea in the Palm Court yesterday. You know," he said, laughter in his voice, "the last time we had lunch—the *only* time we've had lunch—was one day at the country club in Grande Rivière. I'll bet I can tell you what I ate, too—a grilled cheese sandwich with sweet pickles and a root beer float. Guess what? I don't think I'll have the same thing today." He picked up the wine list. "Would you prefer a red wine or a white?"

"How on earth do you remember that?"

"Because I'd never had lunch with you before. Just admired you from afar, I guess. So it was a special occasion. And to tell you the truth, that's what I almost always had for lunch then. Besides, it was the day I dropped the cat in Mrs. Appleton's lap, and I couldn't forget that. My mother was really mad—furious. Even more furious when I refused to apologize. But then she made me, so I did. But you know something? I didn't mean a word of it." Andrew laughed.

"That woman was an unreconstructed bitch. A true bitch. If they'd had a dog show at the country club, Frances Appleton would have won worst-of-breed. I don't know how George survived her."

"George?"

"Her husband. He married my mother, you know, after Frances died. God knows, he was entitled to a little happiness after all those years in Purgatory." She looked at the table. "I do remember now," she said, idly toying with her knife on the cloth. "I remember that day—the day of the cat." Suddenly she laughed. "I loved it. I thought it was hilarious. And I'm sure your mother was furious. How is your mother, by the way?"

"Bob Griswold was there, too," Andrew said. "You didn't tell me whether you'd like red wine or white."

"Red, I think. Somehow I almost always prefer red." Andrew found what he hoped would be a suitable wine—something with a little distinction but nothing ostentatious—and the steward took his order without apparent disdain. "Now about your mother? She was very glamourous, you know."

"Oh, she's fine; coming to New York the end of next month. She's in Sarasota now, just back from Hawaii. Or maybe she's still there. I can't keep up with her schedule. My Aunt Elizabeth says it exhausts her just reading about it. They write letters all the time, back and forth with all the news. You know: 'Today

I'm having two foursomes for lunch, and this evening I'm going to dinner at the Tolsons'. I'm reading *Buddenbrooks*, awfully long but very good. Yesterday Ella and I went to the Playhouse to see *The Bad Seed*—a terrible story, I didn't like it much, but it's nice to support the theater—and tomorrow a few of us are driving down to Fort Myers for the day and maybe to Sanibel. Ruth wants to go shelling there. . . .' You get the idea," he said. "Her sister Clara died a year ago." Daisy murmured sympathetically. "She'll outlive them all, I know. The fact is, she's amazing. She's given up golf, but other than that she's probably much the same as you remember her."

"Given up golf? I can't imagine her doing that."

"You did. I can't imagine that." He paused. "Well, she was in an auto accident a few years ago and broke her shoulder. She's fine now, just can't swing a club the way she used to. So she stopped. Restricts herself to push-ups."

Daisy laughed.

"You think I'm kidding? You should hear her exercise routine. She may be seventy-eight this summer, but nobody would guess it." He paused. "You know, I remember that day we had lunch, very clearly. I was really thrilled to have lunch with you. I didn't like it when Bob Griswold showed up. I wanted you all to myself."

"And here I am," Daisy said, "a few years later, but here nonetheless. And of course, all to yourself. Hard to believe, isn't it?" Her finger stroked the stem of her glass. "You look quite different from those days, Andrew. Grown-up. Handsome. A mustache like Lucien Wolfe's." She laughed. She laughed a lot, Andrew noticed. "Very much at home in the world. Quite a change from the strange little boy in short pants at the country club in Grande Rivière. Quite a change. Still, I'd recognize you anywhere."

"Strange?"

"Well, curious, perhaps. You were a curious little boy, as I recall—quite different from your brothers."

"They were older."

"So was I," Daisy said. "And now I'm even older. I've changed a lot too, I'm afraid."

"No, you haven't. You've not changed at all—except for the golf."

"Perhaps I haven't." She thought for a moment. "I'm not sure that any of us changes that much, except on the surface."

"I don't know," Andrew said. "I'm not sure about that. Do you ever see Bob Griswold?" he asked. "Margie—my brother David's wife—"

"I remember."

"—she tells me he gets to Washington from time to time, on business for the Edison."

"I've never seen him."

The steward arrived with the wine. "Tell me," Andrew asked, after he had tasted it and played out the little ceremony with the sommelier, "did you use to wear sharkskin dresses when you played golf?"

"Andrew, what a curious mind you do have." She paused, looked at him with a mild, amused surprise. "I *knew* you always did."

"Well I just wondered. It's one of those words that stuck in my mind. It seemed so peculiar—dangerous and exciting at the same time. I thought it must have something to do with the skin of sharks, but I couldn't figure out how. I'd never seen a shark, of course." Andrew laughed. "I don't think we had any in our river." She really is extraordinarily attractive still, he thought, peering at her across the table: she could easily pass for forty.

"No," Daisy said, "they weren't in the river." She took a sip of her wine. "You order a nice wine, Andrew. Well, yes, I imagine I did wear sharkskin. We all did. I don't suppose I've thought of that in years. For tennis, too. Those pleated tennis dresses—such a damned nuisance to iron. Fortunately, we had help."

"Yes. The Indians," Andrew said. "Your grandfather was always trying to improve them." He laughed. "That's what Michael Aldrich used to say."

Daisy grunted. "The Governor was very much for improvement, especially for others. It was his Emersonian mode." Curious, Andrew thought, that she referred to him by his title.

"Michael Aldrich is in town too, you know."

"Yes," Daisy said. "That was mentioned in the article in *The Sunday Times*. He's directing your play."

"He's directed all of them," Andrew said. "Do you remember Rose?"

"Rose? Oh, yes, Rose. Of course. The Indian girl who worked for your mother."

"Do you remember when she scalped her husband? I wasn't supposed to know about that, but I did."

"Of course I remember. No one on the Island that summer could forget that. She caught him in . . . well, let's say in an awkward position with Lena. It was the buzz of the summer, or one of them. There was lots of buzzing that summer, lots of things to buzz about." She took a drink of her wine and looked at him. "Probably you knew all about them, all those things you weren't supposed to know about."

"No," Andrew said, "not all."

Daisy smiled. "Oh, I doubt that much escaped you. Mrs. Appleton certainly didn't."

"You were funny about her," Andrew said, "and I liked that. You told me she was having apoplexy in the ladies' room, and I didn't know what apoplexy was. Bob Griswold said I should do it again, drop another cat on her, but you said no, that once was enough. He said it was never enough."

"Yes, well, I've forgotten so much of those years," Daisy said, "and without a great deal of regret, I have to admit. I must have left Grande Rivière not long after that. It was much more exciting in Washington—working for the O.S.S., bumping into Mr. Dulles in the hall." She laughed. "I felt I was winning the war single-handed. Well, no—not single-handed, but there were so few of us, and we all knew one another. Like being part of a family. It was a wonderful cooperative effort—a great spirit. In those years the O.S.S. was absolutely the place to be—not like the C.I.A. today. We worked like beasts. No thought of sleep. But let's talk about you." She bent toward him and affected a conspiratorial whisper: "Let's talk about sex and violence." She leaned back and laughed throatily. "That's what we're supposed to be talking about, not the O.S.S."

"We are?" Andrew took a drink of his wine. A drop ran down the side of the glass and spread a thin red stain on the cloth beneath it.

"You remember. That was to be the subject of your luncheon conversation," Daisy said, fingering her pearls. They were impressive pearls, Andrew thought.

"But that was with my agent. Strictly for her benefit—or

rather, mine, in the end. Agents love that kind of talk, you know. It makes them think money. Besides, what would I know about sex and violence? Let's look at the menu."

"Oh, rather a lot, I imagine," Daisy replied, turning her eyes to the menu. "I've seen your plays, you know. *Riverhead?* Very polite on the surface, of course. Like you, Andrew."

"I like surfaces," Andrew said. "I like dealing with them."

Daisy raised her eyes from the menu and looked across at him. "I think I'll have the prime rib. Very rare, please." She set the menu aside and touched the tip of her fingernail lightly to the table. "But Andrew, surfaces so often reveal what they purport to conceal, if you know how to look at them—clothes being the prime example." Andrew felt suddenly, acutely conscious of the body, his body, that sat there coiled beneath his suit, under his shirt and tie, in his shoes and socks, his underwear. He looked so ordinary, he thought with some amazement, like every other man in the room: nothing outrageous here, nothing to ruffle the surface of the world. He moved his hand across the tablecloth.

"The surface of this table, for instance," Andrew said, rubbing the cloth lightly between his fingers, "how the light reflects on it. Look at it. It's immaculate—or it was until I spilled my wine. If I were a painter—a Dutch or Flemish painter, I think— I'd try to catch it."

"Vermeer," she said.

"And the light in your pearls, too. It's a question of seeing. . . ."

"Or of peeling. Like an onion, the skin of an onion—"

"Always another surface beneath it. Layer after layer of onion." Her skin, he noticed, was surprisingly translucent even with its glaze of tan, and the enigmatic, unblinking eyes that met his gaze were very gray.

"Well, eventually you get to the bottom of it, and with the onion that's, of course, the end of it. But Andrew, it's more than a question of seeing. You also have to know where to look." She took another drink of her wine and broke into a broad smile. "Shall we check under the table"—she moved her hand as if to lift the cloth—"to see what's hiding there?"

"Surely that's not necessary in a place like the Ritz," Andrew said, going along with her joke. "No cockroaches, certainly. Nothing untoward. At the most just an old wine cork. Shall we order? I'm famished." Andrew beckoned the captain and busied himself with the details of their meal, which arrived shortly thereafter.

"And how is your family?" Daisy asked, vigorously attacking her roast beef.

"Oh, they're fine. Enjoying London. They were going to the Tower today. Lady Rysdale told Julie she had to see the Crown Jewels."

"So you've seen the old fraud. She *would* be interested in the jewels. Grisly place, the Tower, except for that lovely, austere chapel. The rest of it is just too bloody."

"Rather like this beef," Andrew said, looking down at his plate and over at hers, at the meat glistening in its bloody sea. He thought suddenly of the holiday dinners of his childhood in the dining room in Grande Rivière and of his father's striking the knife against the sharpening steel with sure, swift strokes before he carved the holiday offering. He could hear the sound of steel striking steel and see their plates, garlanded with heaps of dead game; see the porcelain animal eyes gazing down at them from the platters and dishes on the plate rail that bordered the room. It had been a handsome room, he supposed, solid, fixed. He looked back at his plate, suppressing a shudder. "Did they cook it, do you think?"

"Rare, isn't it? Cannibal rare, as Tom Sedgwick used to say. Yes, our ancestors were very skilled at devising implements of torture, very ingenious. I suppose we still are. Only the instruments have changed. The countess wouldn't be interested in that, of course, but I rather think the earl might. When did you see her, and what did she want? Tell me all the juicy details. I want a delicious story." She picked up her fork and resumed eating.

Andrew told her about their lunch at Lady Rysdale's the day before, and how the conversation had taken rather a turn when Ann inquired after the earl.

"Marvelous!" she exclaimed, cutting into her meat. "I knew I could count on you. How did Ann happen to bring him up?"

"That's what I asked her. She didn't know about His Lordship's predilections, but the rest of them did."

"His toys in the attic. Who was there?"

"It was one of her lesser lists, I think. A couple of titled nitwits from the Cotswolds who couldn't get their minds off their breeding stock—all that animal coupling; I suppose that's what gave Ann the idea: subliminal suggestion—and a funny Anglo-Irish spinster, Sybil something-or-other, something hyphenated. Her son Patrick was there, too. He seemed to take it fairly calmly, said they hadn't seen Dad for a bit." Andrew laughed.

"I don't suppose they have," Daisy said, putting down her knife and fork. "Has anyone? The Huntingtons heard he's in Morocco. I would have thought he'd choose somewhere a little more 'disciplined,' myself—Switzerland, maybe, but I suppose too many people might see him there. But enough about that old pervert."

"Well," Andrew said, "you did say you wanted to talk about sex and violence."

"Touché!" She raised her glass. "Let's talk about you."

"Me?"

"Instead. Or as well as—even together with—whichever you prefer." She took a drink of her wine.

"Touché, yourself," Andrew said.

"You don't seem to be eating your meal." Daisy gestured toward his plate.

"I'm not very hungry, I guess." He glanced down at it, saw he'd scarcely touched it. "Actually, I'd rather talk about you. Where's your husband?"

"Curtis? He's in Washington. He doesn't like London much. He's seventy-nine, you know."

"No, I didn't know. I'd no idea." Andrew stumbled, flustered. "I mean, I've never met him. He wasn't around that day I saw you in Washington with Mrs. Steer, and he wasn't with you in New York."

"He spends most of his time in Washington and France—he has a château in Burgundy, thanks to the generosity of his first wife: she was filthy rich—and in the summer we go to a crumbling pile of stones outside Boston—in Magnolia, on the North Shore. He seems to like ruins. His interests and mine have . . . well, diverged is how I think I'd put it. He pursues his, and I pursue mine. We meet for dinner." She laughed dryly. "He has a very good cook. You should meet him. I think you'd like him."

"*He* has a good cook?"

"Well, we have a good cook, but really he cares more about that sort of thing than I do. Yes, you must meet him. You must come to Magnolia this summer. The food is execrable—the cook won't travel—but the place is interesting. A ruin, but not a rustic ruin. More gothic."

"I have an affinity for ruins," Andrew said.

"You'd like this. It's an old family place—though not at all like the Island."

"The Island's not the Island anymore," Andrew said. He raised his glass and took a drink. "It's not even rustic now, just a wreck. The bridges have crumbled, the docks are rotting. No one goes there. We stopped going the year I went to college and my parents started spending most of the winter in the South. My mother said she could manage two places but she wouldn't run three, and my father was tired of rowing back and forth." Andrew pictured his father in the boat. He smiled at the memory. His father had been very firm about the proper way to handle a boat in the current, and when he'd finally allowed Andrew to row himself—Jim the Indian had taught him secretly—his father had insisted that Andrew do it his way, the right way, directly into the current and then straight to the shore, with no meandering. "The Sedgwicks' island is about eroded away," Andrew continued, taking another drink, "almost cut in half—maybe it is by now. Remember their weeping willow, how its fronds used to trail in the current? It went years ago. And the Sedgwicks' guesthouse, on pilings over the water? How I loved to spend the night there! I used to pretend I was sleeping on a boat, listening to the sound of the waves lapping, the voices on the water. The last time I was actually on the Island—almost twelve years ago, for drinks at the Sedgwicks' right after I was married—"

"I remember," Daisy said.

"You remember?" Andrew was perplexed.

"Yes, I was there."

"You were?"

"Yes."

"How could I have forgotten that?"

"Your parents had a big party for you and your bride—at the country club. She was very pretty. I remember the dress she was wearing, the most extraordinary dress for Grande Rivière—a beautiful white silk, very simple—and a string of pearls."

"My mother's," Andrew said. "She lent them to her for the occasion. She ruined the dress not long after—wading in the ocean one night in Florida." Suddenly he smiled. It had been a happy night.

"Oh, that's a shame. Everyone was at that party—all the old crowd—and everyone was enchanted by her."

"That was the year the Sedgwicks lost their guesthouse," Andrew said, returning to his story. "A winter storm had taken it away and washed the pieces up on one of the islands downstream. They just left it there." He paused for a drink of wine. "Oh, you can still see the Island from the shore, but really it's as if the old place vanished along with the people—and most of them have, actually. I rowed around it once, a couple of years ago, with Julie. I wanted to show her the scene of the crime"—he laughed—"but there was nothing really to show. The docks were so bad we couldn't tie up the boat. The place scared her. She thought it looked haunted—all those crumbling houses, the roofs sagging if they weren't already staved in. She didn't even want to go ashore. It meant nothing to her. Michael's mother, old Mrs. Aldrich— she's still alive but in a nursing home somewhere—tried to sell the thing for years; now Michael says they're trying to give it to the state but the state doesn't want it either." The waiter refilled their glasses and took the empty bottle away. "When was the last time you were there?" he asked.

"Oh, not in years and years. Not since Mother died. Yes, ten years. I've not been back since. There's nothing in Grande Rivière to lure me."

"I was long since gone. I would have been thirty then, the year of my first play. The year my brother John died."

"So you're forty."

"*Just* forty," Andrew said. "Early this month."

"Imagine. You don't look it."

"I don't act it, either," he replied.

"Good. We'll get along well," she said. "Andrew, I'm fifty-three—for another ten minutes, anyway—and I've learned that life is much more interesting if you forget about age. Until it hits you by surprise—attacks in the night, you might say. Then there's no denying it. You know the song: '*What though the night may come too soon, there's years and years of afternoon*'? Gilbert and Sullivan."

"Really," Andrew said. Fifty-three, he thought. Once it would have seemed so old. It still did, in a way, but differently.

"You were only a girl back then," he said, surprise in his voice. "Younger than John!"

She laughed. "Only chronologically." She put down her fork and looked at him. "I still *am* a girl, Andrew. I'd hoped it was obvious."

"Oh, it is." He laughed. "It's quite obvious. On the surface. I told you I was interested in surfaces."

"We must go to the National Gallery," Daisy said, "to see their two Vermeers. He'll show you surfaces, timeless surfaces, and lead you under them, too. We'll do it tomorrow afternoon, about two. Are you free?" Andrew thought he would be free. "There's a lovely Van Eyck, too—the famous one of the wedding, with the convex mirror in the background. Do you know it?"

Andrew thought he knew it. "The bride is pregnant, isn't she?"

Daisy laughed. "She certainly looks it. Very." She raised her wineglass, held it in both hands and looked at him over the rim, studying him directly. Suddenly she said, "Tell me, Andrew, are you happy in your marriage?"

Andrew's gaze floated off toward the windows and out into Green Park. How beautiful it was, washed in the afternoon mist and that glowing pewter light peculiar to London in April, a light that seemed to come not from the sun, which hadn't been visible for days, but from the very air. It made the rich brilliant yellow of the daffodils even more intense, and the yellow of the daffodils, the green of the grass seemed to pulse and shimmer with the shimmering air. It was more than pretty; it was sharp. "Yes," he said, his eyes returning to the woman before him; "yes, of course."

Over coffee they agreed to meet at the gallery the next afternoon at two. "Ann and Julia could join us later for tea," Daisy said.

"That would be nice. I know Ann would like to see you."

"It's unlikely she'd remember me. She's only seen me twice."

"Twice?"

"The first time was at that party you seem to have trouble recalling, the big dinner your parents gave for you and Ann at the country club—almost as grand a party as their silver-anniversary dance. But you probably scarcely remember that. You were a very little boy. And now I must be going." She drained her glass. "The Huntingtons are expecting me for tea."

When he had settled the bill, Andrew walked her to the entrance and watched while the doorman helped her into a taxi and directed the driver to her destination. She seated herself in the car and slowly, almost languidly withdrew her legs—lovely and long, he noticed, beneath the dark sheen of her hose—into the taxi's dim interior. She turned briefly toward him and, laughing, blew him a kiss as the car pulled away from the curb and she directed her gaze ahead.

Andrew walked slowly back along the park toward the shelter of his hotel, a soothing Victorian place on Basil Street in Knightsbridge. Ann and Julia had not yet returned from their excursion, so he called to make another appointment with his agent—for Saturday now, between rehearsals—which this time he promised not to break. He talked briefly with Michael Aldrich and agreed to meet him at the theater late the next morning, and when Ann and Julia arrived, full of excitement and things to report, he roused himself from the bed where he was lying and the three of them went down for tea. "Well, Julie, how was the Tower? Did you like the jewels?"

"Oh, yes, Daddy," she said. "There were a lot of them. Why doesn't the Queen wear her crown?"

"She does, but only when she's all dressed up."

"Oh." She sounded disappointed. "Well, we saw the Beefeaters. They were nice. And these big black birds!"

"The ravens," Andrew said, "waiting for their feeding."

"And we saw where they murdered the little princes, and where the prisoners wrote their names on the wall. Tell me why they did that again? I forget."

"Which?"

"Murdered the little princes."

"Richard III wanted to be king, and the princes stood in his way. He was a bad man."

"We saw the Norman chapel, too," Ann said. "Remember how quiet and beautiful it was, Julie?"

"Yes, it was nice. But Daddy, have you seen those things they used to kill people with? They were *terrible*! They killed a *lot* of people! They chopped their heads off with axes and then they put them on poles so everybody could see, and those huge birds ate them!" Andrew imagined the piked heads lolling high in the air and the ravens hovering, pecking at their blinded, empty eyes. He shuddered at the horror, and felt suddenly sad. Julia looked genuinely distressed. He reached out his hand to comfort her. "And they did worse things, too. They—"

"Julia," Ann said, "we saw some nice things. The boat trip was fun, and the view from the river was wonderful. We decided to take the boat from Westminster," she explained for Andrew. "And remember St. Paul's, Julie?" She turned back to him: "It's even more beautiful than I'd remembered. The choir was rehearsing. We sat down for a few minutes and listened. Magnificent. I wish you'd been with us."

"Yes," Julia said, "we saw some nice things. But London is a pretty bloody place."

"Julia, let's think about something pleasant. We haven't heard anything about Daddy's day. We're waiting," Ann said to him, and Andrew told them about his day.

"Tomorrow can we go to Madame Tussaud's?" Julia asked when he had finished. "I want to see the Chamber of Horrors."

Andrew laughed. "You would," he said, and he and Ann laughed together. "It'll give you nightmares, Julie."

"It'll give *you* nightmares," Ann said.

"Well, we'll see. I've really got to meet Michael Aldrich at the theater in the morning, and we're going to meet Daisy Curtis— the old friend of mine I just told you about—for tea. I think we'll go to the Connaught. That would be spiffy. Maybe we'll see the Chamber of Horrors on Friday, instead. That would be better."

"Promise?"

"I promise."

That night, after they had had some soup and salad sent up to the room—everyone was tired at the end of the day, and no one was hungry after their late tea—Andrew told Julia a story about an armadillo from Mexico named Anthony and a friendly cobra from Egypt named Ralph and a kangaroo named Emily, and how they voyaged across the seas, visiting many strange and exotic lands and suffering many mishaps along the way but surviving them all and having a good deal of fun, too, before they finally arrived safely at their destination, which was Australia, Emily's beloved homeland. Andrew didn't want Julia to have nightmares; he remembered his own childhood terrors well enough: he wanted to soothe her before she went to sleep.

"Are cobras friendly?" Ann asked when she came into Julia's room to straighten up while Andrew was telling the story.

"This one is," Julia said. "Ralph is very friendly. He lives in a basket. He never bites anybody. He just scares bad people. They're like a family. They take care of each other."

"Quite a family," Ann said, laughing.

"Well, they love each other, anyway. It's Daddy's best story. Promise you'll finish it tomorrow night, Daddy?"

"I promise. We can't leave them dangling there on the Pyramids," and he tucked her in and kissed her good night.

Later, when they were in bed, Ann asked him about his lunch with Daisy. "Haven't I met her?"

"Yes, at a party in New York—the time we met the countess. I don't remember why we were there."

"Some theater thing, probably," Ann said.

"She was blond, attractive. Married to an old guy in the Foreign Service. Retired now."

"I don't remember him."

"No, he wasn't there. He's a lot older—older than my mother." Andrew laughed. "Maybe he should have married her. Of course, my mother was already married."

"She's not now."

"But he is. Anyway, when I was a kid Daisy was married to a man named Phil Meyer."

"Now I remember," Ann said. "Yes, Phil—the man you liked. She was at the party your parents gave for us the month after we were married. At the Sedgwicks' for drinks before the party, too."

"Yes. Her mother had a place on the Island. Her grandmother, too, but she'd died a long time before that."

"She was the chic divorcée from Washington."

"Only she wasn't divorced. She'd been married to Curtis for a long time by then."

"And you kept calling her Daisy Meyer. Phil Meyer was there too—not at the Sedgwicks', but at the country club." Ann laughed. "Your parents thought it was very awkward."

"Probably. They didn't deal well with divorce. As I recall, you thought it was a little strange too."

"Oh, come on!" She gave him a skeptical look. "We all rowed over to the party. Mrs. Sedgwick wanted to sing hymns."

"She always wanted to sing hymns. *'Time, like an ever-rolling stream'*—that's the only line I can remember. My grandmother liked it too."

Ann sang the rest of the line: " *'Bears all its sons away.'* That's from *'O God, our help in ages past.'* I don't think her husband was there then, either."

"No. He wasn't. I've never seen him." He reached for her hand.

"I seem to remember that your father didn't quite approve of her. Wasn't there some scandal?"

"Well, you know my father. She always had a lot of men around her—Nick Farnsworth, my brother David . . . he used to play tennis with her, and my father didn't like that much. And then there was Bob Griswold . . . Anyway, she left Grande Rivière when I was a little boy. And now she is very definitely a woman of the world. Like you." He laughed, teasing her. "Come closer, you're liable to fall off the bed." He pulled her toward him and kissed her fingertips. "We could make love," he whispered; "that could be fun."

Ann chuckled. "We could, but I'm afraid Julia would hear us."

"Oh, come on. She's sound asleep in the next room."

"No, she's not. I hear her stirring. And we might as well be in the next room ourselves. These rooms are like closets. How they call this a 'small suite' I'll never know." She was rummaging around on the table beside the bed.

"What are you looking for?" Andrew asked.

"The hand lotion," Ann replied. "Oh, here it is." She poured some on her hands. "Besides, I'm exhausted. You'd be exhausted too, if you'd been traipsing around London with Julie all day instead of having a fancy lunch at the Ritz. By the way, how much did it cost us?"

"Oh, about the price of a crown jewel," Andrew said, kissing her and turning out the light. Later he woke up tossing in the unfamiliar bed. His stirring roused Ann. "I can't seem to sleep. Sorry."

"What are you worried about?" she asked.

"The play, I guess. I'm thinking about the play." Then in the softness of the night they began to make love, slowly and quietly, before Andrew returned to his sleep.

"You'll never guess who I saw yesterday," Andrew said to Michael Aldrich at the theater the next morning.

"So I won't," Michael said. "Who?"

"Daisy Meyer. Daisy Meyer from the Island when we were kids."

"Daisy Meyer? For God's sake! Where?"

"In the British Museum. I went there to see the Elgin Marbles and she just showed up."

"Didya fuck her?"

"Yes, sure, Michael. Right there in the British Museum. On the bench in the middle of the Elgin Marbles. A great performance. Everyone applauded."

"Encores?"

"Only one."

"Well, you're doing better! A little hard on the knees—but I guess it beats the golf course in Grande Rivière. Or the tennis courts. Ask your brother David about that, or that other guy, that lawyer. What was his name? Yes, Bob Griswold." He shook his head, bemused. "Old hole-in-one Daisy, fancy that! Banging her in the British Museum. Did she get off on it?"

"Oh, shut up," Andrew said.

"I would. That could be kind of fun, you know. The idea turns me on. I like older women. And all those bodies, all that marble—God, Andrew, knock it off. You'll get me aroused. I'll need a box lunch."

Andrew laughed. "Michael," he said, "you went to a fancy Episcopal prep school. They were supposed to make you into a nice boy. What happened?"

"I read the Greeks. They'll ruin you for life."

"Yes, I know—all that sex and violence."

"Love it," Michael said. "That's what you need, sweetheart. A little lowlife. That's what this play needs, too."

They were sitting in the darkened, empty theater watching the actors rehearse on stage. It was odd, Andrew thought, how dusty and lifeless a theater seemed when it was empty, and how the glare of the work lights, which someone at that moment switched on, instantly rinsed the stage of all illusion: the solid, rather gentle room up there was merely crudely painted, flimsy canvas; the actors without their merciful cloak of makeup and costume small and insignificant, pale and ordinary in their ordinary clothes—smaller than life, Andrew thought. He heard a breaker trip and the house itself was instantly flooded with light, a light so intense and harsh that Andrew covered his eyes for a moment, and when he opened them the effect was ruinous. The gilded plaster masks that ornamented the proscenium arch were chipped and ugly, the carpet worn, and the faded velvet seat beside him—once burgundy, he supposed, when Queen Victoria reigned—emitted a little puff of dust when he set his clipboard on it. Even the cupids cavorting on the ceiling were grotesque caricatures, an inept painter's idea of the imagined real thing. How could anyone think this a glamourous business? Andrew asked himself, brushing off his hand. In the light, the painted, paneled hall was in fact grimy.

"My mother," Andrew said, "thinks my plays are quite low enough. She'd like to see me produce something a little more elevated, something she could take her friends to without shuddering. At least they don't play in Grande Rivière."

"Well, sonny, a man's first duty is to kill his parents."

Andrew reached for his clipboard, leafed through the sheets of paper, looking for a note he'd made. He glanced at Michael, continued searching. "Which one?"

"Both. Otherwise, they'll kill you. But you already have. You just don't know it yet."

"Yes, of course, Michael." He found the note. "How about just burying them?"

"Not enough."

He'd felt the note was important, but it meant nothing to him now. He couldn't even figure it out. Annoying. "Still, you may have a point—this play needs something." His ambition was to write sometime a play that would in fact be stripped of illusion, that would grant no pretty concessions like costume and scenery and lighting, that would tell the immense stark truth starkly— and still be beautiful. He wasn't sure that he could do it. Beckett could, but look at Beckett, plagued by misery and boils, his life given over utterly to the terrible grim vision that ruthlessly drove him. He might as well be living in one of his ash cans. The engine of the imagination grinds on without pity, Andrew thought. Still,

Beckett had grandeur, and he could laugh—or at least make others laugh. Maybe that was what Andrew was trying to evoke, grandeur rather than beauty, beauty being so easily confused with the merely pretty. Andrew thought of the book he had bought years ago—for the title, really, which appealed to his romantic youthful mind, his easy *Weltschmerz*, his disorder and early sorrow: Unamuno's *Tragic Sense of Life*. He'd never really read the book—too much work—but its final sentence was indelibly graven in his mind: "And may God deny you peace," the sentence read, "but grant you glory." There was, he thought, precious little glory in this place, or beauty either: just dirt. He felt as if he already needed another shower. He turned to Michael —"I suppose that's the problem if your parents kill themselves, or die too young"—then back to his clipboard.

"Yes, it deprives you of your rightful duty." Michael shifted in his seat. "Well, of course your mother would think your plays were 'quite low enough,' as you put it. You made her wear the scarlet letter in *Riverhead*. She thought you'd caught her in the act and the whole world would know. She hasn't seen anything yet."

Andrew made another note. He'd try to be more explicit this time, so he could understand the context when he looked at it again. "Know what?"

"That that guy on the Island was dicking her. That guy with all the Indian stuff from Canada and Mexico. Lucien Wolfe."

He looked up. "Oh, for Christ's sake, Michael! Nobody 'dicked' my mother." He was so tired of hearing it; probably not so tired as his mother, though, he thought.

Michael laughed. He laughed uproariously. "You sound like an eight-year-old," he said. " 'My daddy wouldn't do that to my mommy.' You can bet your ass somebody did, and you can hope one of them was your daddy. So Luke Wolfe was another. Big deal."

"I don't think so," Andrew said.

"He sure thought about it," Michael said, "and so did she."

"And how do you know that? You weren't the moose head on the wall."

"My daddy told me," Michael said, mimicking a child's singsong. "That's okay, Andrew. Don't cry. He banged Daisy Meyer, too."

"Can't you talk about something else?"

"Can you think of a better subject?"

"Lunch. I'm hungry."

"We could talk about the play. That's a good subject. It needs work. From you. Let me remind you: we're opening Tuesday. That's five days away."

"I know, I know. I can't stand to think about it anymore now. I'll think about it tomorrow, I promise. I'll work all weekend. Ann and Julia are spending it in Hampstead, with the Spensers. They knew I'd be busy. Can we have lunch? I'm still hungry."

"We'll send out for it. How about some clams?" Michael looked at him. "Bearded clams." He laughed. "They'll stir your memory."

"Whatever, it has to be quick. I'm meeting Daisy at the National Gallery at two. We're going to look at their Vermeers."

"Holy shit! Are you and Daisy planning to break in all the museums in London? You'll have quite a trip."

Andrew ignored him. He picked up his pad and made a few more notes.

"In that case, maybe you'd better have some oysters." He beckoned to one of the boys standing around. "A plate of oysters for the lad here," he said. "A dozen, I think. Big ones. He needs his strength. I'll have the same—and a bottle of Montrachet or something. Maybe I'll join you later at the gallery," he said to Andrew. "I'll direct. You need a director, you know."

"We're meeting Ann and Julia at four for tea at the Connaught. Why don't you join us there instead?"

"Going solo, heh? A brave lad," Michael said.

Andrew walked from the theater toward the gallery on Trafalgar Square, wandering the side streets and circling here and there if a path appealed to him. He had time, he thought: there was no rush; he was not anxious; and he wanted to avoid the noise and the traffic and the fumes—at least as much as he could, on a street in the middle of London in the middle of the day in springtime. He wanted clear air, and a patch of sunlight. It was an ordinary day, he thought, a Thursday, just a Thursday, like any other Thursday. He looked at the life around him—people going briskly about their business, people laughing and chatting and seemingly intent on their own concerns: the usual vignettes of happiness and misery and boredom and haste that the city, any city, presented. Though scattered flowers bloomed, the pale northern sun of early April still gave off a trace of winter's light, and yet, as he walked idly along, his mind adrift in the urban sea, concentrating on no particular thing, the trees, he noticed, seemed imbued with a particular sharp intensity. Probably some peculiar deflection of the sun's rays at this latitude, at this moment in its climb from Capricorn, he thought. It was the bark that struck him, how deeply grooved it seemed, as if this singular tree were painfully carving itself with excruciating slowness in high relief; and then the stones, even the stones seemed charged with life, pulsing in the waves of light. There was something intensely sensuous about it; sensual, even erotic. He felt an urge to touch the tree, to hug it; embrace the stone. He paused to look, to see if his vision was failing him though he knew it was not. Suddenly he thought of the designer he knew—a brilliant, magical designer—who had gone to Glyndebourne one May to work on the sets for an opera, and how, as he was walking through the park one afternoon he was suddenly seized by a frightful pain in the chest—a more intense pain, he said, than he could ever have imagined—and he stumbled and fell to the ground and his world blacked out. He'd thought he was dying, and he almost did; it had been a massive heart attack. But what he saw as he fell—not what he was looking at but what floated there on the edge of his vision and he had somehow recorded—was the tulips, the masses of white and red tulips waving in the park that he remembered when he awoke gasping in an oxygen tent in a hospital bed in England. "It was an ordinary day," he later told Andrew, amazement in his voice, "just an ordinary day like today. And the tulips were in bloom." Well, it was too early for tulips, Andrew thought, smiling a little ruefully, and he resumed his course along the Mall, around the square, past the lovely, Classical portico of St. Martin-in-the-Fields with its bums littering the steps and music emanating from within, and directly to the Gallery and Daisy's damned Vermeers. Really, he thought, he was too busy to be spending his afternoon lolling about a picture gallery when his play, he knew, needed attention, too old to be fiddling around like this, looking at pictures on a sunny afternoon when there was work to be done. He picked up a little map as he entered the museum, determined the location of the Vermeers, and, as he slowly made his way through the stillness toward them, fell slowly, resistantly under the spell of the silence.

The room, when he got there, was empty and still. He glanced at the two Vermeers—the one a woman standing and the other a girl seated, at a musical instrument, the virginals—and waited. Art galleries were, he thought, finally rather magical places, resonating silence: all those quiet, mysterious figures on the walls, their enigmatic pigment eyes gazing into the viewer's own—at least here, in these two particular paintings. He returned the woman's look. A conjuror's trick, he thought. Weird how a person never sees his own eyes, except by reflection. He looked more intently into the eyes of the paintings. The standing woman's were somewhat shaded, and she stood with her back to the light, her fingers on the keys. The girl—her fingers too on the keys—faced the light, and there was something, well, something faintly suggestive about her face, her look: like a seventeenth-century Lolita, he thought, almost lewd for such seeming innocence, and certainly knowing. But they were only paintings, not even very large paintings; both of average size, almost small, telling no story but describing a fugitive moment long gone, and the light in them catching the stillness, the mystery of the moment. When he thought about it, Andrew realized that he liked looking at paintings, looking into paintings, but he could never say exactly why. He recalled a painting he had seen once—not even the original, just a photograph of it in a catalogue—*Anticipating the Eventual Emergence of Form*, the title of a book he'd remembered Mrs. Steer's reading when he was a little boy. The coincidence had astonished him at the time, though he didn't suppose there could be any connection between the painting and the book. As he recalled it, the painting showed a hand parting the folds of a curtain, but the mysterious thing about the painting was its perspective: the curtain's falling between the viewer's eye and the entering hand with its tantalizing promise to reveal.

"Hello." The voice was soft, startling him. "Hello, Andrew." It was Daisy, standing before the entrance to the room. "I knew you'd like them," she said, speaking in the same soft voice and gesturing slightly toward the two Vermeers. Her dress and her stockings, Andrew noticed, were the color of the silk on the woman in the painting, something the color of mushrooms, and the jacket she wore with them was of a deeper shade and piped in blue—Delft blue, he supposed. He wondered if she left anything to chance.

"Hello, Daisy," he said. "Yes, I like them. You've dressed for the occasion."

She gave a little shrug and laughed. "You're very observant." She turned to the paintings. "I knew these surfaces would interest you—the way the light falls on their gowns, the drawn shade next to the light-filled room, the way nothing *seems* to be happening in either picture, as if the whole scene were merely an interruption, a woman interrupted at her playing. Did you notice the paintings in the background, the paintings within the paintings?"

Andrew looked back to the pictures. "No, I hadn't noticed. I was too busy looking at their eyes."

"The Cupid," she said, pointing to the lady standing, "is supposed to be an emblem of fidelity."

"Well, the other one certainly isn't," Andrew replied, looking at the painting that was partially visible on the wall behind the seated girl. It showed a laughing woman playing a lute, her breast almost bared, looking into the eyes of a bearded man whose hand grasped her shoulder while an old crone apparently negotiated the deal. "I think I'd describe it as"—he paused—"lubricious. Downright wanton. It seems to tell a story in contrast to . . ." He suddenly seized upon it: "the violence of Caravaggio against the silence of Vermeer." Andrew was pleased by the comparison; it almost sounded as if he knew something about art.

"It's called *The Procuress*," Daisy said. "It belonged to Vermeer's mother or mother-in-law, I forget which."

He glanced at her. "You seem to know a lot about all this."

"I make it a point to. It's what I do—among other things."

"What you do?"

"Yes, Andrew, what I do. Did you think I merely swung a golf club? I told you I don't do that anymore. I make things—objects—out of marble, and"—she laughed—"sometimes mud. Sometimes other things, too. That's why you happened to find me yesterday at the British Museum. I go there whenever I'm in London. I like the energy of the marble—"

"Not to mention the energy of the Greeks."

"—to see how the Greeks controlled it, making it flow as if it were liquid."

"I'd like to see how you control it," Andrew said.

"Perhaps you will someday."

"You were dressed for that occasion, too." His gaze had returned to the paintings. "And you're wearing your pearls again, like the women in these paintings."

"So I am," she said. "Vermeer and I are fond of pearls. He painted pearls on a lot of women. I remember your mother's. They were very fine."

"I guess so," Andrew said. "They'd been my grandmother's."

"I quite admired your mother back then. I've not seen her in years, of course. She was a lovely woman."

"Yes," Andrew replied. "So is my wife." He looked more closely at the paintings, at the shadows in the rich satin of the women's dresses. The folds of the dress of the girl in blue seemed almost an abstract pattern of color, as if an iridescent, inky liquid had been spilled from a bottle onto the canvas. His mind flashed to the thick, textured bark of the tree he had seen, and the light of its anguished grooves and shadows.

"Tell me, Andrew," Daisy said, standing beside him, facing the paintings, "do you think your mother had an affair?"

"Her words exactly, after she'd seen *Riverhead*. 'Tell me, Andrew, do you think your mother had an affair?' When she refers to herself in the third person, you know you're in trouble. Well of course I don't think she had an affair! It was a *play*, for God's sake! It had nothing to do with her." What the fuck is going on here, he asked himself—first Michael Aldrich and now Daisy Meyer, Daisy Curtis, whatever the hell her name is. He was annoyed.

"Yes. I know. I saw it. Which was not why I asked."

"Then why did you? That woman was not my mother."

"Oh, Andrew," Daisy replied, "You're a grown-up now. You're not little Tommy. It's time to be a grown-up. People do have affairs, you know—this woman in the picture, perhaps." She indicated the woman standing before the Cupid.

"I thought the Cupid was an emblem of fidelity," Andrew said.

"That's what the experts say—but fidelity to what? To love itself? I like that idea. See the little card he's holding, the little note card? They say it's a love letter"—she chuckled—"but they don't say who it's to, or for that matter, who it's from. Maybe the Cupid represents fidelity, lasting love, that sort of thing. But maybe that's the opposite of what she's got on her mind." Daisy darted him a quizzical little smile, rather, it seemed to Andrew, like the smile on the woman in the painting. "Whatever's on her mind," she said, "it doesn't seem unpleasant."

"Quite a balancing act."

"Yes, it is."

"*Was*," Andrew said. "It was Vermeer's act. He's dead. There doesn't seem to be any doubt about the other picture, though, what's on that child's mind."

"There's always room for doubt." She hadn't turned from the objects. "Maybe Vermeer meant that painting behind her—"

"Sheer carnal lust," Andrew interjected.

"—as a contast to the purity of the young thing at the virginals." Daisy laughed. "That's what the experts say."

"Your experts should open their eyes. That young thing looks ready to slip off her chair at a moment's notice and roll."

Daisy laughed again. "My, you do sound grown-up now. Tell me, what did you say when your mother asked you the awkward question?"

"The same thing I told you: that woman is not my mother." Andrew began to smile at the memory of his mother's call that afternoon, some days after she had seen the play and returned to Grande Rivière.

"Now you seem amused," Daisy said.

"Because of my mother," Andrew said, "because of what she said next."

"What was that?"

" 'Well, I suppose at my age I ought to be flattered that someone might think so.' That's what she said."

"You see, Andrew," Daisy said, laughing aloud, "it is possible to be grown-up. A marvelous response, perfect—she didn't even answer the question."

"I noticed."

"Well, Proust was set off by his mother's kisses—or lack of them. You could do worse, I suppose. Have you read Proust?"

"Not really. I've tried a few times. Sort of like Virginia Woolf. She was always noting that she was reading Proust, or about to read Proust, or picking up Proust again, or trying to read Proust. I'm saving him for my old age. Anyway, why do you ask?"

"Vermeer makes me think of him. Proust talked about his 'special radiance'—*le rayon spécial*—and the work of the artist, to discern beneath the surface, to dive under—"

"And retrieve?"

"At least explore."

"That takes courage."

"He didn't say it was easy. That's why he used *travail*—'ce travail de l'artiste.' "

"So you're at home in French too."

"Practice. It got fairly passable when Curtis was stationed in Paris all those years. I'll have to find the passage for you sometime; it's quite remarkable."

"In the meantime," Andrew said, "let's find that Van Eyck you were talking about yesterday, the one with the pregnant bride," and together they left the limpid stillness of the Vermeers to find *The Arnolfini Wedding*.

"But it's tiny!" Andrew exclaimed when they came upon it. "It looks so big in photographs. And her dress is so green—as if it's about to vibrate. I guess I've only seen reproductions of it."

"Yes," Daisy agreed, "you do expect something larger, something closer to life-size. But no, it's just a small, very precise and meticulously detailed painting—but fascinating. Look at the convex mirror on the wall. See what it's reflecting?" They moved closer to inspect it.

"Why, yes! It's reflecting the backs of the bridal couple, but also the tiny figure of the witness! The artist. With his name above it." He paused to examine it. Her jacket brushed against his arm. "The word and the image," he said softly. "Amazing." His voice drifted off. He could sense her warmth, and hear her breathing, feel her moist breath on his shoulder. He moved back a little. "It works like a microscope."

"And there's someone else, too, at the door," Daisy said. "Another figure. The artist's companion."

"The painting is the telescope and the mirror is the microscope," Andrew said. "Or the other end of the telescope. Yes! Like looking through the opposite end of the telescope. Two ways of seeing."

"There's a third way," Daisy said."

"What's that?"

"With the naked eye. The real thing. The rest is just an illusion."

"But a helpful one," Andrew said. "It's useful. It lets us see, lets us regard the world from a certain distance, you know. And beneath the surface, too—your words, Mrs. Curtis. Otherwise, why did we come here?"

"To see one another, of course."

"Oh." Suddenly there was a commotion in the corridor. Andrew turned, startled.

"Caught you!" It was Michael charging across the room toward them. "Hey!" he exclaimed. "I thought you were looking at the Vermeers. Hello," he said to Daisy. "I'm Michael Aldrich."

"And this is Daisy Meyer," Andrew said, recovering himself. "Daisy, meet Michael. From the Island."

"Yes, of course," Daisy said. "I remember you clearly, though you've changed a good deal. You were a couple of years older than Andrew here. I've not seen you since you were a boy— about nine, I expect—but I knew you were in town. And the name is Daisy Curtis. Tommy keeps forgetting himself." Daisy laughed. "I don't think he welcomes change."

"The name is Andrew," Andrew said. "We all seem to have a little trouble remembering who we are." He cleared his throat. "We were looking at the Vermeers, but we moved on to *The Arnolfini Wedding*." He gestured toward the painting on the wall.

"Glum-looking pair," Michael said. "What are they doing— getting married in their bedroom?" He looked at the bed in the corner of the painting, and then back to the bride. "It looks as if they've already been in it. That girl is one pregnant bride. She's about to go into labor, for Christ's sake!"

"Michael was thinking of joining us for tea later," Andrew said to Daisy. "I guess I hadn't told you that—but he must have changed his mind."

"No, I didn't change my mind—just decided to track you down here. It's part of my role as Andrew's director," he said to Daisy, "to keep him in line. And I may have changed a lot, but you don't seem to have changed at all. You always were a knockout."

"Michael docsn't beat around the bush," Andrew said.

"I haven't seen you since the summer of 1938," Michael said, "the summer they dredged the channels between the islands. I was crazy about your grandmother. Really, I had kind of a crush on you, too. You were"—he lowered his voice—"the older woman." He laughed. "But not much older. That was the summer your grandfather got married."

"Yes," Daisy said. "To my 'aunt,' the ghastly Bellanova. My grandfather may have fancied himself the distinguished former Governor of the state, but really"—she laughed—"he was just an old fool. Imagine! Marrying his adopted daughter! She was scarcely older than I. If he did nothing else, he kept the gossip pump primed that summer. There was nothing else to talk about, to my mother's eternal shame and my grandmother's horror."

"Oh, sure, there must have been something else," Michael said. "There was Andrew's brother David and my cousin Madge. That gave the old ladies something to worry about, didn't it, Andrew?"

"You missed the real excitement," Andrew said, "the summer after, when Rose scalped her husband. That was the summer you had to stay in Madrid."

"With my parents away, I was the terror of the American Embassy." Michael chuckled. "I gave 'em more trouble than the spies. They were spy-crazy that summer. Saw one under every bed—or in it."

"With some reason," Andrew said.

"Yes, sure. I was really mad when my parents wouldn't let me come home with them. I often wonder why they did that."

"Do you want me to tell you?"

Daisy laughed.

"Don't bother. I might be able to figure it out. That was 1939, the summer the war broke out, and everything was in a hell of a mess. Even on the Island. I heard all about it, eventually."

"And the summer after that, I was gone," Daisy said.

"Speaking of going," Andrew asked, "why don't we? Is anything keeping us?"

The three of them walked through the rooms toward the entrance, and straight into Ann and Julia heading toward them. "Found you!" Ann exclaimed, a little breathless. "Julia and I've been at the Abbey, and we decided to walk over here to see if we could catch you before you left. I was afraid we'd be late for tea

—but then I knew that Andrew would be," she said, teasing him. "He always is."

"Stop telling our secrets," Andrew said. "Daisy, you remember Ann. Ann, this is Daisy Mey—Daisy Curtis."

"Ah, the young bride," Daisy said. "Yes, of course, I remember. What fun!"

"How nice to see you, Mrs. Curtis." Ann had shifted to her genteel mode. Andrew could hear it in her voice. Sometimes her voice could sound insanely genteel, he thought. It was a terrible act; he wished she'd drop it.

"Please," Daisy said, "no 'Mrs. Curtis'—just Daisy. It's a dizzy name, but use it anyway. You'll make me feel antique."

Michael laughed.

"Hello, Michael." Ann was still being genteel.

"And Daisy," Andrew said, "this is Julia." She looked so fresh and glowing, Andrew thought, like a little pearl. He wanted to hug her, but then he always did. He gave her a squeeze on the shoulder instead.

"Ah, my lovely Julie," Michael said, picking her up and swinging her toward him. "Kiss me, and I'll be your prince forever"—he nodded toward Andrew—"instead of this old toad." Julia laughed with delight.

"Don't trust him, Julia," Ann said, laughing. "Toads are always making promises."

"I never met a toad I didn't like," Daisy said.

"Yes, but you gotta watch 'em," Michael said. "They'll give you warts. Remember that, Julie."

"Let's go," Andrew said. "Let's go to tea," and the five of them left the Gallery arm in arm and quickly found a taxi on the square.

"I like this place," Julia said as they entered the Connaught. "It's cozy," and for all its grand reputation and imposing façade the hotel did give an impression of comfort and intimacy, the kind of comfort and intimacy—a quiet, paneled clubbiness, really —that money, discreetly but generously applied, can achieve.

"You'd be a fool not to," Michael Aldrich said, "and you're no fool, Julie." They arranged themselves in a pleasant corner of the lounge and ordered tea. "How'd you like the Abbey?" he asked her.

"It's beautiful," Julia said. "It's so old. It's my favorite place in London so far. People were doing these rubbings, and there were all these big stone boxes with kings and queens in them. Tomorrow I want to ride on a double-decker bus and go to Madame Tussaud's. Daddy will take me, won't you, Daddy?"

"She wants to see the Chamber of Horrors," Andrew said. "I'm afraid I'll have nightmares"—he laughed—"but yes, I'll take you, Julie. I've already promised. We'll ride on the double-decker bus to the Chamber of Horrors."

"Take care of your daddy, Julie," Michael said. "We don't want him to be scared."

Julia giggled.

"I think I can handle it," Andrew said.

"Did you enjoy the Gallery?" Ann asked.

"They have some pretty pictures," Andrew replied.

"I wanted Andrew to see the Vermeers," Daisy said. "I thought he would find him . . . compatible, I suppose. The Gallery has his two last paintings."

"So he never resolved the question . . ."

"What question, Daddy?"

"Oh, I don't know," Andrew said, "there's just something faintly disturbing about them, about those pictures—unresolved, maybe, despite their—I guess—perfect composition."

"You said it was a balancing act," Daisy said as the tea tray was set before her.

Andrew continued his musings. "As if they formed two parts of an arch, but with the keystone missing."

"We're being so serious," Daisy said, laughing. "Well, he is the most extraordinary painter—absorbed in surfaces."

"And in light," Andrew said. "Yes, they're beautiful, scrupulous paintings. Quite mysterious for all their apparent clarity. Full of light and stillness. As if time had stopped. We'll have to go," he said to Ann.

"Not before this guy gets some work done," Michael said to her. "We're still fiddling around with this play, and he's fiddling around London. I think he's forgotten we've got an opening coming up—next Tuesday. Right, lad?" Michael rolled his eyes and laughed.

"I told you he's a playboy," Ann said. Michael was joking but Ann, light laughter notwithstanding, wasn't.

"You told *me*," Andrew said. "Probably you forgot to warn Michael. I'll work all weekend, Michael. I've already told you that. Don't worry about it." A playboy! He'd worked like a mule back in New York to finish that play, and the kind of work they were doing now was easy compared with that, simple tinkering and polishing—"fiddling around," in fact. "Well, you know me," he said, "I'm a great fiddler." He laughed. "You can't beat fun, as my father used to say. Remember that, Julie."

"Perhaps we can all go to the opening," Daisy said, pouring tea and handing a cup to Ann. "You look so young, Ann—hardly old enough to be the mother of Julia."

"She's old enough," Andrew said. "Actually, I'm not old enough to be a father."

"We must always allow for the miraculous," Daisy said.

Michael Aldrich laughed. "Yeh, sure. Actually, he's a virgin. He just pretends to know more than he does. Can't you tell?"

"What's a virgin?" Julia asked.

"It's a sweet young thing like your daddy," Michael said, and everyone laughed. Probably, Andrew thought, she had a good idea of what a virgin was; she was just testing their reactions. He was on to that trick—asking a question you already knew the answer to—having tried it often enough himself as a boy. The memory made him smile.

"Then who's Vermeer?" Julia asked.

"He's a Dutch painter," Daisy said, "who lived about three hundred years ago in Delft. That's right across the English Channel in Holland. He worked painfully slowly."

"Like me," Andrew said, interrupting her. "That must be why you thought I'd find him compatible."

"He painted only a few pictures," she continued, "but those few are very beautiful. Full of blues and yellows and light, and pretty women like your mother. That's why I thought your father would find him compatible." She laughed.

"The way I'd always imagined your house," Andrew said, "all white and yellow with the sun streaming in, and with flowers. Blue and white and yellow flowers. And a string of pearls on the table."

"I think he's writing another play," Michael said. "It sounds like a description of the set. I can always tell when Andrew's getting an idea. The string of pearls gives it away. That's the kind of touch he likes to add. You know, apparently offhand, nothing significant—just the obsessive little detail that brings the whole house of cards down. Better watch your necklace, Daisy. You too, Ann. He'll introduce the thief any minute."

"Give me a break," Andrew said. "I haven't finished with this one yet."

"Your pearls," Daisy said, nodding toward Ann's—"they're lovely."

"Thank you," Ann said, glancing down at them. She had roped them twice around her neck. "Andrew gave them to me when Julia was born. Actually, they were his mother's. She gave them to him to give to me."

"Well, of course," Daisy said. "I remember them. In fact, I mentioned them to Andrew today. The pearls on the Vermeer women brought them to mind. But you didn't tell me I'd be seeing them this afternoon, Andrew."

"Pearls look pretty much like pearls to me. Ann's were my grandmother's. I think my grandfather gave them to her when my father was born, and my father gave them to my mother one Christmas. It was the Christmas I got my desk, my rolltop desk. That was the best thing about it. That, and a funny little book on the Sargasso Sea."

"That's my desk now," Julia said.

"The very one," Andrew said. "Everything comes with a history, baby. I did love that desk. It had a drawer that locked."

"But Daddy lost the key. A long time ago he lost the key."

"We'll have to have one made for it." Andrew was discreetly brushing his crumbs into a little pile near his plate. "Every little girl needs a safe place for her secrets." He wondered why he could never manage to break a piece of bread without scattering crumbs everywhere; other people did. There were no crumbs around Daisy's plate, he noticed, nor around Ann's; it must be a secret girls learn in school: the art of eating without leaving crumbs. Julia hadn't learned it yet; her place was littered with crumbs too, like his.

Ann leaned toward them, cupped her hand discreetly to her mouth, and asked, "Are you hearing these two men over here?" She gestured slightly to her left. Two youngish men, in their late twenties or early thirties, perhaps, wearing what appeared to be identical pin-striped suits though of different sizes, were having tea with a pretty girl in a dress the color of melons. One of them was ruddy and looked as if he'd recently gained some weight; the other was very tall and thin. He was sitting with his legs extended and his head thrown back, and he was whinnying in that characteristic, equine way of certain Englishmen, as if he'd learned it not at his mother's knee but from his horse's mouth. His shoes, though, were scuffed. Their conversation appeared to consist entirely of unintelligible grunts, high, nasal, humorless laughter, and a single, continually repeated interjection: "quite."

"Do you have any idea what that conversation is about?" Ann asked.

"That's not a conversation," Michael replied; "they're just trying to establish each other's class."

"Trying for the upper hand," Andrew said. Sometimes he really didn't like the English, the way they pranced and simpered —or London either. Odd he should feel that way, since at other times he felt quite at home here, as if he were among his own people, sharing a common set of assumptions.

"Which is which?" Ann asked.

"The one with the scuffed shoes is the top man," Andrew said.

"How do you know that?" she asked.

"Oh, because—Who said it? I don't remember—the middle classes, they polish their silver too much. Applying that elevated principle to shoes, I'd say he's got the upper hand. Probably they both went to some fancy public school, but the chubby one was there on scholarship—on sufferance." He laughed.

"Andrew always did have an active imagination," Ann said, "as his mother says."

"And he was a high-strung child, too," Andrew added. "Don't forget that."

The Englishmen seemed so comical, Andrew thought, in their anthropological preening, like roosters in a barnyard—and all for the benefit of that comely-looking hen with the soft breasts and the melon silk. Andrew hated himself when he thought like that. He felt like a spy, like an astronomer fixing his lens on another planet. Probably the two Englishmen were no more comical in what they were attempting to establish than Ann and Julia and Daisy and Michael and he—in whatever they were trying to establish. He was so tired of scrutinizing other people's behavior, analyzing their motives, not to mention his own. For a moment he wished he were someone else, somewhere else, and that he dealt with something else, something abstract, something that meant exactly what it was and no more. Music. Suddenly he longed for music. He wished he were home in New York, playing at the piano. "I wish they had a piano here."

"You're thinking of the paintings," Daisy said—"the women interrupted at their music."

"The concupiscent virgin and the woman of the world," Andrew said, "playing at their keyboards."

"Beauty," Daisy said,

"is momentary in the mind—
The fitful tracing of a portal;
But in the flesh it is immortal."

"What's that?" Ann asked.

"It's the keystone," she blurted out, laughing. "It's Wallace Stevens, actually: 'Peter Quince at the Clavier.' "

"Oh, yes. I remember," Ann said. "But T. S. Eliot was my poet."

"*Four Quartets*," Andrew said, "to continue the musical theme."

"I guess you learn that stuff at Vassar," Michael said to Daisy.

"I don't know how to tell you this, Michael," Daisy replied, "but I didn't learn that stuff at Vassar. I served time there for a year and a half, but I was not educated there. I'm self-taught." She smiled. "Like you."

"I'm a Harvard man," Michael said. "Highly educated."

"He majored in bad thoughts," Andrew said. "Graduated *summa*."

"It's a gift," Michael said. "I found my vocation early. Now Andrew, here—he's a late bloomer."

"How does that poem go?" Andrew asked. "I can't quite remember it. But I remember that it fascinated me."

" '*The body dies; the body's beauty lives.*' That's the next line," Daisy said.

Suddenly the beginning of the poem came back to him in a rush:

Just as my fingers on these keys
Make music, so the self-same sounds
On my spirit make a music, too.

" '*Music is feeling, then, not sound,*' " he said, softly uttering the next line.

"Like the paintings," Daisy said. "Resonant."

The phrases rang in Andrew's head:

And thus it is that what I feel,
Here in this room, desiring you,
Thinking of your blue-shadowed silk,
Is music.

He pushed his plate away. His appetite had vanished. "Is nothing safe?" he asked, making a joke.

"Well, yes," Daisy said. "The North Shore, for instance. Very safe and very quiet. The only noise is the sound of the sea. And occasionally"—she laughed—"the crumbling of a stone. I was talking about that to Andrew yesterday at lunch," she said to Ann. "Curtis has a place there. At Magnolia." Curious, Andrew thought, that he'd never heard her refer to him by his first name. "You must come, all of you. This summer. It would be a favor to me, really. It's insufferably dull, otherwise. All those rocks—"

"And the wild, demonic sea," Andrew interrupted, and then wondered why. "Daisy says it's very gothic," he explained. "Something the Brontë sisters might have dreamed up."

"Oh, oh," Michael said, "danger afoot."

"It would be exciting," Daisy said, "and fun. Julia, you'd love it. The Stone House looks like a ruined castle—very romantic, from a distance. It was built by Curtis's grandparents when they'd made their pile. The pile's unfortunately quite thoroughly diminished now, but the ruin's still there and the house is full of relics—old dresses from the 1860s, tons of Victorian costume jewelry, lots of things for a girl to play with."

"Is it like the Tower of London?" Julia asked. "That's a castle."

"Oh, it's not like that at all," Daisy said. "Nothing so massive and regal as that." She laughed. "And not quite so well maintained."

"No vultures?" Michael asked.

"No guards either," Daisy said.

"We'll have to bring our own," Ann said. "By the way, what's your husband's name?"

"Curtis?" Daisy asked. "Oh, it's Frederick," she said, sounding surprised. "Frederick Thomas. Freddy, as his cronies call him. While I'm thinking of it, you'll be hearing from the Huntingtons. They'd like you to come to dinner. Maybe we could do it after the opening. That's a thought. Would you like that, Andrew—a little supper after the show? Michael?"

"Yes, I think I would. How about you, Michael?"

"Fine. I think there's already been some dickering with a couple of restaurants, but we could stop the dickering easily enough."

"We'd have to include the cast, though, and the production staff," Andrew said. "It's their night. Could the Huntingtons handle that? It would be a big party."

"I think so. I think they'd love it, actually. I'll check with them."

"What do you think, Michael?" Andrew asked.

"Fine," he said, "if you can handle it."

"It would be fun to go to that place," Julia said, "that place . . . where is it?"

Ann was wiping Julia's fingers with her napkin. "Mrs. Curtis's place? On the North Shore?"

"Yes. I'd like to sleep in a castle."

"Beware of strange princes, Julie," Michael said. "Remember what I said. Besides, you're mine forever."

"Perhaps you'd better come along," Andrew said, "just to keep watch." He glanced at his watch. "And perhaps we'd better be moving along, too. It's quite late." Out of the corner of his eye he noticed strange blurred shapes flickering on the overturned bowl of Julia's spoon. He looked more closely. The bowl was functioning as a convex mirror, he suddenly realized, and the shapes were not blurred at all but sharp: the minuscule, distorted, and intensified images of the five of them around that table. How absolutely uncanny, he thought, his eyes fixed on their tiny shapes reflected in the silver spoon; how eerie it was.

"The trio is still at it." Michael nodded toward the two Englishmen and the pretty girl at the next table.

Andrew looked up. "I guess they haven't established anything yet."

"And look at all that we've accomplished," Michael said, rising from his chair, kissing Ann and Daisy and Julia, each one, on the cheek. "Take care, my friends, and see you soon."

When Andrew asked for the bill, the waiter told him it had already been paid. Michael had taken care of it.

"Come here, Daddy," Julia said, after she had gotten into her pretty flowered nightgown and was ready for bed, "it's time for my story. You have to finish the story."

"The story?" Andrew asked.

"You know the story," Julia said. "The story you started last night. The one about the armadillo and the snake."

"Ah, yes," Andrew said, "Ralph the Cobra, and Anthony Armadillo, and the Kangaroo named Emily. *That* story. Well, let me see," he said, patting the blankets around her and sitting down beside her on the bed, "where did we leave them?"

"In Egypt. On the Pyramids. They were in trouble."

"Yes," Andrew agreed, "they were in grave trouble." But what was it and how do I get them out of it? he asked himself. "Abdul, the guide, was angry, right?"

"That's right," Julia said. "He was very angry because Ralph was showing Anthony and Emily the Pyramids and the guide caught them and he was mad because he thought he was the only one who could show people the Pyramids. He wanted money and they didn't have any."

"Oh, yes," Andrew said. "And he'd chased them out of the secret chamber in the deep heart of the Pyramid where the Pharaoh—that's the ancient king—was buried, down the long, dark tunnel which seemed to Anthony the longest, darkest tunnel in the whole world because Anthony couldn't move as fast as Emily and Ralph so he was even more scared than they, and then they hopped and crawled and slithered, each according to the ability nature had given him, out of the carefully concealed door and up the Great Pyramid, with Abdul, the ferocious, the red-eyed guide, in hot pursuit."

"Yes, and Abdul was afraid of Ralph. He was afraid he'd bite him, and then he'd die."

"Though Ralph had never bitten a single thing yct."

"How did he eat?" Julia asked.

"He could open his mouth very wide and he just swallowed things whole without chewing. He was a vegetarian, you know, and very gentle. Really, he liked to eat cotton bolls. They were his favorite food. There were a lot of them in Egypt, so he never went hungry. Sometimes he liked a nice piece of fruit or a nut, now and then a spinach salad with mushrooms but without the bacon. He didn't like meat at all. That's why he'd never bitten anything, that and because he had a kind heart," and Andrew, warming up to the story, settled down to telling it.

"Well, you see," he said, "Ralph, who was highly intelligent and also very cunning, knew he could easily disguise himself as a piece of string. He could just go completely limp, and since the Pyramid was very large, there were lots of places where someone might have dropped a piece of string. A piece of string would be very unobtrusive on the Pyramid, virtually unnoticeable. But Ralph was worried about Anthony, and even more worried about Emily, and they were moving so fast, slithering, crawling and hopping for dear life, that they were running out of breath. And besides, Egypt was Ralph's country and he felt, since he was the host, that he had an obligation to make his guests feel comfortable —or at least safe. But suddenly Ralph noticed that Anthony was much the same color as the Pyramid, and of course there were many chinks between the huge stones. Some of the chinks were quite large. So he told Anthony to crawl into one of them and remain very still. 'Abdul will never find you,' he said. 'His eyes are bad. But be sure to remain very still. Don't move at all. I'm going to stretch out and pretend I'm a piece of string, but I'll be close by and watching.'

" 'What about Emily?' Anthony asked.

" 'I'll think of something,' Ralph said, as Anthony quickly crawled into the crack Ralph had found. 'Don't worry.'

"But secretly," Andrew said, "Ralph was very worried about Emily. He just didn't know what to do about her yet, and it was hard to hide a kangaroo. She wasn't exactly small, you know, and also she was carrying Ralph's basket—you remember, the basket he lives in?—and he would need it eventually. Fortunately, though, Ralph noticed a discarded camel blanket—really quite a lovely Persian rug—lying on one of the great stones, and he had a sudden inspiration. 'Emily,' he cried hoarsely, 'get into this, quick.' And Ralph helped Emily drape the camel blanket around her, though he wasn't really very good at that. Still, Ralph did the best he could, and gave her excellent directions. He told her to wrap it around her head and let a lot of it hang over her face. He didn't want to tell her," Andrew said—"he was afraid it might hurt her feelings—but a kangaroo's face looks pretty much like what it is, even though Emily was unusually attractive for a kangaroo, so Ralph thought the best thing to do was to cover it. He made a few minor adjustments to her new robe—really, he thought, she looks quite spiffy—and told her that until darkness fell she was to pretend she was an old lady in a camel blanket begging for alms. 'Put my basket right here at your feet,' Ralph said, reminding her not to let her feet show at all because her feet, of course, would give her away just as much as her face, and to remain as unobtrusive as possible. 'I'll keep an eye on you,' he said, 'and we'll stay here until nightfall. Then we'll make our escape.'

" 'Where'll we go?' Emily asked.

" 'Shush,' said Ralph. 'Don't say a word. If someone drops a coin in my basket, just nod your head but don't say a word.' And Ralph quickly slithered a short distance away, selected a stone with a tiny crack for the tip of his tail and flopped out straight as a string, keeping one tiny eye just a little bit open so he could watch over Anthony and Emily while Abdul raved and ranted all over the Pyramid. Needless to say, Abdul was furious. He searched everywhere. He even poked Emily, but she didn't move, and when she didn't, he put his hand in her basket. Probably," Andrew said, "he thought she was blind. At first Ralph thought maybe Abdul was going to give her a coin, but then he realized that Abdul was too mean for that. You know what he was looking for?" Andrew asked. "He was looking to see if there were any coins he might take *out* of the basket. Wasn't that rotten of him?"

"Yes," Julia said, "it was. So then what happened?"

"Well, so Ralph was hanging there all strung out but with plenty of time to think because the day was far from over."

"What did he think?" Julia asked.

"He thought about what they'd do next, and about how much he liked his new friends and about how bad he felt that they were having such a terrible time in Egypt, his native land. Here he was, just trying to show them a few sights, and they'd all gotten into a frightful mess. Ralph thought maybe it was time to leave Egypt, to continue the journey they'd decided to make together. So when night fell, as it eventually did, and the wild-eyed, red-eyed Abdul had long since disappeared, Ralph unstrung himself and slithered over to Emily. 'Pssst,' he whispered, his tongue flicking the way snakes' tongues do, 'the coast is clear. You can come out from under the camel blanket now.' And he congratulated her on doing such a clever impersonation of a beggar lady —why, some nice tourists from Spain had even dropped a few coins in her basket, which, as we know, was actually Ralph's— and together they hopped and slithered, slithered and hopped over to Anthony, who emerged from his crack when Emily poked him. Ralph said, 'I have this interesting plan.'

"Well, to tell you the truth, Julie," Andrew said, "Anthony and Emily were a little skeptical of Ralph's plans, since it had been his plan to show them the Pyramids in the first place and that was how they'd gotten into so much trouble, but they listened politely anyway."

"What was his plan?" Julia asked.

"His plan was that under the cover of night they should make all haste toward Suez, which is the canal between the Mediterranean and the Red Sea, and that there they should board a suitable boat—choosing it with extreme care, of course, and with regard to its destination—and make their way toward Australia, Emily's beloved homeland, where they would all be safe. And that is the end of the story for tonight," Andrew said. "To be continued."

"Daddy, have you ever been to Australia?"

"No, but I know that Emily and Anthony and Ralph will love it there. It's their kind of place."

"Why?"

"We'll figure that out another time. It's long past your bedtime." He kissed her. "I love you, my baby—you don't mind if I call you 'my baby,' do you? I know you're practically a grown-up lady."

"That's okay, Daddy. I love you."

"I love you too," he said, "very, very much," and Ann, who had been listening in the next room, came in to kiss her good night.

"I like your story, darling," she said, returning to their room

and putting her arms around him. "It's a lovely, crazy story"—
she chuckled—"like you."

"What's so crazy about me?" Andrew asked the next morning.
He and Ann were still dressing, getting ready for the day, and
Julia, already dressed and feeling very grown-up, had pleaded to
be allowed to go down to the dining room before them, by herself. She was hungry, she said, but really it was not breakfast she
sought but the feeling of being a person on her own in the world,
apart from her parents, who remained, nonetheless, comfortably
within reach upstairs. Julia seemed to have quite thoroughly
charmed the people at the hotel, and certainly she was charmed
by them. They doted on her, and Andrew and Ann knew she
would be safe and that she would feel very grown-up indeed.

"What *are* you talking about?" Ann replied.

"Well, last night," Andrew said, smiling a little sheepishly,
"you said my story was crazy—like me."

"This confirms it." She shook her head. "I said it was a lovely,
crazy story, and it is—it made me laugh. I love it, and so does
Julia. It sort of grows on a person." She laughed. "Like you."

"Like a wart," Andrew said.

"Yes," Ann said, "sort of like a wart. Does the toad need a
kiss to turn him into the handsome prince he really is?"

"The toad always needs kisses, but I'm not sure they're strong
enough to turn him into a prince. They'd have to be pretty potent."

"Mine can be quite devastating."

"You're such a flirt." He reached for her. "I always said you
were the best kisser I knew."

"You're not supposed to know any other kissers," Ann said,
coming into his arms. "Remember that."

"Oh, I will, I will." She kissed him. "How could I forget it?"
he asked, returning her kiss. "But you *did* say I was crazy. How?"

"To paraphrase J. P. Morgan," Ann said, teasing him still, "if
you have to ask, you probably can't afford to know."

"Perhaps not. Anyway, it's your turn to tell me a story."

"But you're the storyteller, darling."

"I want to hear about Susanna and the Elders."

"What ever for?"

"Just tell me. You know the Bible better than I. Besides, I

think it's in the Apocrypha, and in the True Church you accepted the Apocrypha. We regarded it as dubious, you know, so I never really learned the story."

"Well," Ann said, "Susanna was a beautiful young woman married to a prosperous man of Babylon, I think, and she was—"

"Accused of adultery?" Andrew interrupted.

"Unjustly accused," Ann said. "Really she was a virtuous woman. But the nasty Elders spied on her bathing—"

"And they lusted after her," Andrew whispered hoarsely.

"She rejected their advances—"

"They were angry?"

"Very. They accused her of adultery instead."

"Just like a man," Andrew replied. "By the way," he said, suddenly remembering, "what was that 'playboy' bullshit yesterday? You told Michael I was a playboy."

"I was only joking, for heaven's sake."

"It wasn't funny," Andrew said. "You've gotten me confused with your father."

"That's not funny either. It is not at all funny. My father was not a playboy."

Well, he was, Andrew thought; he didn't do a damned thing but play blackjack and poker—and the stock market to support his habit; he was pretty good at that. But Andrew didn't say anything: he'd made her angry enough. "I'm sorry," he said. "I didn't mean it." Besides, he wanted her to continue the story. He reached over to hug her. "You haven't finished telling the story."

"The Elders were hypocrites. They said they'd seen her lying under a tree with a young man, which was a lie."

"What happened?"

"They were going to kill her, but I think there was some discrepancy in the description of the tree, and Daniel, who was a wise young man and close to God, caught the discrepancy and proved that the Elders were lying."

"What happened to the Elders?"

"They killed them instead." Ann laughed. She usually recovered quickly from her anger; more quickly than he. "Now it's your turn: why do you want to know?"

"I was thinking about the Wallace Stevens poem 'Peter Quince at the Clavier,' the one we were talking about at tea yesterday. It plays on that story, but I couldn't remember it exactly. I remember the poem, though; it's been coming back to me."

"Well, let's not hear it now. I've got to get Julia and me ready to go to the Spensers' for the weekend, and we've got to get down to the dining room. We can't leave her there alone forever."

"She's having the time of her life," Andrew said, "and probably ordering up a storm."

When they came into the dining room, Andrew suspected that Julia was secretly a little sorry to see them—she had obviously been enjoying the attention—but then he reminded her of his promise to take her to Madame Tussaud's, and that prospect excited her. It was what she wanted most to see in London. After breakfast, leaving Ann to explore London on her own, Andrew asked the hall porter for directions, and together he and Julia rode off on the double-decker bus to Madame Tussaud's and her Chamber of Horrors, which turned out to be less horrible but more grotesque than even Julia had expected.

While Andrew and Julia were gazing at the caricatures of horror in Madame Tussaud's bizarre and grisly waxworks—Jack the Ripper, Bluebeard, and Nelson's thunderous dying aboard H.M.S. *Victory*, of all things—it was decided, between Ann and Daisy and Mrs. Huntington, that the Huntingtons would give a buffet supper after the official opening of Andrew's play on Tuesday. Andrew wasn't sure he was up to it. He wanted nothing so much as to be out of London. He was beginning to despise the place. It was making him sick. The weather had taken a turn for the dismal, which required only a slight adjustment from its unspeakable early-April normal. He was sick of the accents. He was sick of the snobbery. He was sick of the daffodils. He didn't want to be in London when the tulips bloomed. He felt feverish. He was sick, he realized, of everything, including this play that he'd spent every waking moment on since his morning with Julia at the waxworks, and God knew how many hours and days before that. Ann said it was just his usual before-the-opening nerves, but it was more than that. He longed for New York. He didn't want to have to remain in London because of the play or anything else. He'd wanted to spend the weekend with his family, not at the theater in Sloane Square. Now he wanted to return with Ann and Julia at the end of the week to the comfort and safety of his house, even though his house was not a house at all but an apartment he could ill afford in New York City.

"I don't want to be in London when the tulips bloom," he told her.

"*What?*" Ann asked. "What a weird thing to say. That won't be until May. We're going to Bermuda in May, remember? With the Walcotts. He wants to discuss your career."

"Assuming I survive April. I'm sick."

"You're not sick. You've just got a little cold, or one of your allergies."

"Maybe it's an allergy," Andrew said, seizing the hope. He felt like a baby, and he knew he was acting like one. "I'm not used to these London pollens."

"Unfamiliar pollens. That's probably it."

"You don't sound very interested. Here I am burning with fever in this awful place. And this room is either frying or freezing. God, you'd think the English could master a simple thing like the thermostat. How do the Spensers stand it? They've been here all year! I want to go to bed."

"The Spensers love it. They hate to go back. Well, if your mother were here she'd tuck you in and give you a croup pill. But she's not here." Ann touched her hand to his forehead. "You don't feel the least bit feverish to me. And you look the picture of health. But if you feel well enough to make your opening, perhaps you'd better think about getting dressed."

"You too," he said. "It would be nice to be on time for my own show. For once. It's been my lifelong dream."

"Well, then," Ann said, "we shall try to make your dream come true—if you're sure that's what you want," and they began to prepare themselves and Julia for the evening. Andrew wouldn't have an opening without Julia's being there. She was going to the Huntingtons' too, for a little while. Mrs. Huntington had arranged with Ann for a woman who worked for her to take Julia back to the hotel later and to stay with her until they returned.

"I can't find my studs," Andrew said. He was standing in his shoes and trousers, suspenders flapping, his shirt open and cuffs hanging loose over his hands. "Where the hell are my studs? God damn it," he exclaimed, "have I lost my father's studs?"

"Here they are, Daddy." Julia handed him the box. "They were right there on the bedside table."

"Your father's going blind too, along with everything else. Thank you, Julie. You've always been a whiz at finding things," and it was true, she was. If he had mislaid his keys, she knew where he had left them. If he was trying to find a book on the shelf, she could show him; she seemed to have a print of the entire library fixed firmly in her mind. "You look real pretty," he said, admiring her. "Just like your mother must have looked before she got old and grisly." He laughed, and called toward the bathroom where Ann was dressing: "Right, Ann?" He turned back to Julia. "I love your hair that way, Julie. Alice in Wonderland, but shorter. And of course, prettier." He was fumbling with his cuff link, having gotten it halfway through the cuff and then run into difficulty. "I'm messing up this shirt," he said. "This day is not going well at all."

"Here, let me do it," Julia said. "My fingers are smaller," and she nimbly threaded the link through and then moved to the other cuff and finished the job. "Can I do the studs?"

"No, I think I can manage them by myself," Andrew said, "but thanks," and he finished dressing and sat down on the bed with Julia to wait for Ann.

"Will you play a game of cards with me?" Julia asked.

"Okay," he said. "Get the cards." But by the time Julia returned from her room with the cards, Ann was emerging from the bathroom.

"Mommy," she said, "you look *beautiful!*"

"The child is right." Andrew rose from the bed. "You do. You always do." She stood there for a moment, a drift of blues and greens, her swirling presence filling the room like music, like silk. He paused to look at her. "The colors of the sea," he said, then made a kind of melody of it: "with patches of sunlight and shadow—and a cloud of blue perfume." He sniffed the air. "This must be what Bermuda is like. I take it all back: you've not gotten old and grisly at all." He laughed. "You've gotten"—he searched for the word and, finding it, softly uttered it—"ravishing. Yes, even more ravishing with time." He took her by the hand.

"They're the colors of Mommy's ring," Julia said, pointing to Ann's ring with the sapphires surrounding the flawed emerald cut like a teardrop. At the time Andrew had bought it, a belated engagement ring after the success of his first play, a flawed emerald was the only emerald he could afford; now, he realized, he couldn't have afforded that. But he had come to see that the beauty of the stone, its mystery, lay in that small, visible, murky scar in the stone's green depths.

"And the colors of her eyes," Andrew said.

"I planned it that way," Ann said, laughing, moving her extended hand toward her breast. "Should I wear the pearls"—she took them from the table—"or not?" She held them before her.

"I don't know," Andrew said.

"Wear them, Mommy," Julia said.

She turned to face the mirror. "I'm afraid they're too much." She moved them away from her dress so they could compare the effect.

"Oh, no, Mommy. Wear them. They're beautiful. And the clasp matches your ring."

"What do you think?" Ann asked him.

He looked at her reflection. "I don't know what to think. You look nice either way."

"Then wear them, Mommy," Julia said, and Ann looped them once around her neck.

"Would you help me with the clasp?" He fastened it behind her, looked up to see her smiling at him in the mirror. She gave the pearls a little shake, and they rippled smoothly from her shoulders. "Hand me my bag, would you, Julia? And my arrow? I've got an idea." She fastened the arrow to the bag, looked at it sparkling there against the silk, and laughed. "In case I need a weapon." She turned to face him. "There. I'm ready."

Andrew kissed her lightly on the throat, inhaling her fragrance. "You smell so good."

"You look so good," Julia said. "You look so good together. My mommy and daddy are the most beautiful married people in the world. This is exciting!" she exclaimed. "Let's go. I can hardly wait."

"I can," Andrew said. "But let's do it. Time to face the music. *'She sighed, for so much melody.'* That's another line from that Wallace Stevens poem we were talking about the other day at tea." He began reciting it as they closed the door of their rooms and walked down the corridor toward the stairway:

"Upon the bank, she stood
In the cool

Of spent emotions,
She felt, among the leaves
The dew
Of old devotions.

I dropped into a bookstore yesterday and looked it up. Now I can't get it out of my head:

"She walked upon the grass,
Still quavering.
The winds were like her maids
On timid feet,
Fetching her woven scarves,
Yet wavering.

"A breath upon her hand
Muted the night.
She turned—
A cymbal crashed,
And roaring horns."

Andrew felt a tingling on his skin. "End of the recitation," he said. "Go to the head of the class, Tommy. That's a good boy."

"Now it's my turn," Ann said as they walked down the stair-case. She seemed suddenly full of eagerness for the evening ahead, almost joyful. "And my lines are more appropriate:

"Let us go then, you and I,
When the evening is spread out against the sky—"

" 'Like a patient etherized upon a table,' " Andrew interrupted, "which is exactly how I'm beginning to feel."

Ann continued her recitation as they walked across the lounge—

"Let us go, through certain half-deserted streets,
The muttering retreats
Of restless nights in one-night cheap hotels
And sawdust restaurants with oyster-shells:"

—stepped through the doorway—

> "Streets that follow like a tedious argument
> Of insidious intent
> To lead you to an overwhelming question. . . .
> Oh, do not ask, 'What is it?' "

—and into the waiting taxi. She turned toward him and smiled. " 'Let us go and make our visit.' Now that's what I call appropriate," she said as the taxi drove off.

"That's what I call timing," Andrew said.

"But it applies perfectly to what we're doing."

"Life imitates art," he replied, gazing out the window at the blur of the passing street.

"I had to memorize the whole poem for a course in college, and I still"—the taxi lurched in the traffic and she lunged toward him and grasped his arm, her pearls, luminous in the dim interior light, swinging from her breast—"know it. Please, driver," she said, tapping at the glass that separated them from him, "we don't want to transfer to an ambulance."

"No," Andrew said. "I may need to leave in one, but we'd like to arrive in some degree of style."

She squeezed his arm. "I'm excited for you, darling. I know it's going to be wonderful."

"So do I, Daddy," Julia said. He took her hand, and in a few moments their car had navigated the short distance and they were deposited in front of the theater, where a little crowd had already gathered on the pavement under the sparkling marquee of the Royal Court. There was Michael Aldrich, and there was Andrew's agent, Pamela Stickney, towering above the crowd. He waved to the Spensers. Janet was wearing one of her peasant dresses—Bedouin, it looked. He smiled. There were various people whose faces he recognized from his work and whose names he ought to remember but did not: he was terrible with names; sometimes he thought he hardly knew his own.

"Andrew, darling," Pamela shouted, starting like an antelope toward him. "And little Julia! Ann," she exclaimed, showering airy kisses all around, "what a vision! You've made it! We were beginning to wonder if you would," she said to Andrew—"but then, you're always arriving at the last minute." She turned to Ann. "Is it his sense of timing?"

"My sense of timing is confined entirely to the stage," Andrew said. "It doesn't apply to my life."

"Quite true. Otherwise you wouldn't have stood me up for lunch last Wednesday. Imagine canceling a tryst with one's agent, who seeks only your welfare and enrichment, darling. What ever could've been more enticing?" She laughed, and turned to Ann. "Andrew has promised us an evening of sex and violence. Are we going to be disappointed?"

"I've no idea," Ann replied. "He doesn't give me private readings. Only an occasional snatch of what he's working on. Rehearsals and previews are off limits."

"Sweetie," Pamela said, "are you withholding something?"

"My life is an empty book," Andrew said.

"Not empty," said Michael Aldrich, who'd come over in the midst of the conversation. "It's just written in a strange language that hasn't been deciphered yet. But we're working on it. Hello, Ann. Hello, my lovely Julie. What's on your tiny little mind?"

Julia giggled. Ann asked, "What shall we call it?"

"Call what?" Julia asked.

"The empty book," Ann said.

"How about *Looking for the Rosetta Stone*?" Michael gave him an innocent kind of smile.

"Well, when you find it, let me know," Ann said, laughing. "I've been trying to figure it out for years. But about the play: you must tell me, Pamela. Surely you're familiar with it."

"Oh, yes. Of course. Marvelous." Pamela had an accent that went wonderfully well with her appearance, which was rather pale, very tall, and very upper-class. She was about thirty-five, Andrew knew, but a casual observer might have guessed her to be anywhere from thirty to fifty. She looked more like an English "lady" than any English lady Andrew had ever seen, though he knew that she'd grown up somewhere in the North of England, the daughter of a farrier, in a house that hadn't a single book, let alone a nodding acquaintance with anything so grand as a lord or a lady. But her mother was determined and extremely ambitious, and Pamela had been a quick and serious study, winning a scholarship to a fancy school for the daughters of the ruling class. They'd made her life miserable, but she'd learned the thing that mattered most to her mother: an accent that thrilled, even awed her, despite the fact that her mother could scarcely understand it. Her father had died drunk and more miserable, hating his wife and resenting his daughter. Still, Pamela was very funny, and very realistic, and when she was a little drunk, which was not often but occasionally, she would lapse into the accents of her birthplace and tell stories that made them all laugh. But not now. She was very much the lady now. "Why, I've even seen a preview," she said, "and peeked into a rehearsal or two while Andrew was in the midst of his serious 'fiddling,' as he calls it."

"He's impossible when he's writing," Ann said, "though no one else would ever know it. And I'm never sure of the results until I see the play. Sometimes"—she laughed—"I'm not entirely sure then."

"I'm merely a clerk, not a critic," Pamela said, looking over their heads and waving gaily to this one and that. "The *Telegraph* is here," she said, blowing a kiss to an enormously fat man who looked like a rumpled suit on a bad day, "and there's that whore-hopper from *The Times*. Halloo, you lovely thing," she called to him. Andrew chuckled. He felt himself beginning to warm to the occasion. Somehow he always did.

"Who's that one?" Andrew asked, indicating a man in his early fifties but trying desperately to avoid looking it, who had the top-heavy stance of someone who'd spent most of his waking hours sweating and heaving on a bench press, and the rest of them under a sunlamp. A younger fellow, also in evening clothes, stood attentively by his side. "The one talking to Lady Rysdale and her son." Andrew waved to the countess and Patrick.

"To the playwright!" the countess called across the crowd. "To the next generation's Tennessee Williams!" She raised her hand in a mock toast, and Andrew shuddered but smiled. He was determined to seem grown-up this evening.

"That's Nigel Rogers from the *Daily Mail*," Pamela said. "He wants to be Nigel Rogers from *The Observer*. The tart on his arm must be the new boyfriend." She whispered: "He requires from his boyfriends that they gaze adoringly when he's speaking but never utter more than a word, and also lash him a bit at the end of the evening. Lightly, of course. That's the fun part—a mild whipping like mother used to give. Nothing to scar the lovely body. He and the surgeons have worked too hard on it." She called over to him: "Nigel, you genius, you look like a work of art!" Nigel beamed back at her. "I was thinking of *The Picture of Dorian Gray*," she said, bending toward Andrew. "You know, he's got a closetful of evening clothes in different sizes to outfit his young men. He wouldn't want them to look too obviously what they are. But you must talk to some of these people, Andrew. Charm the bloody bastards." She stretched to her height and looked beyond him. "My, what's this?"

Andrew turned. An elegant black car—not a Rolls but a Bentley, he noticed from the hood ornament, wishing he did not notice these things—was gliding to the curb. It was Daisy, of course, with the Huntingtons in their car. At least, Andrew assumed it was their car. When he thought about it, he wouldn't have expected Daisy to arrive in anything less. Well, when he thought again, she might have taken the tube. Yes, she could have done that. She liked comfort, all right, but she also liked to surprise, and when she alighted from the car, rippling softly in the light from the marquee, she did.

"It's Daisy Meyer," Andrew said, "an old friend of Michael's and mine from childhood, and the people she's with must be the Huntingtons. They're giving the supper afterward. I've not met them, but we all will soon." He moved toward them.

"Hello, Andrew," Daisy said, extending her hand. "It's your big night. And such a pleasant evening, too, for a change. Are you excited?" Without waiting for an answer she began making introductions, and soon there was a flurry of "How d'you do's" and "How nice to meet you's" all around.

"She looks like a storm cloud about to drop its load," Michael whispered to him. "And I've forgotten my lightning rod." Beneath her cloak Daisy was wearing a dress of an extraordinary color, like pewter, with the muted sheen that molten metal takes on as it cools, and suspended from the pearls she seemed always to wear was a single large aquamarine that had the liquid clarity of a tropic sea.

"Maybe you won't need it," Andrew said to him as the crowd began to move in response to the bells summoning them inside, and in a few moments they were all swept into the theater to await the curtain. Never, Andrew thought, taking his seat with Ann and Julia in the last row, had he felt so vulnerable, so fragile, and a few moments after the curtain rose he left his seat to stand with Michael Aldrich in the darkness at the back of the house. Soon they were joined by Julia. "I love it, Daddy," she whispered, squeezing his hand. Andrew returned her squeeze, but could not speak.

"Why did you choose that title, that particular address, Mr. MacAllister?" Mrs. Huntington asked him as they were riding in the Huntingtons' car to their house.

"*Forty-One East Seventy-third*? Because it's an address that doesn't exist," Andrew replied. Mrs. Huntington was merely being polite, but Andrew didn't want to talk about it. He did not like his play. He didn't like it at all, though the audience had seemed to. At least they'd laughed when they were supposed to. It seemed, in a way, a travesty with all the horror going on in the world that he should be writing witty dialogue, perversely witty dialogue, the kind that fell so lightly, so painfully from his pen, to put into the mouths of a bunch of overbred but underdeveloped New Yorkers suffering through a city-wide strike. The proposition was interesting enough, he supposed: what happens to people when their accustomed services stop, when they have to haul their own garbage and deliver their own mail and they can't get a taxi on the street or a train in the subway and the trucks aren't delivering. Life without Bloomingdale's. It was all lies, he thought, but then every play was: a collection of dialogue of a certain length, spoken by undereducated actors purporting to be what they weren't, and telling a false story that aimed through its lies to arrive at something that might reasonably be called true. Andrew cared very much about the truth, no matter that it eluded him. "Perhaps I should have called it *Civilization and Its Discontents*," he said, wondering why he should hate himself for doing the only thing he knew how to do, the only thing he did well.

"You seem rather pensive, Mr. MacAllister," Mrs. Huntington said, "for having just scored such a success."

"I've never ridden in such a fancy car before." Andrew was sitting on the jump seat facing the three women, Mr. Huntington beside him on the other. "I think I could get used to it." He looked toward his daughter, who was sitting in front and talking excitedly with the driver. "Julia looks pleased as punch. She's having the time of her life."

"Success always makes him sad," Ann said. "It's one of the sweet mysteries about him."

Andrew laughed. "It's not a success yet. Success requires a lot more than a good opening."

"But it's a very fine play," Daisy said.

"Thank you," Andrew said. He had finally learned to be gracious about compliments, to accept them without argument. "And thank you, too, for giving this party, Mrs. Huntington— and please call me Andrew. Everyone has worked very hard— the actors, the staff, everyone. They're thrilled to be invited to your house. So am I. I much prefer a quiet supper to one of these"—he was about to say "rat fucks," but restrained himself —"one of these after-the-opening feeding frenzies in some de- signer shark tank."

"Well, Mr. MacAllister"—Mrs. Huntington laughed—"the party hasn't started yet. I hope you won't change your mind. And yes, I shall call you Andrew if you'll call me Barbara. And here we are." The Bentley purred to a stop before a broad bow- front Georgian house—a grand house, really, its windows gleam- ing with lights—on Cheyne Walk, overlooking the Thames. *"Brightness falls from the air,"* Andrew thought, gazing at the spar- kling scene. In a moment they were all piling out of the car and into the house, where the party was already beginning.

"It's going to be a beautiful party," Ann said, taking Julia's hand as they mounted the stairs to the drawing room, "in a beau- tiful house."

She was right. It was a sumptuous house. Julia was wide- eyed. "Daddy, this is fun!" she exclaimed softly. She loved par- ties, and so did Andrew, once he got into them. He always found something to interest him.

"Let's hope we can avoid another discussion of Viet-Nam," Mrs. Huntington said. "I'm quite weary of bearing the responsi- bility for our country's transgressions—and these endless recapit- ulations of the Calley trial! At least that's finished. The British, you know, can be awfully self-righteous."

"They speak from a position of moral inferiority," Andrew said. "It makes self-righteousness highly gratifying."

Mr. Huntington, who seemed a quiet but amiable man, looked puzzled.

"I was thinking of their colonial past," Andrew explained. "Not that any of us speaks from innocence."

"Oh, yes, of course," Mr. Huntington said. "As Chesterton put it, 'Morality is like art; you've got to draw the line somewhere.' "

It was Andrew's turn to be puzzled. He wondered if, perhaps, Mr. Huntington felt that in his play he'd not drawn the line with sufficient strength and determination; or drawn it in the wrong place. Lines dissolve when systems break down, he thought. There seemed little chance of the Huntingtons' system breaking down, however; quite clearly theirs was a well-regulated household running smooth as their Bentley on the grease of money. There was nothing quite like a shitload of money, Andrew thought, to smooth life's little bumps and ridges. It seemed to make drawing the line easier—for them, at least. Andrew didn't have much time to be puzzled, though. He could see that Lady Rysdale was about to zero in.

"I know," he said to her: "it's 'the next generation's Tennessee Williams.' Lady Rysdale, if you knew how much I dislike that particular comparison, brilliant as he is and flattering as it may be—" Andrew felt a firm nudge against his shoe. It was Ann, bringing him back to his senses.

"He's quite impossible after he's seen one of his shows." Ann was trying to salvage the situation. "It puts him in a terrible funk; but we're going to bring him out of it," she said, accepting a drink from the tray that was being passed. "Lady Rysdale, would you like some champagne?"

"Why, thank you," she said. "What a festive evening! But Mr. MacAllister, your play is smashing. Smashing! Frightfully witty."

Yes: smashing; frightful. He looked at her. No, he thought, she was too stupid. "Thank you, Lady Rysdale. I'm glad that you liked it. Could I have some whisky, please," he said to the waitress. "With ice." Ann shot him a look. "I'm afraid I need something stronger," he said to Lady Rysdale. "Just like Tennessee Williams," and suddenly he burst out laughing. "I'm teasing you." He was coming out of it. "Really, I'm grateful that you liked the play and I hope lots of others will agree with you." The waitress returned with his whisky. The bows of her eyeglasses swept up like beating wings, a small cluster of rhinestones spangling each corner. My God, he thought, designer eyeglasses! On a servant in this house! Perhaps the Huntingtons didn't know where to draw the line either, or simply didn't know how. He wished he could question her, interview her.

"Visky, sir," she said. She had a slight accent, German or Scandinavian, and she issued the statement as if she were barking a command, maybe hurling a challenge. "Vit ice." Andrew smiled. Life was preposterous. She had had her hair not simply done but "styled," and colored the steel of her glasses.

"Do you suppose she's a baroness in exile?" Andrew asked.

"Pardon?" Lady Rysdale said.

"The waitress. Did you notice her? She looks as if she's a refugee from a castle in Prussia. And sounds it, too. She'd win hands down at a sale in Saks." He shook his head in amazement.

"Oh, no," Lady Rysdale said. "I hadn't noticed." Well of course she hadn't; a countess didn't notice a servant. "I suppose that's why you're a playwright: you notice such things." Andrew could see that she found it a bit bizarre, but probably chalked it up to the expected eccentricities of the artist. He wondered what she chalked her husband's eccentricities up to. Bad company in the House of Lords, maybe.

"Dear Lady Rysdale!" It was Pamela, striding toward them. "How stylish you look! Splendid as the Queen herself!" Lady Rysdale demurred. "Well then, at least the Queen Mother." Pamela flashed her a dazzling smile. "Who is Patrick's charming friend?" Pamela indicated a young man talking with Julia, Daisy, Patrick Rysdale, and one of the actors from the play at the far end of the room. He was, Andrew thought, the same young man who had been with Nigel Rogers at the theater. "Lovely as a model," Pamela said, without waiting for a reply. "Now we must move this man about." She took Andrew by the arm and led him off. "You may thank me later."

"Ann won't. We can't leave her with the countess. She doesn't like me to leave her at parties—at least this kind of party. And what is this 'Queen Mother' bit?"

"Delicious, wasn't it? Don't worry about Ann. I'm sure she can hold her own. Besides, I see Mrs. Huntington and your friends from Hampstead already coming to the rescue, should one be needed. You just come with me," and she began circulating him around the room, telling him who was who, introducing this one and that, prompting him with the right questions, pausing to chat with various members of the cast and production staff.

"You do know how to work a crowd," Andrew told her, with some admiration, as they approached Julia and Daisy and Richard Squires, an actor in the play. "This lady is something to watch," he said to them. "How are you, baby?" he asked Julia. "Are you enjoying yourself?"

"We're having a perfectly wonderful time," Daisy said, "and Julia is entertaining us all. Backstage stories."

"No secrets, I hope."

"I don't know any secrets. You don't tell me any," Julia replied.

"That's because they're secrets," Andrew said. "I think you're teasing me, Julie."

"This girl has lots of secrets," Richard said, "but they're hard to pry out of her."

"And you must keep it that way," Daisy said. "Thanks for taking us backstage after the show, Andrew. I'd never been backstage before, and I know the Huntingtons loved it. I was fascinated. Such an enormous amount of technology and skill and expertise—genuine skill and expertise—to create what is, in the end, an illusion."

"And effort," Andrew added. "You left that out. Amazing, isn't it, how much sheer terrible effort projecting an illusion requires? It never fails to impress me too. Every time. And Richard, let me repeat it: you were great. Good to see you, Patrick. Thanks for coming."

"Andrew, this is David . . ." Patrick stammered, "David . . . I'm sorry, I seem to have—"

"Roper," the young man said, extending his hand, "David Roper. I'm really thrilled to meet you."

"Don't be," Andrew said. "It's just me. But I'm glad to meet you too."

"Weren't you with Nigel at the theater?" Pamela asked him.

"Yes, but he had to go to the paper to write his review. I talked to Patrick at the theater, and he asked me to the party. Nigel introduced us," he added. "I hope it's all right. I feel embarrassed."

"Let's hope it's all right with Nigel," Pamela said, "and he'd better write a good one." She turned to Patrick. "I didn't know you were a friend of Nigel's, Patrick."

"Oh, yes," Patrick said. "Quite."

Andrew chuckled and looked at Daisy, who smiled back. "David, there's always room for an unexpected guest at a party like this," he said. "You fit right in. I'm sure no one has even suspected." The Teutonic waitress with the designer eyeglasses approached again. She served the group, and then, proffering the tray to him, said in the same imperious tone she had used before, "Visky, sir."

He stared at her. "Thank you, ma'am," he said. She held his gaze for half a second, and moved on. "I wonder which barracks she was in charge of at Auschwitz. By the way, Julia, isn't it way past your bedtime? I think you'd better be leaving soon."

"Do I have to go, Daddy?"

"Yes, Julia, you've got to." He looked at his watch. "But okay, ten more minutes—and then you *really* must." He put his arm on her shoulder and drew her to him.

"Here, have an oyster," Michael Aldrich said, approaching with Janet Spenser and Ann, a plate of oysters in his hand. "They're good for you. Maybe you'll find a pearl. Lots of pearls here." He was gesturing toward Ann and Daisy. "That's a big mother," he said, looking at Daisy's aquamarine.

Andrew laughed. "Same old Michael."

"Julia," Ann said, "you're tired. We've got to see about getting you home."

"We'll be happy to take her." It was Janet Spenser, looking plain and solid as ever despite her colorful robe. "And my, Andrew, Philip and I are *so* proud of you!" She clasped his hand in both of hers and stared deeply into his eyes, smiling earnestly, insistently. "So very proud." She rubbed his arm.

"I'm not tired," Julia said. "Daddy promised me ten more minutes!"

"True, I did. She's having a good time," he said to Ann, taking his eyes for a moment from Janet and her astonishingly toothy smile. "And thank you, Janet. I appreciate it. I hear Ann and Julia had a wonderful weekend with you and Philip. Oops! I'm caught in your jewelry." He tried to extricate the buttons on his sleeve from the heavy chunk of silver that hung from her wrist. Metal of one Third World group or another was always hanging from Janet Spenser. "What is it?" he asked. "Indian?"

"Guatemalan," she said. "Huehuetenango. Here, let me do this. You can't do it, dear, with a drink in your hand." She handed his drink to Pamela and began fiddling with her bracelet and his sleeve. "The most wonderful peasant woman—so placid, so wise—just took it off her arm and *insisted* I have it." She smiled at him again. "It was so moving. They have so little. Of course, I paid her for it."

He looked at Pamela, shrugged, and laughed as Janet continued her efforts. "We're hopelessly entangled."

"I'll fix it," Julia said. "I'm good at that," and in a moment he was free.

"Thanks, sweetheart." He patted his daughter. "I was afraid for a minute there that Janet would have to take me home with her. Thank God you're not wearing your Bedouin bells, Janet. I'd be tinkling in your tow all night. We might have had to get married."

"You wouldn't get lost, darling," Pamela said, returning his drink. "We'd just follow the bells."

"Too late now," he said.

"Well, dear friends, if you need us to take charge of Julia, we'd love to do it," Janet said. "Anytime."

"That's nice of you, Janet. I think Mrs. Huntington's already made arrangements for Julia, but we may need to take you up on it anyway. But let's let her stay a little longer—okay, Ann? I don't know what she's been telling these people, but she certainly had them laughing. What were you telling them, Julia?"

"She'll never tell," Michael said.

"Richard," Ann said, "I was telling your wife how good you were tonight. Now I'll tell you directly: you were wonderful."

"Just wonderful," Janet Spenser said, the wide, intent smile still fixed on her face.

"Thanks," Richard said, "and I'll tell you: so was your husband. So *is* your husband. He wrote a great part for this actor."

"I'd like to talk to you about your play." It was the young man who'd come with Patrick.

"While you're doing that," Ann said, "I'll go find Mrs. Huntington and tell her that Julia should be leaving."

"If she's planning to send her home with the ogre of Auschwitz, tell her I won't let her go," Andrew said, hugging Julia to him. "Janet and Philip will take her to Hampstead."

"Oh, really, Andrew, don't be silly."

"I mean it," he replied.

"Then, darling, you tell her."

"I will."

"I can relieve your minds," Daisy said. "That woman doesn't work here. I believe Mrs. Huntington got her from an agency for the evening."

"I'll find our hostess—" Andrew said, laughing, "just to make sure. Will you excuse me, please?" and he went off to look for Mrs. Huntington. He didn't see her in the drawing room or the adjoining sitting room. He asked the butler, "Have you seen Mrs. Huntington?"

"I believe Mrs. Huntington has stepped away for a moment, sir," the butler replied.

"Thank you," Andrew said. That seemed quite obvious, but it hardly answered the question. Andrew stepped away himself, continuing his search. The door to the library was ajar, he noticed, and he glanced in. There, to the left of the door, her back toward him, was Mrs. Huntington, her expensively clothed arm slashing the air.

"Chester," she exclaimed, her voice harsh and angry, "stop doing that! You're acting like an ass!"

Andrew quickly attempted to withdraw, but Mr. Huntington had already seen him. "Come in, Mr. MacAllister," he said, rather adroitly under the circumstances. "Barbara and I hope you're enjoying the party."

Andrew wanted to shout: But Mr. and Mrs. Huntington, your system! So smoothly running, so beautifully maintained, so lavishly greased. Please. Don't let it too break down. I mean, my play was only a play, a fantasy, an illusion; this is your *life*! You've drawn the line, remember? And you've drawn it, ordered it, beautifully. Andrew was genuinely distressed. They had seemed so . . . so in control of their creation. He said instead, "It's a terrific party, but I'm afraid it's time for Julia to leave. I hate to trouble you, Mrs. Huntington. Our friends the Spensers have offered to take her."

"It's not the slightest trouble," she said. Mrs. Huntington too was good at recoveries. "I'll find Stevens now and we'll send Julia home with his wife."

"Is his wife German?" Andrew asked.

"What a funny question," Mrs. Huntington said. "She's as English as Marks and Sparks. Excuse me. I'll be only a moment," and she left them in the library, a small and, Andrew had thought, comfortable retreat in the Huntingtons' grand house.

"What are you enjoying most about London, Mr. Mac-Allister?" Mr. Huntington asked. He was a somewhat florid man, as if, perhaps, he might lean a little heavily on the bottle, but thinner than his sturdy wife, with a shock of black hair where his wife's was silver. Andrew wondered if he dyed it.

Andrew thought for a moment. "I suppose I'd have to say the Elgin Marbles," he replied, "or maybe the Vermeers in the National Gallery. Yes, certainly the Vermeers too—and that marvelous Van Eyck with the convex mirror. I guess it's a toss-up."

"You'll have to talk to Freddy Curtis about the Marbles. He's quite an authority on classical sculpture."

"Daisy's husband? I've not met him."

"Oh, but you will, won't you? I understand you're going to visit them at Sharksmouth this summer."

"Sharksmouth?"

"Yes, the Curtis family place on the North Shore. In Massachusetts."

"My God," Andrew said, "how did it get such a terrible name?"

"Something about the rock formations, I believe," Mr. Huntington said. "They're thought to resemble the jaws of a shark. You'll have to ask Daisy about it."

"I think I'd be afraid to," Andrew said, laughing. "Sharksmouth!"

"Andrew, Mrs. Stevens will be taking Julia to your hotel," Mrs. Huntington said, returning to the room with a woman who did indeed look as sensible and as English as Marks & Spencer and who was not, to Andrew's immense relief, the Prussian martinet.

"Thank you," Andrew said to the butler's wife. "It's very kind of you."

"It's a pleasure, sir," she said. "She's a lovely child."

"We must find her," Andrew said, and they all left the library, Mrs. Huntington drawing the door closed after them, and returned to the party. A few minutes later, Julia went back to the hotel with Mrs. Stevens in the Bentley. Julia never wanted to miss anything, and he knew she didn't want to leave, any more than he wanted her to go, but he was proud that she didn't make a fuss about it. She'd even remembered to thank Mrs. Huntington. After all, she didn't get to ride in a chauffeur-driven Bentley every day. That must have given her something to look forward to. If he'd been eight years old, he would have loved it. As far as that went, he could still get a kick out of it at forty.

"Mr. MacAllister, I'd really like to talk to you about your play." It was David Roper, the critic's friend, seeking him out at the buffet table.

"Suddenly I'm famished," Andrew said, "and these oysters are different from the oysters we get at home. They're delicious." He ate another. "But yes, if you're really interested I'd be happy to talk to you about the play, as soon as I've had something to eat. Here"—he handed him a plate—"I'm sure you could use a little food yourself."

"I feel like an interloper," the young man said, taking the plate and heaping it with slices of duck.

"You're no more an interloper than I," Andrew replied. "We could use the library. It's quiet there, a good place to talk. If you really want to talk." Andrew looked at him. "I'm serious about my work, you know. I don't talk about it with everybody." They walked through the crowd toward the door that Mrs. Huntington had closed. "I sometimes think," he said, opening it, "that it's time for me to go into my room and shut the door. But it seems a terrible thing to have to turn off the world in order to deal with it." They walked into the library. "My usual approach is to make enough noise to drown it out. Well, what is it you want to know?" Andrew asked, putting his plate on a table in the corner and seating himself.

"I would have thought that your usual approach was to keep moving," the young man said. Andrew glanced up at him. "You know, to elude it." He drew a chair to the other side of the table, sat down, and picked up his fork.

"The absence of motion is death," Andrew said. "Haven't you noticed?" He looked at the man more closely. Who is this David Roper? Andrew asked himself.

"Isn't that what you're writing about?" the young man asked, his fork still poised midway between plate and mouth.

"What?"

"Death?"

"Entropy, maybe," Andrew said, laughing lightly. "Actually, I'd rather thought it was the opposite." He was beginning to wish he'd never gotten into this. "The play is a comedy, remember?"

"The dialogue is funny, some of it—a lot of it—if that's what makes a comedy. Are you trying to pretend you're Noël Coward?"

"No," Andrew said, his laughter fading. "I'm not. I'm trying to pretend I'm Andrew Thomas MacAllister, son of James and Emma of Grande Rivière, resident of New York City, currently in London with his wife and child. That's who I am, and that seems quite enough for the moment. It's a tough act. Who are you?"

"I'm just Patrick's friend," David Roper replied, finally raising his fork to his mouth.

"I thought you were that critic's friend—what's his name?—Nigel, Nigel Rogers. The iron-pumper."

"Iron-pumper?"

"Someone who lifts weights," Andrew explained. "But you must be more than somebody's friend."

"Oh, yes," he said, "I'm more than that. You don't like weight lifters?"

"I've no opinion on the subject," Andrew replied. "I don't spend a lot of time thinking about it. Any time, really."

"It develops the body. Like food."

"I'm too busy working on the head." Andrew picked at an oyster with his fork.

"This duck is good," the young man said. "Crispy." He began attacking it voraciously. "I'm hungry as a horse. The Greeks believed in the body. They started the Olympic Games."

"They believed in the mind, too," Andrew said. "You've heard of Plato? Aristotle? Socrates? Their drama festivals? Really, I don't think it's a question of belief."

"What is it a question of?" the young man asked, pausing in his meal.

"It's a question of what is, of what exists. That's what the Greeks were interested in."

"Yes," David Roper said. "That's why they liked bodies." He resumed eating. "Look at the Elgin Marbles."

"I have. I don't think they were interested in 'muscles' per se. It was an idea of beauty that seized them."

"I thought the drama festivals were orgies."

"Every idea has to begin somewhere," Andrew said lightly, his eyes moving about the room. "Sex and violence is one place to start, I suppose." He thought suddenly of Medea, of Oedipus and Agamemnon and the rape of Leda by the great winged swan. Yeats's stark, unanswered question flashed to his mind—

Did she put on his knowledge with his power
Before the indifferent beak could let her drop?

—and he felt suddenly sad. Yes, he thought, that's where they all start.

"Show me an idea," the young man said. "Show me an idea that doesn't begin in 'sex and violence.' "

"It seems likely that you might not recognize it if I did. Anyway, what inspires an idea is less important than how it develops and where it goes." Andrew sighed. "We must all transcend our beginning, David. The evidence that ideas exist is all around us."

"What's the evidence?" he asked.

"Civilization," Andrew replied, rising from his chair. "Tenuous and fragile as it is. And infinitely precious. See these books?" He gestured toward the shelves. "That's evidence. Somebody made each one. A lot of people, actually. And more people have read them. And a few of those who read them understood, and were affected by them. That's how it works. That's civilization, and these—all these things around us—are its artifacts: those bindings, this lamp, that old table, these Chinese porcelains, even that ugly English painting over the fireplace. I used to be more radical, but I'm coming around. Essentially, we're just caretakers—or, at least, first."

"That piece of marble too?" David Roper indicated a rounded black marble sculpture in a niche between the bookshelves at the other end of the room.

Andrew glanced toward it. It was raised from the floor on a white fluted column—Doric, Andrew thought, and old—and squatted there at eye level, massive and smooth and black, though it couldn't have been much more than two feet high. When he looked again he wondered if it was made from one piece of stone or two. It was formed into two lumps, anyway, the larger one polished and somehow balanced atop a smaller, rougher block that was polished only at its rounded tip. The polished stone looked soft, and smooth as velvet. "Yes, that too."

The young man walked toward it and passed his hand over it. "It feels pretty sexy to me," he said, stroking it, "for being so civilized."

"Maybe it hasn't been tamed yet," Andrew said, moving to the door he'd opened earlier. He stood with his hand on the knob. "Let's go. I've just remembered that I don't like this room much."

"You've just described it as the heart of civilization itself, and now you don't like it?" David Roper seemed incredulous. "And you've hardly talked about your play."

"Oh, yes, I did. You just didn't realize it."

"You've scarcely eaten, either," the young man said.

"I left that to you, I guess. I wasn't as hungry as I'd thought," Andrew said, "and I have to get back to the party and act like a proper guest. That's one of the lesser costs of civilization—acting like a proper guest." Suddenly he laughed. "But before we go, I'll leave you with something that just flashed across my mind:

"Beauty is momentary in the mind—
The fitful tracing of a portal;
But in the flesh it is immortal.

That's called an idea," he said. "Think about it. It's your kind of idea. Oh, yes, and the next line, too: *'The body dies; the body's beauty lives.'* " He glanced out and waved to Philip Spenser, who was making his way toward him, pipe clamped firmly between his jaws. "We're in luck!" He beckoned him in. "Philip, this is David Roper. He's interested in ideas. David, this is Philip Spenser. Philip's here teaching classics on an exchange program. He knows all about ideas and civilization." It was amazing, Andrew thought, but even in a dinner jacket Philip looked reassuringly tweedy and comfortable. "Tell him all about it, Phil. Gotta go, David. Pump that iron. Talk to you both later." Should he have a drink? Andrew asked himself as he left the quiet room and returned to the motion of the party. No, he answered, he shouldn't, but he took one anyway. After all, he thought, whisky is one of the more pleasant achievements of civilization, and the thought amused him.

The party had not subsided. "The Huntingtons may regret they invited all these theater people," he told Daisy, coming across her by the large French doors that opened onto a flying staircase to the garden. "We stay late."

"Some are still arriving," Daisy said, indicating a man rushing into the room, his eyes darting.

"I think that's Nigel Rogers!" Andrew exclaimed. "What's he doing here? Critics don't come to these things. Or at least they don't in New York."

Nigel spotted Pamela, who was standing near them, and made his way directly to her. "Where's David?" he asked, loud enough for the room to hear.

"David?" Pamela said. "Oh, David—the young man who came with Patrick. I've no idea, darling. We'll ask Patrick. Oh, Patrick," she called to him, "come here. Nigel is looking for your young man. He seems to be lost. Where have you put him?"

Andrew walked over to them, Daisy beside him. "He may be in the library," Andrew said, "acquainting himself with the artifacts of civilization. That's where I left him."

Pamela arched an eyebrow. "Nigel, this is Mrs. Curtis, and with her is Andrew MacAllister, the playwright of the evening."

"How do you do?" Andrew didn't much like meeting a critic immediately after an opening; it was embarrassing to both of them.

"Hello," Nigel said. "Where's the library?"

"It's over there"—Andrew pointed—"through those open doors," and Nigel abruptly departed, Patrick at his heels.

"You were in the library with the critic's young man?" Pamela asked. "When it was time for Nigel's spanking? Don't mess with the trade, dear." She stopped and looked at him. "What ever for?"

"He wanted to talk about my play," Andrew said. "You know, sometimes I like to talk about my work, if a person seems genuinely interested, so I did. He's smart, actually, but very young. Younger than he knows. And perhaps not so smart as he thinks."

"Smarter than Nigel, I expect," Pamela said.

"Too smart by half, maybe," Andrew said. "There they go now. Nigel looks ready to chew nails."

"It's not nice to talk about what Nigel chews, Andrew," Pamela said.

Daisy laughed. Andrew looked at her. For all her elegance, for all her grand style, despite that enormous glittering aquamarine that she was lightly fingering, there was still something girlish about her. Somehow, he had never quite thought of Daisy as girlish before. "They're heading this way," she said.

"Only Nigel," Pamela said. "Patrick and David seem to be heading for the exit."

"I *hated* the play," Nigel whispered hoarsely to her but clearly enough for anyone within earshot to hear, and without stopping he turned on his heel and scurried after them.

"I'm so sorry, my dear," Pamela called after him. "So frightfully sorry." To them she said, "I am, actually, but less for the play than for Nigel. He makes such a fool of himself, and he can't seem to help it at all. Anyway, Andrew, I greatly admired the play—quite loved it—and others will too. You'll see. I think you're going to have a pleasant success." She raised her glass. "To your success!"

"Yes," Daisy said, raising her glass to his, "to your success!"

"Oh," Andrew said, "Let's just start with something modest —like survival."

"I shouldn't worry about surviving, darling," Pamela said. "It'll take a lot more than Nigel to sink your ship."

"I wasn't worried about Nigel—it's just my general sense of dread. I think I need some air. Excuse me," he said, opening the doors to the garden, "I really have to have some air," and he parted the curtains and slipped out into the cool night, drawing the door to behind him. He was careful not to shut it entirely; he didn't want to lock himself out. He looked back through the curtains into the magnificent glowing room and the room beyond it: a series of rooms, one opening into the other like one of those Dutch perspective paintings. He stood there a moment, watching the party swirl and eddy beyond the softening scrim of the curtains. It was like a kaleidoscope turning, he thought, all colors and forms in slow, continuous motion. Like a dance to a soundless music. The stairway curved down and faded into the hidden garden. He walked down a few steps, admiring the old iron balustrade, and paused to look at the darkened shapes below. How strange and unfamiliar a garden looked at night, he thought, like a mysterious uncharted land. He heard the door open. He looked up. It was Daisy a few feet above him. She looked toward him, and in a moment slowly descended. She stood on the step above him in silence for a moment and then said, "I decided I needed some air too." Her dress brushed against him. He looked to the garden below, trying to discern a familiar shape. "What are you dreading?" she asked.

"Oh, you know—opening night, the notices, all that."

"But it's over," Daisy said.

"Not yet, it's not."

"I don't believe you're worried about the notices at all," she said. "I believe you're worried about something else entirely."

"I worry about everything."

"Are you worried about me?"

"Of course."

"Why? I don't bite."

"Really."

"You say that in a way that falls somewhere between a question and an exclamation."

"I guess that's how I meant it," he replied, turning toward her.

She took a cigarette from her purse and handed him her lighter. "Would you give me a light?"

"I didn't know you smoked."

"Only occasionally. Sometimes at parties."

Andrew finally produced a flame, and cupping his hand around it, extended it toward her. She bent toward him, her necklace swinging free.

"You're a very mysterious man," she said. Andrew returned the lighter to her, and she slipped it back into her bag. The bag was the same fluid color as her dress. She moved down a step and stood beside him but facing away, toward the garden. He grasped the rail behind her.

"Not so very."

"Oh, yes," she said. "Very"

"I guess, then, I want it that way." Why are you doing this? he asked himself, not sure whom the "you" referred to. Her dress flowed like glycerine against his hand. He watched her smoking.

She smoked so casually, he thought. There was something terribly sensuous about the way she did it, without urgency or need. When she had had enough, she let the cigarette drop from her fingers to the garden below, and he watched it burn for a second or two before the damp earth extinguished it. He took another drink from his whisky and set it unfinished on the step above him. Light emanated softly from her dress, her pearls, her magnificent gleaming pendant aquamarine. He grazed her back with his arm and let it remain there, touching lightly. They gazed silently into the darkened garden. She shifted position on the steps. He could feel the pressure of her body against his arm, and he raised his hand to her shoulder. He was in a foreign land; it didn't count, he thought, as he slowly turned her face toward him and kissed her. He was in a strange garden, and beyond her shoulder he could discern, between the shapes of yews, strange looming figures, marble presences reflecting the light from the house. He kissed her again. She tasted not of smoke but of apples. He kissed her hair, and her eyelids. He kissed her mouth. She kissed so softly. He touched her ear with his lips, and he could feel the strength of her thigh against his hand, the thick silk of her back, like fur. He felt the softness of her breasts against him, and he felt himself sinking, sinking into her softness, and he did not know if what he felt was pleasure or fear or both, but he did not stop. He could feel the bones of her hips and the smooth roundness of her belly. He moved her head and kissed her throat, the nape of her neck, her shoulder, her arm, the soft perfumed flesh inside her elbow. He put his foot on the step above him and pressed her against the inside of his thigh. "Stop," she said. "Stop."

"You didn't want me to do this?"

"I want you to stop. I'm going to smoke a cigarette."

Andrew watched her smoke for a few moments in silence. He thought suddenly of Lucy, two or three years ago in the bar of the St. Regis, and how delicious she had made smoking seem, as if she got the most extreme sensual pleasure from it. Lucy in the sky with diamonds. He hadn't smoked for years at that point, and then Lucy took a cigarette and leaned across the table toward him, waiting for him to light it. Ann was there too, and a number of others. It was late in the evening, and they had all been drinking a good deal. There were various separate conversations going

on at the long table, and Andrew watched Lucy smoke in that
seductive way she had, as if the act itself and the slowly curling
puff of smoke hinted at pleaures yet unknown, and at the same
time protected her behind its hazy veil—a smoke signal and a
smoke screen at once. She was a very beautiful and a very intelligent woman, and she knew it. She had extraordinary red hair,
beautiful red hair, and shortly, Andrew knew, she would be
leaving for her suite, which was not hers but the man's she was
then living with, a famous film director whom she married soon
thereafter and soon after that divorced when he took up with the
star of the new movie he was making. He always did. Andrew
didn't like him; he was boorish, and Lucy was beautiful. Once,
in Los Angeles, she had sent him a dozen white roses. That night
in the St. Regis, he had finally reached over to her, taken the
cigarette from her hand, and sucked in the smoke. And later that
night, from a phone booth, drunk, he had called her room at the
St. Regis and said, "I know what you're doing there, Lucy, and
stop it!" Lucy had laughed. It had seemed funny at the time. A
few days later he was smoking again.

"May I have one of your cigarettes?" He clenched his eyes
tight. She reached into her bag and handed him her pack and the
lighter. He took one out and looked at the tube of tobacco, felt its
familiar cylindrical firmness. He held it for a moment in his
fingers, then raised it to his mouth and lit it.

"I thought you didn't smoke."

"I don't," Andrew said. "I deny anything." The cigarette gave
him a rush, making him dizzy. He saw in his mind the trilliums
blooming in the wild garden at his parents' house the day of his
brother's burial a decade before. The day was as fine as any day
in May he had ever seen in Grande Rivère. How beautiful the
trilliums were, white and pink and huge, exotic and fresh as
orchids, and how terrible the day his brother's corpse was lowered into the ground near his grandmother's. He had never seen
anything like those trilliums before, and he had never seen them
blooming since. He inhaled deeply, sucking in the smoke, and
felt another dizzying rush. He stood beside her, scarcely touching. Their two cigarettes glowed in the dark; the fragrance of her
hair floated on the night. He reached over to her and took the
cigarette from her hand and dropped them both into the garden.
"Come here," he said, and he took her head in his hands and

kissed her. "Here," he whispered. He put one arm around her waist and kissed her again, several times again, tasting smoky apples. She touched his leg with her hand, and he put his foot back on the step above and held her firmly against his thigh. The light shimmered on her dress, luminescent, strange, like the ominous figures in the garden below, like softly glowing noiseless creatures under the sea. He pressed her to him. Suddenly the glass he had set on the stair crashed to the garden below. He looked up startled, as if he'd heard a shot, and as he looked up, the doors he'd passed through earlier were flung open and a voice shouted, "Sanka, madame? Sanka, sir?"

Andrew felt he must be someone else, an actor standing on a stair, the shattering of the glass ringing in his ears, the commanding, imperious voice of that ghastly bitch of a waitress clanging in the air, the grid of the fabric of Daisy's dress burning on his palm and the taste of apples lingering in his mouth, the taste of apples and cigarettes and something else—oysters or clams, he thought, whether from his mouth or hers he did not know. And behind the waitress he could sense the presence of Ann.

"We've been looking for you," Ann said. "Isn't it chilly out there?" She turned and went inside.

"No," Andrew said. "I needed air," but she had already gone.

"Sanka, madame? Sanka, sir?" the waitress repeated. She pronounced it to rhyme with "honk-a."

"No," Andrew said, climbing slowly up the steps. "No. We don't want any," and he returned with Daisy to the Huntingtons' continuing pavane. She looked as fresh and gleaming as ever, he thought. He wondered what miracle she had performed; he felt exhausted and wanted to leave. He looked for Michael and spotted him standing with Ann and the Spensers, but before he could make his way toward him he was stopped by an elderly woman.

"Oh, Mr. MacAllister," she said, "I so enjoyed the play. I had to tell you. I'm Mrs. Carroll, a friend of Mrs. Huntington's. Thank you for a fascinating evening. Not entirely cheering, but fascinating."

"How do you do?" Andrew said. Out of the corner of his eye he saw Michael heading his way, followed at a little distance by Ann. "And thank you."

She extended her hand to Daisy. "Mrs. MacAllister?"

"Oh, no," Andrew said. "This is Mrs. Curtis."

Daisy laughed. "I'm old enough to be his mother."

"Hardly," Andrew said. "And this is Mr. Aldrich, who directed the show. Michael, this is Mrs. Carroll. And this is my wife," he said as Ann approached. "Ann, meet Mrs. Carroll. I'm very glad you liked the play. Would you excuse me for a moment?"

"Where are you going?" Ann asked.

"To the bathroom."

"Just where I was heading," Michael said, taking him by the arm. "That's a ball-breaker, isn't it?" Andrew's eyes flitted about the room. The waitress was still passing coffee. "That 'Mrs. MacAllister' bit."

"I've got to get out of here." Andrew took a cigarette from a little urn on a table as he passed.

"What's the matter with you? You don't smoke."

"If I knew, I'd tell you. Or maybe I wouldn't. In any case, I don't want to talk about it."

"Okay, okay," Michael said. "Cool down."

Andrew's eye fell on the butler. "Could you bring me a whisky, please?"

"Certainly, sir."

"I thought you were going to the bathroom," Michael said.

"I changed my mind. On second thought, maybe I haven't." Andrew took his whisky and found his way to the bathroom. He took a drink. He gripped the sink and stood looking at himself in the mirror, leaning into it. The familiar face stared back at him. He looked at it blankly. He smiled. He frowned. He licked his lips. The face didn't look any different. He turned away and flushed the cigarette down the toilet and returned to the party, looking for Ann. "I think we should leave," he said.

"Yes," she said.

"We'll find the Huntingtons."

"Don't forget Mrs. Curtis." Ann looked at his drink. "Don't you think you've had enough?"

"Probably." He took a drink from his glass and then another before he set it down, and together they went in search of their hosts.

"You know I don't like these things," Ann said. "All these English women talk about is gardens, dogs, and children. Or else how exciting it must be to be married to a playwright—that Mrs.

Carroll, for instance. I don't tell them how exciting it really is.
I'm sick of smiling."

"I'm sorry," he said. He felt sick.

"Good show, old boy," Philip Spenser said, patting his arm
as he passed. "Good show. Janet and I are leaving now. We'll talk
to you later."

"Thanks, Phil. I'm glad you could come. I'm sorry we didn't
have a chance to talk." He hurried on. They found the Huntingtons chatting with Pamela. "It's been a very special party, Mrs.
Huntington," Andrew said, "but Ann and I are going to leave
now. I want to thank you both for doing all this."

"You're not going to wait for the reviews?" Pamela asked.

"We already know one of them," Andrew said. "I'll see the
rest tomorrow."

"You're to call me Barbara, remember?" Mrs. Huntington
said.

"Barbara"—Ann leaned toward her; their cheeks brushed—
"we've had a wonderful time. It was very kind of you to do this.
Truly it's been a beautiful party."

"We're all Americans in London," Mr. Huntington said, taking Ann's hand, "and we must stick together." He kissed it. "You
must come again, my dear."

"That would be lovely, Mr. Huntington," Ann said. "I'd love
to see your garden in the daylight."

"We'll have tulips soon." Mr. Huntington was still holding
her hand. "I've got the earliest tulips in London," he said, squeezing it. "And, my dear Ann, you must not call me 'Mr. Huntington.' It would be easier if you'd call me Chester."

"For reasons known best to my husband," Ann said, "he
doesn't want to be in London when the tulips bloom. But I'd love
to see them, Chester. Are you the gardener?"

"I'm the gardener," he said.

"Chester is very proud of his garden," Mrs. Huntington said.
"I'm sure he'd love to show it to you some afternoon. How long
will you be in London?"

"We hope to leave Friday," Andrew said.

"Although that doesn't seem very likely at the moment," Ann
added.

"We'll arrange something before then," Mr. Huntington said,
more to Ann than to him. "I'll send the car for you."

"And we'll send you home in the car now, if you're really determined to leave," Mrs. Huntington said.

"Oh, please," Andrew said, "there's no need to do that. We can still catch the Spensers. They'll give us a ride."

"It's no problem," Mrs. Huntington said. "And the driver can return with Mrs. Stevens."

"Well, thank you very much," Andrew said, "and thank you again—both of you—for everything."

"Goodbye, darling," Pamela said. "I'll talk to you in the morning. Perhaps we ought to have lunch, you and Michael and I—Ann too, naturally, if you don't mind listening to a lot of theater talk, Ann. Promise you won't break it this time, Andrew." She kissed him, then kissed Ann. "Goodbye, my lovelies."

As the Huntingtons were walking them to the head of the stairs, Lady Rysdale rushed over to them. "Would you drop me off on your way?" she asked. "I can't seem to find Patrick."

"Of course," Andrew replied, and the three of them descended the stairs, took their coats, and stepped into the Huntingtons' car, where they rode in silence through the silent streets.

"You didn't tell me you'd stood up Pamela Stickney," Ann said as they were walking to their rooms in the hotel. "Was that the day you had lunch with Daisy?"

"I didn't 'stand her up,' " Andrew replied. "I simply changed the date. And yes, I guess it was that day. I told you about it, about running into her in the British Museum."

"What were you doing out there with her?" Ann asked.

"Out where?"

"In the garden, of course."

"Nothing," Andrew said, loosening his tie. "Getting some air is all." He reached into his pocket for the key.

"You've always been a terrible liar." She laughed as she said it.

Andrew opened the door to their rooms and found Mrs. Stevens sitting vigilantly in a chair while Julia slept in the other room. He thanked her and handed her the pound he'd put in his jacket pocket, adding two more from his billfold. Probably she worked for virtually nothing, he thought; people like the Huntingtons never paid their servants: they believed it a privilege granted to the lower classes to serve as props in their own grand façade.

"Oh, I can't accept that, sir. It's much too generous," she said.

"It's not generous at all." Andrew pressed the notes into her hand while Ann went in to check on Julia. "The Huntingtons' car is waiting to take you home, and thank you again very much."

"Yes," Ann said, returning from Julia's room, "many, many thanks."

"I wish you great success, sir," she said, "and a happy life for all of you."

"Why, thank you, Mrs. Stevens," Andrew said, touched by her concern.

"You're a lovely family. There aren't many lovely families these days, everything so topsy-turvy and all."

"How sweet of you," Ann said, patting her shoulder as she opened the door. Ann stood there for a moment watching her go down the corridor. "You know, darling," she said, shutting the door and leaning against it, "you'd feel better if you told me about it."

"Stop acting like my mother."

"She's old enough to be your mother."

"Hardly," Andrew replied, taking off his tie.

"Maybe that's what you want."

"That's not what I want." He looked toward her. "Is that what you want to be?" He emptied his trouser pockets onto the chest of drawers and stacked the coins by size.

"No, it's not. I'd like to be your wife. Would you unzip me?" She set her bag with its sparkling arrow on the table and turned her back toward him.

He unzipped her dress and unfastened her pearls and handed them to her. She set them on the table and stepped out of her dress, dropping it onto the chair before going into the bathroom. Andrew picked it off the chair and hung it up—he did it with care; it was a beautiful dress, he thought—and then took off his jacket. He felt something unfamiliar in the pocket. He pulled out Daisy's cigarettes and her silver lighter, and his heart sank. He put them behind his billfold, then hung his jacket in the closet and began to remove his studs.

"I do love you, you know," Ann said, coming out of the

bathroom in her slip. "You're my main man." She came over to him and put her arms around his neck. "Give me a kiss."

He kissed her on the cheek. His mouth was very dry.

"No, a real kiss."

He kissed her again, on the lips this time. His lips felt like paper.

"I think we should talk about it." Her voice was full of cheerful teasing. "You really would feel a lot better."

"About the play?" Andrew asked, without much hope.

"You should have called that one 'Mack the Knife.' No, not about the play." Her arms were still around his neck, and he was leaning against the chest of drawers. "About what you were doing on the stairway to the garden. With Daisy Curtis. You remember Mrs. Curtis?" She was being very gay and flirtatious. "I think you're a little sweet on Mrs. Curtis."

"Yes, I remember her. I stepped out for some air. She came out to smoke a cigarette."

"I think there was more smoke than that. Andrew, I'm your *wife!*" She flung her arms away from him.

"It's very late," he said. "I'm very tired,"

"*You're* tired!" she exclaimed, her voice rising. "Do you think this is what *I* wanted to do? Do you think this evening has been all fun for me? I *hated* your party."

"That's nothing new. You almost always do."

"And then you go off into the garden with that . . . that . . . whatever she is, and leave me to entertain your stupid friends, to accept your compliments, to answer questions about you. Or you're off in the library with that disgusting, that disgusting piece of slime who's hanging on your every word like a drooling puppy." She shuddered. "I'm sick of it. I'm sick of being humiliated. I'm sick of leading your life."

"More likely you're sick of me."

"Right now, yes."

"I'm sorry," he said. "Really, I'm very sorry. It's not so easy for me either."

"You'd never know it."

"It just looks that way. Come here." He waited. "Please?"

"No," she said softly, "I don't want to."

"A minute ago you wanted a kiss, and now you won't touch me?"

"Your hands are dirty," she said. She had begun to cry.

"Are you drunk?"

"No, I'm *not* drunk! Are you?" She picked up her nightgown and went back into the bathroom. "Don't bother to answer."

He finished undressing and lay down on the bed. When Ann came out of the bathroom, her face washed and stripped of makeup, in her bare feet and green nightgown, a nightgown she'd had since before they were married and that was one of Andrew's favorites, she looked very young and vulnerable, and Andrew felt very sad. "You look beautiful in that nightgown," he said. "Like a young Greek goddess in her pleated robe. Like Iris. If only you had wings."

"Iris?" She picked up her bag and removed the arrow, passing by the bed on her way to the closet.

"The messenger of the gods. I love you, you know."

"I love you too." She was calm now.

"I'm sorry that I hurt you."

"Yes," she said, stopping at the chest of drawers. "I'm sorry about it too. What's this?" She picked up the cigarettes and lighter.

"I was lighting someone's cigarette and I guess I forgot to return them."

"You're not smoking, are you?"

"No."

"You wouldn't smoke, would you?"

"No."

"I can't bear it if you smoke again. I won't stay around and watch you kill yourself the way your brother did. I couldn't stand it."

"*You* couldn't stand it?" He reached toward her from the bed. "Do you remember the trilliums the day he was buried? The trilliums in the garden at my parents'?"

"No, I don't remember them." She looked at the lighter, rubbed it between her fingers.

"They were incredibly beautiful," Andrew said, his voice hushed, his gaze drifting into the distance, his mind filled with the sharpness of the memory. "So huge and clear and vivid."

"Where did this come from?" Ann asked. She waited. "Does it belong to Daisy?"

Andrew looked over to her. "I think so."

"You *think* so! Her name is on it!"

"Yes, it's Daisy's. I lit her cigarette."

"Well, at least you didn't lie about that. And you didn't lie about the smoking either—did you?"

"No," he said. "I didn't lie."

"That's good, because I'd know. You tried to fool me before, when you started smoking again three years ago, and it didn't work then. It won't work this time either."

"Are you going to see Mr. Huntington's tulips?" he asked.

"I don't think they're blooming yet."

"He said he had the earliest tulips in London."

"Yes, but he didn't say they were this early. Well, if I go, I'll let you know how they're coming." She got into bed.

"I hope we can leave on Friday," he said, turning out the light. "I very much hope we can leave on Friday."

three

How bright the day looked, how clear and penetrating the light, Andrew thought as he walked to the theater the next morning; and how muddled his mind. No longer anything unusual about that, of course; he was growing accustomed to it. Yet no one pointed at him, no one even looked at him strangely. No one seemed to notice anything peculiar at all about this man who called himself Andrew Thomas MacAllister and who was walking down Basil Street in a blue blazer and flannel trousers, a trench coat over his arm. The policeman on the corner did not approach him and take him gently by the elbow to lead him out of harm's way—his own or others'; in fact, he nodded pleasantly. A kindly man. Andrew wanted to thank him. Faces could be very deceiving—like words, the words that mattered so much to him. Too much? he sometimes asked himself. More than simply the tools of his trade, they provided the structure and form and fabric for his life, they were its very fundament, and what slippery little things they were, and costly, too. Wasn't it

Emerson who'd said that reality had a sliding floor? It didn't sound very Emersonian—maybe he'd been having a bad day—but all forms are fluent, as he'd also said. Andrew thought he should have been a mathematician, playing in a self-contained, self-defining universe with its own rigorous set of rules. Numbers seemed so reassuringly solid and real, utterly without ambiguity, without bullshit. Without meaning, too, at least in the slippery sense that words had meaning. They were what they were, and that was that. Two and two had to make precisely four. Nothing else. Of course, even as a child he'd wondered why the necessity, to his father's great chagrin. And then later, in his chaotic college career, after he'd given up on Hegel and the conundrum he felt he'd grasped for a moment—the reality is the real, and the real is the ideal—and then unfortunately lost, he'd flung himself briefly at calculus, hoping to find an exact definition of physical space—to describe a curve, say, so that it was exactly what he said it was and none other. Andrew had an affinity for arches and curves. Calculus had made sense to Mrs. Steer, who when he was a boy used to amuse herself and mystify him with her sheets of strange signs and symbols, but to him none of it made any sense at all after a while, no solid sense, anyway. They were just squiggles and numbers—some of them, for God's sake, irrational—and as tricky as anything else; trickier, maybe. What was so real about numbers? They didn't exist in nature. Even mathematics came down finally to intuition. Perhaps he should have been a builder, he thought, pausing to look at the oddly quaint houses surrounding Cadogan Square. Yes, he would have liked that. He wasn't much good with his hands, but he might have learned. He wouldn't have been the fastest carpenter in the world, but he would have been careful. He would have cared about mortises and tenons and plinth blocks and caps, about corner beads and shoe molds, about mitering joints so they fitted together just so. He could have absorbed himself in the details of crown moldings and picture rails and wainscot, and the art of coping. He would have loved the tools that enabled him to transform something from the image that shimmered in his mind to a real thing, a solid thing he could hold in his hands or touch with his fingers and see with his eyes. His grandfather had done it; why couldn't he have? There might have been some lingering affection in his genes for the touch and feel and smell of wood and iron and stone. Of course, his grandfather had gone bankrupt, too, and disappeared to the West to seek another fortune, which he'd never found. Andrew wasn't supposed to have known about that, but he did; his Aunt Elizabeth had told him. He wondered what his grandfather had been like; he wished he knew. Andrew had never laid eyes on him, but he did have a funny little table from his Aunt Clara that he'd made with meticulous care, all beautifully inlaid with rosewood and satinwood and tulipwood, woods he didn't recognize except for the ebony and the mahogany, but which he knew were there. It must have taken him years to make that table, Andrew thought. But for Andrew, the choice had already been made, years before. He would never make anything so substantial, so solid, so real as a table; his work was all illusion, a conjuror's trick, magic or pure hocus-pocus, depending on his frame of mind. He wanted to scream, but he couldn't muster it; couldn't muster the courage, he supposed.

"Michael," Andrew said when he found him at the theater. "Thank God."

"For those reviews, you want to thank God," Michael said, clapping him on the back and hugging him. "I mean, not bad, my friend, not bad!" Michael was beaming. "*The Telegraph* was great! *The Times* wasn't so bad, either. You and I haven't done this well in a while." He laughed. "Andrew, my friend, we may have a hit on our hands. You may have done it! Think you can handle it?"

"I hope so," Andrew replied, making himself laugh. "I'll do my best."

"I'll tell you, pal, if you can't dazzle 'em with your brilliance—"

"I could baffle 'em with my bullshit?"

"One or the other. Your choice." Michael laughed and hugged him again. Yes, Andrew thought, one or the other. "Of course," Michael said, "the Brits didn't quite get it, but then they never quite do. But they got it enough."

"It's strange about America and Britain," Andrew said. "Either we envy each other and try to imitate, usually the worst, or we condescend. I wonder if we ever really *see* each other . . ." or, he thought, if we just see what we want to see. Maybe that's all anybody does. In some perverse way, love—hate, too—is independent of its object. Quite impersonal. Free-floating feelings needing to fasten on something.

"Well, we're a bit pensive this morning, aren't we? Don't worry about the reasons. Just remember what Oscar Wilde said: 'I don't mind what people say behind my back, as long as they don't tell the truth.' But they did tell the truth, my friend, and it's there for all London to see."

"A few minutes ago I passed that hotel where he waited to be arrested—the Cadogan Thistle. Have you ever been in it?"

"Nope. Never. Pamela's on her way over. She's read the reviews and *she* is taking *us* to lunch."

"That reminds me," Andrew said, "I want to send the Huntingtons some flowers."

"How about some tulips, a huge bunch of tulips?"

"He claims he's got the earliest tulips in London, but I don't think they're blooming yet."

"We'll show him tulips," Michael said. "I'll get the manager to take care of it. He'll find the best blooming tulips in London."

"I suppose they fly them in," Andrew said. "They can't possibly have them here yet. No, I don't want to send them tulips. How about some fancy azalea? Yes. One of those azaleas that look like trees. What do they call them? Topiary, that's it. A topiary azalea. The English are supposed to be bananas about azaleas, and the Huntingtons are bananas about the Brits. They must be, to live in this filthy climate."

"Filthy? It's a great day out there. Sun shining, daffodils blooming, and a long beautiful line at the box office. I think I'll throw in some caviar, from the cast and crew. A nice pot of fresh fish eggs from Fortnum and Mason. I'm feeling excessively marvelous this morning."

"Can we make sure the stuff arrives this afternoon? I'll write a note to go with the azalea. You can take care of the caviar." Andrew pulled out his pen and one of the file cards he always carried and put together a few properly grateful words for the Huntingtons.

"Does m'lord have a color preference?"

"Oh, white or yellow, I think. Do azaleas come in yellow? White or yellow would be nice. Is there an envelope around here?" Michael handed him an envelope. "You know," Andrew said, "I hate this place."

"What place?"

"London."

"How can you hate it? It likes you. Except for Nigel Rogers. That was a pisser. Not that he didn't warn you. What did you think of it?"

"I haven't read it."

"Maybe you shouldn't. Maybe you're not old enough. Anyway, it was truly dumb. Like him. All muscles flexing and a tiny little head. That guy's brains are between his legs." Suddenly Michael shot him a quizzical look. "You haven't read it?" He paused, studying his face. "Andrew, have you read *any* of the reviews?"

"Yes, of course."

"Which?"

"What difference does it make?" Andrew asked. "I'm tired."

Michael exploded. "You haven't read a fucking one! What the hell do you think you are? They are *great* fucking reviews, reviews like you've never had, better than *Riverhead*. Some of them are even intelligent, and you haven't read one!"

"Ann read me some this morning," Andrew said, turning the envelope over in his hands.

"Give me that envelope," Michael said. "Sometimes, Andrew, you're an arrogant bastard. Well, you just haul your poor tired little ass over here and sit down and read them." He led Andrew to a chair and threw the papers in his lap. "You're tired! You asshole. *We*—not just you—*we*—we've busted our balls over this thing—the actors, the stage manager, the business manager, the lowliest miserable gofer in this place—and you're goddamned well going to go up to them before the show tonight and act thrilled if it kills you. If you can't be pleased for yourself, you can be happy for them—or at least pretend. They *love* you, for Christ's sake. They're grateful to you. Why they should be, I don't know—but I won't tell them. Read the reviews. I'm going to take care of the caviar—and your tulips, of course."

"Azalea," Andrew said.

"Oh, yes, an azalea, a *topiary* azalea. White or yellow. Forgive me. I hope I didn't disturb His Lordship too much."

Andrew read the notices. They were indeed good. He was pleased, of course; he certainly would have been unhappy if all the critics had hated the play. Instead, except for Nigel Rogers, all of them were enthusiastic and a couple of them glowing. Rogers didn't seem to have understood the play at all. He'd even confused the Upper East Side with Chelsea, and managed—Andrew burst into laughter when he read it—to drag in a comparison, unfavorable of course, to Tennessee Williams. Andrew wondered if what Nigel Rogers really hated was Patrick Rysdale's clamp on his boyfriend.

"Andrew," Michael said, returning and taking a seat beside him, "what's going on with you?"

"Nothing."

"That's the fourth great lie."

Andrew reached into his pocket and felt Daisy's cigarettes and lighter. "I don't know." He toyed with the lighter in his pocket. After a moment he took it out, and the cigarettes, and lit one.

"Where did you get those?" Michael asked. He took the lighter from Andrew's hand and looked at it. "This belongs to Daisy."

"It seems to have her name on it," Andrew replied.

"So do you," Michael said. "Why are you doing this?"

"Doing what?"

"Smoking this cigarette." He reached over, took it from his hand, and put it out. "Playing with fire." Andrew didn't reply. "You know the fire I mean. I'm not talking about Daisy's lighter. I'm not even talking just about her cigarettes. I'm talking about the big D herself. You disappeared with her last night. What were you doing out there on the balcony?" Andrew didn't say anything. "Banging her, I suppose. The museums must have whetted your appetite."

"Yes, of course," Andrew said, picking up a clipboard. "It was a bit brisk, what with the weather, and a bit precarious, what with the stairway, but I gave it my best shot. I knew you'd be counting on me. I didn't want to disappoint you." He laughed.

"And then there was that critic's little beauty. You disappeared with him as well. Did you fuck him too?"

"Oh, yes. Him too. In the library. A little more comfortable in there, but a bit nervous-making, what with Nigel baby lurking around the door. Or was it Patrick? I'll tell you a secret if you promise never to tell." Andrew lowered his voice to a whisper. "We had a threesome. Boy, can that boy fox-trot! Well," he said, returning to his normal tone, "now you can understand why I'm tired. My curtain went up at the end of the show. Between the library and the balcony, it was an exhausting performance. A very long night."

"Only two acts," Michael said.

"But they were arduous. I'd like a little sympathy, please."

"Sympathy? Did I hear 'sympathy'?" It was Pamela Stickney, sweeping toward them. "Darlings!" She kissed the air around their cheeks. "All London is weeping for you. The Queen herself read the reviews and is distraught. Princess Margaret is under sedation again. The Prince of Wales is in seclusion. The Duchess of Windsor is flying over from Paris. All for you, my angel. Do you like my cape?" She twirled before them in a feverish creation of burgundy and mustard.

"It's you, Pamela," Andrew said, laughing, catching her as she fell backward into his waiting arm and turned her face toward him. She batted her eyes. "None other. Unless it's Bette Davis. Maybe Gloria Swanson. A bad movie, if I ever saw one. Hollywood, 1939."

"How about Ginger Rogers, Fred? I always wanted to be Ginger Rogers. Or else the Duchess of Targyll, that delicious little slut. I think I might enjoy being a slut, darling. Have I missed my calling?" She rolled her eyes like a vamp and flung her weight against his arm, kicking her leg up and holding it in the air.

"I don't know," Andrew said, straightening her up. "Maybe basketball. Center, I think. Or forward. You can be pretty forward, Pamela."

"Don't be rude, dear." She took a few steps and turned again. "Actually, I bought this ravishing little garment just this morning, anticipating a little income at last. Now, Michael, would you tell me why our boy needs sympathy? He's only the envy of London, and it seemed this morning half the city was trying to reach him."

"Because all he can do is joke," Michael said. "It's a terrible affliction. I think it could be fatal."

"Well, let's laugh about it over lunch," she said. "The poor thing's looking a bit peaked. I think he needs a little beef broth before the matinée. I'm taking you to a divine little haunt of mine, something very special. Will Ann be joining us?"

"No, she's dropping Julia off at some friends' in Hampstead —the Spensers; you met them last night: he was the ruddy fellow, the one who managed to look tweedy in a tuxedo, and she was the tall woman in the peasant getup—and then she's going to see Mr. Huntington's garden. Or at least, I think she is. I guess that's tomorrow. He called as I was leaving and she seemed to be arranging something with him on the telephone."

"Oh, yes—to see the famous tulips," Pamela said as they left the theater.

"They're not blooming yet," Andrew said, scanning the street for a taxi.

"I wouldn't count on that, dear. It's his fertilizer, he told me. That old lecher is an expert fertilizer. Why, he even offered to fertilize me! Not, however, in the garden. After he'd lured me into his library. Sweet of him, wasn't it?"

"Whatever turns you on," Andrew said as a taxi pulled to the curb and Michael opened the door.

"Excessively sweet, I thought. I told him I wasn't a tulip."

"Just a long-stemmed rose," Andrew said.

"And the rose is taking us to lunch," Michael said, opening the door. "Can you believe it?"

"The check is in the mail, too," Andrew said. "I'll believe that when I see your bills on the table, Pammy."

"One size fits all," Pamela said cheerily, pulling the folds of her garment around her and climbing into the cab.

"Sure," Andrew said, handing her the part of her cape that still hung from the taxi. "I won't mention the third great lie."

"The third great lie?"

"That's 'Of course I won't come in your mouth,' " Michael said. "Andrew knows all about lying."

"I can't believe I offered to pay for this," Pamela said.

"I know"—Andrew pulled the door closed behind them— "it's against nature."

"Andrew, my dear," Pamela said after Michael had excused himself to make a phone call and their plates were being cleared, "you've scarcely eaten a thing. A taste of melon and a bite of prosciutto will not sustain you through the matinée. And this lovely wine! Virtually untouched. Is something wrong?"

"No," Andrew said, "nothing's wrong. I'm just not hungry."

"A touch of the hangover, perhaps?"

"Maybe that's it," Andrew said, laughing. "I should have avoided the whisky last night. My father always claimed that nobody ever got drunk on Scotch, but experience has proved him wrong."

"That's what we do, dear: prove our fathers wrong."

"I thought we just killed them."

"Andrew, are you all right?"

"That's Michael speaking. His words."

Pamela studied his face. "I have just the thing for you. Champagne. Its effects are magical. I insist we have a nice bottle of champagne. To celebrate. And to nurse you back to health. I'm worried about you, darling. So is Michael."

"Did he say something?"

"No, he wouldn't. But he didn't need to. A woman knows, lovey. I don't believe it was the whisky you drank last night. You didn't have that much, did you? Just enough for a pleasant buzz. You seemed your usual bright and charming self."

"Well, and don't I seem my usual bright and charming self today?"

"A little distracted, I think. *Distrait*, as the French say. But never mind, a glass of champagne will take care of it." She beckoned the captain and placed her order. "Mother's own remedy." She laughed.

"I thought it was nature's," Andrew said. "Nature put the bubbles in, not Mother."

"But Mother found a use for it. Now about you."

"I suppose I'm thinking about the play. I've been working hard, at last." He felt the weight of the lighter in his pocket.

"You're exhausted, that's the problem?" Pamela sounded hopeful. "Naturally. It follows the anticipation of opening night —the exhilaration, too." She stopped and stared at him. "Unfortunately, I don't believe it."

"But there is no problem," Andrew said. "What is this with you and Michael?" He was exasperated, but he laughed. He reached in his pocket, pulled out the cigarettes and lighter, and held them in his lap. "My only problem is that I've scarcely seen Ann and Julia, except for last night. I need some domesticity and peace." He laughed again. "My last relief from this play was Madame Tussaud's horror show."

"Some relief!" Pamela exclaimed. "That may have done it."

"And our quick lunch on Saturday, of course. It's always a relief to have lunch with you."

"You're such a flatterer," she said. "As well as a tease. That was all business."

"Comic relief, I meant," Andrew said.

"Shall I unleash my whip? I knew I should have worn my leathers."

"No, my dominatrix, save that for the critic from the *Daily Mail*."

"Tut, tut," she said. "Further naughtiness will be rigorously punished. And if Nigel'd heard that, he'd send his young man after you. Or I shall. I suspect the boy might like that, actually. But I think it would be just the thing you don't need at the moment."

"Actually, Pamela, our lunch last Saturday was helpful. You are a very smart lady—despite appearances. And now I'm thinking about New York. I feel I've still got work to do on the play before it's ready for New York. If it ever is. I hope somebody will pick it up there. I'm desperate for money, as usual. Maybe Sam Walcott will. He likes my work. Michael's, too."

"He'll like it even more now. And certainly somebody in New York will pick it up, as soon as they've read these reviews. We'll see a producer or two presently, I expect. They'll be booking their flights before the weekend. Producers are like the swallows in autumn, you know: they all fly to the same telephone line. And here come the bubbles."

"Jouvet-Perrier, ma'am," the steward said, extending the bottle for her inspection.

"Here comes Michael, too," Andrew said. "We almost got away with it," he whispered. He slipped the cigarettes and lighter back into his pocket.

"Away with what?" Michael asked.

"With the champagne." Andrew said. "We thought we'd have it finished before you got off the phone." He turned to Pamela. "He must have sniffed it."

"I have an infallible nose," Michael said. "Especially for trouble. You know that, pal."

The steward filled their glasses. "We're not drinking to trouble," Pamela said, raising her glass. "we're drinking to a long and happy run at the Royal Court—"

"You'll need it"—Michael laughed—"to pay for this lunch, remember?"

"Michael, be nice," Pamela said. "And to New York. And to you, Michael, and to Andrew and his return to health." She took a healthy drink of her wine. "Delicious!" She took another.

"Not a moment too soon," Michael said, raising his glass, "for all of the above."

Andrew smiled and raised the glass to his lips. "I ought to be going soon," he said. "I want to get some work done before the show tonight."

"The boy is ready to work!" Michael exclaimed. "I'll never stop that. What about the matinée?"

"I have a lot of work to do before I leave." His mouth felt like paper. "I've got to leave on Friday. We're booked on a flight."

"I don't see how you can get out of here on Friday. You've got to see the play a couple more times, at least. I want you to take a serious look at the second act. You've got people to talk to. No," Michael said. "Really, Andrew, there's no way. It's already Wednesday."

"I hope you're not right." Andrew felt dismayed. "But we've got to get out of here. Julia's got to get back to school."

"They could go on ahead," Michael said.

"Oh, no," Andrew said. "I can't be here alone. You know"— he laughed—"I'm not old enough." He started to rise from the table.

"We'll take care of you," Michael said. "We'll tuck you in every night."

"And tell you a story, too," Pamela said, "a nice bedtime story."

"Don't forget the milk and cookies," Andrew said. "I can't go to sleep without my milk and cookies." He stood up. "Would you excuse me for a moment?" He followed the path Michael had taken earlier and found a telephone and the Huntingtons' number on one of his file cards and dialed it. "I have your lighter," Andrew said when Daisy had come to the phone. "Would you like it back?" And then he went into the men's room and lit one of Daisy's cigarettes, inhaling it tentatively, tentatively again, then deeply. He shuddered and dropped it to the floor, grinding it out on the tiles. The smoke had made him dizzy. The room was all gleaming white tile and porcelain and glass, brilliant under the merciless fluorescent glare and spotless except for the remains of the cigarette he had crushed. He studied his own puzzling face in the mirror. He thought he detected a tiny line of white below his pupils. He'd heard somewhere that the white's showing below the pupils was a bad sign, a very bad sign. Probably he'd read it in one of those fraudulent health magazines that he sometimes fell for, full of alarming signs and sulfurous pineapple cures. Did he look pale? It was hard to tell in the cold, colorless room. Its intense whiteness shimmered eerily. It was frightening, almost blinding. Like snow, he thought. He was snow-blind. He thought of Amundsen and the hapless Scott and the terrible trek to the Pole. That would make an interesting play. He splashed water on his face and examined it again in the mirror. It gave nothing back.

He returned to the table. "And you'd give me a good-night kiss, too, wouldn't you?" he asked, laughter in his voice. "And you certainly wouldn't spank me if I were bad."

"Oh, I don't think we could promise that," Pamela said. "That's the fun part for Mother Stickney."

"Well, if you can't promise that, then I'm not sure I could stay."

"Promise him anything," Michael said.

"Okay, I'll stay if I have to."

"But give him a spanking," Pamela said in a stage whisper.

"On that threatening note, I'm going to run," Andrew said. "I've got a few errands to do. I'll have to miss the matinée, but I'll be at the theater early tonight. I'll see you there, Michael. And Pamela, I'll see you whenever—before I leave, certainly. Any ideas about the play, let me know. And thank you for lunch." He picked up his glass of champagne and finished it. "To you, my friends, with gratitude. Really," he added, and kissed Pamela on the cheek and patted Michael's shoulder, then suddenly kissed him too, on the cheek, before he turned and abruptly left the restaurant.

The sunlit morning had turned into a dense and cold afternoon. He got a cab at the door and on his way to the Huntingtons' he wondered if he could be seeing snow in the air. "Driver," he asked, "is that snow?"

"I'm afraid so," he said. "Just a trace. It's like that at this time of year—you never know what the day will bring." Yes, Andrew thought, I feel the same way. He could feel his mind fading, and his eyes seemed to blur. He concentrated his gaze on a speck of lint on the back of the driver's seat. By the time he got to Cheyne Walk, the wind from the Thames was blowing damp and chill. But inside, the house was warm. "Hello, Stevens," he said, with a kind of jovial good cheer that astonished him, "nice and warm in here." Too warm, he thought.

"The furnace is broken, sir," the butler said, taking his coat. "We can't seem to regulate it. Mrs. Curtis is expecting you in the library," and Andrew climbed the splendid staircase and crossed the drawing room and passed through the open doors and entered the library.

"Your azalea is lovely," Daisy said, putting down her magazine and rising from the couch. "I sneaked a look at the card," she explained. "The Huntingtons are out until evening and I couldn't resist. I did resist dipping into the caviar, though I looked at that card too."

"That's good. It would have been a struggle for me. Where is it?"

"The azalea? At the foot of the stairs. How could you miss it? It's the size of a redwood. The caviar is in the refrigerator."

"What color is it? The azalea, not the caviar."

Daisy laughed. "Rather a cream color, with a touch of deep pink at the center. Very beautiful. Very succulent. The biggest flowers I've ever seen on an azalea. I can't imagine where you found it."

"I didn't. The theater manager did. I'm surprised it arrived so soon."

"The English are good at that," Daisy said.

"I'm afraid it will expire before the Huntingtons get back, it's so hot. I'm suffocating in here. What ever happened to the Huntingtons' furnace?"

"I don't know," Daisy said. "We can't seem to stop it. A repairman is supposed to arrive tomorrow. The English aren't so good at that, at sending out repairmen to fix mysterious things like furnaces. I suppose they think we shouldn't have them."

"Probably they do, since most of them don't seem to. And why on earth do they have a fire blazing in here? Can't we open a window?"

"There's always a fire in the library, regardless of the temperature. It's another of the peculiarities of the English. They don't approve of furnaces, but they do approve of a decent open fire sizzling politely in the grate. Especially in the library. But we're not obliged to curl up next to it. That's why I've been sitting over here, with my back to it. On a different occasion a fire might be cozy. However, I've asked Stevens to curb his unnatural English instincts and not throw another log on it. I told him we would be quite warm enough without adding fuel. Take your jacket off," Daisy said. "You'll be much more comfortable." She sat down on the couch.

"I'd still like some fresh air," Andrew said. He unbuttoned his jacket and moved toward the window, parting the heavy curtains and fumbling with it. "I can't get it open."

"Neither could I," Daisy said. "It appears to be stuck. Things are not entirely what they seem in this extraordinary house. I guess you'll have to take your jacket off unless you prefer to sweat like a bull. Excuse the earthy image."

"Was Ann here today?"

"No. Unless she was here this morning, which hardly seems likely. The Huntingtons left before noon. The heat drove them out."

"What's this?" Andrew asked, pointing toward the pieces of black marble squatting one above the other on the pedestal. "Maybe I should hang my jacket on it—cover it up. It doesn't look as if it belongs in the Huntingtons' house."

"Really? Why not?"

"Oh, I don't know, it's just that it's so sort of . . . sort of . . . *rounded*, I guess. Primitive. And sitting on this rough, this rough *block*. The Huntingtons' taste seems more classical, like the column. More linear. Apollonian, I suppose."

"And this is Dionysian?"

"Yes, I'd say so. It feels primitive but it's not. It just has that feeling. It's quite a sophisticated piece, I think. Yes"—he laughed

—"a primitive sophisticate, or should I say a sophisticated primitive. I suppose that's a contradiction in terms. A smart caveman, anyway." Andrew laughed again and turned his back to it.

"I did it."

"Did what?"

"I made it. I told you I make things. I think I specifically mentioned marble." She rose from the couch. "Here, give me your coat. I'm sorry you don't like it." She took his coat and laid it over a chair. "Chester especially is quite taken with it."

"You made it?" He stared at her, incredulous.

"Don't I look like an artist, Andrew? Don't I look as if I 'suffer' enough? Too chic? Not sufficiently radical?" She laughed.

"Well, I wouldn't know that. I don't know much about art. Or artists." Had he said that? He wanted immediately to bite his tongue. Daisy rolled her eyes. He laughed. "But I know what I like, as they say." He was sounding more stupid by the moment.

"When people say that, they really mean they like what they know. Surely you're beyond that."

"I hope so. I was trying to make a joke, actually. It didn't work." He glanced over his shoulder toward it. "You made it? My God! It's awesome."

"God, as they say, had nothing to do with it." She returned to the couch. "You could sit down."

"Not the Queen's nice Anglican God, anyway." He turned to face it. "Maybe the god of Stonehenge." He stared at it for a moment. "My God!" he repeated, almost in a whisper, shaking his head and looking from the sculpture to Daisy and back again. "I didn't say I didn't like it; I said it was awesome. You're full of surprises." He moved toward the bookshelves. "Actually, I noticed it last night. But if you'll forgive me, it does stick out in this room."

"Like a sore thumb, you think?"

"No, not like a sore thumb, just a thumb. A *big* thumb. It looks *very* heavy. It looks massive. It looks . . . I don't know." He turned toward her. "How did you handle it?"

"Handle what?"

"Well, the stone."

"I wasn't tossing it around the studio, Andrew. Marble is fragile, for one thing; it breaks easily. And for another, I couldn't lift it. Strong as I am. But there are techniques for handling stone, like anything else. You learn them—just as you learn the techniques for handling words."

"Words have no mass, no density. They're not substance."

"I don't know how you can say that, doing what you do, knowing what you quite obviously know."

"Is it obvious? It's not obvious to me."

"Yes, Andrew; I don't know how to tell you, but it *is* obvious. No matter that you try to hide it."

"Well, is this one piece of stone?"

"No, it's two."

"How did you get it to balance?"

"There's a rod joining the top to the base. You can't see it, but it's there."

"Really?"

"Yes, really," Daisy said, laughing. "You do have a lot of questions."

"Well, I'm curious," Andrew replied. "I'm always curious about other people's work."

"That's how it was done. The rod holds it together. Perhaps we should open that caviar. I *love* caviar. The Huntingtons wouldn't mind. I'll tell them I was seized by lust. We don't have to eat it all," she said. "Or if we do, I'll get another pot tomorrow and put Michael's card with it. They need never know. I'll get it," and she left the room.

When she had gone, Andrew passed slowly by the sculpture. He sat down on the couch facing it and crossed his legs. The light from the fire behind him moved across the smooth black stone, shimmering softly like the Aurora Borealis against the black night sky: the Northern Lights, he suddenly thought, from long ago— he hadn't seen them in years. He rose and walked over to it. The piece was hardly figurative, yet it seemed like a figure, it *felt* like a figure; looked, in fact, as if a knee and part of a leg might be emerging from the rounded mass, and from behind, the mouth of a fish—no, a dolphin's mouth, Andrew thought, because of the lips. A thin white filament ran down the leg, as if the marble in its molten state, in its metamorphosis, had been touched by an electrical arc. He put his fingers on the stone, shockingly cold in so hot a room, and traced the vein. He moved his palm across the stone's curved surface, feeling its smooth folds and ridges. It seemed almost soft for such a hard substance—like velvet, like butter. He peered closely at it. There were two nearly lateral scars—deep gashes, really—chiseled into the rough-hewn base just below its polished tip. Curious, he thought, examining the scars. More than curious. Violent. He heard a clanking in the heat pipes and shivered as Rilke's urgent, grim command came to his mind: *"You must change your life."* How could he shiver in so hot a room? He loosened his tie and walked over to his jacket and reached into the pocket for Daisy's cigarettes and lighter. Ah, Rilke. The line, he realized with mild surprise, had been inspired by the luminous torso of an ancient, youthful Apollo. *"You must change your life."* He laughed. Frightening. He returned to the couch and lit a cigarette. He felt less dizzy this time; he must be getting used to it. The softly glowing, paneled room was suffused with amber light, the wood and the carpets very mellow. The lampshades, he noticed, were fringed. They must be silk: only silk diffused such a soft light. He put Daisy's lighter and ciga-rettes on the table before him and straightened his tie. He looked around the library, wondering if there might be a whisky tray. It would be nice to have a drink, he thought as somewhere a radiator clanked again.

"Sorry I took so long." Daisy put the tray she was carrying on the table where Andrew had sat the night before, the round table near the entrance, and closed the doors. "It's so hot in the house I decided to change into something more tropical." She carried the tray to the couch, her white shirt and silky black trousers flowing loosely around her. Andrew pushed the ciga-rettes aside so she could set the tray of caviar—and a small frosted decanter, too—on the table before them. Her pearls swung free as she bent over to put it down. "Everything's iced," she said, looking back at him, "except us. Loosen your tie, you fool. Here, give it to me." She took it and placed it on the table behind them. "You must be cooking." She sat on the edge of the couch and began to spoon the glistening black eggs onto a cracker. "Speak-ing of cooking, the cook's in a terrible sulk. We're not allowed in the kitchen, you know. That's her domain. But I often break the rules of the house. I can't always bother with the protocol that the English are so devoted to, and the Huntingtons are more English than the Queen. Would you pour the vodka? We're being Russian this afternoon."

"Good. I'm tired of England," Andrew said, taking the decanter and pouring the vodka into the two small glasses she had provided. "Czarist, I'd say. This isn't your standard Marxist spread."

She passed him the caviar and a napkin, and raised her glass. "Congratulations," she said, "on such splendid notices, on such a fine play—and," she added, "for pocketing my lighter. Thank you."

"Thank you?"

"Well, yes," she said, "because, being a gentleman, you were forced to return it. If you hadn't taken it, it's doubtful you'd be here now, in the inferno." She looked at him and laughed, and bit into her cracker thickly spread with caviar. "You know—the hyperactive furnace of the Huntingtons."

"Oh."

"You're not eating your caviar. It's beluga. Michael sent the very best. And delicious."

Andrew looked at the black lumps glistening on the cracker in his hand. "My appetite seems to be failing today," he said. "I think I'll become a vegetarian."

"Surely not before you've tasted this," she said.

He took a drink of his vodka and contemplated the cracker. He was afraid he might drop it. He decided to eat it whole. "No spills," he said, swallowing the cracker in his mouth. "I'm always spilling things," he explained. He finished his glass. "It was a tiny glass," he said. "No more than a thimbleful." He indicated Daisy's lighter and cigarettes. "May I?"

"Certainly," she said, taking his glass and filling it.

He reached across her for the cigarettes and lighter. The glass flew from her hand and the vodka ran down her leg. "Oh my God!" he said. "Hell! I'm sorry. I can't believe how clumsy I am." He rose from the couch, grabbing a napkin, crouched before her and dabbed at her leg. He was shaking.

"A little dry-cleaning fluid is all," Daisy said, pulling up her pant leg and kicking off her shoe. Her shoe was very black, with little beads of jet around the edge where it met her foot. Andrew squinted at the beads. "It'll evaporate in a flash," she said. He touched the rich black suede of her shoe—it felt like fur—picked it up and put it aside. Her stockings were black too.

"I'm sorry," he said, still crouched before her, still holding the useless napkin.

"Get up," she said, nudging him with the point of her shoe, the single shoe she was still wearing. "Get up."

Andrew rose.

"Sit down," she said.

He touched his hand to the silk of her leg—lightly, only grazing it with his fingers—and moved, felt himself pulled, toward her. He felt the heat rising in waves from her leg, from the couch, from the room, and saw, swimming before his blurring eyes, the luster of the pearls gleaming against the softness of her throat, the rippling whiteness of her shirt. They filled his eyes, entered his eyes, as he pulled her to him and he sank into her throat, her neck, her breasts, the soft curve of her now bared belly and kissed it, and kissed it again. He lifted her shirt and kissed her breasts and the space between them and the warm moist flesh beneath them, and inhaled her perfume. Dimly he saw her reach up and unclasp her pearls. They slipped slowly from her hand to the table, clattering like bones as they fell, as he fell, gravity lost, slipping in a murmur of silk into the dizzying void. All forms were fluent. Above him now, her fingers moved spiderlike down his body. "No," he whispered, "no." "Yes," she said, lingering over the sound, taking his cock in both hands and hovering over it, staring intently. "Ha," she said softly, triumphantly, taking it in, enclosing it, consuming it. He groaned. He could feel the tiny pricks of her teeth. "No," he whispered again, to whom he did not know, as they slid to the floor. Her body above him flowed like silk; her teeth were pearls. He kicked off his shoes, then his trousers, and squirmed to pull off his socks. He was naked, except for his shirt. He wanted to be naked. She put her hand beneath his balls and clasped them, and with her other hand reached under his shirt and pressed down on his breast, her finger touching his nipple. His skin tingled. He heard himself moan. "Take off your shirt," she said, scarcely looking up. He pulled at it. He heard a button pop. Her yellow hair streamed from her head to his body to the patterned carpet, shimmering. He reached for her hair and pulled her mouth away from him and up to his mouth. He pressed down on her. She tasted of caviar, and the astringent tingle of vodka. He licked her eyelids closed and nibbled at her lips and mouthed the soft space under her chin, and slipped his other hand beneath the flowing silk of her trousers and pushed them off with his foot. He pulled his arm out of his shirt and crouched naked beside her, over her, extending his arm and pressing her hair to the carpet, and with his other hand, his right hand, parted her legs. He looked. He put his face into her soft hair and kissed her there, and opened her soft lips with his fingers, then his tongue, tentatively, flicking at her, tasting her salt taste, smelling her salt smell. He moved his other hand lightly across her face—a blind man—over her lips, and slipped his fingers into her mouth, across the edges of her teeth. He felt her teeth grazing his fingers, her tongue playing at his fingertips. The jaw was the strongest muscle in the body. Or was it the thighs? He moved back on his haunches, knocking the table, and heard her pearls riffle softly to the floor. He looked down at where his hand was, where his tongue had been. He bent down again and lapped her like a furry animal. He narrowed his eyes and looked up directly at her face. "I'm going to fuck you," he said with a kind of grim determination, opening her hands and pressing them against the floor. He raised himself up on her. "I'm going to fuck you *now*," he said roughly, and he pushed her legs apart with his knee and looked down and amazed, aghast, saw himself disappear within her.

He opened his eyes to see a tiny section of the carpet, a fragment of an exquisite Persian garden wound with lacy tendrils and flowers of the finest muted hues. It must be very old, he thought. He stared at it for a few moments, marveling at its delicacy, and traced his finger along a stem. There was something else, too, in his narrow frame of vision. Oh, yes. Fine yellow hair spraying into the picture from the left of the frame, and a piece of his shirt with a loop of pearls trailing off it across the top right. Its folds, the form it had taken when it fell, reminded him of the folds in the dress of the girl seated at the virginals. The whole made an interesting composition: on the field of patterned carpet the wisps of hair, the folds of cotton, the loop of beads, and there on the right, almost at the bottom, the lost button.

"What are you doing?" Daisy asked.

"Looking at the carpet," he replied, placing her pearls on the table, picking up his shirt and the button, and raising himself from the floor. "It's very beautiful."

"It looks as if you're putting on your shirt," she said.

"Yes," he said. "I am. I have to get to the theater." He buttoned his shirt and smoothed his hair. He pulled his underwear from the tangle of his trousers and began to dress.

"Would you give me some caviar?" Daisy asked, sitting up and leaning against the couch. He slipped the button into his pocket and fixed a cracker and set it on a plate before her. He picked up her trousers and laid them on the couch and straightened her shoes. She was holding her shirt. He found his socks and put them on. A radiator clanked. "The furnace is still grinding on, I hear," Daisy said, slipping into her shirt and fluffing it. She nibbled at the cracker. A pearl of caviar glistened on her tooth.

"Apparently," Andrew replied.

"It's very difficult to dress gracefully," Daisy said, reaching for her trousers and rising from the floor. Her shirt billowed loosely around her.

"Still," Andrew said, "you manage to do it." He retrieved his shoes and sat on the couch to put them on while Daisy glided into her trousers. In a moment she was fully dressed and fastening her pearls. "Very deftly," he added. The glass he had knocked from her hand lay unbroken on the carpet near the niche. He walked over and picked it up, then sat down beside her on the couch, placing it back on the tray.

Daisy dipped her finger into the caviar and licked it off. "Well," she said, "now we're back where we began. Everything in its place." She smiled. "Would you like some caviar?"

"No, thank you," Andrew replied. "Yes. Not quite."

"*What?*"

"No, I don't care for any caviar, thanks." He laughed. "I suppose I did sound a little confused. I was responding to your other questions."

"But I asked only one," Daisy said.

"I guess you did," Andrew said. "Let's forget it. It's not worth explaining. I don't even remember what it was now, what I meant."

"I suppose I ought to replace the beluga," Daisy said. "That would be the civilized thing to do, wouldn't it? Are you sure you won't have some?"

"Quite sure, thanks. I'm already late, and I promised Michael

I'd be at the theater early." He adjusted the table in front of them. "There," he said, "that's better." He reached behind him for his tie and walked to the chair where Daisy had put his jacket. "Well, Mrs. Curtis," he said, standing before her, his jacket on, "thank you for the afternoon."

"What is this 'Mrs. Curtis' shit?"

"It was a joke, a feeble joke. I thought it would help put everything in its place."

"But I've already put you in your place," she said, laughter in her voice. "Must I do it again?"

"I don't think that will be necessary. I'm a quick study. I learned my lesson. Did you?"—he laughed abruptly—"Whatever that might be." He looked across the room, suddenly startled. "What are those?" He was staring at the niche at the opposite end of the room. She followed his gaze.

"Why, they're tulips, of course. Chester Huntington's obsession. Or one of them." Andrew walked toward them, stopping a few feet away. "Aren't they magnificent? I've no idea where he finds them." They were white, arranged in a huge porcelain bowl that stood atop a column identical to the one supporting Daisy's sculpture.

"Was Ann here today? She was talking to Mr. Huntington when I left the hotel. I thought they were arranging something."

"You've already asked that," Daisy said. "I don't believe so. She may be coming tomorrow. I do recall that he wants to show her his tulips. Some have etchings." She laughed. "Chester shows his tulips. Not usually in vases. I meant the ones in the garden. They're just about to bloom."

Andrew looked at the bowl of flowers. "There must be two or three dozen of them!"

"Didn't you notice them last night?"

"No. I'm suffering from snow blindness."

"But there was no snow last night. It was unseasonably pleasant, remember?"

"That's right. I didn't see them, in any case. I missed that painting over the fireplace, too. Actually, I didn't miss it but I didn't see it. Unless they've changed it today. Did they?"

"I don't believe so," Daisy said.

"Last night I thought I saw an ugly English landscape there. But this is not ugly at all. I really must be going blind." He

walked over to the fireplace. "It doesn't even look English. It's"
—his voice was hushed—"magnificent." He stood before it.

"Cézanne," Daisy said. "One of the forty or fifty he did of his
famous mountain."

"Yes," Andrew said, "his miraculous green mountain. Mont
Sainte-Victoire."

"Miraculous?"

"I meant 'marvelous.' But it was miraculous to him, I think."

"Lovely, isn't it? Although I'd say it's more purple, reddish
purple, than green. That's the other end of the spectrum."

"More than lovely," Andrew said, gazing at it. "It looks green
to me, but you're the expert. And now I've really got to go. What
time is it?" He looked at his watch. "Oh, God, I'll have to run to
make the curtain! And I don't want to bump into the Huntingtons." He walked toward the doorway.

"They went to the country," Daisy said, walking with him.
"You're probably safe for a few more minutes."

"Well," he said, "goodbye, then." He put his hand on the
knob. "Goodbye, Daisy. I hope they get the furnace fixed." His
chest hurt. He felt as if he were suffocating, as if there were
something in his throat and he couldn't swallow. "Or at least a
window open."

Daisy laughed. "I'm sure they will. Thank you for returning
my lighter."

"Oh, you're welcome." He paused. "I didn't expect . . . I
didn't expect . . . this."

"You didn't?"

Andrew stood there, his hand still on the knob.

"Wouldn't you like to open the door?" she asked. "You'll be
late."

"Oh, yes, of course," he said, turning the knob. He bent
toward her and kissed her on the cheek. "Goodbye, then," he
said. "Goodbye." He opened the door. "It's hard to say goodbye
gracefully," and he left the library and escaped through the drawing room and down the stairs. He quickly scanned the entrance
hall, looking for a likely place for his coat, and saw, suddenly,
the azalea. He stopped in front of it.

"Are you looking for your coat, sir?" Andrew jumped at the
disembodied voice behind him. He turned. It was Stevens, holding his coat before him.

"Yes, thanks," Andrew said, "I am." He reached to take it.

"Let me, sir," Stevens said, helping him into it as Andrew stood transfixed before the gigantic azalea. It was indeed the largest azalea he had ever seen, and its creamy petals trembled exotic and huge in the heated air. *"You must change your life!"* The colors spun before him, the green of the leaves, the thick cream and deep pink throats of the blossoms. He felt a sharp pain behind his eyes and rubbed his forehead with his hand. "Will that be all, sir?"

"Oh, yes, thank you, Stevens. I'm sorry. I seem to have a headache suddenly."

"Would you like some water, sir?"

"No. No, thank you. I'm fine. Really. I've got to get out of here," he muttered. "Just a little air, that's all."

The butler opened the door. "If I may, sir, Mrs. Stevens tells me you have a lovely daughter."

"Julia. Thank you. Thank you very much. Good night. Good night, Stevens." The snow had stopped, leaving no traces, but the wind from the Embankment blew damp and chill. The river was dark. Andrew shivered, and began walking. He needed air, needed to think of nothing. A tear ran down his cheek. He supposed it was the wind. He wiped it away. In a moment or two, another appeared, then one on the other cheek. Strange. He didn't bother to wipe them away. He walked the back streets for a while, and when he finally stumbled upon King's Road, he proceeded directly to Sloane Square and the theater. The curtain had already gone up on the first act.

"You're late," Michael said when Andrew arrived breathless in the greenroom. "Where the hell have you been?"

" '*Another opening, another show,*' " Andrew sang out, breaking into a little dance. There was no response. "Gee, Mr. Aldrich, what's the matter? Don't you like my act? You're a big director. I'm just a Broadway baby. Please, sir? I can't go back to Iowa. My mother won't take me in, not after what those nasty . . ." Michael remained expressionless. "All right, I got lost. I couldn't find a taxi."

"You were supposed to be here before the show tonight. You were too busy to make the matinée. God damn it, I am mad. I am fucking goddamned mad."

"Sorry," Andrew said. "Sorrier. Sorriest. I got lost! I couldn't help it."

"Of course you couldn't. You can't be expected to find your way around London alone, a simple Broadway baby like yourself. Did you say you lived in New York? Oh, but you're from Iowa. Well, now that you're here, take off your coat and stay awhile. Pay us the honor of a visit." Michael took his coat. "You look a mess! What happened? Were you lost at sea? Or just in a May-tag?"

"Look, I'm sorry I'm late. I'll watch the rest of the act. I'll come back at the first intermission. I'll stay till the end of the show. I'll stay till the end of the run, for Christ's sake! I'll even go to supper afterward, if anybody's interested. Let me think, what else would you like—five days of penance? I'll do it. Mortify the flesh and all that."

"Think you could last five days?" Michael asked.

"I'd give it my best shot, but nobody's perfect. By the way, you're charging supper to the production, aren't you?" He sat down on the arm of the battered couch. "I'm broke. And I hope I'm not paying for that azalea. It must have cost a bundle." He got up. "Listen, I don't want to stand here talking. I want to catch the end of this act. You know: I want to work." He moved quickly to the door and stopped. He turned to Michael. "I promise I'll be great after the curtain. I'll give my best impersonation of myself. A rousing performance. It's not a bad act, really. Takes a lot of technique. I'm not a Method actor." He thought for a second. "Maybe sometimes I am." He stepped halfway out the door, and stopped. Again he turned back. "Please watch it with me, will you?"

"Which? Our show or your own particular magic act?"

Andrew laughed. "Our show. Something to divert your attention."

"Don't worry about my attention getting diverted. But yes, I'll watch it with you. I don't think I should let you out of my sight. You might get lost."

"I might," Andrew replied.

"If you're not already."

"If I'm not already. Let's go."

The show seemed better to Andrew than it had the night before. So did the audience: more attentive, more serious. He distrusted audiences, particularly first-night audiences, and all the hyperbole and self-congratulation and hoopla—wishful thinking, most of it—that surrounded an opening. Everyone telling the toad he was a prince of a fellow. That could be fun, of course; Andrew didn't mind a little sparkle and glitter—but it wasn't the real thing. Someone had to see the real thing, to see it clearly, see it clear. He tried to concentrate. That was where the work came in: a matter of seeing—and seeing and seeing. Of course, you had to know where to look. In his work, at least, Andrew usually felt that he did; he wasn't so sure about his life, though he tried not to let it show.

After the final curtain, after Andrew had gone backstage and gotten through the usual ritual of hugs and kisses and theatrical excesses, after he'd had a few words with virtually everyone in the show or connected with it—from the stagehands to the prop man to the wardrobe assistant to each actor—and he felt they had all been properly congratulated and appreciated, he and Michael and Richard Squires, the actor he liked, together with a few others from the production, walked over to a nearby café for supper. The place was familiar; they'd been there often.

"Well, I have to admit it despite myself," Michael said as they approached the restaurant, "you delivered. When you get your act together, it's quite an act. It would convince almost anyone."

"I try to rise to the occasion."

"Now for your five days of penance. You can do that with a pad and pencil. Really, though, the show's a hell of a lot better than it was last week. I'm pleased. I may even forgive you. It's amazing what a line or two here and there can do—and bloody endless hours of rehearsal."

"Practice," Andrew said, opening the door, "practice." The place was noisy but amiable, and the long table that Michael usually reserved offered a good vantage of the room. The actors liked that, liked being seen. And tonight their mood was jubilant.

"Our kind of place," Richard said, taking the arm of an actress from the show, seating her against the wall next to him, and scanning the crowd. Andrew took a chair on the other side of the table, his back to the room. "Not so grand as the digs of those friends of yours last night, Andrew, but quite swell enough."

"They aren't really friends of mine," Andrew said, "they're sort of friends of friends."

"Friends of a friend, I believe," Michael said, sitting down beside him.

"I think they really liked having that party. It made them feel, oh, slightly risqué or something. Bohemian, I guess. I don't think we were their usual crowd. You know how those theater people are. They all live in funky little flats in funny places like Greenwich Village or Soho and do God knows what to each other. Unspeakable things, probably. They may even smoke dope—or worse. Let's order. I'm famished." Andrew picked up a menu.

"The Huntingtons don't look as if *they* do much to each other," Richard said, taking a cigarette from his pocket and lighting it. "I think they're missing a lot. Unspeakable can be rather delightful."

The waiter came and took their order. "Hey, Richard, give me one of those cigarettes," Michael said.

Richard offered him the pack. "Actually, I'm quite fond of unspeakable things. The error of my ways, and all that. It's saved —saving—my marriage."

"It ruined mine—the first one," Michael said. "Got a light, Andrew?"

"No."

"Lose your lighter?" He reached for some matches and lit his cigarette. "Of course, that particular error got me the second, but she turned out to be a different kind of mistake. It was the error of her ways that got to me."

"You know how some people are between jobs?" Andrew asked. "Michael is between wives. Richard, if you're passing out cigarettes, would you hand me one too?"

Richard put the pack on the table. Michael clapped his hand over it. "Don't give him one!" But Richard was already turning his attention to the actress beside him.

"No, damn it. I want it. You took one. Why can't I?"

"Because I know how to smoke and you don't. I have five cigarettes a week—maybe—and when you smoke you have five an hour."

"Daddy," Andrew said, taking the cigarette, "I'm a grown-up now."

"It's a nice thought." Michael turned to him, speaking softly. "Why are you doing this? Have you forgotten your brother?"

"No, I haven't forgotten." The waiter approached. Andrew

looked across at Richard. "Here's the food. That was quick. I don't know about anybody else, but I've got to have some food. I've hardly eaten all day." He put the cigarette down without lighting it.

"Wednesdays are killers," Richard said, shifting his attention from the actress for a moment. "It's the matinée. The show went better tonight, I thought."

"Harder on you guys than the rest of us," Andrew said. "Your work is just beginning—we hope—and ours—mine, at least—is about finished." He began eating.

"Andrew here had a rough day," Michael said: "champagne at lunch and then he got lost in your city. A hell of a matinée. Lucky he survived it."

"It's a big city," Andrew said, beginning to eat. "Full of strange turns."

"I think he met a sorcerer at one of them."

"And everybody drives on the wrong side of the road."

Richard laughed. "Maybe a sorceress, with any luck." He turned back to the actress.

"Yes, the wrong side of the road. You know," Andrew said, "I had the strangest experience last month. In Colorado. I was out there for a conference, a truly crazy conference. They bring all these people together and put you on panels and make you talk about things you know nothing about. Weird. But they paid my way. I thought it would be a free ski trip."

"In the Rocky Mountains? That's exciting. Did you ski?" the actress asked.

"No. I changed my mind and went back home."

"What was weird about it?"

"Oh, what can I say? The sun rose in the west. That's what was weird about it."

"But the sun comes up in the east." She sounded very earnest.

"That's what was weird about it." He put down his fork. "I just had this belief—no, this *conviction*—that the sun was rising in the west."

"He must have been stoned," Michael said. "I've told him not to do drugs. He can't handle them."

Andrew laughed. "That may have been part of it." He resumed eating and turned his attention to the group. Suddenly he wanted to amuse them, make them feel good about the play and their roles in it. He felt a rush of gratitude; without them there would be no play to see. He even felt grateful to the actress Richard was fancying—Valerie something-or-other—the one who seemed so puzzled by his remark. A bit of a bimbo, he thought, but a pretty bimbo, a sweet bimbo.

"All right, Andrew," Michael said, turning toward him when the meal was over, "I want to know what you were up to today. I don't want any more of your evasions, I don't want any more of your excuses. No jokes. This time I want to know, and we can stay here until you're ready to tell me. Don't say you're tired. I've got all the time in the world." He put his foot up on a rung of Andrew's chair, leaned back, and looked at him. "I'm waiting."

"We've got company. We're supposed to be talking to them."

"They're all talking to each other. See? Nobody's paying any attention to us. And I'll bet you anything Richard's about to leave with that blond number. We could be in church. Think of me as your confessor."

"I don't want to talk about it," Andrew said.

"As I said, I'm prepared to wait. Like a cognac? Good night, Richard. Good night, Valerie."

Andrew waved good night. He turned to Michael. "I don't think so. I've had more than enough to drink today. Wine. Champagne. Vodka. God! Wine again right now. And you're suggesting cognac?"

"Now we're getting to it. Vodka. You always give yourself away. Anyway, I told you I've got an infallible nose for trouble. Where'd you have it? And what else did you have. Tell Uncle Mikey."

"Well maybe I just don't feel like telling Uncle Mikey. Did somebody appoint you my guardian? Or just my shrink? I quit Dr. Rip-off, remember? Years ago."

"How did the azalea look? Suitable?"

"Why don't you ask me about the caviar? If you think I'm falling for that trick, you must think I'm pretty dumb."

"You mentioned it. You said you hoped you weren't paying for it. I figured you must have seen it—you know, when you lost the lighter. So what were you doing, then?"

"I was buying a gift for Ann, among other things. I'm the Easter Bunny at our house."

"Where is it?"

"Where is what?"

"The gift the bunny bought."

"Oh. I couldn't find one."

"You couldn't find one? In London? That's like saying you couldn't find a hooker on Broadway. What did you really do? I want you to tell me. I'm worried, Andrew. Genuinely worried."

"I told you. I went over to Regent Street. I looked around the shops. I wandered around Bond Street, down Piccadilly. I went to Harrods, Beauchamp Place." Andrew imagined himself doing all those things. "And then I walked over to King's Road and eventually the river. I was thinking about the play. Honest to God."

"It was snowing. For such an observant guy, you're beginning to miss a lot."

"I know. I got snow-blind." He laughed. "That's how I got lost. You know, I really am very tired."

"And you want me to let you off the hook."

"Yes."

Michael stared at him for a moment, looked over to his wineglass, picked it up contemplating it, and looked back at him. "You know, Andrew, most people think you're a very fortunate guy."

"Lucky."

"No, not just lucky. Fortunate. You've got a beautiful wife, a beautiful child, a great apartment. Enough money. A house in the country, for Christ's sake."

"Almost enough money."

"And talent. You're smart. You've written a very funny and a very serious play, and what looks to be a successful one. As Pamela said this morning, you're the envy of London."

"You know Pamela. We have to allow her her excesses."

"Ann envies you. Even I envy you, and I love you, you know."

"Ann envies me? Don't be silly. I couldn't stand that."

"Yes. That's pretty apparent. Especially at times like last night."

"How can she envy me? She's my *wife*! She knows me at my worst. What does she envy? That's crazy."

"That's probably part of it: she knows you at your worst. And then she sees all this glamour, this crazy world we travel in. At least, it looks glamourous from the outside. Champagne lunches, opening nights, all these people fawning over you, telling you how great you are, telling *her* how great you are. And she *knows*. You know how it is when you live with somebody: they know. Nobody's telling her how smart she is—at least, nobody in your world—and she is smart."

"She knows me at my worst, and she knows the rest of it is lies."

"But it's *not* lies. It's part of it. Part of you. It's what people see." Michael covered Andrew's hand with his own and roughly shook it.

"I can't help what people see. I can't help what they do. I can't help it if someone flatters me. I don't want anyone to envy me. I don't like it." Andrew withdrew his hand. "I can't deal with it."

"Baby, you'd better learn. As I said, even I envy you, and I love you. I love you and I envy you, but I wouldn't want to live your life. It's easier to direct, and that's crazy enough." Michael slowly shook his head and looked off across the room.

"Can we go now?" Andrew asked.

"Yes, we can go. We can share a taxi."

"I thought I'd walk. It's not very far."

"No, I insist. You went for a walk before and look what happened. I don't want to let you out of my sight. Anyway, it's on the way to my hotel, more or less," and they rode off together. "What happened in Colorado," he asked, "when the sun came up in the west?"

"It was really strange. I don't know how to describe it except that I was standing on this tower of this crazy house in the mountains, near Nederland, I think, and this guy—a crazy guy, very funny, very good-looking, an actor, he'd built the house—was showing me the mountains from this tower that he'd built, said we had to see the sun rise. It had been snowing. His wife had taken the dog and gone off at dawn in her evening dress to drive the school bus. Crazy! We'd had a hell of a ride up there. He said it was about ten minutes from Boulder, but it turned out to be a lot more than that. It seemed like an hour. I was in the back seat of his Volkswagen with another lunatic, a brilliant guy from Chicago who kept raving on about Alfred North Whitehead and William James and Martin Buber and the definition of evil and so on. He was drunk out of his mind. Stoned, too, probably. So was the guy who was driving. When we drove back down the mountain in the morning, in his wreck of a car, and I could see—even with this excruciating hangover—where we'd been in a snowstorm in the middle of the night, on the edge of a gorge, a chasm, really, our lives in the hands of this totally crazy, totally engaging nut who drove like a bat out of hell, I was scared shit-less. But I made my panel—a little late, just like tonight, but I made it"—he laughed brightly—"and I said something that apparently sounded convincing about the madness of My-Lai re-flecting the madness of society, about the question of individual responsibility—our usual clichés." He shrugged, amused, sur-prised. "Anyway, they said it was my best panel."

"Did you say everybody's guilty, that it was society's fault?" Michael gave a wry laugh. "You know, 'all must share the bur-den'?"

"No, I said it was the individuals' involved. To say the actions of a Lieutenant Calley were simply the extreme manifestations of a sick society, as someone there said, of course—all that social-psychosis bullshit—as if what they did was something to be ex-pected, something natural, inevitable, even, says nothing; at least, nothing useful." Andrew was getting excited, relieved to have a subject he could handle. The words poured out of him. "The guys weren't starving. They weren't killing for bread. They were killing out of lust. They killed children, for Christ's sake. Horribly. It was an orgy. Okay, none of us is innocent, but not all of us are equally guilty. Those guys—victims, maybe, but not innocent victims—"

"The world can't afford such innocence."

"I think I even threw in a reference to Martin Buber, some-thing about choice, courtesy of the burnt-out case in the car." He laughed. "Nothing is ever lost."

"Wrong, Andrew. Our innocence. 'It is not only our misfor-tune but our business to lose our innocence.' The words of a smart lady, my friend."

"Who?"

"I think it was Elizabeth Bowen."

"You have to think about that one." Andrew paused. "Our business, hmm? I'm sure I could have worked that in. Probably I quoted Yeats: '*the blood-dimmed tide is loosed, and everywhere the ceremony of innocence is drowned.*' I usually do."

"It has a nice grim ring to it. Very appropriate."

"That's why we need art."

"To spice up our chatter?"

"That too." Andrew laughed. "But it's also socially useful."

"Tell the President."

"It allows us to vent our fury, maybe even our love, without destroying everything in the process. Unlike war and revolution."

"Be sure to tell Nixon that one; he'll be real interested. But you still haven't told me about the day the sun came up in the west."

"It just came up, that's all. A burning orange ball over the mountaintop. And I was facing west, and I saw it. It was my birthday."

"Change of life. Hormones—that must explain it."

"Yes, of course. Your insights, Michael, are truly stunning."

"What did you do?"

"I shuddered."

The taxi pulled up to Andrew's hotel. "You haven't told me about today, either—the truth about today." The driver quoted the fare. "We'll wait to see the young man through the door," Michael told him. "I said I'd tuck him in." He turned to Andrew. "We'll talk again. We *will* talk. I ought to walk you to your room, but I'd feel too foolish."

"I'll make it, I promise," Andrew said.

"I've heard your promises before."

"I'm too tired to get lost," Andrew said. "I'm on automatic pilot. Good night. And thanks. I'm glad you appreciated my show."

When he got to the room, Ann was sleeping. He took off his clothes in the darkness, dropping them on a chair. He looked into Julia's room. She wasn't there. "Oh, my God!" he said, gripping the doorway. He ran over to Ann, shook her. "Julia! Julia! She's gone!"

"Stop shouting and come to bed," Ann said, her voice full of sleep. "She's spending the night in Hampstead, remember?"

"No, I don't remember. Are you sure?" He was shaking, and beads of sweat broke out over his body.

"Of course I'm sure. She's with the Spensers. I told you that. Come to bed, darling. You'll freeze. I'm going back to sleep."

Andrew went into the dark bathroom and leaned against the

basin, catching his breath. He slapped water on his face, and tried to probe the dark mirror with his eyes. He picked up a towel and dried himself off, then walked over to the bed, standing there for a moment before very quietly climbing in. He didn't want to disturb Ann. In her sleep she snuggled against him. For a time he stared at the ceiling, watching the lights from the window flicker across it. He got up and pulled the shade tighter. Then he fell into a thick sleep. It was still dark when he woke up, sweating. He'd been dreaming, but he couldn't remember what. The room seemed very warm, and his pillow was wet. He looked at his watch. It was almost four—the fell of night, he thought. He went into the bathroom and took a shower, and then returned to bed.

"Well," Andrew said, coming slowly out of his sleep to feel Ann's fingers tickling his thigh, "we're feeling awfully frisky this morning, aren't we?"

"It's a lovely morning," she said. "I checked. The sun is shining again, the flowers blooming. I've had a shower. I feel wonderful. And you. You looked so innocent, so contented and sweet —just like a young boy—that I decided to see if you were real and not just a dream. I had to come back to bed to make sure. Are you, my tousle-head?" She pulled his head toward her and looked into his eyes.

"Am I what?" Andrew asked. "Your tousle-head?"

"Real." He turned back. She was making little circles on his thigh with her fingernail. "You already *are* my tousle-head. That's belonged to me for years. The question is, are you something I dreamed up or are you real?"

"I think so. Do I feel real?" He buried his head in the pillow.

"Let me feel it. I'll tell you in a minute."

"Don't be rude," he said. "I'm sleeping."

"Oh, no, you're not. You're just hiding. You *were* sleeping, and so peacefully it was irresistible. I had to disturb it." She continued running her finger over his thigh. "I think my little tousle-head is getting excited."

"That's not possible." Andrew's head was still buried in the pillow, his mind still half asleep.

"Oh, yes, it is." She curled her body around him. "I'm a spoon and you're my soup."

"We haven't had breakfast yet," he said, coming more awake, lifting his face from the pillow, giggling. "I never eat soup for breakfast." He pulled the pillow over his head.

"You don't have to, darling. I said you're *my* soup. We're all alone, you know."

"We are?" He moved the pillow and looked at her.

"Julia's with the Spensers in Hampstead, remember?"

"No, I didn't remember," he said. "Hey, where are we? Oh. Oh, yes. London." He turned back. "Help! What are you doing in my armpit?"

"It's not your armpit. It's mine. You gave it to me a long time ago. Before we were married. Remember?"

"I take it back. I want my armpit. It may be a little dank, but it's my very own and precious to me. We're in a hotel. I'll call room service." He reached for the telephone. "Maybe they've got one in the supply closet that nobody's using. You could have that."

"I don't want somebody's smelly old armpit from the supply closet." She leaned over him and pushed the telephone out of his reach. "I already have yours. You can't take it back. I won't give it back."

"Why do you need another armpit?" he asked, pulling the blanket up to his chin. "Nobody needs three armpits."

"Oh, yes," she said. "But I don't have three, I have four. You keep forgetting. You gave me *both* armpits. I don't know why you can't remember these things."

"It's easy." Andrew moved his hand and clutched his arm tightly to his chest. "I have a memory problem. That's it! Amnesia."

She pried his fingers away. "It's nice having four armpits, two of them furry and two of them smooth. Every girl needs four armpits." She wriggled her finger under his arm and tried to tickle him. "Well, time for soup," she said. "It should be about ready. Let me check."

"Armpit soup doesn't sound very good."

"I wasn't talking about *armpit* soup," she said, grabbing the covers from him and diving under them.

Andrew jumped. "Stop it," he said. "That's mine."

"Wrong again," she said, peering up at him, the covers like a hood over her head. "Your memory is getting terrible. I'll refresh it. Before we were married you gave me this"—she tickled the back of his knee—"and this"—she rubbed her hand across his chest—"and this"—she touched the inside of his elbow—"and all sorts of other things besides. Your belly button, for instance. That was very sweet. I did love having your belly button." She tickled it. "Still do."

"I must have kept something in reserve."

"Oh, yes, you did. You kept these"—she jiggled his balls—"and this"—she tapped his penis. "But they became mine as soon as we were married. I told you as soon as we were married I'd have all the rest of you. It was your wedding gift."

"It was? I thought I gave you that pin. That arrow."

"That belonged to your mother. It didn't count."

"I don't see why not. You like it. It's pretty. What did I get?" he asked, reaching between her legs. She jumped back.

"You got a ring." She tapped her ring to his. "Remember?"

"Yes, I remember."

"So it's coming back at last."

"It's beginning to."

"So is this," she said, feeling his penis.

"It has a mind of its own." Andrew giggled. "But didn't I get anything besides a ring?"

"Wasn't that enough? I did give you my belly button but I seem to remember you dropped it, so I took it back."

"I guess I was satisfied with one. One was enough. Hey, I don't have anything left. That's not fair."

"Yes, it is."

"How do you get to make all the rules?"

"Because," she said. "Just because." She pressed his penis between his legs.

"Ouch!" Andrew grabbed her hand. "Behave yourself, or I'll cut off your leg and beat you with the bloody end."

"What a wicked thing to say." She lifted the covers from her head. "I'll have to punish you for that."

"Please," Andrew said, "I didn't mean it. I was desperate. I meant, I love you so much I could eat you with a spoon." He reached to hug her. "I got mixed up. Honest. That's what I really meant."

"But that's what *I'm* going to do," Ann said. "Right now." She threw the covers off the bed. "As soon as I find my spoon.

Oh, here it is." She pulled an imaginary spoon out of the air and began to make spooning motions over his body. "I'm getting closer," she said, moving down. Andrew grabbed for the bed-clothes. "You won't need those." She pulled them from him. "Here we go!" She took his penis in one hand and began to spoon at it, making slurping noises with her lips. "It won't hurt a bit."

"That's what they all say."

"That's what they *all* say?"

"It's just an expression, you know. Hey! Be gentle. That spoon feels sharp. Cut your fingernails." He grimaced. "You want something to eat, I'll give you something to eat."

"I've got plenty to eat," she said, spooning away.

"You can even swallow it."

"You know I *never* do that. Shall I finish this now, or leave a little for later?"

"Come here, you little bitch." He reached for her hand.

She looked up. "Little bitch? Andrew! What a way to talk! To your own precious wife. Little bitch, indeed!" Suddenly she brightened. "Well, this little bitch is going to chew her bone. Ha, ha."

"Jesus, this is making me nervous."

"Say your prayers."

"Please, God, leave something for lunch."

"Lunch!" She jumped back. "What time is it? Oh, *hell*! I'm afraid it's late. Let me see your watch." She reached for his wrist and turned it over.

"What's the matter?"

"I'm supposed to have lunch with Chester Huntington and see his tulips. He's coming for me at eleven thirty, and it's almost that now. We've been playing all morning. Actually, you've been sleeping most of it. You must have been tired."

"I was."

"I like playing in the morning. I don't want to stop now." She hugged him. "I guess I'll have to, though. I guess I'll have to leave a few crumbs. Sorry. I'll finish it up later." She laughed and looked down at him. "Not much left now, anyhow." She nuzzled his shoulder. "It's been a lovely morning, darling. How did your day go?"

"My day?"

"Yesterday."

"Okay, I guess. I don't remember."

"You don't remember?" She got up and riffled through the closet, pulling out a dress and rejecting it with a shake of her head. "You *have* been working too hard." She took out a blouse and skirt and threw them over a chair. "You didn't hang up your clothes last night. You always hang up your clothes."

"Well, Michael and I had lunch with Pamela, and then I saw the show again and went to supper with Michael and some others. It must have been pretty late when I got back."

"It was. You woke me up looking for Julia." She moved to the chest of drawers and put on her brassiere.

"You're even prettier without your clothes."

Ann laughed. "You'd forgotten she was spending the night with the Spensers. This selective amnesia could be dangerous." She kissed him as she passed by the bed. "Do you suppose it's fatal?" She was getting into her skirt.

"I got some work done, anyway."

"Lunch and supper." She went into the bathroom. Through the open door Andrew could see the reflections of her face in the angled mirrors. He watched her put on her makeup. "That doesn't sound like work."

"That's the trouble. My work doesn't sound as if it's work. These days it sounds as if all I do is eat lunch or something. It's a rich diet. Speaking of lunch, isn't it awfully early for lunch? Why is he coming so early?"

"Chester is taking me on a little tour of London first, then we'll have lunch." She came out of the bathroom, smelling of perfume. "We have a little date." She laughed gaily and began to dress.

"What's he serving? His tulip?"

"That sounded just slightly rude." The telephone rang. "That's probably him now." It rang again.

Andrew swung himself to the edge of the bed and reached for it. "Saved by the bell."

"Who? You or me?"

"Me," he said, picking up the telephone. "Yes? Yes, I'll tell her. Thank you." He hung up. " 'Sir, Mr. Huntington is waiting in his car for Mrs. MacAllister.' "

"He'll just have to wait a minute. Call back, will you, and tell them I'll be there in five minutes?" Andrew relayed the message. "I'm sorry," she said, "about our argument the other night."

"Yes, I am too."

Ann was dressed now, and putting on her earrings. She rummaged through her little bag of jewelry. "I think I'll wear your mother's arrow."

"Why don't you wear that gold feather I gave you?"

"No. I think I like the arrow." She held it up to her blouse.

"You'll pierce my heart," he said.

"Now remember," she said, fastening it, "this is Thursday. You're working all day. I'm going to Hampstead tonight. Julia and I are spending the night with the Spensers. We'll go to Mass. You know it's Holy Thursday. Don't come back to the hotel and shout for the police. We'll both be at the Spensers', returning around noon or a little later." She laughed. "That will be Friday. Do you think you can remember all this?"

"I wanted to leave Friday. We have the tickets."

"You know that's impossible. You won't be ready to leave the city by noon tomorrow. Anyway, I've already changed the tickets. We're leaving Sunday from Heathrow. Maybe we could go someplace for the weekend, or at least for a day. Someplace close. Rent a car. We could visit one of those English gardens—Sissinghurst, maybe."

"How about Camden Court?"

"Camden Court?"

"I was joking. That's where Lord Rysdale came unraveled. My favorite countess' missing husband. Patrick's daddy. The guy you so tactfully inquired after at lunch last week."

She laughed. "Oh, yes. That creep. Probably we should avoid Camden Court."

"Probably we should avoid gardens. I'm afraid of tulips. We could go to Stonehenge. I'd like to see that. It's not terribly far. Maybe we could leave London late Friday afternoon."

"Do you think you could handle driving on the left? Well, you call me this evening and let me know if you can get away. You have the number." She paused. "I'd better write it down, just in case."

"Hug Julia for me." Andrew still lay on the bed. He pulled the covers up to his chin. "Tell her I miss her."

"You're shaking," she said. "What's wrong?"

"I'm just cold, that's all."

"Take a hot shower. It'll warm you up. Darling, I have to leave." She kissed him.

"I know. So do I. I'm sure his tulips won't be blooming yet."

"We'll see," she said. "I'll let you know. Goodbye."

A few minutes after she had gone, the telephone rang. Andrew didn't answer. He huddled in bed for a while, the covers pulled tightly around him. The play opened on Tuesday, he told himself. Then this must be Thursday. The year is 1971. The month is April. The opening was the sixth; therefore, today is the eighth. I am a grown-up man entering my forty-first year—God!—and this is the first day of the rest of my life. Okay. There are things I have to do. One: I have to find a gift for Ann and a gift for Julia. Two: I have to go to the theater for the second-act rehearsal. Three: I have to call Pamela. Four: I have to see the show tonight. Five: I have to get up and put my feet on the floor. He got up and walked into the bathroom and brushed his teeth. Then he took a shower. He could hear the telephone ringing again. When he got out of the shower he walked to the bed and sat down, wrapping himself in the bedclothes. He picked up the phone and called Pamela.

"Sam Walcott's been trying to reach you," she said—"and Michael too. He wants Michael to go to Bermuda with you. Have you talked to him?"

"No."

"Well, they're clawing at you, darling. What did I tell you? They all went to the Russian Tea Room for lunch and came back and picked up their telephones. They're like the swallows in autumn, you know."

"Yes," Andrew said, "all flying to the same telephone line."

"I tell them you'll be in New York next week. Michael too, I imagine."

"Yes," Andrew said, "next week. I'm not sure when Michael's going. Ann and I are leaving Sunday now. Maybe we'll drive to the country for a day and leave the car at Heathrow."

"That sounds lovely," she said. "What is that strange noise?"

"Noise? It must be my head rattling."

"Really, darling. Shall I send over a tinsmith?"

"No, send a dentist. My teeth are chattering." He put his hand to his jaw to steady it. "It's freezing in here."

"It's lovely out there. Go out and see."

"I will. Goodbye, Pamela, if I don't see you."

"Goodbye, lovey. We'll be in touch. I want you to take care of yourself, now."

"I will. Goodbye. Thank you," he called into the phone, but she had already hung up.

Andrew thought of Rilke—"*You must change your life*"—and the line that preceded it: "*for here there is no place that does not see you.*" He couldn't seem to get fragments of poems out of his head, nor could he remember anything whole. He thought of the time when he'd been on the boat, in the merchant marine on enforced absence from his second college, and he'd passed the hours trying to reconstruct some of the poems he'd studied while he spent his days mindlessly, contentedly chipping paint from the bulkhead as the ship plowed through the azure southern seas. The seas weren't exactly azure, either, except on a very good day in July or August; they were steely gray and cold. Nor were they filled with dolphins. They weren't even southern. They were in fact the Great Lakes, not seas at all. The rest was just his fantasy. He'd been affected by Conrad and Melville. It was a challenge, then, trying to piece together an ode of Keats or remember Yeats's Byzantium poems, a Shakespeare sonnet or the lines that followed Hart Crane's "*Green rustlings more than regal charities drift coolly from that tower of whispered light*"—whatever—and a pleasure, although it had rather astonished the first assistant engineer whose watch he stood when he came upon Andrew one afternoon and asked him what he was mumbling and he had turned away from his chipping, looked the first assistant straight in the face, and said, " '*Once out of nature I shall never take my form from any natural thing,*' " and returned to his chipping. Of course he wasn't crazy then, so far as he knew; just a youthful seaman who liked to read. It wasn't a pleasure now, only an amazement when one line or another popped admonitory and unbidden into his head. Pecked to death by dead poets, he thought as he dressed; sky diver attacked by starving birds: a headline he'd seen somewhere. In retrospect, the boat had been a floating asylum, and barely floating at that—a ship of fools propelled by mighty engines; but he hadn't quite realized it at the time: he'd just thought his fellow seamen, fugitives to a man, were a bit wacky. The merchant marine had been a lark, more or less, and then he'd returned to another college. Well, he could always go back to sea; he still had his papers stashed away somewhere, just in case. And, he thought, unless he got going, that might well be the case.

He left the hotel, nervous and on edge. He seemed able neither to go back nor to go forward, yet he could not keep the world forever at bay. He walked to the theater and looked in on the rehearsal. He changed a word or two; he supposed it was an improvement, but none that anyone would ever notice. The play was all right, but he was bored with it, and bored with himself. At least there was a line at the box office. That was what counted. He could be Shakespeare, and still that would be what counted. Of course, it had counted for Shakespeare too.

"You seem awfully uninterested today," Michael said. "Almost irritating. Exasperating, in fact. Like a kid who's been in the house too long. You know, when your mother finally chases you outside because she can't stand you around any longer?"

"Is that a hint?"

"Merely an observation, shit-for-brains."

"Well, I'm feeling childish today, bully."

"Baby! I think I'll smack you." Michael made to punch him. "You flinched!"

"Dink!" Andrew smacked his arm. "Wart-nose!"

"What in the hell are you two lunatics doing?" It was Richard Squires coming down from the stage.

"You always were a little brat." Michael shoved him. "Brat! We're having a fight, just like old times," he said to Richard. "And I'm beating him up, just like old times."

Andrew shoved him back. "Geek!" He stuck out his tongue and made a face. "You always were a geek. And a bully, besides!"

"Mamma's boy!" Michael turned his head to Richard: "Andrew's not playing with a full deck today."

"Turd-face! Full deck, huh?"

"Fart-head! I thought I ought to explain your behavior."

"Turnip-brain! Look, dog-breath, I'm running out of epithets." Andrew called to Richard: "Want to join us? It's very cathartic. Not exactly what Aristotle had in mind, but cathartic nonetheless."

"Fools, both of you," Richard said, laughing. "Who would believe it, two grown men, two eminent men of the theater, acting like ten-year-olds."

"Wrong! Seven-year-olds," Andrew said. "I just wanted to be a little boy again. Besides, I was trying to amuse Michael." He lowered his voice. "He doesn't *have* a full deck, you know."

"Listen, joker, I'm sending you outside to play. Run along now. Go play in the street. Make it a busy one. The grown-ups have things to do."

"They always have things to do," Andrew said. "I've got to go outdoors anyway, so there. Yes. Today I've got to find something for Ann and Julia."

"Don't get lost," Michael said.

"I won't. But if I should, tell them to look for the man in the bunny suit. And I will be back for the show tonight."

"Would you like to grab something to eat first?"

"I'd like to, but I don't know. It depends on how much I get done today. I'll call you. See you later." Andrew started off, paused and turned—"Alligator"—and walked out in laughter.

When he got to the square, he stopped, wondering which way he should turn. Harrods wasn't far. He could surely find something at Harrods. He walked to the store and looked around. A lot of stuff, he thought, a bewildering place. What was it Buber said, some connection between evil and a plethora of choices? He poked around the displays. He thought about buying himself a hat, but didn't. He thought about writing a play about life on a freighter, or about the trek to the Pole. He was more interested in the Pole. He bought a fantastic Easter egg and had it sent to Pamela. That's a start, he thought. Then he bought three smaller chocolate eggs with chickens inside them for Julia, and had them sent to the hotel. He was improving. He could get the hang of this. There was something solidly reassuring about the crunch of the machine gliding across the charge card, something exhilarating, giddying when he thought about having to pay for it. What else could he buy? He could buy Ann an Easter egg too, one of those eggs that opened. He seemed to be fixated on Easter eggs. He went back and bought her one. Surely there was something else. He bought himself a pocket comb. He was always sitting on his combs and breaking them. This one looked like tortoise but was really plastic. Expensive as tortoise, though. The trouble with pounds was that they seemed like dollars, only they weren't; they cost more. England was very costly. Still, an Easter egg didn't quite seem an adequate gift for a grown woman, unless he put something in it. A chicken wouldn't do; jewelry was out. He'd find something, but not in Harrods. He was tired of Harrods, so he left and decided to walk along the Brompton Road. Lots of fancy little shops there. He wandered in and out of a few. Not a whole lot to excite the imagination, except, suddenly, on a tiny side street, a curious little pen shop. Andrew could spend hours gazing at fountain pens, examining them, testing them and discovering their quirks, brooding about the most suitable color of ink, the most appropriate point. His father had given him a fountain pen once, for his birthday, about the only real gift he remembered his father ever buying him. He was in second grade. At the time, he'd never used one; he hadn't learned script yet— cursive, they called it—but he did treasure that beautiful black pen in its fancy white case. He'd had it for years, and taken very good care of it. Once when he was still quite small he'd dropped it point first on the floor, but he'd managed to fix it himself. But then one summer day, years later, when he was in the merchant marine, he'd dropped it for good. It had fallen through a hole in his pocket as he was climbing from the tender to return to the ship after a few hours in port. He'd stood there gripping the ropes of the ladder and watched the pen fall spinning through the air like the winged fruit of a maple, and break the surface, the gold clip and band around its cap flickering in the dappled, sunlit water until it twisted slowly out of sight and sank in Duluth harbor. He could still feel the loss he'd felt that day. However, he didn't see that he could justify buying himself yet another fountain pen; he had more than enough, more, really, than he ever used. But maybe he could buy one for Ann and put it in her Easter egg. Andrew went into the shop and fell quickly under its spell.

It was an odd little place; almost funky. It felt ancient, Rosicrucian, as if it had been lifted from the sands of the Nile and magically deposited on a little side street off the Brompton Road. In the murky light Andrew could discern three or four display cases filled with pens: old ones, new ones, lacquered ones, gold and silver ones, fat ones, skinny ones, richly ornamented ones, plain ones—an amazing variety. He peered into one of the cases. A clerk appeared, noiselessly, from the shadows. He was quite a young man of an unusual color, faintly African. He seemed to be a sort of apprentice to the older man in the green visor who sat behind an enclosure in rapt concentration on the repair of an instrument. The clerk slipped his hands into thin white cotton gloves, almost gauzy, and without speaking took a pen from the case to show Andrew, and then another and another, laying them out on a piece of velvet. He handled the pens as if they were infinitely precious, yet he was strangely matter-of-fact about it. He began to talk, his voice scarcely inflected, about the merits of one over another, the quality of the nibs, the advantage of eighteen-karat gold over fourteen, how eighteen-karat had a different sound as it passed over the paper, and a different feel, too. He filled a pen and demonstrated for Andrew, making a series of scrolls across the foolscap. The ink smelled slightly acrid, metallic. Andrew felt dizzy, intoxicated by the fumes. The clerk used words like caresses, like incantations, with more regard for their sounds than for their meanings. Andrew was amused, fascinated, bemused by the mellifluous flow of words; the clerk was a magician, a sorcerer, an alchemist, and he knew it. He handed him the instrument. The pen was dark, but ornamented with silver in a kind of fanciful Art Nouveau style, and there was a curl to its clip. Andrew took the pen and wrote his name, heard the point move across the surface of the paper. He turned it over in his palm while the Svengali's flow of words continued unabated. His mind felt like cotton wool, of an amazing lightness but at the same time soporific, too heavy to move. He stared at the clerk and let his words wash over him. Finally he emerged. He felt as if he were slowly coming from the depths of the sea, from a great ocean. But he couldn't afford the pen, and he left the shop. He walked on, half a block or so, but kept pausing. It was a ravishing instrument. He looked back, then turned. "All right," he said, entering the shop, "you've hypnotized me, Dr. Mesmer. I'll take it." He paid for the pen with travelers' checks. The clerk placed it carefully in a box and wrapped the box in paper the color of sepia with a darker, paisley design on it. "Your package, Mr. MacAllister," he said.

"How do you know my name?"

"You wrote it," he said.

"Oh." Andrew slipped the package into his pocket and left the shop. He felt giddy, and a little guilty, spending all that money on a fountain pen. Ann didn't even use one, probably didn't like them. They weren't very practical. He could feel its weight in his coat pocket. Maybe he'd find something else for her. He continued walking along the Brompton Road but veered off it unaware at some point—it must have been at a fork; these London streets were very confusing—and after a few twists and turns found himself in an increasingly residential area dotted with cafés and a few curio shops.

"Welcome to Earl's Court, Mr. MacAllister." Andrew turned, startled out of his reverie. Who on earth would know his name here? He couldn't tell where the voice was coming from. "What brings you here, to my neighborhood?" It was David Roper, the critic's friend, the fellow from the party, suddenly beside him. "I thought you hung out in the fancier parts of town. This isn't very fancy. More raffish. You're a long way from home."

"I don't discriminate," Andrew said. "I thought I was walking on the Brompton Road and suddenly I wasn't. And oh, yes, hello. Don't call me 'Mr. MacAllister,' please; it makes me nervous. Is this where we are—Earl's Court?"

"Just a hop from my flat. It's easy to lose your way here. The streets appear to change their names at random: same street, different name. That's what happens to the Brompton Road. But there's a kind of barmy British logic to it. You know," he said, "we never really finished our conversation the other night."

"We didn't?"

"No. You were telling me about civilization, remember, and then you decided you didn't like it."

"I decided I didn't like it?"

"Well, you were describing the glories of the Huntingtons' library, said everything in it represented an achievement of civilization, was precious, and then you decided you didn't like the room very much."

"Not precisely the same thing."

"Close."

"You're not the usual run of shad, are you?"

"Usual run of shad?"

"Shad is a fish, a type of herring. I don't think you have it here."

"Meaning?"

"It just means not ordinary, different. It's a New England expression—Maine."

"Oh. I suppose I'm not. I was thinking of making a pot of tea. Would you join me?"

"Why don't we step into one of these cafés?" Andrew suggested. "I'll treat you."

"We're only five minutes from my place, if that. Let me buy some biscuits." Before Andrew could respond he had darted into a shop and emerged in a few moments carrying a paper sack. "Now that I've got the biscuits, you'll have to come." He smiled. He had a very beguiling, boyish smile. "Otherwise I might think I wasn't nobby enough for you."

"Oh, please!"

"I can't offer you the Huntingtons' library, but I can offer you a chair and a cup of tea or whatever. It's only a room, and not a very civilized one, either"—he laughed—"but I like it. I hope you will too. Come on."

"Well, if you put it that way, yes, thanks. I'll come."

The room, when he got there, was astonishingly white, and very plain. It was not at all what Andrew had expected. Its simplicity made him think of one of those gleaming whitewashed houses on an island in Greece. There was a chair with a piece of thin blue cotton draped over it, a small table next to it, and a lamp behind it; two large windows, and across from them, in the corner, a bed covered with a kind of Indian batik throw and some pillows; a simple table with an alarm clock on it—one of those old-fashioned clocks with the bell on top—a poster from a gallery show on the wall, a few books on a shelf near the bed, a big candle on a saucer, and one extraordinary thing: an enormous iridescent blue butterfly in a lucite case.

"I've only been here a couple of weeks," David said. "That's why it's practically empty. I took it for the light. And because it has its own bathroom. The place I lived before, you had to wait in line for the bath, and it was like a cave, dark as a tomb."

"This one isn't," Andrew said. "It's almost dazzlingly bright."

"I just finished painting it last week. Let me draw the blinds.

The light glares at this time in the afternoon. It hurts the eyes."
He pulled the blinds. The room remained filled with brightness,
but the brightness was diffused by the translucent fabric of the
window shades. "And now I'll put the water to boil." He opened
a door to reveal a burner on a shelf and a tiny makeshift kitchen.
"Please sit down. I'm sorry there's not more choice."

"Choice?"

"Of a place to sit, I mean."

"Oh. Oh, yes. This is perfectly fine." Andrew sat in the chair
and looked around the room. The floor was beautiful—a soft
golden-orange pine, it appeared. It looked American. Andrew
wondered if there were many pine floors in London; but perhaps
it wasn't pine at all: he wasn't an expert on wood. There was a
small, well-worn rug on it of a Persian design—from a flea market, probably. The room might have been simple, but it was
pleasing. Spare more than simple. "I like your place," he said.
"It's not what I would have expected."

"You didn't expect to like it?" David was standing at the
burner, taking the teakettle off.

"I didn't say that."

"What did you expect?"

"Oh, something more . . . Actually, I've no idea. I don't
know what I expected. I didn't expect to find that incredible
butterfly, for instance." He gestured toward the wall between the
windows. "I've never seen anything like it, any butterfly that big
or that brilliant. It's unreal." He saw suddenly the ancient ruin
he'd visited once with Ann—years before, when it was still possible for an American to visit the place—a small, exquisite temple
in the Cambodian jungle that they'd reached after half a day first
in a jeep and then a bullock cart. The temple was said to be pink
—a soft rose sandstone—but it didn't look pink; it appeared to be
a dull brownish gray and, from the distance, disappointing. Then
suddenly as they approached—they and their guide were the
only people there—the whole façade sprang to gorgeous, splendid, vibrant life in a gathering murmur, a whisper, a rush of
wings, and the drabness was transformed in a flash to brilliance
as the butterflies, thousands and thousands and thousands of
them, their incredible wings unfolding and for a moment beating
there resplendent against the stone, took flight into the shimmering air above them, revealing the rose of the temple.

"You seem nervous."

"Nervous?" Andrew said. "No, I'm not nervous."

"Well, distracted, maybe. Somewhere else, at least."

"I was in Cambodia."

"Cambodia?"

Andrew laughed. "Oh, I was just thinking of some butterflies I saw there once. Yours reminded me." He gestured toward it. "I'd almost swear its wings were moving. It seems to breathe."

"It's beautiful, isn't it? You could take off your coat. It would be all right. Here, let me take it."

"I think I'll keep it on for a minute. I feel cold. This room is like a whiteout."

"The tea will warm you up. It'll be ready in a minute." He brought it over to the table. "So. There we were in the library, discussing your work."

"I don't think we talked much about my work."

"A little. We also talked about Greece and the Elgin Marbles, remember? And that piece of marble you thought hadn't been tamed yet—the black sculpture on the pedestal. Other things, too—the origin of ideas, for instance. And then you brought in your friend. He was supposed to inform me about ideas or civilization or something—smarten me up a bit—but he didn't. Mr. Huntington came in before he had a chance. He told us who the sculptor was. Would you like milk and sugar in your tea?"

"Yes, thanks. I don't remember."

"You don't remember? Well, you were a little testy that evening. I remember that."

"I guess I vaguely remember. I was testy?"

"I think you thought I was a little forward, maybe, button-holing you like that about your work, then arguing with you." He poured the tea. "You could have something stronger. I think I've got a little whisky here. Some whisky in your tea would warm you up right. How about it?"

"Thanks. That might be good."

He added some whisky to the mug and handed it to Andrew, then fixed his own. He pulled a couple of cushions off the bed—"These are my chairs"—and sat on one, propping the other against the wall and leaning back. "Tell me about yourself."

Andrew laughed. "There's really not much to tell. You probably know most of it, anyway. I write plays and live in New York. Were you born in London?"

"No, in Wiltshire. My parents live there still, and I have a sister who works for the BBC and another who lives in the States. They're older. I'm the black sheep. Would you like a cigarette?" He offered Andrew the pack.

"No, thanks. I'd eat a biscuit, though. I don't think I've eaten anything all day."

"I completely forgot!" David jumped up and opened the package of biscuits, putting a few on a plate. He set them on the table beside him. "How about taking off your coat now?" Andrew stood up and gave him his coat. "I'm sorry I don't have more to offer you. You must be hungry."

"Not really. But I will take one of these, thanks." He ate the biscuit and took another. David lit his cigarette and put the pack on the table next to Andrew's chair. "Help yourself," he said.

Andrew looked at the package of cigarettes, feeling the slow longing, the sink of dismay. "You smoke Dunhills," he said. "Very spiffy."

"Not usually. Rothmans or Woodbines are what I buy. To tell you the truth, I picked these up at your party. Try one."

"Maybe I will." He lit the cigarette. "Do you work?"

"Oh, yes," the young man said, "but as little as possible. Would you like a little dope? I have some very nice Moroccan."

"That's all I need," Andrew said. David rose again and took a tin box off the shelf by his bed. "So what do you do when you work?"

"A little of this and a little of that. Right now I'm selling things at flea markets. And sometimes I take people—Australians, mostly—on coach tours of England. Sometimes I deal a little of this"—he sprinkled some marijuana on a tray and began to roll a joint—"and sometimes I paint. Pictures. That's what I like to do, what I really do, but there's not a great demand for my work at present."

Andrew glanced around the room. "Where are your paintings? Why don't you hang some?"

"They're all stacked in a room in Wiltshire for the moment. So I'm buying junk and selling it at flea markets. I'll be doing one Saturday. You should come."

"I can't. I'm leaving London tomorrow, I think."

"That's too bad." David returned to his cushion and kicked off his shoes.

"Too bad?"

"We're just getting to know one another." He took a hit. "I could be your guide, show you a London you've probably never seen."

"I don't need a Virgil. Anyway, I'll probably be back."

"You're a mysterious man. Hard to fathom."

"So they say."

"They do? Who else?"

"Oh, I don't know. It's just an expression."

"Like 'not the usual run of shad'?"

"Something like that, yes."

"You know, for having written a play that's getting all this attention, these terrific reviews—"

"Except for your friend's, the iron-pumper's."

"—that grand party, and so on, you seem rather at odds with yourself, rather sad." He laughed. "Not at all the usual run of shad."

"Really? And how am I to defend myself against that charge?"

"There's no need to. Would you like a toke?"

"No, thanks. I don't deal well with drugs."

"The finest Moroccan doesn't turn you on?"

"That's not the problem." He took the joint from David Roper, looked at it, and raised it to his lips. He sucked in the smoke.

"What does turn you on?"

Andrew felt suddenly very heavy. "Oh, I don't know, my friend." What was he doing? he asked himself; why was he here? He tried to gather control. "What turns you on?"

David Roper sat there cross-legged on the cushion, his pale blue eyes looking at him, a trace of a smile on his face. "At the moment, you do."

"Oh."

"Oh?"

"That's what I was afraid of."

"What's there to be afraid of?"

"Everything." The air itself felt heavy; only the light was weightless. "Please. I know this sounds odd, my friend. You are my friend, aren't you? It can't help but sound odd. I am very tired. Very, very tired. It's all been too much. Would you mind? May I just lie down here for a little? I'll make it up to you, I promise."

"Well, certainly. Let me take your jacket."

Andrew stood and walked slowly over to the bed. "I just want to lie down," he said. David took his jacket and pulled the throw back from the bed. "Not in it," Andrew said, "just on it," and he knelt on the bed and stretched himself out across it. His voice seemed to be coming from somewhere else, from a great distance. "I'm intoxicated by the fumes," he said.

"I'm sorry. This is strong stuff. I should have warned you. It's a hash joint, probably opiated."

"No, not those fumes." He shut his eyes. "Other fumes." Andrew could feel David Roper fumbling with his shoes, removing them. He covered him with the throw. He paused, then reached toward the end of the bed and pulled up the quilt, wrapping it over him. "Thank you," Andrew said, moved by the gesture.

"You might be cold."

"Thank you." He heard the sound the clock made, the look of the table, the wings of the butterfly; and sensed somewhere David Roper hovering over him, his fingers resting lightly on his arm. He could hear his breathing. He heard his own voice coming from a great distance. "I have to sleep."

"Yes."

He opened his eyes to the whiteness of the room, like Colorado, like speeding down the mountain when the snow is falling and the light is flat. No shadows. No definition. Warmth suffused him. He pulled his arm out from the quilt, threw the quilt off him, and the throw. Far away he heard a siren. A man in a white robe stood near him. A plume of smoke rose from the cigarette in his hand and curled slowly around his head. He stubbed out the cigarette. The robe fell open. The floor seemed to slant. Curious how the floor slants. The siren faded. The whiteness filled his eyes. He heard the sound of the clock, the long clear silence of the table, the iridescent beating wings. "I took a shower," the man said. Beads of water glistened on the curve of his breast, his placid thighs. He was a young man, fair, almost hairless except for the curls around his head and the darker curls clustering the smooth center of his thighs. He looked so vulnerable. "May I sit down?" He pulled the robe loosely around him and sat on the bed.

"Yes," Andrew said, his cheek pressed into the quilt. "I heard the water." He had not moved. "The way you were standing a moment ago, it looked like *David*."

"I am David."

"Not that David. The statue *David*. Snug. The way your hand was. Curved. Open. Nature doesn't make a straight line. Not a perfectly straight line, anyway. Isn't that odd?"

David Roper picked up his hand. "It's okay," he said. "Really, it's okay."

"Is it even true, I wonder. Crystals of quartz, for instance. They look straight. I'll have to find out."

"You have unusual hands," David said, turning Andrew's in his own.

"I'm not sure I can deal with this."

"You'll have to start. It's easier once you start. I won't hurt you."

"I know. Where did you get that butterfly?" The light was falling from the white room.

"I don't really remember. I found it a couple of years ago in a box of stuff I'd bought to sell, but I couldn't bring myself to part with it." David reached over him to the shelf and lit the candle.

"I can understand that. It's very beautiful."

"You know you're talking about everything but the issue at hand."

"The issue at hand?"

"The issue between us. Whether we're going to make love or not. I'd like that, you know."

"I thought you did things with that critic, Nigel Rogers."

"Did things?" He laughed. "You mean sexual things?"

"I guess that's what I mean."

"I suppose that's what everybody thinks. Actually, no. I don't 'do things' with Nigel. Or with Patrick Rysdale either, if you were wondering that."

"That's too bad."

"Why is it too bad? I don't think it's too bad."

"Probably Nigel thinks it is. Patrick too, for all I know."

"You're getting off the issue again, Andrew. You're very clever about getting off the issue. But I won't let you."

"I see." He paused. "I don't think I can deal with that issue." He turned on his side and raised his arm and touched the young man's head. "Your hair is very soft. Fine. Like a baby's curls."

"You remember what I told you at the party, about your approach to the world?"

"No."

"You said your usual approach was to make enough noise to drown it out. I said I thought it was to keep moving, to elude it."

"So you did."

"But at the same time, you reach out to embrace it. Like right now. You just reached out to touch my head."

"Yes. It's a lovely head, actually; a beautiful curly head, worthy of a statue. When I first saw you, I assumed it was empty."

"I'm more than just a head."

"Yes, well, the rest of you is worthy of a statue too. You are a very beautiful man. You must know that."

"But I'm not a statue, see." He bent toward him and kissed the corner of his mouth. "I move."

"You kissed me," Andrew said, with a kind of mild surprise.

"Yes, I did."

"I've never been kissed by a man before."

"Is it different?"

"Yes. No. I don't know."

He opened his robe. "I'm flesh, see. Not stone." He picked up Andrew's hand and put it on his breast. "Feel it." He moved it to his thigh. "Taste it." He kissed him again, very softly. "Touch it." He put his hand on the curve of his penis, resting so casually, so easily against his groin.

"Yes," Andrew said. He could hardly hear himself speak. "Yes, you are." He could feel the fine hairs beneath his hand, and the warm blood moving. "So am I, and I'm easily hurt."

"How are you hurt? What hurt you?"

Andrew sat up. "I'm terribly sorry. I'm afraid I can't deal with this. I'd like to, but I can't." He stood up. "I must go. Really I must. I'm sorry." He picked up his jacket and put it on, then his coat. "Why did you say that?" he asked.

"Say what?"

"Turning you on."

"It was hanging there," David said, "hanging there in the air.

I thought it might help clear it. But Andrew, my friend, you asked it."

"Oh."

"It still is."

"Is what?"

"Hanging there."

"I'm sorry," Andrew said again. "I can't deal with this. It's too much."

"What did you expect?" David Roper asked, standing with him at the door.

"I no longer expect," Andrew said. "Goodbye." He leaned toward him and kissed him on the lips. "Thank you."

"Thank God," Andrew said, settling into his seat on the plane, listening to the sound of the engines warming up: "free at last. I am very, very glad to be leaving London."

"I *love* London, Daddy. It's a lot more exciting than New York." Julia was sitting by the window, looking out.

"We can hope so," Andrew said. "We can surely hope so."

"We're not off the ground yet," Ann said, "and we're already three hours late. These flights *never* leave on time. But I'm glad you're feeling better. The Easter Bunny can't be sick on his own holiday, can he, Julia? You make a very nice Easter Bunny, darling. It's your rabbit ears. What do you suppose was wrong?"

"Just a twenty-four-hour flu of some sort, I guess."

"You must have needed the rest. You were sleeping when Julia and I got back from Hampstead Friday afternoon, I couldn't wake you when we came back for dinner, and then you slept the entire night. We were afraid you had sleeping sickness. But I'm glad you woke up Saturday morning. It was glorious to spend the day in the country. I was getting sick of soot. And we missed that terrible Good Friday traffic, at least. You should have seen the streets Friday afternoon! Total madness. It would have taken us hours to get out of the city. Especially having to drive on the left."

"I only clipped two hedgerows, and I navigated all the round-abouts. I was quite proud of myself, under the circumstances."

"So were we," Ann said.

"You were good, Daddy."

"Thank you, Julie. Now if this plane would just take off." An engine backfired. "Jesus! What was that? Ann! Say your rosary or something. I forgot—you don't do that anymore. Say it anyway, will you?" The plane began to lurch toward the runway. "This thing'll never make it off the ground. I knew we should have gone by sea. I wish we'd gone by sea."

"For heaven's sake, Andrew, what's gotten into you? You're developing a phobia an hour—fear of tulips, fear of flying, you *must* have an aisle seat."

"Only for takeoff. Well, I'm not playing with a full deck. Isn't that what you said? No, it was Michael. Or maybe I've got some extra cards."

"Wild cards, I think."

"Anyway, I never know what keeps these things afloat—do you? It's against nature."

"They have storms at sea, you know. And icebergs. Remember the *Titanic*."

"Thanks. I'll try to go down singing," he mumbled, clutching his armrests as the plane gathered speed and left the ground. " '*Gather Thou Thy people in, free from sorrow, free from sin.*' "

"That's not Easter, darling. It's Thanksgiving." She laughed. "Your daddy!" she said to Julia, but Julia was still looking out the window, watching the takeoff.

"I know it's Thanksgiving. It just popped into my head. I'm feeling thankful. We survived takeoff. We're in the air, on the way home. Speaking of phobias, did you see Mr. Huntington's tulips? We've been such tourists that we've hardly talked since you left the hotel Thursday morning. Somewhere I lost a day or two." He paused. "Were they blooming?"

"Why do you suddenly sound so glum?" she asked. "Only in a bowl in the library. The tulips he's so proud of are still in bud. You'll be relieved to know that. But I expect they're blooming by now: that's the bad news. By the way, did you see their incredible Cézanne? Imagine having a Cézanne in your house!"

"Imagine having lived near that mountain."

"It's so still, so . . . *there*."

"Still? I remember driving across Provence once, years ago, and there was this strange geological formation—a great long ridge like a cliff cutting across the landscape, brooding over it— and finally it began to dawn on me that this was, this was . . .

his holy mountain. Only it hardly dawned on me then. It didn't really mean much to me at that point; I just thought it looked a little out of place. Strange in the landscape."

"And there it is, in the Huntingtons' library."

"Rilke said Cézanne stood dumb like a dog before the object. I like that."

"And so peaceful."

"Yes," Andrew said. "More or less. Like the mountain on our wedding trip—until we started to climb it. It looked so placid from the lake, so solid. Remember how it loomed, and how the lake reflected it? We could go back. Maybe this summer. Let's."

"That would be nice."

"I wish we could. I hope we can. We could climb it again— while I still have some breath left."

"Shall we have a Bloody Mary?" she asked as the steward approached. "To celebrate Easter?"

"Can I have a Coke?" Julia asked.

"Yes, you may," Ann said. "You should say, '*May* I have a Coke?' "

"Don't forget the 'please,' baby." They ordered their drinks. Andrew made them doubles. "It's likely we'll never see the steward again," he said. "Might as well fortify ourselves in advance, like good Boy Scouts."

"Boy Scouts?"

"Be prepared," he said. "Julia, would you like a little story?"

"The kangaroo story?"

"Yes. Ralph the Cobra and Emily the Comely Kangaroo and Anthony Armadillo. That one."

"Tell me."

"Let's go to the bathroom first. Ann, you can have the aisle seat when I get back. You might want to get out. I don't mind sitting in the middle for a while." And when they returned, Andrew settled down to telling the story.

"Well, so," Andrew said, taking his Bloody Mary, "there they were, making all haste toward Suez. You remember the plan Ralph had devised to get them out of Egypt? That they should bid farewell to the Great Pyramid, which hadn't turned out to be all that thrilling an experience for them—"

"It was pretty thrilling, Daddy. They almost got caught."

"True. All that happy an experience, I should have said,

though they were happy being together, happy that they had through a series of amazing but fortunate coincidences found one another. Anyway, Ralph had decided that under the cover of night, while Abdul the Fierce, the red-eyed guide, was sleeping near the Sphinx and next to his camel—by the way, his camel didn't like Abdul very much either, and would have much preferred to be sleeping next to another camel—they decided they should make all haste toward Suez, and there they should board a fine white ship and relax in their deck chairs while the vessel plowed through the Red Sea and into the Gulf of Aden, across the wild Arabian Sea and into waters yet unknown but carrying them ever closer to Australia, which, as we know, is Emily's beloved homeland and their ultimate destination. She would never feel out of place in Australia, where kangaroos are quite common. She was tired of being stared at, as if she were some kind of freak. In Australia, some—many, in fact—had considered her quite fetching, ravishing even, with her soft brown eyes, her smooth coat and lovely moist nose."

"Why was her nose moist?"

"That's the way kangaroos are. You know how dogs have wet noses when they're healthy and happy? It's the same with kangaroos. It has to be admitted, though, that her nose had a few dry moments there on the Pyramid. And of course, they weren't at Suez yet. It was still night. First they had to cross the Nile. That proved to be no problem."

"Why not?"

"They got a ride on a felucca. That's one of the distinctive little boats that ply the Nile. The river never sleeps, and there's always a boat going about some nefarious business or other. Ralph selected what he thought was a particularly river-worthy craft and approached it. Well, of course the boatman was terrified; cobras are not the most beloved creatures in Egypt today, though they were revered in the time of the Pharaohs. 'Scat, foul serpent!' he shouted, picking up a stick and trying to hit him. 'Shoo, blasted snake!' Fortunately, Emily intervened in her most fetching, most persuasive manner. She explained that Ralph was not your ordinary run of snake—a complete vegetarian, in fact, who ate only the odd cotton boll and was, in addition, a true friend to the needy—and that they were on a mission of vital importance which required they cross the Nile forthwith. She

reached into her basket. 'Oh, sir,' she said, 'kind, lovely sir'—he
was not lovely at all, but never mind—'pray assist us in this
matter of the gravest urgency.' You remember the coins the nice
Spanish tourists had dropped in Emily's basket, thinking she was
a beggar lady? Emily remembered them too, and she took the
coins from her basket, which was actually Ralph's—that's where
he slept, remember?—and gave them to the boatman. 'A little
baksheesh for the charming gentleman,' she said. That's a tip,
Julia, money for a favor. The boatman was very pleased, because
people in Egypt are extremely poor and always grateful for a little
money. 'Wel*come*,' he said, 'wel*come*. Call me Ahmad. Please to
hop aboard,' which Emily did very easily. Kangaroos are excellent hoppers. It was harder for Ralph, and finally he gave up and
just slithered aboard in his usual fashion, watched very closely
by the skeptical eye of Ahmad. And then came Anthony, who
chose to crawl. He couldn't hop, either. 'What's this?' the boatman said, pulling his galabeya up around his knobby knees and
looking down at Anthony. 'What kind of lizard is this? You didn't
say anything about a lizard!' 'Not a lizard at all,' said Emily with
immense *sang-froid*. That means she was very cool about it. 'This
is Anthony. Anthony Armadillo.' 'How do you do?' said Anthony, just a trifle disdainfully, and he found a snug dry spot in
the corner and curled up into a ball in the manner of armadillos
generally when feeling insecure. He was quite a sensitive armadillo, and he did not at all like being referred to as a common
lizard. Emily was rather proud that she had negotiated the whole
deal so well and also that she could respond so deftly to the
boatman's invitation to hop aboard, and she stood quite grandly
next to the tiller as the boat swept across the Nile. For a moment
she fancied herself as Cleopatra—'*the barge she sat on, like a bur-
nished throne*'—surveying her domain. She didn't want to miss
anything, you see; she didn't expect to be back in Egypt anytime
soon. Then too, Ahmad insisted she stay near him. He didn't
trust Ralph, who was stretched out in the prow, keeping an eye
on the farther shore. Ralph didn't care about seeing the sights,
having lived in Egypt his entire life and seen them all many times,
and although he was sad to be leaving his homeland on the Nile,
he felt it necessary to concentrate his mind for the journey ahead.
The trek across the desert could be very difficult. They would
have to move very fast to get to Suez by dawn, unless they were

fortunate enough to hitch a ride. It was important that they reach Suez by dawn."

"Why?"

"Why? Well, when the sun comes up the sands of the desert get very hot and burn with an unholy fire, causing the dreaded phenomenon of the mirage, which utterly confounds the mind, not to mention muddling one's sense of direction. You see, a mirage is not something that's there; it just appears to be there. It's not real, but it might as well be. It could be very dangerous if they saw a beautiful green oasis shimmering on the desert and they raced to get to it and then it disappeared. Or if they thought they saw Suez but it was just a mirage beckoning them in the wrong direction. You understand?"

"Yes."

Ann turned to him. "Are we going to Sharksmouth? Do you want to go to Sharksmouth?"

"How did you know that's what it's called?"

"Chester told me."

"Daddy, go on with the story."

"Just a minute, Julia," Ann said. "I want to talk to Daddy for a minute. Do you want to go?"

"I don't know if I could deal with a place called Sharksmouth."

"I don't know either, but you seemed eager enough to go when we were all at tea."

"That was ten days ago."

"What's Sharksmouth?" Julia asked.

"It's Mrs. Curtis's place in Massachusetts," Ann said. "It's on the way to Maine."

"I want to go, Daddy. Can't we go? It's like a castle."

"I don't know," Andrew said. "We'll see. We haven't really been invited yet. We may not be."

"Well, she asked *me*. She said I'd like it. She said there were lots of things I could play with."

"Yes, well, we'll see. We'll have to think about it."

"You and Mommy *always* have to think about things. That's all grown-ups do." She picked up her Coke and turned to the window.

"What did you think of her sculpture?" Ann asked.

"Her sculpture?"

"The one in the library. The black marble."

"Oh. Oh, that. It was all right, I guess."

"I thought it was quite good. I was surprised. I hadn't thought of her as an artist."

"I guess it was kind of surprising. Was it hot?"

"Hot? I don't know." She looked at him quizzically, then laughed. "I didn't take its temperature. It didn't look hot. Maybe I should take yours. Are you feverish? What a crazy question!"

"I meant the room."

"No, not that I remember. Why do you ask?"

"It seemed hot the other night, I guess."

"Chester said their furnace had run amok after the party, that the whole house felt like a broiler. It was so bad they went to the country for the day, but it was fixed by the time I got there." She finished her glass. "Not a bad Bloody Mary. Shall we have another? Maybe a single this time?"

"May I have another Coke?"

"Why don't you have some juice, instead? You could have the same thing we're having," Ann said, "but without the vodka."

"I'd rather have apple juice."

"Okay. Ann, see if you can flag a steward. I sent them an azalea. Did you see it?"

"No, I didn't notice. Chester said that Michael'd sent them caviar—he didn't mention the azalea. We finished the caviar—Chester said his wife would say we were being naughty, but it was so delicious. There wasn't a whole lot left, anyway. Somebody'd already opened it: we just finished it off. There's really no comparison between fresh and canned. If you make a little money from this play, we'll have to get some. To celebrate. With champagne. Or vodka. Some really good iced vodka. That's what Chester served."

"Did you eat it out of the same dish?"

"What do you mean, the same dish? Like dogs? Why do you sound so shocked? We ate it out of a dish. With little spoons. I don't know if it was the *same* dish. What same dish?"

"The pot it came in, I guess."

"You certainly want all the details. Yes, we did eat it out of the pot. I guess if you've got Petrossian's fresh beluga, you don't hide it. And we spread it on little crackers. And when it was finished I scraped the pot with my finger and licked it. Anything else?"

"Did you sit beside the fire?"

"Yes, my dear. Right next to it. Very cozy."

"That's good."

She turned toward him, cocking an eyebrow. "Chester's quite hot."

"So I hear."

"Where do you hear that?"

"Pamela said he told her his secret's in the fertilizer, and then he offered to fertilize her. You know, he doesn't show his etchings; he shows his tulips. He's famous for his tulips, right? And they pop up every spring. It's the sap rising."

"I think he's rather sweet."

"I didn't say *he* was a sap. He must have something going for him—something that's not immediately obvious. Here are the drinks."

"Cheers," Ann said, raising her glass. "Well, he's very flattering. More than flattering, he pays attention. Most men don't pay any real attention to a woman. But Chester focuses on you. He makes you feel quite special."

"Attention is a powerful aphrodisiac."

"He told me the most amazing story about Frank Potter. The writer? You know the one. He does all those interviews, gets people to say the most amazing things, politicians especially. Have you heard it?"

"How would I know? You haven't told me yet."

"You'd know if you'd heard it. Frank is now Francesca, or will be shortly."

"What?"

"That's what I said. Father of three becomes mother of same; wife now best chum. 'Just girls together,' writer claims."

"Sounds like a headline from the *National Enquirer*."

"It probably will be soon. He's not exactly unknown. A young journalist Chester knows—"

"I think the Huntingtons collect people. I suppose they're more interesting than objects, in the long run, though less enduring. They've got some pretty interesting objects, too. By the way, when are you going to Miami?"

"On the twentieth, a week from Tuesday. I'll be back Saturday morning, probably—maybe Friday night. The conference ends Friday."

"Wear your heart."

"My heart?"

"Your amber heart. The one I just gave you. I don't want you to forget me."

"That would be hard. But listen to my story. So this up-and-coming young journalist was a protégé of Potter's, though he'd never met him. They'd just corresponded from places like Tanzania, where the young man—George something-or-other, think he now works for the *Times* or the *Observer*—was posted. Potter had once written him a letter praising an early story. The fellow was trying to decide whether to become a geologist or a journalist, and Potter became his mentor, turned him toward journalism. Anyway, they'd never met, but George was back in England and Potter invited him for tea. They'd talked on the telephone; he sounded normal. Potter lives mostly in Devon, I believe, and George was on a few days' hike, trekking around the moor. Apparently Potter has a lovely house on the edge of it. George shows up at the appointed hour and knocks on the door. This very elegantly dressed woman answers it—high heels, hose, pearls, rather heavily but beautifully made up—and George says, 'Good afternoon, Mrs. Potter. Is Mr. Potter in?' And the woman says, 'Come in, George. I am Mr. Potter.' "

"I don't get it."

"Neither did George. He was thunderstruck. But Chester says he's a quick study and recovered nicely. They had a lovely tea."

"Potter is a transvestite?"

"No, he's having surgery. He's becoming a woman."

"Don't be silly."

"I'm not being silly. That's what he's doing. He keeps running to Morocco for a snip here, a snip there. I think when George met him he hadn't yet had the final cut, but he was on hormones and practicing for his new role. Probably it's all over by now. Potter's writing a book about it."

"Good. I'll be sure to read it."

"He's very serious."

"He's insane."

"No, he's not. He wants to be a woman; he always felt he *was* a woman."

"Well, he's not. It's possible to be serious and insane, you know. I'd say he's seriously insane—suffering from an extreme manifestation of the Tiresias complex, a bizarre and fortunately rare neurosis. I should write it up for Dr. Karnov. Maybe it hasn't been discovered yet."

"You don't understand."

"No, thank God. What did he look like?—the walking wounded? Did George report that?"

"He said he wore a green-and-black brassiere that looked as if it were stuffed with socks."

"Where the hell did he find that—Frederick's of Hollywood? And how did George know the color of his brassiere? Did they get that intimate—on their very first date?"

"She wore a sheer blouse. He could see through it. He said she was very feminine, but with a rather husky voice."

"Surely they can do something about that. I mean, what do we have doctors for?"

"You're just mocking it. You just can't believe a man would *want* to have his balls cut off."

"No, I can't. Should I?" He finished his drink. "I think I'll go to sleep. But Julia, let's switch places first. I know the middle seat is made for you. I believe it has your name on it. See?" and he wrote her name with his finger on the back of the seat.

"Aren't you going to finish my story?"

"Later, angel." Andrew took Julia's seat by the window, adjusted a pillow, and closed his eyes. What had he forgotten? Lately he seemed very good at forgetting. But yes, he had made the play Thursday night. There was nothing more he could do with that at the moment. He'd called Pamela to say goodbye— for the second time. He'd remembered to do that, though he'd forgotten he'd already done it once. That was Friday morning, after he'd found gifts for Ann and Julia and before he'd gone back to bed. He'd played a good Easter Bunny this morning, hiding the eggs around their quarters in the funny old inn in Wiltshire —virtually a rabbit warren itself. Altogether, he thought he hadn't done a bad job of it. Julia liked the Ouija board; he'd known she would. Maybe he should ask it a question or two himself. Ann liked her heart. So did he. It was a natural formation, the man said, of clear, almost crystal, amber, streaked with red, very nearly but not quite transparent—like a cube of ice. A small misshapen pendant heart. An odd thing to put in that silly chocolate egg from Harrods. The man who'd sold it to him—an older man with a wisp of white hair in a tiny shop off Piccadilly—seemed to know as much about amber as there was to be known. Reserved at first, but when he began to tell about his various pieces—they were very beautiful, some of them, and very rare—he'd spoken with reverence, awe even, as if he were a priest and the shop a temple and these its sacred objects. Andrew had listened to the man talking, watched him pick up the amulet, turn it in his hand, and then slip it into Andrew's own warm palm. He'd wrapped his fingers around it. He liked the resinous warm feel of it, its smoky quality. Amazing that a living thing had exuded it and time had done the rest. It had made him sleepy, and he'd returned to the hotel and bed. He'd slept for a long time, dreaming strange fierce dreams—about ancient Mexico, he thought, and the Yucatán. When he was a boy there'd been a man who used to go to Mexico. Once he'd given him a book about it, and later a wooden mask with tiny slits for eyes that he'd rather liked, even though he couldn't see when he put it to his face; the slits were too small. He'd imagined the Aztecs using it for their sacred dances, in their ghastly bloodly sacrifices when they would cut out the hearts of their bravest warriors and offer them to the implacable god. And the vessels were so beautiful, too. Well, you wouldn't offer a beating heart to a god on just any old plate. Sometimes, the man in the amber shop told him, they'd boiled the hearts in copal, a sort of amber. What goes around comes around, Andrew thought. And those birds—what were they called?—those feathered snakes. Mr. Wolfe had had a couple of them, great stone figures, in front of his house on the Island. He wondered if they were still there. Andrew knew he'd remember the name, if he could delve deeply enough. It would come to him; he'd known it once. He remembered so many things. Even yesterday, when he'd come out of his slumbers and gotten the car from the rental garage and they'd all left London. Yes, he remembered yesterday. It had been a pleasant day, driving west—a good idea. And then, late in the afternoon, in the fading light, the shock of Stonehenge: rounding a bend and looking across at the bleak chalk downs and suddenly there, far in the distance, the monoliths rising stark and fearful from the plain. What ghastly compulsion had driven them, what dreadful force inspired them to raise those enormous, ponderous slabs inch by excruciating inch, adjusting them, moving them—some, the bluestones, the leaflet said, from the end of Wales—it must have seemed like the end of the earth—through an entire millennium and more, on that barren site on the Salisbury Plain? And at what sacrifice, and whose? Andrew shuddered to think. Charred bodies were buried in holes around it. There were daggers carved on one of the stones. Just in the last century—he thought he'd read it somewhere—they'd buried three living men under the piers of a bridge near Glasgow. Gave it strength. Could that be? It wasn't all that long ago. He was sure he'd read it; and they'd done the same thing fairly recently in Germany, too. Of course, they'd done it furtively. They used to do it all the time, and not so furtively, either. Was there anything else? No, not that he could think of. He would sleep now, and he burrowed deeper into the pillow.

"May I borrow your pen, darling?"

"What?" He struggled from his drowsiness.

"Sorry to wake you, but I need your pen. I have to fill out our customs declarations. Do you have anything to declare?"

"My what? Oh. Oh. No. Nothing. Nothing but a Ouija board."

"You must have bought more than that."

"My heart. Your heart. It's an antique. There's no duty on it. Wear it. They'll never notice."

"I still need your pen. You missed dinner. I didn't want to wake you."

"Oh, okay. Thanks." She held out her hand for his pen. He reached into his pocket. There were three of them. He usually carried at least two. He found the felt-tip and pulled it out. "Here," he said.

"What about your raincoat?"

"I forgot. Yes. You have the bill, I think. I wonder how they felt, those Stonehenge people, if it was cloudy on Midsummer morning, or raining, and they couldn't see the sun rise over that Heel Stone. It must have happened a lot, in this climate."

"Nervous, probably."

"Calamitous, more likely. You know why they call it Mid-summer's Day?"

"Isn't it obvious?"

"Well, it's not the middle of summer; it's the first day of summer. The longest day of the year. That used to puzzle me when I was a kid. How could it be longer than any other day? All days were supposed to have twenty-four hours. I didn't realize that when they said 'day' they meant 'daylight.' But they used to reckon that summer began on May Day. It makes more sense. That's when they drove their cattle from their winter quarters to their summer grazing land."

"On May Day?"

"Yes, you know: 'Hooray, hooray, the first of May! Outdoor screwing begins today!' "

"Andrew, for heaven's sake!" She shot a glance toward Julia and back at him.

"And you thought it had something to do with May baskets, I'll bet. No, it all has to do with light. It's the only thing that matters—light and the absence of it. Everything flows from that. The Stonehenge people knew it. We've forgotten it."

"You're forgetting earth, air, and water."

"Earth smothers you, air freezes you, and water drowns you."

"Yes, and light blinds you, then burns you. That's a fairly dire way of looking at things, if you ask me, since we couldn't live without any of them."

"I suppose." He looked out the window, then at Julia between them, at Julia studying her Ouija board. "How'd you like another installment in the strange and marvelous adventures of Ralph the Cobra and Anthony Armadillo and Emily the Fair, the Comely Kangaroo? Let me get a cup of coffee. Then we'll have the story."

"Are you forgetting anything else?" Ann asked.

"No, you know I don't forget anything."

"You forget lots of things. You forgot to call me in Hampstead Thursday night, and who knows what else. You'd forget your name if I weren't around to remind you."

"Would you try to get me some coffee, please? Well, Julie, as you know, it was important that they reach Suez by dawn, which they did. They hitched a ride in the back of a truck. Ralph determined that the truck was going in the right direction and

Emily flagged it down while Ralph arranged himself rather gracefully around her neck, as if he were a scarf or something, and
Anthony slipped into the basket. That was really quite generous
of Ralph, to let Anthony use his basket, but he could hardly
pretend to be a brooch. Anyway, the truck stopped. It was a
pickup truck, you know, with an open back. 'Hey, Mo,' Emily
said, because it was a very common name in Arab lands, 'want to
buy a little perfume? Joy? Chanel Number Five? Arpège? I give
you very good price. Special price, Mo, just for you.' 'Are you
crazy, lady? Flagging me down like this in the middle of the night
to sell some phony perfume? I've got a boat to meet in Suez. Beat
it, lady.' He looked at her again. 'Pssst,' he whispered, 'there's a
snake around your neck.' 'Snake?' Emily asked. 'Oh,' she said,
'You must mean my boa. Handsome thing, isn't it?' She fluffed
it up a bit. 'Found it at the souk in Cairo.' The driver rolled his
eyes and gunned his motor. Ralph thought Emily was getting a
bit carried away with this fluffing business, but then as the truck
started off, Emily Roo—her preferred designation—in one splendid and graceful bound, hopped into the back of it, where the
three of them snuggled down cozily together for the bumpy ride
to Suez. The driver never knew.

"In the morning, in that cool early light before dawn, Ralph
and Emily and Anthony arrived at the mouth of the great canal,
and before the truck had pulled to a stop, they hopped blithely
off, Emily carrying the basket with Anthony in it, Ralph casually
coiled around her neck. As soon as they hit the ground, Ralph
uncoiled himself, Anthony crawled out of the basket, and they
all shook their kinks out—it had not been a very comfortable ride
—and made their way to the very edge of the water. Although
the light was dim, it was nonetheless apparent that a beautiful
white ship was at that very moment unloading a little freight.
Oddly enough, some of the freight seemed to be going into the
back of the truck they'd just ridden in, which Ralph found rather
suspicious, but never mind. He couldn't solve all the problems of
the world. Besides, he couldn't believe their luck. Floating there,
haughty and aloof on the jade-green sea, was the fabled *China
Hand*, the most elegant, the most grand, the most luxurious flag-
ship of the Orient and Pacific Steamship Company. No more
trying to catch a little shut-eye on the stony Pyramid, Ralph
thought; no more fleeing ferocious guides or crossing the palms

of scrofulous boatmen with silver, no more jostling in the back of pickup trucks. No. No more of that. 'Prepare yourselves,' he said, 'for a life of deck chairs and ease, for tiffin in the morning and tea in the afternoon, and soft linen bed sheets in the perfumed night. Ah, the sweet scents of Araby!' Ralph felt triumphant. To what fresh bliss he had brought his friends, he thought. From what dangers and disappointments he had led them. He was, I have to say, a bit of a romantic."

"What's tiffin, Daddy?"

"It's a late-morning snack—just a little one, a cup of bouillon, perhaps, to tide you over from breakfast until lunch."

"Okay, so then what happens?"

"That's it."

"That's it? That's not very much."

"That's all for now. My story bank is running low."

"Daddy needs a rest," Ann said. "He'll get back to it." She turned to him. "Phil Spenser asked how your therapy was coming."

"He *what?*"

"He asked how your therapy was coming." She laughed.

"How kind of him. And what did you tell him? That I'd run out of anecdotes?"

"I knew that would set you off. I told him you'd given up Dr. Rip-off years ago. He knew that. But really, he is very kind. He likes you. He was just being solicitous. They have a lovely family life."

"How do you know? Their children aren't with them. The last I heard, Sarah was going to Oklahoma to radicalize the oil workers. I imagine the workers loved that."

"That was last summer. She's very concerned. A Quaker activist. You shouldn't make fun of her."

"It's easier to radicalize the workers when you don't have to be one. But frankly, I think it's insulting."

"His question?"

"No, that's just offensive, but you know how I am. What's insulting is the idea of flouncing out to Oklahoma with your Mao suit and your trust fund to educate the proletariat on your summer holiday. Those guys working the oil fields are not exactly the greatest victims of injustice in the country. Nor are they stupid. Sarah's lucky they didn't make her one."

"One what?"

"A victim. What's Peter doing? Taming the Black Panthers?"

"He gave them his trust fund. Janet's father must be spinning in his grave."

"He did?"

"The day he turned twenty-one he marched into the Morgan Bank and signed it over. What he could, anyway. He couldn't get rid of all of it. He doesn't have control of the rest until he's thirty-five."

"When he's thirty-five, he may be grateful for that. But at least what he did wasn't frivolous. I have to admire that. I don't know that I could have done it. I don't know what good it'll do, either, but that's another matter."

"Well, it wasn't a whole lot of money."

"A little money is a whole lot more than none. And speaking of therapy, I assume the Spensers are still doggedly at it."

"I don't think you should make fun of them. At least they're trying."

"They certainly are. Like Sisyphus. Who are they pushing now? Who do they think I should see this time? You might as well tell me."

"Well, actually, she was telling me about these two wonderful women—nurses, I think, who've become therapists. Not Freudian; much more practical. They made them keep special journals. They have a retreat in Vermont, and the Spensers spent a week with them there just before they went to London. Very intensive. Janet said it saved their marriage."

"That took only a week?"

"You *are* making fun of them."

"It's possible to make fun of people you like. I like the Spensers. Janet never saw a sunset she didn't like. Or a horse turd, for that matter. How could I dislike someone like that? It's just that it's too bad about her ears."

"What are you talking about? What's the matter with her ears?"

"Well, you know—her earlobes. It's practically tragic. They've grown so *long*, you know, ever since she went native with her jewelry. Good thing she doesn't wear lip rings."

Ann looked at him for a moment. "Oh, shut up," she said, and picked up a magazine and began to read.

"That's what Michael said. I'm just quoting him. Really, I do like them," he said. "You know that. Beneath their serapes, they're very kind people." Ann didn't seem to be listening. Suddenly she looked up.

"I should tell you that I've invited them to dinner in New York when your mother is visiting. Their year in England is almost over. At least we can count on them not to do something outrageous. I hope we can count on you to do the same."

"What's 'outrageous'?" Julia asked, looking from one to the other.

"It's something shocking," Andrew said. "Like taking your clothes off in public. That would be outrageous."

"Not for you, darling," Ann said.

"Daddy, I want to hear more of the story. What happens when they get to the boat?"

"Now? Oh, not now."

"Please?" She squeezed his hand. "Tell the rest of it before we get home."

"Well, let me think a minute." He looked out the window, into the blackness, wondering. "Okay," he said, "are you ready?"

"Yes." Julia lifted the armrest and snuggled up beside him. "I'm ready."

"Just as dawn was breaking, they boarded the vessel—by the first-class gangway, of course—and found a commodious stateroom on the port side. 'Port out, starboard home,' Ralph said."

"Why did he say that?"

"Because on a ship the port side is the left side, and starboard is right, and it was considered more comfortable to be on the port side heading south and east, which is where they were heading. I think it's supposed to be cooler. But it turned out not to be cool at all. Very soon it became very, very hot."

"It did?"

"Yes."

"What direction are *we* heading?"

"West. It became very hot indeed. They were in tropical seas, you know, and the hot wind from the desert blew across them, riling the waters. But they didn't know that yet. Before that happened they'd settled comfortably into their stateroom—state-

room nine—and then took a stroll around the deck to catch whatever breeze there was available. People glanced at them, but they
were very British people, very reserved, and it would be impolite
to stare or even to register faint surprise at seeing a cobra, a
kangaroo, and an armadillo, all of whom were most well behaved,
on promenade. They found three very nice deck chairs and adjusted them so they would be comfortable and close together.
They could have done quite well with two, or even one, since
Anthony and Ralph didn't take up a great deal of room and they
did like to snuggle, but they all agreed that three would be nicer,
and having a chair of his own would give Ralph an opportunity
to stretch out, which he liked to do in the heat of the day. By the
time they'd settled into their deck chairs, the ship had left Suez
and was well into the Gulf, steaming toward the Red Sea. It was
already very hot. It was also time for tiffin, which Ralph ordered
from the steward. Emily took her tiffin with delicate hauteur.
She smiled very sweetly at the steward, who seemed quite
charmed by her. Things were going very well, Ralph thought,
sipping his broth; very well indeed. Almost, he might have
thought, too well. But it was good to have an uneventful day or
two, a drowsy time at sea, and so it was, just as Ralph had
promised: tiffin in the morning, tea in the afternoon, and perfumed sheets in the stilly, starry night." Andrew paused, lulled
by his story. He looked into the night.

Julia nudged him. "Go on, Daddy."

"For several days they voyaged, leaving the Red Sea and the
Gulf of Aden and into the open waters of the Arabian Sea, steaming toward Bombay, which is in India. This particular afternoon
was torpid, somnolent. All the afternoons were, and so were the
mornings, for that matter. But then the hot wind began to blow
and the ship began to rock, and Ralph began to feel a bit squeam-
ish. I didn't tell you, but he suffers from seasickness. Emily felt
a little rough herself. Only Anthony was unperturbed. Seeking
to make himself as comfortable as possible under the circumstances, and finding nothing entirely satisfactory, Ralph curled
up on a little pile of lightly soiled linen beside the stateroom door
—the bath towels were especially nice and soft and could prove
handy, should he get sick—and burrowed into it. That was a
serious mistake."

"Why?"

"Because the cabin steward came by and picked up the laundry and Ralph was in it and nobody knew it! But as you can imagine, there was considerable consternation in the laundry room. The laundress screamed—'Walter, there's a snake in these sheets!'—and ran from the room. Walter ran too. When they discovered their loss, Emily and Anthony were desperate. They searched everywhere, even looking under the mattresses. What would they do? What ever would they do? And Ralph, what would he do? But as we know, Ralph is a sly and cunning snake, and not without resourcefulness, even sick as he was."

"What did he do?"

"Well, he was hopelessly lost. The laundry was located somewhere in the bowels of the ship, but he had no idea where. He slithered quickly out of there; it was no place for him. He peered up and down the passageway and noticed a sign that said 'First Class Galley.' "

"What's that?"

"It's a ship's kitchen. Hhmmmm, he thought, sliding along the passageway, stopping by the galley door. He waited for it to open, which it did soon enough, and when it did Ralph slithered directly in. It was getting on in the afternoon, almost teatime, and Ralph knew that because of the storm no one would be having tea on deck. It was quite likely that almost all the passengers would be taking their tea in their rooms. The trays were lined up on a long table, and stewards were bustling about preparing them. Ralph snaked quietly along the wall, looking for a tea tray that might have his number on it. Sure enough, there was one with a big 'nine' on it, a pot of tea and three cups, a plate of toast, and some wildflower honey. Hot as it was, they were still serving tea and toast—you know how the English are. The steward was just then covering the toast to keep it warm."

"But Daddy, the English eat toast cold!"

"Yes, but only at home. At sea they like it warm. Anyway, Ralph was poised to strike as soon as the steward moved away. I don't mean 'strike to bite'; I mean strike to get under that lid and curl up on the toast. Which he did."

"How?"

"He climbed up the table leg and sped to the tray with the 'nine' on it, got his nose under the lid, and slithered in. He felt a little sorry that he had to curl up on top of their toast, but he knew that Emily and Anthony would forgive him. After all, it wasn't much fun for him either, sitting on a stack of hot toast on a steamy, stormy afternoon on the wild Arabian Sea, no matter how posh the boat. He'd just finished adjusting the lid when he heard someone coming and felt the tray being lifted. 'This is a very heavy tea tray,' the steward said. 'Don't look,' Ralph prayed —but silently, to himself. 'Please don't look. You won't like it.' Then he felt the tray begin to sway, the steward push the door open, and . . . and"—the plane took a sudden plunge, and Andrew looked out the window—"my God! We're starting to land!"

"Don't stop."

"I have to, baby. We're landing."

"We've got to get our things together," Ann said.

"But I want to hear more. I want to know what happens, Daddy."

"So do I," Ann said. "We've got to find out how Ralph gets out of the toaster. But not now, darling. Daddy will tell us more of the story soon. Now we've got to get our things together." She started rummaging in their bags, putting things away, closing them up, gathering the trash into a little pile. She was always very organized. "Are you forgetting anything?" she asked him.

"I'm forgetting everything," he said.

"What's this?" she asked, picking up an envelope from the floor. "It's addressed to Daisy. It certainly is thoroughly crumpled."

"Oh. It's a note. It must have fallen from my bag. I was thanking her for her help with the party. I forgot to mail it."

"But there's nothing in it."

"I forgot to write it, I guess."

"You could always send it to Washington." She put the envelope with the trash. "Did you ever return her lighter?"

"Yes, I think it was sent with the azalea. Hold on, we're landing. Here comes the runway." He squeezed Julia's hand and watched the lights of Kennedy careen crazily toward them. He shut his eyes tight. Suddenly the plane touched the ground, gave a little shudder and began to glide smoothly toward its stop at the gate. "Thank God," he said. "Back in New York, safe at last. Safe at last."

"Safe?" Ann laughed and patted his hand. "Safe in New York? With all those piranhas in the Russian Tea Room? Imagine!" She chuckled to herself and shook her head.

four

After the curves of London, the rectilinear grid of Manhattan seemed solid and rational. Not so clean, maybe, but at least intelligible. You turned a corner and you knew where you were. Henry, the doorman they liked, had greeted them with his usual cheerful salute; Frank, the elevator man, had a piece of candy for Julia. That was no surprise; he often did. Andrew didn't want surprises. Everything looked the same; everything seemed the same, just as they had left it. There was only one new thing: a bowl of forced white tulips that had arrived that day and which Frank had put on the table in the entrance hall. "Good God, where did those come from?" Andrew asked, startled, still in his coat, as Julia wandered off to check on the apartment, to see that everything was in its place.

"I've no idea," Ann said, picking up the card and reading it. " 'Happy Easter, with love from Mother.' " She began to laugh. "Shall I hide them?"

"How did she know?" Andrew asked, bemused. "How did she ever know?"

"That you were afraid of tulips? Darling"—she put her arms around him—"there's no escape. They'll be blooming everywhere soon." And suddenly she hugged him. "Oh, I do love you, my funny, clever, crazy baby. I do love you, tulip madness or not. I could throw something over them—my scarf, a towel." Her eyes scanned the room. "The rug?"

Andrew looked at her and began to laugh himself, a little tentatively. "I love you too," he said. "I think maybe I can handle a few tulips. I'll try." He laughed again, surprising himself. "Yes, I can handle them." He put his arms around her. "With help, of course." And they stood in the entrance hall together, surrounded by their baggage, their arms around one another, their laughter filling the room. "With a little help." He tried to kiss her. He was happy.

"What's so funny?" Julia asked, returning from her rounds.

"Your father's afraid of tulips," Ann said. "He's afraid of tulips!" She held him tightly, clinging to him, laughing hilariously now.

"But no longer," Andrew said, smiling still. "I'm recovering." He reached down for Julia and put his arm around her, drawing her into their embrace. "I've been reprieved. 'Reprievèd,' " he sang, hugging them both.

"What are you singing?" Ann asked.

"The end of *Threepenny Opera*. He's not going to hang for his crimes, everybody's going to live happily ever after, and that's what he sings: 'Reprievèd.' You gave me the album when we were married, remember?"

"No, it wasn't that album. I gave you some of Weill's American theater songs, I think; but no matter."

"No, no matter," and he hugged them both again. "I'm glad to be home," he said.

"It's good to have you back. Let's celebrate the Resurrection," Ann said. "The Resurrection tonight. I love you, you know. I love you. You're still my main man." She kissed him. "Now we've got to get Julia ready for bed."

While Ann busied herself with Julia, Andrew carried their luggage into the bedroom and then ran out for some milk and juice. When he returned, they sat with Julia in her room while she drank her milk, then tucked her in and kissed her good night. A few minutes later they were in bed themselves. Andrew turned out the light. "I'll be your Easter rabbit," he said, drawing her to him, curling around her like a spoon.

It was a relief for Andrew to settle into the routine of his days, and a comfort. The *Times* showed up at the door each morning, and food on the table each night, as regularly as Julia went off to school and back. In the morning and again in the evening, the apartment, filled with its extraordinary light, was luminous as an Impressionist painting, just as Michael had once described it. He'd opened his mail—nothing of particular interest there; no surprises, for which he was grateful—and resumed his business: the usual hours at his desk, toying with this idea or that, pretending to work, convincing himself he was working; a visit to the Actors' Studio to see a workshop, sometimes a screening in the late afternoon or evening; doing his number for one producer or another over lunch at the Russian Tea Room or Sardi's; an evening plotting at Elaine's with Michael, the Walcotts, and a few others. Sometimes it was fun, of course; he could enjoy that role. The Russian Tea Room seemed relatively harmless; no dangerous fish that he could see. Sardi's was as bad as ever. One night while Ann was at her conference in Miami he'd gotten drunk and thrown up in Elaine's, the first time he'd done that in years. He didn't think anyone had noticed; not even Elaine, who seemed to notice everything. That was a relief. The weather was reasonably pleasant—better than London, in any event; yes, there were worse places to be in April than New York—and after the event that shocked him in Elaine's miserable toilet, he'd begun running again in the park when the weather was good, running or swimming at the Y when it was bad, and drinking very little. His annual spring cleaning, Ann described it when she returned from her conference and noticed his new regimen, his new self. Yes, he was happy to return to the soothing regularity of his days, but of course it didn't last.

For one thing, he had to go to Minneapolis to talk to the people at the Guthrie. They were interested in his play, and he wanted to keep them interested without making any commitment. Interest at the Guthrie would be useful in New York. Interest generated interest. The Long Wharf? Arena Stage? He was interested in all of them; desperately interested, though he tried not to show it. He was hoping to find a producer who might care about his play, actors who would be good for it, and reliable; that it might open by the end of October or early November, that it would be a huge success, and that he would get rich. Well, he knew that it wouldn't be a huge success; a modest success would be all right with him. Could he hope for the Public Theater? Joe Papp seemed interested. Could he hope for something more lucrative? Yes, of course he could hope. A reading was arranged, and Sam Walcott came by to see it. He liked the play; they'd discuss it in Bermuda. But in the meantime the people at the Guthrie actually wanted to make serious talk, so two days after Ann returned from Miami—she'd decided to stay for the weekend, returning late Sunday—he headed out to the airport once again and flew to Minneapolis. As long as he was going, he decided to arrange a lunch with his Uncle Christian, who had moved there several years before, Chicago being just too big and having grown too noisy, and then on his return to meet his mother at La Guardia, saving another trip to the airport. She was flying up from Florida, on her way home for the summer. A heavy dose of family, Andrew thought: his mother, his uncle. But he could handle it. Andrew hadn't seen his uncle since his father's death eight years previously, and although he had a kind of residual affection for him from his youth, he was still feeling rather cold toward him because of the events surrounding his Aunt Clara's death the year before. As Christian was the youngest, Clara had been the oldest in his mother's family, and the richest. When she died and Andrew called to tell Christian that he was flying out for her funeral—it had seemed important that some family besides Christian be there, and it was easier for him to make it than for his mother or his brother—Christian had told him that he didn't want him to come, and when Andrew had told him that he wasn't asking his permission but merely wanted to know the arrangements so he could make his own, Christian had said, "No." He would not be welcome. Christian would be driving up to Flambeau with the trust officer and the attorney, the car would be crowded, and there would be no place for Andrew to stay. He was not opening Clara's house but spending the night with the son of Clara's best friends there, the friends themselves being dead; there was no hotel in Flambeau. "I'm sorry," Christian had said, though his tone denied it, "but that's the way I want it: the three of us only." There were no children. "I can't deal with it any other way." So Andrew had not gone—a decision that still rankled.

He felt a sudden rush of that cold feeling again when he saw his uncle standing there, so white-haired, so immaculate, as he walked through the arrival gate, and he wondered why he'd called him, why he'd agreed to lunch, and why he'd allowed him to meet his plane. He could easily have slipped in and out of Minneapolis without his uncle's ever knowing. But it was too late now. They had lunch in a hotel near the airport. It was as good as anything downtown, Christian said, which if true didn't bode well for dining in Minneapolis, Andrew thought. He would rather have had a sandwich in Christian's apartment, which was in an older building on one of the lakes, not far from the Guthrie itself. Christian was proud of his apartment, and Andrew was curious to see it. The family always said he had a flair for decoration. Christian liked fine things, and so, really, did Andrew, although he sometimes considered it a moral weakness.

"And how was your trip to London?" Christian asked.

"Oh, fine," Andrew said. "The play seems to be doing okay. Julia saw all the sights. The weather was miserable. I guess it usually is at that time of year. Maybe all times of year."

Christian chuckled. "Byron said that the English winter ends in July and begins again in August—*Don Juan*."

"He was right."

"Your mother's looking forward to her visit. I wish I could be there too. Make it a family occasion, the kind we used to have on Bellevue Avenue—how I miss that house! We'd have a grand time."

"That would be nice." Andrew thought for a moment or two. "Maybe you could come while she's there."

"I'm afraid New York always exhausts me. It's all I can do now to make it to Chicago occasionally." He took a drink of his brandy Manhattan, then peered at Andrew across the table. "You know, Tommy, you've done the two things I always wanted to do and never did: have a grand piano and go to Europe."

"Well, why didn't you? You used to make reservations. I remember a long time ago you were going to sail on the *France*."

"I don't know. I suppose I didn't want to travel alone, and there was never anyone I wanted to travel with. I'm not the adventurer Clara was. She was still riding a horse at seventy-five! Imagine! I used to worry about her, going all over the world by herself, taking those risks. She was the adventurous one; your mother's the strong one." He paused and took a drink. "She had to be, to have lived with your father all those years."

"I think she liked living with my father."

"In the beginning, yes. In the end, too, I suppose. I'm not so sure about the middle."

"Middles are always hard." Andrew looked at his drink. He hadn't touched it. He raised his glass and took a sip.

"Life is hard, Tommy."

"That's why it's precious." He put down his drink. He'd ordered dry vermouth and wondered why. Because it seemed safe, he supposed. "You're wearing a nice suit," he said, thinking to please him.

Christian looked down at it. "Do you like it? Thank you. I got it on my trip to Chicago in February. At Field's. In their custom shop. No more suits on sale," he said. "It's an extraordinary risk, taking suits on sale. They cost more in the long run." He shifted in his chair, crossing his legs and adjusting his trousers. Christian, who looked so elegant, so expensively dressed and manicured, was wearing black silk hose without garters. Andrew could see his shiny white shins, spindly, hairless, with tiny blue veins above the drooping socks. Andrew marked his father's decline from the time he'd stopped wearing garters. He had been so adamant about them, about a gentleman's never letting his bare leg show between his socks and his trousers. Andrew never wore garters—his socks stayed up with elastic, usually—but his handkerchiefs were linen still. His father had insisted on that, and Andrew had gone off to college with dozens of them. Most of them, he supposed, he had still, along with his father's now, too—a lifetime supply; the badge of a gentleman. In the unlikely event he'd ever need more handkerchiefs, he'd probably make sure they were linen—a little nod toward his father's sense of what was right. A smile flickered across his face.

"What are you smiling about?"

"Oh, I was just thinking about my father, about how many rules he had, how everything had to go according to his plan."

"That's why he was so angry when David behaved so outrageously at college, and when you did, too. That wasn't part of his plan."

"I'm afraid very little in my life has to do with his plan for it. Or in John's either—at least toward the end. That's probably why he was so angry when John died. He couldn't control that. No matter what he did, he couldn't keep John from dying. And John always seemed so perfect, too, when I was little—the perfect big brother. I idolized him. Once when I was a kid and he was home on leave from the war he took me with him to have his shoes shined and the man thought he was my father. John had him shine my shoes too. Was I ever proud! He seemed pretty special to a lot of other people too, I think."

"I heard from Sedge," Christian said, "after Clara died. That was a surprise! I hadn't seen hide nor hair of him since his father's death. How old was he?"

"John? He was forty-four. That was ten years ago. Ten years next month. What did Sedge want?"

"Money, I think. I think he was sniffing money. He wrote me, said he'd like to come to Minneapolis for a weekend. I simply wrote back 'no' in large block letters on a postcard. 'NO. NO. NO.' " Christian pursed his lips into a smug, defiant smile. His beautiful hair—purest white like Clara's, and thinning, too, like hers—had been cut and combed out over his forehead, like one of the later Caesars. It looked a little ridiculous, Andrew thought.

"Why did she leave him out of her will? She remembered everyone else. She remembered his sister. He was the only one."

"I think she thought he was weak. Morally weak. Married, divorced; married, divorced again—all before he was twenty-five. He doesn't have our Bigelow starch. Not like his sister; more like his mother. Like the Sedgwicks. Clara couldn't abide weakness."

"She held everyone to a very tough standard."

"Like your father. That's why they got along so well."

"He wasn't eighteen when my brother died, and life with his mother was no picnic. Shall we order? I think I'll have the liver. Lots of iron, you know."

Christian examined the menu. "I'm trying to decide between the chef's salad and the creamed chicken." He looked up. "The Sedgwicks always were peculiar. Look at Emily's brother—he was never right. Molested someone or other when he was fourteen and never seen since. They had him put away immediately.

Eventually cost them all their money, their entire fortune, or so Emily claims now. One day he was there, and the next day he wasn't. But you wouldn't remember that. It happened around the time you were born. And then Ella Sedgwick's sister's committing suicide. Right in the Sedgwicks' house.

"I didn't know about Emily's brother until after I was grown. I didn't even know she had a brother until he died. Isn't that preposterous? I was in high school then. And I never did know about the suicide. Her legendary Aunt Jenny? When did that happen?"

"You must have been a baby. She was staying with the Sedgwicks after her divorce. They passed it off as a heart attack."

"We were always passing something off as something else." It was the family pathology, Andrew thought; if it wasn't pleasant, or proper, or nice, pretend. Or ignore it. One way of getting through the night, he supposed. "Have you decided what you'd like?"

"I think I'll have the creamed chicken. It's always good here. Her son did the same thing."

"What?"

"Killed himself."

"Ed? He did?"

"You remember him? Yes, Emily's cousin Ed. A bachelor, but not like me. Depressing. A very depressing person. No spunk. He could never find himself. He lived in Chicago when I was there. I saw him occasionally."

"What did he do?"

"Stuck his head in the oven."

"Oh, no." Andrew's heart sank. He looked at his drink. "Yes, I remember Ed. I always liked him." He looked up. "He was nice to me when I was a kid. He took me around the Museum of Science and Industry one day. Took me all over Chicago on that trip. I probably wore him out. He was nice to me when I was making such a mess of college, too, and my father was so mad. I was always grateful." He felt very sad. "I thought he died of some kind of sudden brain disease."

"Yes, but not quite as they said. Nothing sudden about it, except the end. Like Emily's pneumonia. Drunk all the time and they said it was pneumonia! The only person who believed that was your mother." Christian chuckled.

"She always looks on the bright side. She thinks it's being kind."

"Your mother thinks your life is very glamourous, you know."

"It's just another life. We each did what we chose to do."

"But she always says, 'Poor David.' Tommy, what *will* David do when Grande Rivière finally dries up and there's nothing left to ship? It's a good thing your father started that business when you got married. You and John were supposed to be part of it too."

"I know. But then John died, and going back to Grande Rivière was the last thing I ever intended to do. The very last thing."

"I'm sure Margie's money is gone. She and David spend like fools. Never take a bus if a taxi will do. And what they didn't spend, that lawyer took. What was his name? Oh, yes—Bob Griswold. Never trusted him. There must have been a lot of money, too. The Slades were a very fine family once. Old Mr. Slade—Margie's grandfather—lived in an elegant house down near the docks—an abandoned wreck the last time I saw it; probably torn down by now, along with so many other things up there. A pillar of the Presbyterian Church, but he spoiled his sons terribly. Let them smash the Christmas ornaments in the cupola! Imagine! Not one of them amounted to anything. Playboys. Drinkers, too. And the women they married! The same."

"Margie's mother is supposed to have been nice."

"But look at Maxine Slade. Nothing but a tramp."

Andrew laughed. "A dope fiend, too. I always liked her. But I liked her better before she kicked the habit."

"Well, you would." Christian chuckled. His eyes twinkled suddenly, and when he spoke it seemed half chiding, half—half what? Envious? "You were always intrigued by the things your mother didn't want you to know about."

"Attracted to them, too. Mrs. Slade seemed so sad after that. She just drank coffee and stared out the window. She'd wave when I'd walk by, but she'd never talk to me. Cured, but crazy. And then she died. I went to her funeral, the first funeral I'd ever been to. Hardly anyone was there. Reilly the yard man, and their two daughters. Mr. Slade was dead. Margie went too. I was in high school then. It was the first time I'd been in her house in years. And she never left it." Suddenly he laughed. "I always liked the Sedgwicks, too—especially Emily's mother. She had a wonderful laugh. Once I was even crazy about Emily, when she and John were first married, before I got tired of her dream world." He laughed again. "I think I must have an affinity for madness."

"That's a dangerous affinity." The twinkle had disappeared. "It's a good thing for Margie that she's adopted."

"Not having to carry the Slade genes, you mean?"

"I wouldn't have put it that way, but yes. Family matters, you know. We're very fortunate to have the Hopkins' blood, our mother's blood. Except Louise. I don't know what happened to Louise. She wasn't like the rest of us—always different."

"Well, she had children."

"I wonder sometimes if she was brain-damaged."

"That's how I feel."

"What?"

"I was making a joke. A feeble joke." Andrew took a drink of his vermouth. He remembered his Aunt Louise. She'd been married to a farmer. His parents used to take him by their place sometimes when he was a child. He'd never liked it much. It seemed he was always stepping in a cow pie, and he'd felt uncomfortable around his cousins, who were older and never seemed to mind the shit in the pasture—and all around the house, for that matter. They must have thought he was a terrible prig. When he was very young, they'd had neither electricity nor running water, only oil lamps and a hand pump in the kitchen and another one outside. He remembered how the water had tasted: bad. In those terrible harsh winters, he suddenly recognized, his Uncle Arthur must have had to carry water to the animals. It had never occurred to him then. Every single day. Up the hill to the barn, and back down for more. Twice a day, probably. That was devotion. Louise had died a few years ago, but she'd hardly known where she was her last ten years, except that before she got too addled she'd always insisted on going to church. It gave her some kind of consolation. She seemed to know where she was then, at least intermittently. Arthur would drive her in from the country, sit there following the service, and try to keep Louise from wandering wherever her mind was going as she followed the mysterious sacrament moving within her head. Andrew's mother had given Arthur a couple of dresses so Louise would have something suitable to wear. He'd nursed her all those years, attending to her every need. Clara had wanted to put her in a nursing home, and pay for it, of course, but Arthur wouldn't allow it. He might not have been much of a provider in their sense, but eventually they'd had to admit he was kind.

"Louise got sick in the flu epidemic back in 1918," Christian said. "She was half in a coma from November to March. Your mother and Clara were off and married. We hadn't seen our father in years. Jonathan was dead out West. Elizabeth and I and Louise were the only ones home. I had to clean her room. I hated to look at her. Mother had the flower shop then. When she came home at night she'd rub Louise's back and speak to her in a soft voice." His own voice softened, and his eyes looked into the distance. He took another drink. When he spoke again, he was back to his usual brisk tones. "When Louise finally woke up, she did just that—just woke up one day. But she was never really right after that. Then she went to secretarial school. I had to read to her so she could practice her shorthand. She was twenty when she woke up. I would have been just eleven. Nobody remembers that, but I do." Christian looked at him. "Strange, isn't it?"

Half horrified, half mesmerized, Andrew felt a rush of warmth and sympathy for this man so full of memories and small defiance, with the startling blue eyes like Clara's, the radiant white hair, and the expensive suits, and he thought what a mean life he had had, and lonely. His Aunt Elizabeth had told him that for the first year of his life Christian was so sickly he was carried on a pillow. "That can't help but do something to you," she'd said. Probably he has no one else to talk to who knows the context, at least face to face. And he must feel he has to be amusing for his young friend Dennis. No one in the family had met Dennis. They all though he was after Christian's money; Andrew wished him luck. His Aunt Elizabeth had said she thought he drove a truck, or maybe worked in a warehouse. "Not our sort, anyway." She'd whispered when she'd said it. Christian said that Dennis helped him hang pictures, move furniture—the apartment was continually being rearranged to make room for a new acquisition—and he took care of things when Christian went to La Jolla for a month or two in the winter. He seemed to brighten his life. Maybe, Andrew thought, they even loved each other, in one way or another. For a moment Andrew wanted to reach out and touch his uncle's hand, but the moment passed, and as Christian turned to the subject of Clara's estate, Andrew felt the chill set in. The trust company. The trust officer. The investments. The taxes. The attorneys. The place she'd leased for years at the ranch in Arizona. The house in Flambeau. As Christian talked on, Andrew noticed the two men in double-knit suits at the next table. They were eating steaks, and smoking at the same time. One was slightly, the other grossly overweight. Everyone in the room seemed to one degree or another overweight. He began listening to their conversation; he hoped they were not hearing his uncle. "We file a report saying there are seventeen thousand units out there and we get three," the younger man said. "It just makes us look stupid. On the road ten days, and look what we get!" Andrew wondered what units they were talking about.

"Does your family mind?" the other, fatter one asked.

"Oh, no."

Families. He could write a play, he thought, and call it *Family Matters*. He rather liked the title. It was hard for Andrew to think of these men with families. He began to feel disembodied, as if he were hovering over the scene at the next table, the scene at his table, an out-of-the-body observer. A sign of schizophrenia, he thought. A bad sign. It was strange to think of the mysterious business of America being transacted in a brown-and-cream-and-turquoise dining room on the edge of Minneapolis. It was not his business. He didn't understand it at all. Units. Everything was units. Units of what? They never said; it seemed to be understood. Andrew had forgotten how distant he felt from this heartland with its hotel coffee shops and dining rooms with frozen fish, and color-coordinated bedrooms like the one he was surely heading for in the hotel downtown. He felt suddenly very alone.

"You know I have to sign everything," Christian said, bringing Andrew back to himself. "That's what Clara wanted and I intend to abide by her wishes. Yes, I sign everything. When it comes to money, I don't trust anybody—not even a trust company." He smiled at his joke. "But I *am* a co-trustee. They have to continue to deal with me." His eyebrows rose. He looked triumphant. Behind his elegant silver spectacles, Andrew could see his brilliant sapphire eyes—beautiful, really; the color of Clara's, of her stone. His mother had that sapphire now but seldom wore it; she preferred her own. "You know, Tommy, your mother fears now that she's rich she won't live to enjoy it, but there's no reason she couldn't go on to ninety. She's almost seventy-eight, and look at her! Running rings around Elizabeth and me. Clara would have, if she hadn't knocked herself out tripping over the rug at the ranch. They're lucky they weren't sued. I'm sure that's what gave her the stroke. If the Bigelows hang on, they really do hang on—but we do have to watch our steps."

"Prone to falling," Andrew said.

"And I intend to."

"Intend to what?"

"Watch my step. Go on to ninety. I'm going to outlive them all, you know. Of course, I *am* the youngest, barely sixty-three. Your generation will have to wait a long time for your share."

There was nothing for Andrew to say. To shift the subject slightly, and seeking, too, to please him, Andrew told him how much he liked the painting of Clara's that Christian had sent him after she died. "It's a fine painting."

"I thought you'd like it," he said. "Clara had an eye for art." He paused for a moment. "Would you like to have my secretary when I'm . . . through with it?"

"Of course," Andrew said, though he didn't know the piece at all—knowing, though, that it was precious to Christian and knowing, too, that he would want it. It would remind him of Christian, the way Clara's painting reminded him of her, and he had a need for mementos. They kept him anchored.

"We buried her in her blue suit, one of her oldest. She must have had it ten years. I suppose she had it on when they took her to the hospital, and the hospital must have given it to the under- taker."

"I didn't even know she was sick. Nobody told me."

"You didn't? Well, there was nothing you could have done." Except for her nurses, Clara had died alone, though the trust officer had called often, and when it was all over he'd seen that her body was shipped north and, later, her things. "She looked very old and frail when I saw her in the funeral parlor. I didn't go to the cemetery. I couldn't have gotten through it. Richard did."

"Who's Richard?"

"Richard Love, the trust officer."

"The trust officer?" Though Andrew supposed he'd felt it was his duty, it still seemed a generous gesture.

"Yes. Richard's been a godsend. He took care of selling the house. He saw to it that all Clara's possessions were shipped down here and auctioned off, except for the few things I wanted and the couple of things I kept out for Elizabeth and your mother and David and you. He's taken care of everything." Andrew thought how Richard must wonder what lurked behind those brilliant, cold blue eyes staring at him across the polished table at the trust company, and how he must wonder about this absent family, so distant from the needs of the living, so attentive to their remains. But he imagined trust officers grew accustomed to such things. "It's too bad she closed the Chicago apartment and kept the house in Flambeau. It would have been a lot easier if she'd done it the other way around."

"I remember that apartment. We spent a Christmas there once." Andrew remembered that Clara had made him eat a soft-boiled egg before he could go to the tree. He'd hated soft-boiled eggs. "They had a dial phone—I'd never seen one—and Uncle Andrew showed me how to use it and let me dial it for him. I liked him."

"Your namesake. Dropped dead on the golf course at the Greenbrier. I'm surprised you remember him. That was thirty years ago. He was still a young man, younger than Clara by three years. That changed all our lives—at least Clara's and mine. How is your liver?"

"Quite good, thanks. And the creamed chicken?"

"Delicious."

"Well, I scarcely knew him, of course, but I do remember thinking he was a lot of fun, and I loved that incredible car with the push-button doors and the spoke wheels. It smelled like my mother's gloves. Oh, yes, and the spare tire mounted on the trunk. Nobody'd seen anything like that in Grande Rivière, that's for sure."

"The Lincoln Continental. Did you know he bought it right off the floor of the Chicago Auto Show? Said it matched Clara's eyes. The day he gave it to her, she drove it through the back wall of the garage"—Christian laughed—"and refused to drive it again. She said there was something wrong with the gears." He chuckled. "She couldn't believe that she'd done something wrong; it had to have been a defect in the car."

"That sounds like Clara."

"It was like Andrew, too—to buy it like that. He was an impulsive man, almost flamboyant. I often wondered how Clara ended up with him."

"But Christian, she did drive that car. I remember. She used to drive it to Grande Rivière in the summers."

"Yes, but only after Andrew died. She sold the Packards and drove the Continental all through the war. Don't ask me why. I think she thought it burned less fuel." He paused. "They were an unlikely match, Clara and Andrew. You knew he was a terrible womanizer. Compulsive."

"No, I didn't know. The family doesn't talk about that stuff."

"It must have been very distressing for Clara. Humiliating. But she never acknowledged it. Never even mentioned it, as far as I know. Once at a birthday party of your mother's he behaved outrageously toward that girl—who was it? One of the young girls on the Island, anyway. Right in Clara's face and eyes. Could hardly keep his hands away from her. She couldn't have been more than fifteen or sixteen. Clara never let on she'd even noticed, but your father was fit to be tied!"

"He would have been. He didn't like scandal. It interfered with his sense of order and decorum."

"What *was* her name? That Addington girl. The one who married the Jew. Daisy, that's it. Daisy Addington, the Governor's granddaughter. That's who he went after. Do you ever see her? I understand she lives somewhere in the East now."

"Who?"

"The Addington girl. Daisy Addington."

"Oh. She lives in Washington. Yes, I've seen her. Mrs. Steer took me over to her place a few years ago. Her name is Curtis now."

"She was a beautiful girl then, but developed rather a reputation, I think—rather fast, Ella Sedgwick said. I don't suppose I've seen her since that grand party your parents gave to celebrate their silver wedding. She wore a white dress. You'd have thought she was a bride! I stayed in the Sedgwicks' guest house that time. I loved it—like sleeping on a boat. I doubt that Grande Rivière has seen a party like it since. The war changed all that."

"Yes, I guess it did. I was awfully young, so I hardly remember." He glanced at his watch. "Well," Andrew said, "I've really got to think about leaving. They're expecting me at the theater this afternoon, and the afternoon, I see, is almost over."

"Won't you have dessert? They make a wonderful chocolate cream pie here."

"Really I don't have time. Can't I drop you off? It's on the way, isn't it? I'll call you before I leave."

As they waited for the check and then Christian's change—he'd insisted on paying for lunch—Andrew asked him about his apartment, and Christian described the latest arrangement of his furniture: the placement of the Chinese rug so the direct rays of the sun did not touch it; the location of the prized secretary, which still did not seem right; the Ming vase that had been a great bargain thirty years before; the faded polychrome figure of an antique saint bought from a prominent collector's estate. "My next move will be to a hotel," Christian said as they waited for a taxi. "I'll simply take a suite of rooms." That would seem sensible, Andrew agreed, and Christian continued nattering on as they got into a taxi and headed downtown. When they arrived at Christian's building, Andrew got out of the car and walked him to the door.

"You've really set me up for a while, Tommy," Christian said, his blue eyes liquid and glistening, a crooked little smile contorting his face. Andrew could not help himself. Overcome at once by revulsion and tenderness, pity and despair, he leaned toward the lonely, aging man in the costly blue suit, the white hair combed over his forehead, and kissed him goodbye at the door.

The hotel room in Minneapolis turned out to be as Andrew had expected: the two double beds, the color television set, the big bathroom with the drinking glasses wrapped in waxed paper and a paper strip over the toilet seat with the little sign "FOR YOUR PROTECTION," but no space for working. He liked the people at the Guthrie, though. They knew what they were doing, and his talks with them were interesting. The prospects looked hopeful, he thought.

The return to New York was uneventful, although it didn't go as Andrew had planned. He'd learned during his two days in Minneapolis that his mother would be unable to make the connection they had arranged. One of her friends had died in Sarasota, and she felt she ought to stay for the funeral. She would arrive the next day instead, even though she hated to travel on Friday, and at Kennedy, not La Guardia. Well, that was all right, Andrew thought; it would give him a day to recover, a day to gear up. He always needed to gear up for his mother's visits, brief though they were and undemanding as she was. He wondered why. He should try to remember how she'd read to him for hours on end when he was sick, and sometimes when he wasn't sick. She'd always had time for that when he was a child, and he was grateful. Still, he had to allow her her stories, and to sit there and listen while she told Ann and Julia about his blond curls, and what pretty little legs he'd had, and how she used to try her hats on his head and that he'd looked better in them than she did, and so on. But after all, she was his mother, and she'd been a good mother, too, on the whole, and he could grit his teeth or bite his tongue when the impulse to snarl some sarcastic remark overwhelmed him, remarks that she overlooked but that were not lost on her. He'd try to act grown-up this time, try to keep from sticking his head into the newspaper while they talked, and not to disappear from the house earlier and earlier in the morning. It took some inventiveness to disappear from the house, since he had no office to go to but the one off the hall to their bedroom. An office could be a wonderful excuse. Sometimes he envied people who went to offices every day, people who had a whole other life outside of their homes, outside of their imaginations; people who had copying machines and long-distance telephone lines and secretaries and paper clips and rubber bands: a real place to go to, with real things to touch and do, and buzzing with the sounds of the world at work. When he worked, there was only the sporadic tapping of the typewriter, the scratching of the pen, and when he didn't work there was no sound at all.

That night when they were in bed, he wanted to tell Ann about his lunch with Christian, about his alternating feelings of horror and—and what? pity? love? desperation?—but she was not in the mood to hear his confession, and even less to give him whatever benediction, whatever absolution he required. "Really, Andrew, you should forget it," she said. "You spend too much time thinking about that stuff. I've got your mother's visit to think about. I'm trying to get you through that."

"Don't tease me. It hasn't even started yet."

"I know. I'm just trying to prepare you. We all know what happens to you when your mother comes." She laughed.

"But if you'd seen him—"

"Also, I've got some reading to do from the conference in Miami." She picked up a book from the table. "I know that doesn't interest you much. All you wanted to know was who I danced with. You've scarcely asked me about the conference."

"Oh, yes. Conflict resolution. Separating the people from the problem. You went out dancing on Key Biscayne, yet—where we kicked off our shoes and waded in the ocean the night you ruined that beautiful white dress. Peau d'ange, they called it. Angel's skin. That's how you looked, too, that night. I remember. We'd had dinner on the roof of that hotel downtown, and when the moon came up the band played 'Moon over Miami.' We danced. Very romantic. And we drank a bottle of that Portuguese crackling rosé, the kind that came in a crock. Lancers, that's it. We thought it was great then." He smiled. "We'd rented a little red convertible. And then we went to Key Biscayne and walked on the beach at Crandon Park. A lot of life in those bushes, I remember."

She looked up from her book. "Andrew, that was ten, eleven years ago. We're living in 1971 now."

"I guess it was. And when midnight struck we went back to being pumpkins in that funny little place we were staying that cost about five bucks a night—something right out of Tennessee Williams, remember?—and we made love. We had fun that time. We were happy little pumpkins. What's his name again?"

"Whose?"

"The guy you danced with. The myopic Swede from our honeymoon."

"His name is Peter and he is *not* Swedish, he's Swiss. We went through all that before you went to Minneapolis."

"I guess we did." He paused for a moment. "Well, you may be right. Maybe I do spend too much time thinking about that stuff. But if you'd heard Christian go on and on and on about Clara's funeral, and Clara's money, and the attorneys and the trust officer and this one's faults and that one's madness and how his sister Louise was never right and how *he* is going to outlive them all!—well, you'd think about it too. He is my uncle; family matters, as he said."

"Darling, think about your play."

"I do think about it. A lot. But it's hard to control my thoughts. My feelings are impenetrable—I mean, impossible."

"You can't help your feelings," Ann said, marking her place in the book, her voice calm and full of reason. Suddenly he felt almost tearful, and overwhelmed by his love, his gratitude for her. She looked into his eyes. "You're not responsible for your feelings, Andrew. But you are responsible for how you act on them."

"Yes." He was immensely impressed, as he always was, by her correctness, and if he couldn't stop thinking about his lunch with Christian, at least he would try to stop talking about it. "But you know, he's all alone. They all are, I guess. I'm sorry. I'll stop. I'll go to sleep. I'm tired out." Ann opened the book again. He heard her turning the pages for a while, but he wasn't aware when she turned out the light.

Still, he kept returning to the subject whenever he sensed an opening: in the morning as they were getting dressed, after Julia had left for school and he and Ann were sitting in the kitchen finishing their coffee, later when he emerged from his office for another cup of coffee. "Why are you doing this?" she finally asked him. "Why can't you forget him? Are you trying to get his money?"

"He doesn't have any money," Andrew replied, feeling sickened, "and he's planning to live another thirty years, anyway. It would be a very long wait. No, he's not rich—just a fastidious man with beautiful white hair and a taste for books." He didn't know why he did it. The engine of the past driving him furiously on, he supposed, the memory of some childhood kindness, of some flash of compassion since extinguished that had passed between them when he was a boy and his father was mad at him about something or other.

"Oh, he must have *some* money."

"A little, I suppose, but not that much. He has a Chinese rug, the income from a trust fund, and an old secretary."

"Is that what we call Dennis now?" she asked laughing, teasing him. "I didn't know he was on the payroll. Besides, I thought he was young."

"I am referring to a desk," Andrew said, but he laughed.

"You know, darling," she said, softening and moving toward him, "your real life is lived with me and Julia and our friends and your work here in New York—not with an aged mother and an old aunt and a crazy uncle out somewhere in the frozen heartland."

"Yes, I know. I'll try to remember that."

"And speaking of your real life, you do remember that you're picking your mother up at Kennedy in a couple of hours? We've got to think about what to do with her while she's here."

"You make her sound as if she's a problem we have to stow somewhere—like a big crate of onions or something."

"Don't be irritating. I'm trying to help you. We should have thought about this days ago, but you refuse. You act as if it won't happen if you don't think about it. Why won't you plan ahead?"

"*Oh! Calcutta!*?"

"Are you joking?"

"Yes. There must be some innocuous play in town—something where the cast wears clothes and they're not calling each other motherfuckers every third line. Not *Oh! Calcutta!* Not *The Boys in the Band*—I guess they finally shoved that one back in the closet last year. Not *Hair*. Not *No, No, Nanette*. *Follies*, maybe? That's new. Good, too, if a little pessimistic. I went one night when you were in Florida."

"Why not *No, No, Nanette*? She'd love to see it."

"Because I wouldn't. I couldn't stand it. I saw *The Sound of Music* once. I'm a mental diabetic and I'd go into shock from an overdose of sugar."

"We're not doing this for you. We're doing it for your mother."

"Yes, but still. I have some standards to maintain myself. Well, there's always a concert. She loves music. Maybe they're doing something at the Cathedral, unless the Bishop has given it to the Weathermen or the Black Panthers for the week. If she heard a chorus of 'motherfuckers' ricocheting around the gothic arches of St. John the Divine with the Bishop in full drag stamping his crozier and shouting 'Right on!' she'd . . . well, I don't know what she'd do, but let's just say she wouldn't be smiling. She wouldn't be slipping large bills into the collection plate. No, the Cathedral is out. Too risky."

"I wish you wouldn't talk like that."

"Why not? Everyone else does. I understand it's the password at the Dalton School."

"We could visit the Metropolitan and take her to tea in the Palm Court."

"That's a good idea. And surely there'll be some nice Mozart or something at Lincoln Center. Maybe Schumann. She likes Schumann. That takes care of one afternoon and one evening."

"We're having the Spensers to dinner with her Tuesday night. They've just come back. I told you I'd invited them. Janet's mother is in town. That will be nice—someone your mother's age. Sarah Spenser's coming too, I think."

"If she's not got a previous engagement to throw a bomb at some bank. Well, she could always radicalize the doorman. Henry'd love it. Or maybe liberate the elevator."

"Would you be serious? By the way, Daisy Curtis called while you were in Minneapolis. She said she'd gotten your note."

"My note."

"She said you told her your mother was going to be in town."

"I guess I've forgotten." Now, why had he said that? he asked himself. He remembered it exactly. *"Dear Daisy, I'm sorry I left London so abruptly and without speaking to you again. Everything got out of hand my last two days there. I suppose I got a little out of hand myself. It would be nice to see you in New York. My mother will be arriving the end of the month. If you happen to be in town, let me know. She'd like to see you. Andrew."* He'd hesitated before closing it. He could hardly say "sincerely," and the other possibilities seemed preposterous, so finally he'd simply signed his name. And then he'd debated on how to address the envelope. *Mrs. Frederick Curtis* didn't seem right, somehow, and *Mrs. Daisy Curtis* was worse. He'd sent it to *Daisy Curtis*. Yes, he remembered the note quite clearly. "But I didn't mean it."

"What? What *are* you talking about? Anyway, I invited her to dinner with your mother and the Spensers. I thought your mother'd be interested in seeing her again. They used to play golf together, didn't they? They can talk about old times on the golf course."

"You invited Daisy Curtis?"

"I told you she called. She said she was planning to be in the city next week—she has some business with her gallery—and would love to see your mother. So I asked her to dinner."

"I don't want a small dinner. I can't deal with a tableful of women: my mother, my daughter, my wife, Daisy, Janet Macramé, and Sarah in her Mao suit. There's no escape at a dinner like that."

"Escape is not the point, and Janet's name is Spenser, Janet Spenser, and she's my friend. Phil will be there. He can be your support group."

"He'll just ask me how my therapy's coming. No, I can't deal with it. We should ask the Walcotts. I'd like to have the Walcotts."

"We'll be seeing them in Bermuda."

"But he's *important* to me! And we have to have Michael. My mother's known him longer than she's known me. She'd think it was strange if he wasn't there."

"Why must we always have Michael Aldrich? I don't want a houseful of theater people. Can't you do anything without Michael Aldrich?"

"No. He's my best friend."

"Maybe you should have married him." She picked up the book she'd been reading the night before.

"I couldn't. He's my legal guardian. It would have been incest or something. What's that book?"

"*Talking It Out.* It's about conflict resolution. Well, I can't deal with a big dinner. I don't have time. You'll have to handle it as best as you can." She leafed through the book, looking for her place.

"You did say we all know what happens when my mother comes. I can't bear the scrutiny. We could make it a buffet. There are lots of people out there we could have over."

She looked up. "I told you I don't have time. And it's too short notice to get a decent group together. I'm going to read now."

"Oh, all right. But it hardly takes any longer to have a big party than a small one."

She looked up again and thought a moment. "Okay, I'll do it if you promise to help. And if you truly resolve to act like a grown-up while your mother's here."

"You will? I'll help. Really. I'll boil rice for days. I'll search the city for the politically correct lettuce. I'll stamp the grapes myself. I'll do anything."

"I think you just want protection."

Andrew laughed. "From whom? Probably I just want to hide in the crowd. And now I suppose I ought to think about heading for the airport. How'd you like to come with me? Then I wouldn't have to park the car. You could read on the way out. I promise not to say a word."

"I think I could do that for you, but you'll have to do something for me, too."

"What's that?"

"Promise to behave until we leave for Bermuda."

"Don't I always?"

"No."

When they returned from the airport that afternoon, and his mother stepped into the apartment, she said what he might have known she would: "Why, this looks just like the house on Belle-vue Avenue." She walked through the foyer and into the living room, looking to her left and right. "Just like the house on Belle-vue. I can never get over it." She'd said something similar on every visit. And Andrew's response was the same as usual, too.

"But it's not like that house at all. Everthing is reversed. The kitchen is in the front. The dining room is on the right. There's no stairway. It's not so big. There's no library. It's not like that house at all." Why did he have to be so argumentative? She'd meant no harm.

"Well, it looks like it to me," she said. "It certainly has the same feeling. Even the furniture. The old dining-room table. And that funny couch of your grandmother's."

"With the feet like a lion's paws. Sometimes I long for plastic." Yes, he thought, it does look like the house on Bellevue Avenue, the house he'd grown up in in Grande Rivière. Although he'd heard her make the same remark many times, he'd never recognized its truth before. It wasn't a truth he liked to recognize. It made him feel as if he were an actor in a play he didn't write.

When the doorbell rang early the next morning, no one was there; but a mysterious stranger—Ann, of course, sneaking out from the service entrance—had left a May basket for Julia, who sparkled with delight when she rushed to the door and discovered

it. And when they went into the dining room for breakfast—not
their usual morning ritual but special because of his mother's visit
—there were May baskets for the rest of them at each place. It
looked a pretty picture, and the air was fragrant with the fresh
scent of flowers in the morning sunlight. It reminded Andrew of
the times they'd gathered arbutus from the matted leaves and
melting snow of the woods on the Island in early May. His
mother had loved those excursions. So had Mrs. Steer. She
would make a picnic of it, and he and Amy Steer and the grown-
ups would sit in the sunlight around the old Indian cemetery in
the clearing and drink the hot chocolate kept warm in thermos
jugs, and the intense sweet fragrance of the arbutus, the smell of
hot chocolate, the damp smell of the awakening field would min-
gle and rise in waves around them. The fresh smell of that sparkling clear air and the thick, heavy odor of arbutus floated in his
memory now with the fragrance of the flowers in the baskets on
the table, the warmer light falling on the rug this morning in their
dining room in New York. May baskets were a tradition in their
house, one that Ann had brought from her own. Andrew loved
that about her, all the customs she liked to observe. Sometimes
he wondered if he'd married her for her customs, which, like her
family—perfect to him, then, and unattainable—had once
seemed so solid and fixed: May baskets and Easter eggs, sparklers
on the Fourth of July and heart-shaped cookies on Valentine's
Day and oyster stew on Christmas Eve, something he'd always
had as a boy. As a boy, he'd regularly left the oysters in the
bottom of the dish. Somehow, oyster stew on Christmas Eve had
always seemed more exciting than the big dinner the next day,
which was a grown-up occasion and formal, and after the anticipation of Christmas Eve and the excitement of the tree in the
morning, never quite measured up. Besides, as his mother had
pointed out when she called from Florida the previous Christmas
and he was coming down with a fever, he always got sick on
holidays. It wasn't true. He'd remembered coming down with
the measles one Christmas, and that was all. He was very irritated.

"Hooray, hooray, the first of May, everybody knows what
begins today," Andrew chanted, sitting down at the table and
taking the basket from his plate and sniffing it. "Very pretty."

His mother looked puzzled but polite; Ann shot him a warning look. His mother reminded him how the Indians used to come to the door in early May selling bunches of the arbutus—trailing arbutus—they'd gathered from the woods. He remembered. "Yes, and our excursions to the Island in the spring, too." He remembered it all. Ann began asking her about her trip, her winter in Sarasota, her friend who'd died. She'd been a dear friend, one she'd met a year or two after his father died. They'd traveled to Hawaii together, and she would miss her greatly. It was very sudden, and clearly it made his mother sad.

"But let's talk about something cheerful," she said. "How was your lunch with Christian? He told me you'd had a wonderful time, that he hadn't had such a good talk in years."

"Terrible."

"Andrew," Ann said, "it wasn't terrible. You enjoyed seeing him."

"It was fairly terrible. He wanted to talk mostly about Clara, about Clara's estate and his triumphs over the trust company."

"I don't know what's wrong with him," Ann said to his mother. "He's always on edge when he's worrying about a play."

"I'm always worrying about a play—either the play I'm writing, the play I'm not writing, or the play I've written. Any old play at all. I worry about *Oh! Calcutta!*, for God's sake. I worry those people will catch cold."

"Could I pour you some coffee?" Ann asked his mother.

"Thank you," his mother said. "You make delicious coffee. I suppose Christian is a little peculiar, but he is my brother."

"Well, at least he hasn't broken anyone's ribs—that we know of. Right, Ann?" Andrew was referring to her brother, the one she'd adored. Still did. He lived in Korea and was married to a peasant who didn't speak English. He'd broken her ribs once. Hardly anyone knew that.

"A man shouldn't live alone," his mother continued. "Women handle it better. Christian doesn't have enough outside of himself to think about, to keep him interested. No wife, no children."

"Strange," Andrew said, "that none of them had any children. Not Clara, not Elizabeth. Just you and Louise."

"It's too bad, really." She looked at him and suddenly laughed. "They don't know what they've missed. Poor Christian.

Sometimes he talks to me as if I'm on my last legs. Speaking of my last legs, I've brought something for you, Ann. Let me get it."

"I'll come too," Julia said.

"I can tell you right now," Ann said when they'd gone out of earshot, "if you don't stop this, I'll walk out the door and I won't be back. You can tell your mother whatever you feel like. She's not been here twenty-four hours, and you're driving me crazy! That's an ultimatum."

"What are you talking about?"

"What do you *mean*, What am I talking about? What do you think I'm talking about?"

"Did you think I was referring to your brother? The one who never masturbated?" He stopped. "Okay. Don't say a word. I'm sorry. I'll get myself together. I'll be back in a minute." He abruptly left the table and went into the bathroom and rinsed his face. Then he opened a bedroom window and stood there for a minute or so, inhaling the May morning, despairing. He loathed his behavior. It was obscene, if it wasn't plainly lunatic. Ann didn't deserve this. His mother didn't deserve this. *Nobody* deserved this, not even he. It was savage. But—he smiled demonically—he served a savage god. He pulled himself away from the window, arranged his face into a civilized smile, and returned to the dining room. He looked at his mother. She did indeed look extraordinary for someone who'd be seventy-eight in a couple of months. And acted extraordinary, too. "What's the surprise, Mother?" He put his hand on her shoulder, determined to be a loving son, a loving husband, a loving father.

"Do you remember these?" She picked up the tissue that held a pair of silver buckles studded with stones. He recognized them instantly. His mother used to clip them on her shoes when she went dancing.

"Yes, of course I remember them. I remember when Mrs. Henderson gave them to you. I remember you wore them one New Year's Eve, and you wore them at your silver-anniversary party. They made your feet sparkle. I thought they were beautiful."

"Tommy, how can you remember all that?" she asked. "You were practically a baby."

"You had a black chiffon dress, and you came down the stairs on New Year's Eve all sparkling. You wore that arrow of Ann's in your hair. Daddy said you were the Queen of the Night. It's coming back. I must have been"—he calculated the years—"almost eight years old. That's old enough to remember. It was the year the war began."

"He's probably right," Ann said. "He does remember things. Not everything, but a lot of things."

"No, not everything. It was the New Year's Eve you scalded your leg. You and Daddy had a lot of people for breakfast and you sat right at this table—right where Ann is sitting now, I'll bet."

"A lot has changed since then," his mother said.

"Not the table."

"Your grandmother's table. We had some good times around this table, didn't we? I'm glad you've got it now. It looks right here."

"There's a hiding place underneath it," Julia said.

"She likes to play there," Ann said.

"So did your father, Julia," his mother said. "Your grandfather, too, when he was a boy."

"It's a family tradition," Andrew said. "Like May baskets. Like your buckles, Mother."

"I'd almost forgotten that Mrs. Henderson, poor thing, gave them to me."

"Why is Mrs. Henderson a poor thing?" Julia asked.

"She'd had her legs amputated when I was very little," Andrew said. "She used to live near us. My mother said that she'd always liked to dance, and it was sad when she had to give it up. It's hard to dance in a wheelchair, baby."

"Well, the buckles are Ann's now," his mother said. "I don't expect to be doing any more dancing myself."

"You never know. You look as if you could still manage a good fox-trot, Mother."

"Oh, I could manage it, my dear, but I've made a decision: my dancing days are over." She laughed. "When you're my age, there aren't too many partners around who can still dance. Even fewer you'd want to dance with."

"Surely there's some nice old widower down there in Sarasota, Mother."

She giggled. "You'd be surprised."

"You're giggling!"

"I think Mother's keeping secrets," Ann said.

"Well, your mother doesn't have to tell everything she knows, but I can tell you some of those old widowers aren't all that nice. Anyway, once I did love to dance, and I loved these buckles. They even look stylish again. You live long enough and it's astonishing to see what comes back. I hope they don't bring back hobble skirts, though. They were impossible."

"Maybe that was the idea," Andrew said.

"I don't know how we put up with them. If they do come back, Ann, don't wear them. I hope you'll wear the buckles, though. You're young. It's your turn."

"It's her turn?"

"Of course I'll wear them. I love to dance. I have some shoes they'd be perfect for."

"Mother, you won't have anything left. Ann has your arrow, your pearls . . ."

"You gave Ann those things, Tommy. I gave them to you to give to her. Anyway, I never considered the pearls mine. They were Grandmother's. And I still have a few things left."

"I wish you'd call me Andrew."

"I don't know why you insisted on changing your name. I still think of you as Tommy. I can't help it. I've tried to call you Andrew, but Tommy keeps slipping out." She reached over to squeeze his hand. "You'll allow your mother that, won't you, my boy?"

He laughed. "I don't think I have any choice. Mother, how'd you like to see *Fiddler on the Roof*? Or have you already seen it? It's not exactly new. Or *Follies*, Stephen Sondheim's new musical? We could go Monday night."

"Why, I'd love to. We did see *Fiddler on the Roof* once, at the Imperial, I believe, here in New York—don't you remember?—but it's worth seeing again. I'd really love to see it again. I think I'd rather see that than the other one you mentioned."

"Are you sure?"

She nodded.

"Okay. Then we'll all go."

"That's the kind of theater I like. Some of these modern things —those depressing situations, that terrible language. I don't understand them at all. I don't understand how people can talk that way. It's the sign of a poor vocabulary, I always said."

"Or a filthy mind." No, he thought, don't start. Get a grip on yourself.

"*Voice of the Turtle*. That was a lovely play. Sophisticated, a little risqué—"

"Risqué? Mother!"

"Well, your mother wasn't born yesterday, you know. I don't mind something a little risqué if it's witty. I simply don't want to go to the theater and be showered in filth, that's all. It's not necessary, and it's not nice. I hope you'll never do that. To me or anyone else."

"I'll do what I have to do, I guess." He felt himself sinking again.

"No one *has* to do that. Look at Noël Coward. Cole Porter. I'd love to see the revival of *No, No, Nanette*."

"Both faggots, Mother, and Cole Porter didn't write *No, No, Nanette*; Vincent Youmans did. I couldn't stand to see it. It's stupid, and as saccharine as *The Sound of Music*. Maybe worse."

"Andrew!"

"I'm sorry."

"Andrew has a long list of things he can't see for one reason or another," Ann said. "You and I could go to the Wednesday matinée, Mother. I'd like to see it."

"Oh, that's not necessary, Ann. You've got your own things to do. There's no need to do that for me."

"But I'd love to. We could have lunch at the Algonquin, and then walk over to the theater. We'll make an afternoon of it."

"Well, I'd love it, of course. I'll take you, Ann. We'll have a nice ladies' afternoon."

"That sounds like fun," Andrew said. He couldn't think of anything else to say. "Does anyone mind if I take a look at the paper now?"

Ann laughed. "It might be a relief," she said, as he left the table.

There was nothing in the paper that interested him particularly, but there was something that would interest Ann: an article about a week-long workshop on resolving conflicts that was scheduled for early August on a private island off the coast of

Maine, only a few miles from their house. The organizers—one of Manhattan's better-connected, trendier ministers and his present wife who'd lived on the West Coast for a number of years experimenting with various therapies—hoped to bring a limited number of people together from different fields to develop not only their own survival skills—they'd live in tents in the woods—but, by geometric progression, the survival of the race: a sort of giddy California encounter without the hot tubs and with an East Coast intellectual tinge. Ann was skeptical of the more mindless aspects of the human-potential movement, but she did endorse its emphasis on the here and now as opposed to what she characterized as his obsession with the there and then, the if and when. She didn't believe that groping or shouting at one another was the way to resolve anything, however, let alone achieve a higher awareness. But Andrew thought this workshop sounded a little more promising. It had an aura of respectability and seriousness about it, as well as the perhaps dubious blessings of the Reverend Mr. Stone. He clipped the article and left it on her desk.

That evening, after the concert at Lincoln Center—a heartbreakingly beautiful recital of Strauss's *Four Last Songs*, and some lieder that interested him less—he said to Ann, "I tried. Did you see the article I left on your desk?"

"Yes," she said, "I saw it. Thanks. It looks interesting. I know you tried, darling—you were good tonight—but you'll have to try harder. Your mother will be here four more days. It's hard for me too, you know, and you hurt me very much this morning. I can't deal with any more outbursts like the one at breakfast."

"I know. I'm sorry. I didn't mean to hurt you. But you did tell me your brother never masturbated."

"Don't be disgusting. Of course I didn't."

"Yes, you really did. A long time ago. When we were first married. That's what you said. And I was dumb enough to believe you. How do you think that made me feel? Not like the playboy of the Western world, that's for sure. More like the pervert."

"Andrew, you do know that you're acting like a baby?" She sounded weary.

"Yes." And a brat, too, he thought. "But I thought maybe Catholics really didn't. Then I heard one of those new priests say that *he* did. It made me wonder if all those stories were true—you know, about the tunnels from the convent to the rectory? A kid in Grande Rivière swore there was one. And I'd thought that Catholics just beat up their wives."

"Stop it!" She was angry again.

"Well, he did. He punched her out and broke her ribs. And he told your mother! God! She must have been horrified! She must have burned a thousand candles after that. Conflagrations in the churches. Months of novenas." Ann looked at him. "I'm sorry. I'm not laughing. It's just that my hysteria level is rising again. But really, why do you suppose he told your mother that? It was very cruel." He didn't need to, Andrew thought. He'd lived his entire adult life in some godforsaken village in Korea, speaking the language and hating the people. He never saw her, though he wrote her twice a week without fail—long, loving letters. And then he'd come home one time, for less than a week, and he'd told her. Probably he was drunk. At that moment he must have hated her—or hated himself. "The poor guy."

"He doesn't know half so much about cruelty as you do. Please leave my brother alone. He doesn't have anything to do with this, with us."

"Maybe he knows something about love—" Andrew said, "or terror. The terror of it." Like Leda in the wings of the swan-god, he thought, or the great engendering swan itself. Creation is not an innocent act.

The dinner, as it turned out, was a disaster; Andrew might have known it would be before it even began. All the omens were inauspicious. Any reputable astrologer, any ordinary diviner of chicken entrails could have foretold it. Even his mother had said there was no need to have a party for her. She just wanted to see them, and she'd be more than happy with a small family dinner. She'd always enjoyed the Spensers, of course, though she'd never met their children, and it would be interesting to see Daisy Curtis after all these years, though she'd not sounded very enthusiastic about it. "I'm more than content playing cards with Julia," she'd said. Well, they should have listened to her; but plans were already under way, forces already in motion, and some two dozen people had been rounded up at the last minute and invited for Tuesday evening. Ann donned her quilted dress that had been made by a farm women's cooperative in Appalachia and had cost an arm and a leg, clipped his mother's buckles to her shoes, and dinner was upon them. Sarah Spenser, smartly dressed in regulation army surplus and fresh from a mass arrest at the Mayday Tribe's attempt to shut down Washington the day before, seemed to have passed out of her Quaker phase into something a little more violent, if the bandolier was any indication. Andrew shrugged. "It's a look," he said to Ann. "Some wear quilts." The dizzy Harvey tobacco heiress they'd invited because he thought his mother would be dazzled by the name and her foundation had given him some money once and—who knew?—might again, decided to bring not her husband but her new psychotherapist, who liked to talk about the quality of his orgasms. They were, he was eager to tell you, at once on a higher and yet more earthy plane than other people's, and they seemed to occur simultaneously and in multiples with the aptly named Hope's. It was part of her therapy. Hope smiled in a bovine way. There was a rumor that her husband got similar treatment from the same source. The therapist volunteered that he was also heavily hung, which was why he never wore underwear—too constricting. One of their guests from Ann's political work said she'd never heard such a boring conversation in her life, and the therapist said, with an audible sneer, "What would you rather talk about? Viet-Nam?" Ann's friend uttered an emphatic "Yes," and turned to another group. Hope continued to smile. Andrew shuddered, rolled his eyes at Ann across the way, and moved on, pausing for a word with Lord Lollipop, a grandiloquent New York broadcast journalist in English shirts—but taking care not to linger; his voice was more compelling than his brain. They called him Lord Lollipop because he was said to share, in addition to his shirt-maker, an awkward compulsion with a famous English newspaper publisher who regularly whipped out his member while riding in taxicabs with new female employees. Only the willing lasted. Andrew felt he'd never heard so many "motherfuckers" in his life, except maybe once at the Cathedral, and most of them came from the mouth of sweet Sarah Spenser, the onetime pacifist before she'd been radicalized by the pigs in a tear-gas attack after Kent State the year before and whose most valuable contribution to the revolution appeared to be the making of MFMs. When Andrew's mother politely inquired, "MFMs?" Sarah said,

"Mother-fucking munchies, dig? We pass them out to the Weathermen at demonstrations, Mrs. MacAllister." Janet, at least, had the sense to be horrified, and she immediately took his mother by the arm and steered her into another, safer corner as she launched into a story about how she'd acquired her jewelry from a simple peasant woman—"so placid, so wise"—in the Wadi Musa, or something. She was wearing her Bedouin bells, and they tinkled as she moved. Later she revealed that Sarah'd said the same thing to *her* mother as the three of them were driving up to the Berkshires for a little respite from the trenches. Fortunately, the Mercedes was on cruise control. Well, at least there were no drugs, Andrew thought, until the heavily hung therapist lit up a joint in front of Janet's mother—no needles, anyway. Probably she was used to it. He didn't think his mother had noticed; even if she had, she probably wouldn't have known what it was. Maybe she didn't know the meaning of the word, either; it was altogether possible that she'd never heard it: anything was. The Swedish couple they'd hired for the occasion—it seemed important that the help not be from some ethnic or racial minority— left early, so aggrieved by the language and affronted by Sarah's political grilling that they refused a tip. But the food was good; it always was, and there wasn't a leaf of iceberg lettuce in sight, though even before César Chávez made it unacceptable they'd never bought iceberg lettuce. It would have meant social extinction. They didn't have to worry about the grape pickers, because they didn't serve grapes and the wine was French. Yes, the food was good; never mind that he'd lost his appetite and scarcely tasted it.

"Was this disaster your idea?" Michael asked him as he and Ann were working to keep the factions apart. Andrew was trying to contain the radical caucus in the dining room, and Ann was entertaining his mother and Janet Spenser's and the more conservative contingent in the living room. There was a sort of demilitarized zone in the columned space between, through which the few who could be counted upon to act civilized with either group passed freely or clung together, forming a natural barrier. The Swedish waitress was serving coffee in his Aunt Clara's demitasses. Andrew was taking a breather, contemplating the scene in the Federal mirror—a family piece of Ann's—above the mantel.

"Well, what are we supposed to do?" Andrew asked him.

"Pretend we live in some dump on Avenue A and throw the garbage on a pile in the middle of the room?"

"I could chant a mantra."

"I've never felt so bourgeois, so counterrevolutionary, so part of the problem as they say, in my life. You could do something useful, Michael. Try to pacify the uprising with a chorus of 'Cumbayá.' I think they respond to music."

"I forgot my guitar. If we weren't on the wrong side of town, I'd say this could almost be a scene from your play. Too bad the Walcotts aren't here to see it."

"Probably just as well. Here on the West Side we call it living theater. It's very hip. It's what's happening. The psychopathology of everyday life."

"Everyday life seems to be disintegrating."

"Oh, I don't know. Everybody's wearing something. I'm in a jacket and tie. Only a few are in battle fatigues, and Sarah Spenser's the only one with ammunition. I hope she doesn't trip—she might detonate." The waitress approached with a tray of coffee. "Suck a demitasse, Michael?"

"What's Daisy Curtis doing here?"

"Ann invited her. She was in town and she wanted to see my mother."

"Come on, Andrew. It's Michael you're talking to."

"Here, have an MFM." Andrew walked over to the table and picked up a plate of mints.

"An MFM?"

"It's the K-ration of the revolution. Mother-fucking munchies. All natural, of course. No sugar, just honey. Ask Sister Sarah—she's right over there. She'll be happy to tell you. You two could talk recipes."

"I'd rather talk to you. Remember that night in Elaine's? You threw up."

"So I did. Good of you to remind me. But I've reformed since. Eat right, enough sleep, plenty of exercise. And of course I take my Geritol every day. I'm off the sauce, almost. Haven't you noticed?"

"You managed to get sick just when I was grilling you about the day you disappeared in London. It's amazing the lengths you'll go to to avoid answering what you don't want to be asked."

Andrew looked around the room. "I should be acting like the host here."

"It's not as if you're prowling around just because you need some strange. Nothing wrong with a little strange now and then. Revitalizes the juices. But you're not getting strange, my friend; weird, that's what you're getting."

"Oh, knock it off. I was keyed up in London, that's all. I'm much better now. Haven't you noticed? I think, though, that I will have a small glass of wine while I make my rounds. Do you want to water it, or is it okay with you if I take it the way the grown-ups do?" Andrew walked over to the table for a glass of wine. "Good Lord!" he exclaimed. "Sarah's trying to escape." She was moving toward the buffer zone between the two rooms.

Michael put his hand on Andrew's arm. "Don't stop her. She could shoot."

"Stop the revolution? Listen, I know which way the wind blows. But I'd better find my mother in case she's headed her way. Come on. I may need help." Together they moved into the living room, where Andrew's mother was talking to Daisy Curtis.

"Your mother was just saying how much your apartment reminds her of the house on Bellevue Avenue," Daisy said, "and she's right. It does feel like your old house. I remember that couch."

"The dining-room table, too," Andrew said. "My God!"—he smiled, bemused—"I'm living the life I was programmed to lead!" The words echoed faintly in his head.

"But I always thought you were programmed to marry Michael's cousin Amy," Daisy said, "Amy Steer."

"I did think they might," his mother said.

"So did my Aunt Varla," Michael said. "So did Amy, I'll bet."

"And what is Amy doing now?" his mother asked Daisy.

"She's working for the government again, the Interior Department, I think. She had a breakdown a few years ago, you know, a bad one—when she was with the C.I.A. She had to be hospitalized—and of all things, the deputy in charge of covert operations turned up in the same ward. They weren't allowed to recognize each other."

"Just conspirators together," Michael said.

"Then as soon as he got out, he went out on his boat and shot himself. That's when Amy left the agency. The suicide was very upsetting to her."

"I suppose it would have been," Andrew said, "after her brother."

"Oh, dear," his mother said. "What a sad thing! His job must have been a terrible strain. I know it was a strain on poor Amy, too—but didn't she go back to college then?"

"She did go to N.Y.U. for a while after that—studying anthropology, I believe—but gave it up. Tried various other things, but never could settle down to anything for long. Finally she came home and moved in with her parents. The whole thing was awfully hard on her. It was hard on Varla, too. Especially after Dick's stroke. He was helpless. Varla took care of him the way she used to take care of her garden, the way she hooked rugs."

"Or played golf," Andrew said. "She liked playing golf with you, Daisy."

"She was a perfectionist," his mother said.

"Utterly single-minded. She did nothing else until he died," Daisy said. "Bathed him every day, combed his hair, talked to him. He couldn't talk back, of course, or move, but otherwise he seemed to flourish. He was Varla's project. Now it's Amy, the only one left." She turned to Andrew. "I told Varla I'd seen you in London. She wanted to hear all about it. She said how much she'd loved talking to you when you were a boy—especially after Amy went to college and you used to drop in on her if you were walking home in the evenings and saw her lights burning. She said she'd rather have talked to you than most of the people her own age." She smiled at him. "I agreed, of course."

"That's nice. I liked talking to her too. I learned a lot from her. She always told me the truth, I think."

"The Steers pushed Amy too hard," his mother said. "She should have been in Tommy's class, but they were determined to force her. That probably had something to do with her problems. It's not good for children to be pushed beyond themselves—especially by two years. When the school wanted to skip Tommy ahead, I wouldn't allow it."

"I never knew that," he said.

"I never told you. I don't think it would have been good for you if you'd known that."

"Probably not."

She laughed and squeezed his hand. "You knew too much already." She looked at Daisy and Michael. "He was a smart little boy."

"He still is," Daisy said.

"But no longer little," Michael said.

"No," Daisy said, "no longer little."

"And Michael," his mother said, chuckling, "you were the mischievous one—always into something. And Tommy—Andrew—was quick to follow."

"Now I keep him in line, Mrs. MacAllister."

"See that you do," she said.

Andrew turned to Daisy. "So, Daisy, why do you live in Washington? I was there the Saturday before last. It's a dismal place."

"Why didn't you call? Were you trying to avoid a confrontation?"

Andrew laughed. "I was just there for the day. We went for the march. There was no time. We took the train down and back. Julia was with me. Michael came along to throw a plastique."

"Where was Ann?"

"At a conference in Miami."

"Well, Andrew, I live there for the light and the space and the trees, not for the politics—certainly not for the conversation. The conversation is largely gossip. Very-high-level gossip, often, but nonetheless gossip."

"That's what a lot of conversation is. It makes it interesting. I love to talk about Michael, for instance—at least, behind his back. And it's interesting to know that that fellow over there"— he gestured toward the dining room—"the one in the battle fatigues conspiring with Sarah Spenser, used to write speeches for Goldwater before he spun three hundred fifty-nine degrees and became a tax resister because of the war. Now he lives off the underground economy on a houseboat at the Seventy-ninth Street boat basin and his old lady, as he calls her, does something with hedge funds on Wall Street. You wouldn't know it to look at her now, but she's supposed to be a whiz at it. That's right. Hedge funds. Wall Street. I think it's called boring from within."

"I'm afraid I don't understand what's going on these days," his mother said. "I like to think I'm modern, and I believe I am, but in some ways I'm quite Victorian. There's a great deal to be said for appearances. For good manners. I don't understand all these protests, these people who won't get a haircut or take a bath."

"Because their hair is long doesn't mean they're dirty, Mother."

Daisy took her cigarettes and lighter from her bag. "When Ann invited me, she said she was having just a small family dinner. Is this their idea of a family dinner, Emma?"

"I told them not to do it on my account," his mother said.

Andrew laughed. "We did it on mine. We just decided to have a few more people." He took the lighter from her hand and lit her cigarette.

"Thank you."

"For what?"

"For lighting my cigarette."

"Oh."

"We tried to bring him up to be a gentleman." His mother looked at him. "To get his hair cut. I wish you would, dear. It could be shorter."

"Nobody's successful all the time, Mother. Writers are like that." He laughed. "You know—longhairs." What did she want, a crew cut? He returned Daisy's lighter. "You wouldn't want to lose this. It's a very elegant lighter. Speaking of fires, I think I should move around a bit and see if there are any I should be putting out."

"Oh, there's Julia," his mother said. "She's out of bed."

"And sneaking into the dining room," Andrew said. "She hates to miss a party. I'd better take care of her."

"She wants to know if you're going to visit us at Sharksmouth this summer," Daisy said. "She told me earlier that if you didn't go, she'd like to come anyway."

"She did?"

"I told her August would be fine."

"Let me take care of her," his mother said.

"No," Andrew said, "I'll do it. Will you excuse me?" He headed off in Julia's direction. "Caught you, baby. What are you doing here?"

"I wanted to see the party."

"But you've already seen it. You were here until we served dinner."

"But Daddy, I wanted to see *more* of it! It's fun. And the noise woke me up."

"You can't fool me, Julie. I'll bet you haven't even been to sleep. Come on, I'll tuck you in."

"Will you tell me a story?"

"A very short one. I've got to get back to the party. I have to pay attention to our guests," and he put his arm over her shoulder and led her back to her room and tucked her in.

"Sit down, Daddy. Tell me some more about Ralph and Emily and Anthony Armadillo. You haven't told me that story in a long time."

"I'll see what I can do, but you have to remember that I can't stay long. A man has his duties. We have a party going out there. But really, Julie, it's nice to be in here with you. I'll get you a glass of milk." When he returned from the kitchen, he began the story. "They were at sea, on the fabled *China Hand*, steaming toward Bombay. Port out, starboard home—remember? And Ralph had gotten extremely sick and found himself taken out of his cabin with the laundry. He'd been resting on a pile of towels. Eventually he found his way to the first-class galley and is now curled up on top of a stack of toast, under the warming lid, which the steward is about to carry to stateroom nine. Or so Ralph hopes. He's not the tiniest snake in the grass and it's a tight fit under that lid, and the toast is steaming, too. A hot day under a tight lid—a very tricky situation. And all he wants to do is make it safely home."

"Where's home?"

"At the moment, it's a stateroom on the *China Hand*, but his destination is Australia, Emily's homeland. They will all be very safe there."

"Do they get to Australia?"

"Oh, yes. One day, Julia, they get to Australia—but you're getting ahead of the story. They have to cross the Equator first, to get to the other side. They're still in the middle of the Arabian Sea, a long way from the Equator or Australia, and it's very stormy and very hot and Ralph is still feeling seasick. The smell of warm toast isn't making him feel any better, either. And the butter is sticky." Andrew could hear the sounds of the party, muffled and indistinct, beyond Julia's door: the voices of the grown-ups, he thought, a kind of rueful smile on his face. Julia looked at him expectantly; he returned to the story. "Well you see, also traveling on the *China Hand* was a very grand lady, the Dowager Duchess of Dork, with her son, the present Duke. They are on their way to Malangprabang, a seldom-visited island kingdom off the Malay coast, where the Duke of Dork, in accordance with the family rule, will for seven years oversee the tea and spice plantations that keep the duchy afloat, more or less. After his obligatory exile—that means something he has to do, Julia, and 'exile' is when you live away from your country—he can go home to Dorkminster Hall, the cold and drafty family seat —really a very nasty place, though large—and live like a fat cat, with all the nutmeg and cinnamon and cardamom his tummy desires, which is a lot. The only good thing about Dorkminster Hall is that it smells like an apple pie because of all the spices, and because the Dowager Duchess insists on having one freshly baked every day. But it looks like a slaughterhouse because for centuries the Dukes of Dork and many of the Duchesses as well have beaten the bushes around the place for stags and quail and whatever game was within shooting distance, and they'd mount their heads and sometimes their whole bodies and stick them on whatever wall or table was available. Over the years the place has become very cluttered, and very frightful, as you might imagine. So they were fortunate to be away from all that, whether they knew it or not. The Duchess didn't, but the young Duke was looking forward to his seven years in exile where the weather is warm and the sun shines every day—utterly unlike England, where the weather is nasty and the sun hardly ever shines, and the toast is always cold, too. He may like it so much below the Equator that he may never return to Dorkminster Hall—who knows?"

"That's not true, Daddy. The sun shines in England."

"Well, yes, I suppose it does. But not very often. And it's very damp much of the time. In any event, they're not in England now but in stateroom six on the *China Hand*, waiting impatiently for their tea. Dukes and duchesses can be very impatient, you know, especially when they've got a good dose of *mal de mer*— that's what the Duchess and the French call seasickness. Moreover, the Duchess was filled with longing for her cozy slaughter-house. She was almost the only person in the whole world who thought Dorkminster Hall was cozy; except for their like-minded friends, everybody else thought it was creepy. But I'm getting away from the story. You know how a 'six' looks much like a 'nine,' but reversed? Well, the steward, who was a very kind man, had a problem with reading. It's called dyslexia. Sometimes he saw a 'b' where a 'd' was, and a 'p' for a 'q,' and vice versa. And sometimes he mistook a 'nine' for a 'six.' You can imagine what happened."

"What?"

"It was terrible. He mixed up the tea trays. He took the tray for stateroom nine to number six. And vice versa. Emily and Anthony discovered it first. There were only two cups on the tray, for one thing, and the toast was cinnamon toast. Emily was already a little seasick, you know, and the smell of cinnamon made her feel sicker still. She had requested plain toast with just a little wildflower honey on the side. Also, she liked her toast with crusts—it was chewier and better for her teeth—and these crusts had been neatly trimmed away. It looked very fancy, but it didn't appeal to Emily, though Anthony wouldn't have minded. He wasn't seasick and he liked cinnamon. They were both too worried to eat, anyway."

"Why?"

"Well, because they'd lost Ralph. He was, after all, their companion, guide, and dear, dear friend."

"What about the Duchess?"

"At the sight of the tea tray the Duchess suddenly became ravenous. Her seasickness vanished. She poured a cup of tea for the Duke and herself, and was eagerly looking forward to her cinnamon toast. She removed the lid with a grand flourish—and there, there before her very eyes, curled up as small as he could make himself, his head tucked under his tail, was Ralph. You'll never guess what she said then."

"What?"

"She said, 'A grilled reptilian, beautifully buttered! On toast! How indescribably delicious!' The Duchess, you know, would eat anything that had ever moved. She didn't realize that Ralph was still moving."

"Daddy, that's disgusting."

"Indeed it was. But so was the Duchess. And Ralph was in a terrible plight. He didn't want to be eaten by some nasty Duchess. He didn't want to be stuffed and hung on some wall in Dorkminster Hall with all the other creatures the Duchess had devoured. Not at all."

"So what did he do?"

"What could he do? He bravely untucked his head from under his tail and said, 'Excuse me, my dear Duchess, there's been a frightful error. Let me present myself. My name is Ralph, currently lodged in stateroom nine with my traveling companions Emily Roo and Anthony Armadillo. I should be extremely grateful if you would put down your knife and fork. I am most inedible.' Needless to say, the Duchess was astonished. Rendered quite speechless, in fact, but she did put down her utensils. 'Thank you,' said Ralph. 'And now, if I may, I'll slither quietly off to my cabin.' The Duchess by now had recovered her composure and her voice. 'How do you do?' she said, moving to stand in front of the door. 'I am the Dowager Duchess of Dork, of Dorkminster Hall in Dorking, Dorkshire—England, of course. You would be most welcome there. Indeed, you would be a significant addition to the Great Hall. I believe it lacks a snake, certainly one of your stripe. Have you thought of becoming a trophy?' 'No, madam.' 'A handbag, perhaps?' 'Most definitely no, madam. I suggest you ring for the steward to rectify this unfortunate error.' But the Duchess had the gleam in her eye. She wanted Ralph more than she wanted her cinnamon toast. She wanted Ralph stuffed, his beauty captured forever and hers to admire whenever she felt like admiring it. She was overcome by desire. 'Strike a pose, my dear Ralph,' she said. 'Strike your most fearsome pose.' 'Oh, I don't believe you'd like that, madam,' said Ralph. 'My most fearsome pose can be very fearsome indeed.' 'Dear boy, I insist.' 'Oh, Mother, don't be a kvetch. Let the snake alone! Please bring me my tea. I'm seasick.' That was the Duke, lying on the couch, still waiting for his tea, and looking very pale."

Andrew was growing tired of the story. "You know," he said to Julia, squeezing her arm, "when I was a kid I always wanted to be out there with the grown-ups, to know what the grown-ups were up to. Now that I know what they're up to, I'd just as soon be in here with you." He could write a play, he thought, and call it *The Children's Room*. All of it would take place there: four or five children, and an occasional adult dropping by from the party outside, maybe bits of conversation coming through the door. Not a bad idea; but where the hell would you find five children good enough to carry a show? Casting would be a problem. A big problem. Producers would not be beating a path to his door. Still, he liked the idea. He pulled himself out of his reverie. "I'd just as soon be in here with you, Julia, but I've got to get back to the party and act like a host. I've been gone a long time. Your mother'll kill me."

"But Daddy, the story! What's happening? You can't leave it like that!"

"Okay. Here it is. The conclusion of tonight's installment: The Duchess had a *plan*. She was determined to capture Ralph for the Great Hall at Dorkminster, or at least for a handbag. But in order for her plan to succeed, Ralph must preen a little, and strike his most fearsome pose. You see, she was counting on his being a bit vain, quite dazzled by his own beauty and hence susceptible to the most fulsome flattery. But first, of course, she had to take care of the Duke. She brought him his tea. 'Please stop whining, you puny weakling,' she whispered; 'I am engaged in business of the utmost importance to the House of Dork. I'm going to get that snake if it kills me.' 'But Mother,' said the Duke, 'it may. It's a very venomous snake.' Neither of them knew, of course, that Ralph was a vegetarian and had never bitten anything yet. 'We'll see,' said the Duchess. 'I'm sure I can charm a snake. After all, I charmed your father, didn't I?' 'He wasn't a snake,' the Duke said. 'That's all you know,' she replied. 'Here, hold this.' She handed him one of her hats, a large and lumpy feathered number with very long veils that she intended to wear in Malangprabang for protection from mosquitoes and other flying bugs. 'The moment I say "Rawalpindi," give it quickly to me. When I have flattered and charmed him, and Ralph is under my spell, we shall wrap him in my veils like a moth in its cocoon, and he shall be mine forever. Oh, what a delicious thought!' she exclaimed. She returned to Ralph, who had by now removed himself from the toast and was resting rather casually on the back of a chair near the door, waiting for someone to open it. He could manage that in a pinch, but it took him a long time and he wasn't very good at it. 'Ralph, my dear,' she said, rubbing her hand along his buttered body, 'I am going to sing you a song, the loveliest song, and while I sing to you, I want you to slowly reveal your most magnificent, most fearsome self.' Ralph thought he'd better go along with the game. 'Very well, Your Grace,' he said, rising up from the back of the chair and weaving gracefully before her, 'I am quite charmed by music, and I should love to hear you sing to me, and while you are singing, I shall astonish you with the splendor I reveal. But first, dear madam, would you crack the cabin door a bit? It's frightfully stuffy in here, and I require fresh air if I am to perform at my best. I cannot give a duchess as exalted and beautiful as yourself anything less than my best. Surely you want nothing but?' She opened the door. Oh, that sneaky little snake! We can see who's doing the charming. 'Please to begin, my dear duchess.' Guess what she sang?"

"What?"

" 'Begin the Beguine.' She thought it sounded like something a snake would be charmed by. In another voice, Ralph thought; in another room, perhaps. But not here, not now. He, after all, had encountered some of the greatest snake charmers worthy of the name; he was, you might say, a connoisseur of snake charmers. You can imagine what he thought of the Duchess. You can imagine what *she* sounded like. Ralph pretended to be charmed, however. He huffed and puffed and rose up swaying before her, flicking his little forked tongue and fixing her with his snaky eyes, and all in time to the music—a difficult trick because she was having trouble with the beat, and more and more trouble. Finally her voice trailed off, and Ralph took up the song. 'Hindustani,' she cried, but rather weakly. Nothing happened. She tried again. 'Singaporè,' she murmured. Where was the Duke? she asked herself; surely Ralph had succumbed to her hypnotic blandishments by now. He must be ready for his gauze cocoon. Another try, weaker still. 'Bangladesh.' The code word seemed to have slipped her mind. 'Rawalpindi, is it you?' 'Aye, Mother, it is I,' the Duke said, as if from a great distance. He pulled himself slowly from the divan and moved toward the Duchess while Ralph continued to sway, singing his own mysterious tune now. On the Duke's head was the hat of many veils. 'Surabaya, Mummy,' he said, 'Savu Sea.' 'Ujung, my son, Pandang.' 'Mindanao.' 'Corregidor.' 'Alabaster.' 'Mustard plaster.' Well, Julia, as you can see, they were hopelessly befuddled. The Duchess began to wrap the Duke in her veils so that he looked rather like a mummy, which Ralph, being a native of Egypt, found amusing, and as she was finishing her wrapping, she picked up on Ralph's strange little tune and began to dance to it. With the Duke and Duchess thus safely occupied, Ralph coiled himself tightly into a Frisbee, called out 'Papua Skidoo,' left the Duke in his mummy suit and the Duchess dancing, and, feeling quite perky, spun down the passageway to stateroom nine, where Emily and Anthony were very, very happy to see him. Their seasickness vanished, the three of them danced a little jig and sent out for another tea tray. And they were careful to show the steward the difference between a 'six' and a 'nine,' but very nicely, so as not to hurt his feelings.

"End of story, baby. I've got to get back to the party now. I've been gone too long; but I love you."

"That was a crazy story, Daddy."

"It was fairly crazy, I guess. The craziest one yet. Good night, precious." He kissed her—"Go to sleep now: I love you" —and slipped out her door and into the party.

"I decided it was time for me to leave the children's room," Andrew said to Daisy when he found her in the dining room talking with Larry Evans, an actor he and Michael were courting. "I see you two have met. We're hoping we can persuade Larry that he'd like the lead in the play so we can convince Sam Walcott that he'd like to produce it. And vice versa. See how it works? I hope you're using your charms on him, Daisy."

"Of course he'd like the lead," Daisy said. "You'd be perfect for it, Larry. The mysterious young radical whose appearance throws everything into sixes and sevens." Daisy called to Michael Aldrich, who was passing nearby: "Isn't that right, Michael? Larry would be perfect."

"I'm not sure I'm young enough for it."

"Andrew's not sure he's old enough to have written it," Michael said, "so there you are. You two should come together in the middle, because Andrew's definitely old enough and you're certainly young enough. It would be a great role for you: attractive, funny, serious at the same time. You're all those things. A great role for you."

"What about the London cast? Might any of them come over?"

"It's possible," Michael said. "We just don't know yet."

"Speaking of London," Daisy said, "do you remember that young man at the Huntingtons' party, Andrew—the one who came with Patrick Rysdale and wanted to talk to you about your play?"

"Yes."

"I had a note from him last week, thanking me for allowing him to crash the party. Of course, it wasn't *my* party. He's coming to the States—"

"Oh, no."

"—and hopes to see me in Washington. He noticed that piece of mine at the Huntingtons' and wants to see more of my work. He's a painter, you know."

"How did he get your address?"

"He called the Huntingtons and got it from them. Enterprising of him, wasn't it?"

"Well, he's interested in people's work."

"I'm sure you'll be hearing from him too. He'd probably make a good actor," Daisy said. "He's attractive enough. You should find a role for him, Michael."

"Give him mine," Larry Evans said, laughing, moving off.

"Oh, no, you don't," Michael called after him: "You're not getting off the hook that easily." He turned to Andrew. "*You* find a role for him. I think he's a bad actor."

"Oh, no, he's not," Andrew said. "He's just young and ambitious. When are you showing, Daisy?"

"My new work? In the fall. He's going to be here soon, though. I forget just when, but it's soon. I'll ask him to tea if he calls."

"He'll call," Michael said.

"He can ask your husband about the Greeks," Andrew said. "He's interested in them too."

"How do you know that?" Michael asked.

"He was talking about the Elgin Marbles at the Huntingtons', and Mr. Huntington told me that Daisy's husband's an authority on classical sculpture. So they have something in common."

"No doubt," Daisy said.

"At least he cares about it. The Greeks cared about it too."

"About what?" Michael asked.

"Oh, you know"—Andrew shrugged—"art. Civilization. It's

preposterous to pretend that it matters here. Do you think that crowd of sanctimonious degenerates running this country from their bunkers in Washington cares a whit? The only art they recognize is the kind of street theater they saw yesterday, and that's because they couldn't miss it. It was in the middle of their streets. The Nixon gang doesn't even care about politics, in any serious sense."

"Really, Andrew," Daisy said, "I'm not so sure those mobs in the streets are all that interested in art and civilization—or politics either. They seem more intent on tearing it up—as if they had a grudge against it. What did the students in Paris accomplish in 1968? They tore up the paving stones that had been there for centuries, that's all, and destroyed some trees and learned that the state will maintain itself, no matter what."

"They almost toppled it, too," Michael said.

"But in Washington, for God's sake, the *liberals* think Viet-Nam is a debatable topic—you know, pro and con, hawks and doves, let's be reasonable. People are dying, Daisy—being hideously, horribly killed; fried in napalm! That's not polite. Sometimes I have to go along with Sarah Spenser. Off the pig, or something."

"You don't really think that."

Andrew looked toward the curtains moving slightly in the air. "No, I guess I don't."

"Sarah Spenser's politics doesn't change anything, unless for the worse. The Viet-Nam Veterans Against the War may. And John Kerry's testifying for them on the Hill. Very nice, very liberal, but very effective."

"Liberals are all for dissent until it gets rude. John Kerry's polite and handsome and everybody's mother loves him. The whole point of freedom is the freedom to be rude, to be unacceptable."

"*Épater* your mother is what he means," Michael said.

"I may have, tonight."

Daisy laughed. "But if you're talking about ending this interminable war, Andrew—"

"They're not talking just about ending the war, Daisy. They're talking about changing the system!"

"To what?"

"Good question. Ask Sarah. Maybe she knows."

Michael snorted. "Sarah Spenser's revolution has degenerated into an exercise in street theater."

"Dionysus emerges in bizarre ways," Andrew said. "We need a recognized bacchanal. An official day of madness. Something to keep people sane for the rest of the year." He paused. "Well, that might take more than a day."

"Give it a week," Michael suggested. "A feverish week of madness and delight, with all bets off."

"Something to keep the egg in its shell the rest of the time. That fellow you know, Michael—William Gibson?—he wrote somewhere that sanity is to insanity as the shell is to the egg." As with so many other things, Andrew didn't know how he felt about the revolution. He knew it was over, though. Sometimes he seemed to take whatever was the contrary view, rather like the revolutionaries themselves—angry children of privilege, by and large, suddenly thwarted and wanting more. More what? Not more goods; they weren't venal, at least. Just more. More attention, maybe; more power, more control. Sometimes, it seemed, just more disorder. Like little Mark Rudd, whose mother, he'd remembered reading in the *Times*, had cooked a dinner for her son the rebel on Mother's Day three years before and brought it down to him at Columbia while Chairman Mark was paralyzing the campus. That was what she'd called him: "my son, the rebel." She'd wanted him to have a home-cooked meal. The little creep had closed the university, and his mother thought he was cute! He was a tyrannical child in wire-rimmed glasses, cultivating the deadly grim look of Lenin and acting increasingly like the Infant of Prague in the midst of a temper tantrum. That was what Andrew thought now; he'd felt differently then. "In '68 I took the train up to Columbia to watch the university fall. I pretended I was in Petrograd in 1917. The Low Library was the Winter Palace. That got the old adrenaline pumping."

"The whole thing peaked with the march on the Pentagon," Michael said.

"That's when Varla Steer brought you by my house, Andrew —the first time I'd seen you in some years." Daisy laughed. "You were in Washington to stir things up. You sounded quite radical —your politics made Varla nervous."

"She didn't like disorder. Anyway, it was a short-lived revolution. The only thing that keeps it flickering still is the government." Once, Andrew thought, it had seemed so promising. He'd read a little Marx. He'd thought he was a socialist; he still thought he'd be a socialist, if he could keep his Chinese lamps. He'd read Marcuse. The assembly line was alienating. He could go along with that. So was his typewriter, at times: the oppression of society was ubiquitous. So should he heed Marcuse and refuse to participate? Should he bomb a bank? Could he get off on that? He knew how to make an explosive, thanks to *The New York Review of Books*. A few years before, it had printed a diagram of a Molotov cocktail on the cover. He thought he still had the issue somewhere, kept for an emergency. Would that make him happy? Would that give "meaning" to his life—or at least a momentary *frisson*? Violence lent a certain exhilaration. What made black power frightening—not what gave the civil rights movement its moral force, but what scared the shit out of the white middle class and brought results—were the fulminations of H. Rap Brown and the riots in Watts, in Newark, in Detroit; the sight of Washington in flames after the assassination of King. Black looters boogying in the streets, snipers in the alleys—now, that was scary. The good Rev. King may have touched people's hearts, but Brown caught them by their throats. Power comes from the barrel of a gun. That article in *The New York Review* said that morality started there, too—a disheartening view if he'd ever heard one. Andrew remembered the night King was assassinated. Ann was working at the McCarthy campaign headquarters and he was home with Julia listening in horror to the news when slowly, floating through the gates and up from the courtyard, he began to hear the sound of singing. He'd opened their bedroom windows, and he and Julia leaned out listening in the spring night. The singing grew louder. "We Shall Overcome." The two of them had stood there for a while, staring into the empty courtyard, listening to the voices and the shuffle of feet; then they'd taken the elevator down to the courtyard and stood behind the iron gates of their building and watched the grim black throng pouring out of Harlem, marching toward who knew where, taking up bystanders as they passed. The singing was soft, and except for the singing and the sound of feet moving, the crowd was strangely quiet. Suddenly he had taken Julia in his arms and a little nervously left the protection of their courtyard, and together they were swept along in the warm spring night, participants, for a couple of blocks, in the great march of history. Later that night the riots had begun, but these people were not riotous; immensely serious, rather. Their power was palpable. Andrew had to believe it was greater than Rap Brown's or Mark Rudd's. Otherwise, civilization was down the tubes. " 'It was the best of times, it was the worst of times,' " he said with a smile. "It is a far, far better thing that I do than I have ever done. It is a far, far better place that I go to than I have ever gone."

"You know where the guy who said that was going, don't you?" Michael asked. "To the guillotine."

"Go with the flow." It was Hope's mindless therapist passing by, a stoned look on his face, on his way to zero in on Sarah Spenser's huddle.

"Well, you could always get stoned," Michael said, "or bore from within. Like that rich priest who's a friend of yours, the one who wants to be a bishop, with forty or fifty million bucks from a guns-and-cookie fortune and whose wife is right now chatting up your mother. Isn't that what *he* claims to be doing—boring from within?"

"He doesn't feel the money is really his; he's just the steward."

"That's what they all say, but you'll notice they've still got it," Michael said. "By the way, I hear his wife's being bored from without—by her editor. She's writing a book, you know, about their life in the South Bronx or wherever the hell they were."

"It was Newark," Andrew said, "and they were there for nine years. When people thought they were crazy to do it. Whatever you say about them, that's a commitment. Fads don't last nine years. It couldn't have been a picnic. And where the hell did you hear that about Kay?"

"Her editor told me. He's one of those guys who likes to do it and then get off again by telling about it. He says it's twice the fun for half the price—like a twofer."

"You can see, Daisy," Andrew said, "that in New York we discuss serious things: social change and the Frankfurt School; the early Marx versus the later Marx and which has had a greater influence on Leonard Bernstein, and was either as influential as Danny the Red; the pros and cons of the mariachi band at the Chávez benefit in East Hampton last summer; the politics of love versus the politics of rage; Norman Mailer and women's liberation—that sort of thing. Whereas in Washington all you people do is gossip."

Daisy laughed, and Michael excused himself.

"Wait!" Andrew called to him. "When are you coming to Bermuda? You haven't told me yet."

"I haven't made up my mind. I'm trying to decide how long you can survive without a director. But don't worry, I'll show up. Sam wants me there, I'll be there. See you later."

"We could sit down," Daisy said.

"I shouldn't," Andrew replied. "I'm supposed to act like the host here."

"But I'd like to," she said. "It's part of your duties as a host to make a guest comfortable. Or are you thinking only of the comfort of the host?" She laughed. She had a lovely, throaty laugh.

"Okay. I'll sit for a moment. If you'll tell me what keeps you in Washington besides the trees," he said, seizing on a topic. "And your husband, of course."

"You wouldn't like it. It's a city of journalists, you know—and lawyers and politicians, all of them quite enamored of themselves. Nothing else matters."

"I'd like the trees. But you're leaving out the bureaucrats."

"They don't count. They just keep the whole thing going."

"I thought that's what the attorney general did. Did you see he announced yesterday afternoon that the city was open, traffic was flowing, and the government was functioning? A triumph for law and order over the Mayday Tribe. Superego knocks out id. Great!"

"Am I seeing another right now?" She reached in her bag for her cigarettes.

"Another what?"

"Triumph for law and order. Would you like a cigarette?"

Andrew stared at her pack. "Thanks," he said, taking it. He reached for her lighter and lit the cigarettes. He had to be moving. The smoke was making him dizzy. High on nicotine. Or maybe contact. A contact high from Sarah, the tax resister, the bonzo therapist, and the hedge-fund lady. The dining room was heavy with fumes. He rose, and saw the party hazily reflected in the mirror across the room, saw his face wavering at the edge of it. He took another look. The glass was bad—smoky—and reflections were murky. That was what gave the mirror its value: it was the original glass. Andrew smiled at the absurdity. "What do you mean?"

"I thought it was clear. But if you'd rather talk about something else, I can do that. The Elgin Marbles? Your new Washington obsession?" She laughed. "France under the old regime? That's pertinent. The Palace of Versailles isn't art; it's spectacle. Art was ancillary there. It's the same in Washington."

"The Hall of Mirrors," he said. "But when it's ancillary, you have no responsibility." He heard his voice coming from a distance. "You become a dilettante, a scribbler. You make pretty things. Its only value is gossip or scandal. Or spectacle. The masks of power." He sounded articulate enough, he thought.

"No. Your responsibility is to tell what you see, if you can. If you can see what's in front of your eyes."

"I suppose." He turned her pack of cigarettes in his fingers.

"Most of the world is too blind, too stupid, or too timid to look."

"I don't blame them." He looked toward the mirror again, and laughed. "You can't always like what you see. That's why they prize a mirror like that. It's hard to tell what you're looking at. Maybe the truth is in the distortions."

"An artist can't work in a hall of mirrors, Andrew. An artist has to see what's there, hard as that may be, not a crooked distortion of it."

"I suppose." He took two of her cigarettes and slipped them into his pocket. "But art always distorts. It doesn't tell the truth. It's hard to speak the truth. There may be only one truth, but it's alive. It has a live and changing face."

"Who said that?"

"Kafka." Andrew laughed aloud. "You can't always want what you get, either, as the woman who cleans for us once said. Really, I should be talking to some of our guests."

"I'm a guest, remember?"

Andrew's eyes scanned the party. "It's a good thing Ann's mother isn't here. We'd have an exorcism in the morning. Maybe we should anyway."

"Are you avoiding me, Andrew?"

"Of course not. I've been talking to you for half an hour."

"You're very good at that: obfuscating the issue in a cloud of chatter. You even make the chatter sound more or less intelligent."

"What are you talking about?"

Daisy looked at him. "What do you think I'm talking about? Nixon's China policy?"

"I can't talk about that."

"Really. I quite liked it. I thought you did too. I admit it was a little surprising." Daisy glanced toward his mother in the other room. "She wouldn't have approved. Nor would mine, for that matter. She would have told me to stay out of the playpen. She never quite believed that children grow up, learn to swim. Mothers are like that, I suppose. At least our mothers, back then."

"Maybe because they didn't."

"Didn't what?"

"Learn to swim."

"Anyway, I loved it. Imagine! Little Tommy MacAllister, getting down on the Huntingtons' rug!" she laughed. "That was rather an odd thank-you note, by the way. What are you afraid of?"

"I don't know," he said, looking about the room. "I don't know. Have you seen my kaleidoscope?"

"Of me?"

"Of course not."

"You answered that awfully quickly."

"Timing. I'm a quick study. I'm recovering nicely. Let me get it." He walked to the bookshelves and returned with the tube of copper and brass. "I found it last year in California. Look through it. You'll be amazed." He put the kaleidoscope in her hand.

"I think your sense of timing is confined to the stage."

"How do you know that? Point it toward the light and look through it."

"I don't know it. It was merely a supposition." She raised the instrument to her eye. "So if you're not afraid of me, what are you afraid of?"

"It's a participatory universe. I'm afraid of my effect on it." He laughed. "Or vice versa. Turn it. You really should be high for the full effect. It can be explosive."

"It's pretty enough without drugs." She began to turn it. "Extraordinary! It's like a Persian carpet." She turned to him, a quizzical smile on her face. "Like the Huntingtons' carpet."

"Oh? I don't really remember. Now I must introduce you to the parson's wife, the lovely Kay—and the parson too, of course, if we can pry him away from Lord Lollipop. Maybe he's hearing his confession—or Lord Lollipop is giving him a voice lesson."

"No, I'm afraid I must be going." Daisy handed him the kaleidoscope. "A lovely thing," she said. "Let me say goodbye to your mother and Ann." She rose. He could smell her perfume. "I'll see you in August, of course. Would you get my coat?" She walked into the living room and Andrew started into the bedroom for her coat, then went into his office and put the cigarettes in his desk. When he came out, he walked her to the door. "I always fall back on Wallace Stevens," she said as he was helping her into her coat. "He said that the greatest poverty is not to live in a physical world, to feel that one's desire is too difficult to tell from despair. May I have my lighter, please?"

He stood there, dumb, his hand on her arm.

"My lighter, please," she repeated, releasing herself from his grasp.

"Oh. Oh, yes. Certainly. Sorry, I forgot."

The next morning, Andrew felt sick. Dizzy, sleepy, a band of pain around his forehead: his usual panoply of symptoms. "You can't be sick now," Ann told him, setting the tea tray down on the bed beside him. "It's your mother's last day here. You've got to spend some time with her."

"You're going to lunch and that dumb show. Why can't I be sick?"

"Be sick in the afternoon, while we're gone, but get up now." She opened the blinds. "Besides, you've got to help me finish cleaning up from the party. The house is a mess."

Andrew shuddered. "So am I. Don't mention that party."

"It turned out all right. I think everyone had a good time."

"I didn't. I had a terrible time."

"Terrible? What was so terrible about it?"

"What wasn't? Aside from the food."

"Well, you wanted it. You insisted. And in any case, it wasn't for you; it was for your mother." She moved about the room, putting things away, straightening up. "But you can't stay in bed over it. You can lie down in the afternoon, provided you're up and dressed when we get back from the matinée. You can't be sick tonight, either."

"You don't *schedule* being sick. Really, I feel terrible."

She stopped and turned toward him, studying his face. "You don't look terrible. What's wrong?"

"I don't know. I've got a headache. I feel dizzy."

"You'll probably feel better when you're dressed."

"I'll get up. In just a minute. Will you pour me some tea? Maybe I'm getting a sore throat."

"Here." She passed him a cup. "Julia's gone to school. Your mother's in the shower. We'll have breakfast in a few minutes."

"I'll be out in a second, I promise. As soon as I've had some tea."

Ann poured a cup for herself and carried it out of the room. "Bring the tray when you come," she said.

When she had gone, he pulled the pillow toward him and curled up around it, clutching it. He felt light-headed, unanchored, as if at any moment he might float off toward the ceiling and beyond, like a helium balloon, one of those balloons you bought from the balloon man in Central Park. He'd heard you could buy other things from the balloon man, too: specifically, Acapulco Gold and Panama Red. Whatever gets you high. He wished he were. Maybe he was: suspended in an altered state. Everything that rises must converge. Some Jesuit said that. They made him stop teaching. Andrew looked up at the ceiling. It appeared very solid. They lived on the top floor; beyond the ceiling was the roof. Sunlight was filtering through the curtains at the windows. It must be falling on the roof as well. It appeared to be a fine May morning, the kind of morning that ought to cancel out the effects of the previous night. What *were* the effects of the previous night? He hadn't drunk very much; he didn't have a hangover. He should feel good, and come out humming a happy tune. Instead, he felt like throwing up; well, queasy, at least. He was worried about what his mother might think about the party. Why on earth should he be worried about that? What would she do if she hadn't liked it—blow the place up? That seemed unlikely. She wasn't Sarah Spenser. He was always surprised, it always gave him a little shock, when he saw how small his mother actually was, smaller always than he'd remembered—tiny, really

—and her hair was grayer, too. Still, she was stylish and stood as straight as she ever had; there was nothing frail or tentative about her—or so it seemed. She looked more like a vigorous woman in her sixties than someone almost eighty, and she'd clearly made an effort to meet and say something relevant to everyone at the party. It really had been a terrible party, he thought, a mix of people that sounded good in theory but that reacted unpredictably in the crucible. Some stray molecule had not been taken into account, had run amok. It was awfully hard to plan a party these days. You never knew what to expect. It was especially hard to plan a party for his mother. Hard for him to take her to the theater, too, or even the movies. They ought to rate things differently: "Caution! Some language may be unfit for mothers over seventy if accompanied by their children, and children under seven if accompanied by their parents." Well, thank God for the Spensers. Except for Sarah, the foul-mouthed bomb-thrower. He shuddered again. Lord Lollipop, so mesmerized by the sound of his own voice, had mesmerized his mother as well. That was good; maybe he'd put her in a trance for the evening, making everything appear in soft focus under a rosy gel. Kay Baxter, who might or might not be screwing her editor, knew how to talk to the ladies' auxiliary when she had to; his mother had loved her. Maybe she talked differently to her editor. Well, at least she could be charming, and she seemed a lot more genuine than her husband, the curate from Central Casting. Maybe he thought that because he had a little crush on her; her editor was not alone. Everything was mixed up. Sometimes he didn't know how he ever wrote plays even, wrote the kind of language he sometimes heard his characters speak, knew the kinds of things they seemed to know. Automatic writing, maybe. I didn't do it, Mother; I was just the instrument. I was brought up Episcopalian, remember? True, I held the pen, but God did the rest. He even filled it. It's all His fault. What a mind He has! Remember Plato? He said it was divine madness. If God didn't do it, the daimon did. Christ, Andrew thought, what a jerk he was being: *If God didn't do it, the daimon did!* But the daimon must have possessed him when he wrote that note to Daisy Meyer. Daisy Curtis. What was she doing there? And what was that envelope with the unfamiliar handwriting that had arrived yesterday in the packet from Pamela? He hadn't opened it, hadn't even read *her* letter. Not his usual behavior. Sometimes letters were an unwarranted intrusion, like telephone calls. You could be doing almost anything and if the phone rings you're expected to stop everything and attend to the call. It wasn't right. He heard Ann calling him. He raised his head from the pillow. "Coming," he called back. "Be right there." He had to get up. They'd be coming for him—or sending the ambulance, maybe the baby-sitter. The baby-sitter might be more appropriate. He threw the pillow to the floor, went into the bathroom, slapped some water on his face and brushed his teeth, then hurriedly jumped into some clothes. When he walked into the dining room, his mother was holding the kaleidoscope to her eye.

"Pretty, isn't it?" Andrew said, seating himself. "I'm afraid I'm too old for kaleidoscopes. But they are pretty."

"I've never seen one like it," she said as she put it down. "Remember the kaleidoscope you had when you were a boy? I wonder what happened to it."

"I don't remember. Maybe that's why I got this one. To replace it. Julia likes it."

"I suppose it went to the rummage sale when I sold the house. I got rid of so much. Your desk. That little swan rocker. I don't think I would have gotten rid of the kaleidoscope, though. I loved it." She laughed, and reached across the table to squeeze his hand. "I was afraid I'd wear it out before I ever gave it to you." Ann arrived carrying a platter. "What a lovely omelette!"

"I was expecting orange jello," Andrew said. "With marshmallows." Ann had once said that that was his mother's idea of a salad. She glared at him. Get a grip on yourself, he thought. "I like it in the morning sometimes," he explained.

"What?" his mother asked.

"Orange jello."

"You do?" She seemed surprised.

"Only sometimes. Ann hardly ever makes it. She says she can't get the right marshmallows. She likes the tiny ones. You didn't get rid of my desk, Mother. We have it. We've had it for years. It's Julia's now."

"Of course. It's standing right there in her room. How could I have said that? I would never have gotten rid of that desk—you loved it so."

"I know what happened to the kaleidoscope, too. You didn't

give it to the rummage sale. I gave it to Ophelia at the country club. Years and years ago—at the end of one summer. The summer of your silver-anniversary dance, actually." He paused, then laughed. "I suppose I thought she could use something pretty— a pretty toy to play with. Running that country club couldn't have been any picnic."

"You gave it to Ophelia? You never told me that. It was your birthday present!"

"Yes. I remember. I liked it—it looked as if it had been sprinkled with confetti—but I'd played with it enough. I thought I was too old for it." He laughed again. "But, you see, I bought another. So I must have changed my mind."

"He changes his mind a lot," Ann said.

"Maybe I've just regressed."

"I think he gave a lot of things away," his mother said to Ann. "Or threw them in the canal on his way home from school." She chuckled. "He was forever coming home from school without his mittens, a scarf—something. He'd say he'd lost them—such an innocent look!—but I never quite believed him. I think he just didn't like them. His Aunt Elizabeth gave him a beautiful scarf one birthday. I put it on him one morning when he started off to school and I never saw it again. You can tell me now," she said to him. "Did you throw that scarf in the canal?" She turned to Ann. "I don't think he liked it." She laughed again.

"I don't remember. I don't remember everything, you know. I don't remember the scarf, for God's sake. Which scarf? I don't remember it at all." He was suddenly irritated. "I was always getting shoved into scarves or mittens or something I hated. Can't we change the subject?"

His mother tilted her chin slightly up and to the side, the muscles around her mouth settling into a pattern he suddenly, deeply, and instantly recognized; and with that tiny shock of recognition he knew what she was at that moment feeling: what he had done to her. He knew it with absolute certainty, not from some faded sepia tableau floating up from the well of his childhood like the photograph of his mother and her friends dressed in Gay Nineties costumes at some half-remembered Ladies' Day at the country club, not the way he recognized certain gestures of his father's in himself—how he'd rubbed his fingers together, for instance, or, at the end, in the oxygen tent, absent-mindedly tapped his breastbone—but from the primitive cellular memory that she herself had embedded—imprinted—there in his own nucleic tissue. He was his mother's son, and he had hurt her, insulted her. He knew that she would never acknowledge it, as if by refusing to remark or even admit his ugly, snappish behavior —could it really have been that bad?—that would somehow tame it and render the insult if not powerless, at least unnoticeable. He supposed that if you spent a lifetime deliberately failing to notice, it would be quite possible to end up not seeing at all. The world became what you willed it, and what was inadmissible remained exactly that. But not quite. The world was not that tractable, and the muscles betrayed you, twitching their own involuntary signals. Before he could speak, make some tiny amend for his outburst, Ann had begun talking. "It sounds like him," he heard her say. Perhaps his mother was right; Ann appeared not to notice anything out of the ordinary. "He'll throw *anything* away that I want, but if I throw something of his away, that's another story —isn't that right, darling? I can't get rid of last Thursday's newspaper without checking. He saves everything." She laughed. "Really, I expect to come across his old teddy bear one of these days."

"My old what?"

"Teddy bear. I expect to come across your old teddy bear."

"Oh. No need to worry. I buried that years ago. In a shoe box. Decided he'd died. It was the summer we were doing bird funerals. Michael Aldrich, Amy Steer, and I dug him up a few days after we'd buried him, to see if he'd decomposed. I was expecting a little pile of cigar ash. But no, not even a maggot. Maybe he was a saint. You know, like that uncorrupted corpse in *Crime and Punishment*, the guy who looked fresh as a daisy when they opened the coffin—smelled sweet as flowers. That was one of the signs."

"Signs of what?" Ann asked.

"Sanctity."

"Oh, yes," she said. "Of course."

"Aren't you thinking of *The Brothers Karamazov*?" his mother asked. "And I thought the body had putrefied. That was the problem. Father Zossima's body smelled, and everyone pretended not to notice. A great embarrassment—for a saint." She sighed. "Well, you fertilize the earth, one way or another."

"I think you're right." He looked at her again. His mother astonished him; one minute she was carrying on about some third-rate Broadway comedy and the next she was correcting him about Dostoevsky. "It is *Karamazov*. I'm getting everything mixed up today. I'm not feeling well. I've got a headache." He got up from the table.

"I wondered if you didn't look a little peaked," his mother said. "You should lie down and let Ann and me finish cleaning up. There's not that much left. We'll have it done in no time."

"No. Really, I don't feel that bad. I'll help, and then I'll see if I can't get some work done. It shouldn't take long." He glanced around the rooms. "The place doesn't look so bad. I expected a lot worse for the morning after that Walpurgisnacht."

"It was a lovely party. You do things so nicely, Ann, and you both know so many interesting people. I enjoyed talking to all of them."

"I'm glad," Andrew muttered, picking up the shards of a wineglass from the hearth. "I didn't." His mother didn't appear to hear him.

"By the way, did you ever get the tulips I ordered for Easter?" She was emptying ashtrays. "You never mentioned them."

"We didn't?" Ann was surprised. "Oh, dear, I'm sorry. Yes, we got them. They were waiting for us when we got in from the airport on Easter Sunday. A cheery welcome home. They were beautiful. And they lasted at least two weeks."

"They were white," Andrew said.

"Andrew had a problem with tulips when we were in London." Ann laughed apologetically. "You know how he can be when he gets something in his mind."

"Yes," his mother said. "It's hard to get it out. It's hard for him to forget anything."

"As long as you people are talking about me as if I'm not here, I'll just load the dishwasher and retreat to my office. The place looks pretty clean to me. Anyway, Mrs. Bridges will be here tomorrow to do the rest," and Andrew went into the kitchen and a few minutes later disappeared into his office, a small room at the back of the apartment with his desk, a daybed, some bookshelves, and a window from which he could see, if he looked between the buildings across the way, a patch of the Hudson flowing. Andrew loved his office, the tabernacle of his desires.

He looked at the photographs propped here and there. They were all old, except for his pictures of Julia. He'd always meant to hang them; but hanging them, fixing them once in place, seemed a definitive and final act, like placing the heavens in their orbits: there the gleaming Venus, here the red-eyed Mars, and what shall we do with Sirius, that little scorcher? God's work, not his. Did he want to face the photograph of himself in his blue beret every time he sat down to his typewriter? No. Did he want his grandmother looking at him from beyond the grave? No. His father looking over his shoulder as he played with words on a page? Double no. On the other hand, he didn't really want their faces to the wall. So they remained propped about the room, changing position now and then, occasionally one retired to or resurrected from the closet. Just getting some of them framed had been a significant accomplishment; hanging them seemed too rich with complications for an ordinary mortal, involving too many decisions and consequences unforeseen. Such hubris would be punished. He picked up the photograph of himself in his father's arms on the dock at the Island and dusted it off. He looked a little like his mother there, he noticed with some surprise, but he didn't have her eyes. His hair was still blond and curly; he couldn't have been two years old. It must have been taken in his second summer. His father looked very young, younger than he'd ever remembered him, although when he thought about it he realized that his father must have been older then than Andrew was now. He must show his mother the picture, remind her; she'd like his golden curls. Andrew had several photographs of his father at various stages of his life, fewer of his mother. She didn't like having her picture taken. But he did have a beautiful tinted photograph of her as a child in yellow ringlets and dreamy, innocent eyes, her opaque gaze floating calmly out toward the expectant world. The picture must have been taken seventy years before, but anyone could recognize her from her eyes; they hadn't changed. He dusted that off, too. He was the only one who ever dusted his office; he didn't let anyone in to clean. Consequently, it sometimes got awfully dusty. It needed dusting, he noticed; maybe more than dusting. He'd do it later. He opened the drawer to his desk and took out the pen he'd bought in London—his most recent amulet. It was a beautiful pen, its barrel of a very deep bloodstone lacquer—not black; maybe a little green in it, or red—spun with filaments of silver, like a cocoon. He'd bought it to give to Ann, but he couldn't part with it. He couldn't tell her about it, either. Sometimes he bought a new pen when he was beginning something new, or when he wanted one for some special purpose. He took out the rest of his pens and lined them up, putting his new one with them. He supposed he still liked the first one best, but it was hard to tell. The French lacquer that he'd bought to use on one of his projects was certainly the most beautiful: it glowed like some precious, molten stone; but the barrel was too slim and therefore harder to handle, and it didn't hold as much ink as the first. The pens were like his children: he loved them all equally but differently, as his mother had tried to explain to him when he was a child, but without much success. He had many pens, but only one child, unfortunately, so she was forced to bear the brunt of his love. He wondered what had happened to the snapshot in the little silver swivel frame that used to sit on his mother's dressing table, of himself as a toddler running toward the camera from her open arms, she in full pursuit behind him. He used to like to spin the picture in its swivels. He put his pens aside and sat looking out the window for a time. Then he got up, went over to the closet, and pulled out the old cardboard box from Field's; the address label was still on it. It had been sent many years ago, before the war, to the house on Bellevue Avenue with something for his mother. Much later he had found the empty box in the attic when he was packing some things to take East, and he'd used it. He opened the box and looked in: a few old letters and papers, the dice from his Monopoly set, a small book and a shoe box at the bottom, this and that —and something carefully wrapped in paisley, what was left, he thought he remembered, of his great-grandmother's wedding shawl that he'd found in a chest in the attic that day and knew that no one would miss. He put his hand on the scrap of paisley and opened the wrapping. There was the telescope he'd been given for his birthday years before, the same birthday his mother had given him the kaleidoscope. That was curious. He supposed it must be the only thing that remained from that day. The telescope Mrs. Steer had given him: he'd remembered that. He hadn't seen it in years, not since he'd decided back there in the attic in Grande Rivière—more than fifteen years ago, probably, and for reasons lost to him now—not to toss it out but to wrap it in an available scrap of paisley and pack it away instead. He brought it to the desk and sat down. He looked at it resting there. Closed, it was no more than ten inches long. He picked it up and extended it; sixteen inches, maybe, at its full length. He raised the telescope to his eye and tried to focus it on the river—harder than he might have thought because the buildings kept getting in the way and the lens was fogged. He wondered if fish would ever return to the Hudson. He examined the lens. It was cloudy. Was it still smudged from childhood fingerprints? He remembered taking great care with it, but then he'd been only eight years old, and he wasn't the only one ever to touch it, either. He took out his handkerchief, blew on the lens and the eyepiece, and carefully wiped them off. That helped, though the view was still a little cloudy. Dust inside, he supposed. He found the path through the buildings and focused on the river again. Not much action there. He raised the instrument a bit and New Jersey appeared. He brought it into focus. They could have New Jersey. New Jersey, he thought, was one gigantic bedroom next to a smokestack; some of the names might sound pretty, but the stench was unendurable. He knew there were lots of beautiful places in New Jersey— he'd been to some of them—but all he could think of when he thought of the state was the smell of Secaucus and Elizabeth, and terrible places like Trenton or Camden—where that Swede lived, that guy with the glasses and the goatee that they'd met on their honeymoon and that Ann had run into again. He was an ex-seminarian; they'd excuse anything: it made it all easier. That old Thomistic tango. The Church comes to grips with Chaucer's real world. Chaucer wins. He moved the telescope a fraction to the right, and suddenly he was looking into a dark blur. He glanced up and realized he must be aiming at the building across the way. He adjusted the focus, and instantly the bricks, even the mortar between them, jumped into sharp relief. The telescope brought the building across the street a lot closer than New Jersey. It was very clear. He put the telescope down and scanned the building with his naked eye. He counted the windows. There were twenty to a floor. He wondered how many apartments that would be. He peered through the lens again. Oh, Jesus! What was that? He put the telescope down. Come *on*! Was this his bourgeois, boring West Side? He didn't believe it. In one of the windows across the street? Where did they think they were—in the Village? It was

Wednesday *noon*! Was it a Jewish holiday or something? He heard Ann calling him. He slipped the telescope into the drawer. There were the two cigarettes he'd stashed away the night before. Funny he hadn't noticed them earlier. Ann opened his door. "We're leaving," she said. He got up and went out of his office. "Okay. Have a good time. I'm just working at my desk. I'll be there all day. See you later."

"You must be feeling better," she said.

"I seem to be," he replied.

"Get a lot of work done," she said.

"Don't forget to take a little rest," his mother added.

"I will, and I won't," he said, laughing and walking them to the door. "Enjoy the show."

He shut the door behind them and returned to his office. He picked up the packet from Pamela. There were things he should be dealing with. He glanced across the street. Prurient, that was the word. It was the word the Supreme Court liked. He was too old to be curious about what went on behind other people's windows; besides, he *knew* what went on. Ann would say it was disgusting, this prurience. That he should have his mouth washed out with soap. No, no, he had it wrong. That was what they said if you used bad words. What would they do if they knew you were looking at bad pictures? Blind your eyes, maybe. And for bad thoughts, well, he supposed they could cut off your head. That would take care of the problem. Remember the Inquisition; it wasn't that far away. Once his mother had threatened to wash his mouth out with soap, and his brother, in fact, had done it. He didn't remember the word, either. Now, of course, everybody used those words. If they were pissing over the balustrade at the back of Gracie Mansion—and he'd seen them do it, in fact had done it himself, standing right next to the Mayor, and it had been a kick—they could certainly say "fuck" at the dinner table if they wanted, and they sure did. They were a lot alike, Ann and his mother. He'd leave his brother out of it; anyway, he was dead. He moved Pamela's packet to one side and reached for the telescope. It was amazing how well it still worked. He looked it over carefully. It had been built to last. They don't make toys the way they used to. This was metal with a sturdy black covering that was supposed to look like leather. It had gotten a little banged up over the years, but it was still in pretty good shape. He put it down and opened his drawer again, looking at the cigarettes he'd taken from Daisy's pack. He took one of them out and sat toying with it, feeling it. He found a match, struck it, and watched the flame. To hell with it. He lit the cigarette. He didn't have an ashtray. He left the room and returned with one. He sat there blowing smoke at the window, clouding the view of the building across the street. It was a taller building than his, but the floors were closer together. That building was eighteen stories, but the ceilings couldn't be as high as they were in his because from his twelfth floor he was looking directly across at their fourteenth. He looked down one floor. There she was again! But she was alone this time. She was just passing by the window in her blue dressing gown, oblivious to his gaze. Should he warn her? And how? She'd never hear him if he rapped on his window. The idea was preposterous. He could make a sign and hang it from his window: STOP! SOMEONE IS WATCHING YOU. He remembered the plaque he'd seen once in a house in Oxford: THOU, GOD, SEE'ST ME. It was a Staffordshire plaque, decorated with flowers: sweet and charming for such a stern message. If he'd had it now, he could put it in his window, remind her, remind her to be careful, that you never knew who might be watching. She probably wouldn't see that either. Anyway, she was just walking around her apartment in her dressing gown, a perfectly innocent thing to do. Perhaps he'd imagined the scene earlier; he'd always had a fevered imagination. He put down the telescope. What had he seen? A woman in blue leaning back in a chair, apparently speaking to someone out of range of his vision while a man crouched at her feet and ran his hand under her dressing gown and up her leg, massaging it, kneading it like a lump of dough. Pretty far up, too. He must have imagined it. The woman looked lovely, young and graceful and blond, a pretty face, almost sweet. A Wellesley graduate, maybe Bennington, who somehow found herself transplanted to the West Side. Getting ready to go to lunch across town with a member of the Junior League. Looking for her pearls, probably. Yes, that must have been it. Of course. She was a provisional member, off to lunch at the Colony Club in her Chanel suit and then some worthy cause in Spanish Harlem. Well. Thank God he'd worked that out. If she'd seen him spying on her, she might very well have called the police: "Officer, there's an outrageous pervert across the street. Send that man to Bellevue." He laughed with relief and put out his cigarette. He reached for Pamela's letter. Everything was fine in London. People were still talking about the play; he knew that. She'd had several calls for him, and several letters which she was enclosing. She didn't want to give out his address to strangers, for which he was grateful. A few people had asked for it, including Nigel Rogers' young man. He was coming to the States. She'd told him Andrew was going to be in Bermuda so there would be no point in trying to reach him in New York. That was nice of her. If David Roper wanted to reach him, he could write care of her and she'd send it on. She didn't know if he had. She didn't like him much, maybe because she didn't like Nigel much. She was still very angry about his review. Andrew leafed through the stack of letters. He didn't feel like reading them now. His hand moved to the telescope. She'd have found and fastened her pearls by this time, and would be giving them a final little flip. Her blouse would be silk, creamy beige, with a floppy bow, and she'd be debating whether she should button her jacket. The leather bag on a chain would match her shoes, low-heeled, sensible, black. There would be just a discreet touch of perfume. She would reek of quality. He wanted to rush out and find her a cab, she was so lovely. He reached for the telescope, but thought better of it. Instead, he picked up one of the letters that Pamela had forwarded, and opened it. Interesting handwriting. He glanced at the signature. It was from David Roper. He put it aside. He didn't want to read a letter from David Roper now. Maybe he should take a nap, rest his mind, get himself together. Then he could tackle the mail. *Leave that poor lady alone.* Anyway, she was probably already on her way to lunch. He stood up and leaned across his desk, peering down to the street. The doorman was standing quietly in front of her building. There was little traffic. Andrew hoped the doorman had gotten her a cab without much trouble. Wednesday afternoons could be difficult; she might have been late. He picked up the other cigarette, decided to light it—it was the last one; might as well be rid of it—and fingered the telescope again, then raised it to his eye, to check, to see if he was right. He focused first on the river, then New Jersey, before edging it a hair to the right, to the blur of her building. He sighted with his other eye to see that he had the right floor. He brought the bricks into focus and moved to her window. Nothing. He could see her blue robe shimmering where she'd tossed it. On the tufted blue boudoir bench, vaguely French, at the foot of the bed. She must be partial to blue. The bed was enormous, king-sized. It hadn't been made. He was expecting something a little more genteel. The room was empty. She must have left, but she'd forgotten to turn out the lights. It was brilliantly lit. Suddenly a figure appeared, from the right. A woman. She was wearing white satin slippers—mules, they called them—and a short white nightie with a little ruffle around the bottom. She ambled slowly to the bed and sat down, and reached up and began to unfasten her stockings. She was wearing garters. A lacy white garter belt! He didn't know women wore garter belts these days. Suddenly she looked toward him and smiled broadly. She did it again, smiling shyly this time. She touched her tongue to her upper lip. My God! He recognized her. The Wellesley girl who was supposed to have gone to lunch at the Colony Club in her Chanel suit and pearls! She took a long time fooling with her stockings and garters, extending her leg, running her hand slowly along it, running it over her breasts, lingering over the nipples, then to her stomach and back to her leg again, rubbing it lightly. Her nails were polished—pink. He hadn't noticed that before. She was still wearing her slippers. They were edged with fur at the arch. She never did get her stockings unfastened. She was rubbing her groin now, her nightie pulled up so he could see a patch of pubic hair. She kicked off her slippers and fell back on the bed. Jesus Christ, she wasn't! She was *masturbating*! Tossing her head from side to side! Golly, she didn't need to do that. He could call her up. Of course he couldn't call her up! He'd never find her telephone number. He didn't know her name. Maybe he could run across the street and describe her to the doorman, pay him a few bucks and go up to her apartment. Knock on her door, say he was the Fuller Brush man, a tool for every need. That sounded like a dirty joke. He could feel himself getting excited. She was still wearing her stockings. *"Take your fucking stockings off!"* He whispered it hoarsely, aloud, startling himself. He looked around to see if anyone had heard. Well, of course no one had heard; no one was there. He looked back to her bedroom. Oh, oh! A man. A young man. In some kind of uniform. She had company. Perhaps the maid had let him in? She ought to fire that maid! He was standing beside her bed, holding a pad in his hand. He seemed to be asking her to sign something. Andrew smiled. It must be the Fuller Brush man, the rat. Someone else had thought of it, and done something about it. Had really gotten into it, in fact, costume and all. He looked nice, as if he should have been in class. Working his way through college, maybe—N.Y.U. She looked startled, frightened; then she reached smiling toward the man. The motion caused the strap of her nightie to slip from her shoulder, exposing most of one breast. She took the pencil from him and signed the pad, smiling still, her eyes on him, not the pad. He touched his hand to his cap, about to leave. She touched her leg again, then his leg, his crotch. She smiled demurely at him, questioningly, and her breast popped the rest of the way out of her nightie. It was a lovely breast, glistening, as if with dew. Fresh as peaches, plump as melons. Pretty as nectarines. Christ, such clichés! He was supposed to be a serious dramatist, and his mind worked like a porn writer's. Right about now he should go jerk off. Oops. "Bless me, Father, for I have sinned." "And what was the proximate cause, my son?" "That twat across the street, Father, the Wellesley grad." "Wellesley is a pagan place. Avoid such occasions of sin, my son. Stick with Marymount girls." "But Father, they're all marrying Jesuits now. Fucking like minks, every last one of them." "That will be three Rosaries, my son. Concentrate on the Sorrowful Mysteries. And chew your food. Next." Without doubt, he was losing his mind. Moreover, he was getting hard. She was fumbling with the man's fly now. That was how it looked, at least. The man had his back to him. His hands had reached for those breasts. He dropped his pants. He wasn't wearing any underwear! Nice little ass, though. Reminded him of David Roper. Well, he'd never seen David's ass—at least uncovered. She was licking her lips, smiling at the man, and rubbing her hands up and down his thighs. She buried her face in his crotch—shit! The lights went out! What a time to blow a fuse. Just when he was about to blow his. He could discern movement in the dim room, but he couldn't tell what was really happening. He moved the telescope to the right, to the next window. No action there, just a man in a baseball cap sitting on the window ledge, gesturing. He must be in the next apartment. Andrew couldn't see anyone else. The man turned toward the window. It was a blue cap, New York Yankees. Then he got up and passed from sight. Andrew turned his gaze back to the girl's apartment. The lights were blazing now. She was sitting on the guy's face! The view from down under. That girl really liked to see what she was doing. No messing around in the dark for her. What a lovely ass she had, peeking out from beneath her garter belt. She was still wearing her white stockings. Just like a bride. Must be some kind of fetish. But the guy was naked now. Jesus! He was hung like a horse. When they made that, they broke the mold. She turned her head toward the window and grabbed his cock, pumping it like a piston. You'd think she was churning butter. Careful, honey, those things aren't made of iron, you know. He may be hung, but he's not King Kong. Not hairy enough; too blond. His face was still buried in her, and his hands were working her, moving around her ass, parting her cheeks. Jesus fucking Christ! He stuck his finger up her ass and suddenly she turned and was going down on him. Way, way down. That girl could take it. Amazing. She ate the whole thing! They had some matinée going here. It beat *No, No, Nanette* by a mile. Andrew hoped his mother and Ann were enjoying their show as much as he was enjoying his. *No, No, Nanette* indeed! Suddenly there was another man, in a suit, carrying a briefcase, standing next to the bed. She flung her hand to her mouth, palm out, fingers splayed, alarm written on her face. And the lights went out again! Holy shit—her husband had come home! Back early from a business trip, he bet. Christ! He might shoot her. Or him. And Andrew'd be a witness! He'd have to testify. He'd have to say that he was just idly scanning the heavens, looking for constellations. Lots of stars visible at midday, Your Honor, really. It's the best time to see the corona. That's the sun, of course. You have to be very careful not to burn your eyes. He'd thought there was going to be an eclipse that day. Wasn't there an eclipse scheduled? He must have gotten the date wrong. But that was what he'd been doing, waiting for the eclipse. He could wear an eye patch to court, just to make it more convincing. Damn near went blind, he could say. You'd be surprised, Your Honor; astronomy is a very dangerous hobby. He put the telescope down. This was definitely not grown-up behavior. On the other hand, what they were doing certainly wasn't child's play. The lights went on again. He was afraid to look. He'd never been a witness to a murder. He should have gone to *No, No, Nanette* with his wife and mother; what any decent son and husband would have done. Well, he supposed he should think of his civic duty. He picked up the telescope. If there was a crime, he had an obligation to report it. He found the window immediately, and put the telescope down at once. This was too much! Her husband was ramming her from behind while she was going down on the other guy—with his cap on her head, he noticed, set at a very jaunty angle. Well, he'd always had an eye for detail, although it was hard to make out the details in that mass of tumbling flesh, hard sometimes to tell what part belonged to whom, there were so many of them. Bodies were so vulnerable, he thought, so easily hurt. He hoped nobody got hurt. He peered through the telescope again. Some kind of doll had gotten knocked to the floor. He hadn't noticed that before. It must have been sitting on the bed. It was a wonder one of them didn't fall. He focused on it. A teddy bear. What a grotesque touch! *A teddy bear*. My God! Does she sleep with a teddy bear? Well, at least it would give her some rest. She wasn't getting much of an afternoon nap, that was for sure. This was hardball, a real workout, tougher than the gym. She wouldn't need her exercise class this week. They were really going at it now, a jumble of changing angles and shifting forms: not the geometry Euclid had imagined. Suddenly she jerked up. Her husband pulled out, the other guy flipped over. She stuck her ass in the air, bent toward the guy she'd been blowing, and buried her face in the crack of his ass. Her husband—he wasn't! He was! He was sticking his dick in hers—in her *asshole*? His face looked grim. The other one turned again to fuck her at the same time—an almost impossible juxtaposition; he couldn't get it in, tried to shove it in. It wasn't working. He'd gone limp. He reached for the man's balls. That didn't help. Lord, what was left? Nothing that Andrew could think of. Unholy geometry. It swam before his eyes, all tumbling shapes and planes like—God forbid!—a kaleidoscope. He was at once revolted by the scene and riveted to it, unable to take his eye from it though he was beginning to feel saddened, and slightly sick; and slowly, very slowly and surely, the camera of his eye dollied remorselessly back and these poor human figures peopling his frame of vision became smaller and smaller and smaller in his sharpening sight. And suddenly they all just stopped. Stopped cold. The lights dimmed a little. The woman looked down at the other guy and laughed, shoving him aside. He sneered at her.

Her husband got off the bed and disappeared, while she swung her legs around and sat on the edge of it and the other guy scratched his balls and reached over to the table for a cigarette, maybe a joint. He pulled the sheet around him—a touchingly modest gesture, Andrew thought, almost innocent. Or maybe he just felt cold. He seemed awfully young. The other man, the husband—oh, yes, of course, the husband!—appeared in an orange robe. He took a toke from the younger man's cigarette—it must be a joint—and passed it to the woman. They all looked bored now, as if they'd been involved in some tedious and tiring task that was unfortunately occupying what looked to be an otherwise pleasant afternoon in May in New York City. And at once the room began filling with people. The man in the baseball cap, the cap reversed now, passed next to the window, filling Andrew's lens, blocking his view. He set a piece of equipment—photographic equipment: it appeared to be a light meter—on the window ledge. Oh, sure. The man from the next apartment. Andrew wondered how he could have been so simple, so stupid. Of course he had been witnessing the making of a movie. Right across the street. Preposterous! Well, he supposed they had to make them somewhere; an obscure apartment on the West Side was as good a spot as any. The man in the cap walked to the bench, picked up the woman's robe, and tossed it at her. She got up and wrapped it around her, moving out of sight. Two other men appeared. One of them was lugging a camera on his shoulder, a big, hand-held movie camera; the other wheeled a Fresnel light into view. No wonder the room was so bright. He pushed another light next to the bed. The director—the man in the cap must be the director—and one of the cameramen moved the bed a little, and then they rolled another camera into place behind it, adjusting it so that it was pointed down directly onto the bed. Of course. A movie. A fuck movie. Were they Method actors, he wondered, or did they rely primarily on technique? What Andrew had been witnessing, what he had been spying on, was not life but art. Like going to the gallery to look at the Vermeers. Life as Vermeer had never painted it—though, Andrew supposed when he thought about it, as Vermeer might in some obscene flight of fancy have imagined it. He would have liked the play of light on the folds of the bedclothes, on the woman's blue robe, the pearls Andrew had imagined her wearing; his painterly eye would have appreciated their concentration on the business of the day, and, of course, the window admitting light. Andrew imagined the quizzical, enigmatic faces Vermeer would have given them. The man in the baseball cap was running around with the light meter now; the two guys were standing off to the side, desultorily playing with themselves and each other, trying to get it up again somehow. One way or the other, Andrew figured. The woman returned, dropped her robe on a chair—the man in the baseball cap adjusted its folds; he had an eye for detail too—and she began to assume various poses on the bed while the cameramen adjusted the lights and the director took sightings through an instrument that looked much like a very small telescope. They were getting ready to shoot again. The two men arranged themselves on the bed, each absorbed in himself now, in some erotic dream of his own devising, in a desperate attempt to strike some fresh new nerve, to dredge up a tingle of desire or at least the necessary appearance of it, while the woman gazed down at her breasts and fingered her nipples. One of the men was playing with his nipples too. The bodies scarcely touched. For all the attention they gave to one another, they could as well have been in separate rooms. The director approached the woman with a jar in his hand and rubbed something—some kind of rouge, Andrew figured—around each nipple, on its aureole. No, that wasn't the word. The word was areola. He gave one of her nipples a little flip with his finger. She slapped his hand away. Then one of the cameramen handed him a spray bottle—the very same kind of bottle Ann used to mist their plants—and he misted her breasts. No wonder they'd looked fresh as dew. He handed it back to the cameraman and took a bottle of baby oil. He spread her legs and the lips between and squeezed some of the oil there, rubbing her, making her glisten—*"like the ooze of oil crushed,"* Andrew thought. He couldn't help it; Hopkins' line just popped into his head. She reached for a book on the table—Andrew couldn't see the title, but it looked like a serious book, like a textbook— and the director took it from her hand. She grabbed it back and he knocked it away from her. It fell to the floor. They left it there. The director handed the bottle of oil to one of the men. He squirted some into his palm and rubbed it onto his penis, then onto the other guy's, the deliveryman's, who rubbed it into his ass, too—they were both getting hard at last—and onto the girl as well. The man tossed the oil out of sight. Suddenly the lights went up again, the cameramen rushed into position—one manning the big camera behind the bed, the other circling around it, closing in with the smaller camera on his shoulder—and they all resumed their work. Andrew put the telescope down and rested his chin in his hand, his elbow on the desk in this room that he worked in, surrounded by his photographs and pens, his totems, talismans, and taboos. Then he got up and went out for a glimpse of sunlight and air, and a pack of cigarettes.

Andrew felt the need of music, and when he returned he found his old Flagstad recording with the London Philharmonic of some Bach and Handel songs. "Sheep may safely graze." That sumptuous voice, that stately chromatic progression so pastoral and simple in its opening, so richly complex in the repetition, wafted through the apartment and down the corridor to his office. *"Sheep may safely graze and pasture in a watchful shepherd's sight."* He noted the irony, the telescope on his desk. Mrs. Steer never had this in mind when she gave him the telescope for his birthday all those years before. Thirty-two of them, he realized. Thirty-two years and two months since Mrs. Steer had given him that telescope and his mother had given him the kaleidoscope that he'd later given away to Ophelia, the black steward at the country club who used to make chicken sandwiches for him when he was sick, and grilled cheese when he wasn't, and root beer floats, and sometimes she would give him a Coke, even though his mother didn't like him to drink Cokes. He looked at the cigarettes, opened the pack and shook one out, then decided not to light it yet. It was the same birthday that his father had given him the fountain pen, although that had come a few days later, when his father had returned from a business trip. He used to go on a lot of business trips, Andrew remembered. And that was the birthday, too, that Mr. Wolfe had given him a Canadian silver dollar for each year of his life. Fortunately for Mr. Wolfe, Andrew had been only eight. He remembered what he'd done with those silver dollars, too, and with the one he'd given him the Christmas before, the last coin minted in 1938 and with silver from his own mine, according to Mr. Wolfe: he'd buried them under a floorboard in the attic, in his secret place, the same day all those years before that he'd packed up the telescope and the other things that he wanted to preserve from his childhood. He couldn't imagine why he'd done that; it had just struck him as right, and at the time it had made him smile. It was odd that he'd never spent them, considering his inability to hang on to money. He supposed the coins were still there, gleaming dully under the attic floor. Actually, they probably weren't gleaming at all. They'd been very tarnished when he'd hidden them there; they must be black by now. The people who'd bought the house, of course, would have no idea of the treasure hidden in the attic, their attic now, nor of the letter that he remembered putting there in that spring of his childhood, a letter that had been addressed to his mother, that had arrived when she was away, and that he'd never given her for reasons inexplicable to him then and not entirely clear to him now. Or perhaps he simply didn't want to think about the reasons. He'd even forgotten about the letter, though not about his secret place, until he'd raised the loose floorboard to hide the coins and discovered it there, the envelope covered with dust. He had knelt down on the floor, bent over, and blown the dust off it without picking it up. The letter had come from Mexico in 1939, and the colors on the stamps were still clear, virtually as fresh and vivid as when they'd been printed: the smoking volcano, the plumed serpent, the huge gray stone head. They'd been protected from the light all those years. Colors don't fade in the dark. He hadn't moved the letter, hadn't even touched it. He'd simply arranged the coins by date, the earliest on the bottom, divided them into three stacks of three, and, taking care not to cover the stamps, had dropped them on the envelope to hold it down. Not that that was necessary; it certainly wasn't going anywhere. He was toying now with the cigarette in his fingers; lit it, inhaled. He realized that the letter must have come from Mr. Wolfe; he'd known it then, too, he supposed, even when he was eight, but hadn't wanted to acknowledge it. The seepage of the past: how strangely it worked. Mr. Wolfe had been rather a mysterious character in his childhood, not one he'd been entirely fond of, despite the various gifts that he'd sent Andrew's way. Mr. Wolfe had taken rather a fancy to his mother—and vice versa, Andrew supposed. He didn't suppose it; he *knew* it. On the Island that summer they were together all the time. It was odd that he'd never heard her mention his name in all the years since; never once. Andrew recalled seeing him at the big party his parents had given for him and Ann the August after they were married—maybe the only time he'd seen him since that summer. The memory was vague. Despite his age, Mr. Wolfe had gone off to Canada the autumn after his parents' anniversary dance, not long after Germany had invaded Poland and Britain entered the war, to join the Royal Air Force. He couldn't have been that old, of course, maybe about forty: Andrew thought he was younger than his mother. He was going to be a hero. Everyone had thought that joining the R.A.F. was a very dashing thing to do. Nick Farnsworth, one of his brother's friends, had done the same thing and gotten killed. Andrew's father had been very upset when that happened, and started working harder than ever. He'd said that was his contribution to the war effort. Mrs. Steer had said that Mr. Wolfe fancied himself Lord Byron. She'd said she hoped he wouldn't try to swim the Channel, though, that the water was over his head and the currents too powerful for a man like him. Those were her words; he remembered that, and the way she'd laughed at the time—with a great whoop. As a child, Andrew had thought Mr. Wolfe a pretty good swimmer, though he didn't do it very often. Except for Mrs. Steer, who was really good and used to swim all the time, Mr. Wolfe was just about the only one of the grown-ups who ever went into the water. His father didn't. His mother never did; she didn't know how to swim. Andrew wondered what his mother remembered—*if* she remembered. Of course she must. If she could remember a toy kaleidoscope she'd given him for his eighth birthday, she'd certainly remember the man who'd shown up that day with a stack of silver coins. The past was trickling back to him; a faulty memory had never been his problem. He wondered if he could ask her about him. He put out the cigarette and picked up the letter from David Roper. He was going to read it. He knew what it would say. He was afraid of what it would say. Flagstad was still singing, another aria now. The sounds floated toward him. "Break in grief, thou loving heart!" From the *Saint Matthew Passion*. He liked, sometimes, hearing music from a distant place, a reminder that there was life beyond his desk, beyond his room. That had been the strangest experience in London. He didn't want to think about it. He didn't know what to think about it, either. He didn't know what to think about a lot of what had happened in London. It had not been his best time. He began to read the letter. Yes, David was planning a visit to the States. He hoped to visit New

York and Washington, perhaps some other places as well. He'd like to see the Byzantine and pre-Columbian collections at Dumbarton Oaks, and visit the gardens there. He'd heard they'd be at their peak then. Pamela Stickney had told him that Andrew would be in Bermuda early in May. He thought he'd arrange a stopover—what? *What?* Andrew stopped reading. He hadn't known it would say *that*. He lit another cigarette and reached for the telescope. He raised it to his eye and, without thinking, aimed it at the window for a last, clinical inspection. He focused on the bodies now littering the bed—like something from a battlefield, after the battle had moved on. The three participants were flung out motionless where they'd fallen; the cameramen and director nowhere in sight. The man who'd shown up with the briefcase was lying face down, his head buried in his arms. Someone beyond Andrew's range of vision—the director, probably—tossed a roll of paper towels onto the bed. The younger man—the deliveryman—reached for it and began wiping himself off. Almost indifferently, Andrew thought. He handed the roll to the woman, who was staring listlessly at the ceiling. She did have a pretty face. She lurched into a sitting position and rubbed her breasts and belly with a wad of towels, slowly at first, then vigorously. She touched her hand to her hair and gave a kind of grimace, then tore more paper off the roll and scrubbed at her head, her face, mouth and eyes. They seemed a little awkward around one another now, like conspirators sharing in a slightly shameful secret, comrades in a crime that made them a little contemptuous of one another at the same time that it had brought them so violently, so nakedly together. Still, they *were* in it together: nobody'd forced them; nobody'd pointed a gun at them. Some of it must have been fun. As his father had always said: if you don't like your work, quit. Nobody'd forced him to look, either. Did that make him a secret sharer? He wondered what the cameramen thought, what they felt. In a sense, of course, *he* was the cameraman—or the director. It had been his movie too; he'd virtually written the script. She passed the roll of towels to the other man, who had changed his position and was now sitting naked at the edge of the bed, in the tungsten glare, the sharp, relentless light—Edward Hopper's light. Andrew couldn't see the man's face, but there was something sad about the pose, something vulnerable—the slump to the shoulders, maybe, the curve of the back. He appeared very vulnerable for a man of his size—not large, but not slight, either. The director appeared; shooting was clearly finished. He dropped the man's orange robe beside him. The man turned to look at it. There was no expression on his face. It seemed utterly blank, exhausted. It was indeed as if Yeats's great cathedral gong had struck and the drunken soldiery were abed—or perhaps they were just now beginning to awaken; it was hard to say. The director moved about the room, picking things up, throwing things into a Bloomingdale's shopping bag. Nice touch, that. The woman was up and in her robe now, her hair pulled back, her face looking scrubbed—more like the Wellesley graduate again, emerging from her bath, maybe. The director began talking to her, gesturing with his arm. She shook her head. She seemed angry. They appeared to be arguing, more and more heatedly. He stepped toward her. She pulled away. He reached out. What did he want? Absolution? He had come to the wrong place: she shrank back, shuddering, as if from something vile. He shouted at her. Shouted what? All of a sudden she swung her arm and slapped him—on the face. Slapped him really hard—*crack!* he could almost hear it; almost feel it burning, on his face. The Yankees cap fell to the floor, and they stood for a moment, a photograph fixed in time, their eyes fixed on one another. The man who'd been sitting on the bed remained slumped there looking quietly on, his robe draped around him. A decent man, Andrew thought. The younger man eased across the bed toward him, resting his hand for a moment lightly, solicitously, on the other's shoulder. There was something very sad about the scene, and the young man's simple gesture ineffably touching. The woman disappeared. The director picked up his baseball cap, tucked it into his belt, and followed her out of sight. In a few moments, the two men had themselves passed beyond the range of his lens, and the room was empty.

Andrew leaned back in his chair, setting the telescope on the desk. Oh, yes, he thought; oh, yes. He knew. He lit another cigarette and sat there looking toward, not focusing on, his window, noticing in the still air the smoke curling slowly upward in little loops and whorls against the glass. Finally he put the cigarette out, raised the window a little to clear the smoke, and left the room. He turned off the record player—Flagstad had long since stopped singing—and went to the piano. It had been some time since he'd played the piano, he realized, and his fingers would know it. He sat down and leafed through his music, looking for the Bach *Inventions*. He always liked to begin with the *Inventions*. He wished he had an affinity for Bach. Instead, he found him extraordinarily difficult; even the *Inventions* he found difficult, and they were supposed to be relatively simple. He played the first four, then the eighth and one of the *Sinfonias*, and played them all again before he stopped: his usual ritual. His fingers were loosening up. He turned back to the stack of music, paused at the Mozart sonata he often played—the easy one, the only one he could play through without hesitation—decided against it, and continued his search. He pulled out *Kinderszenen*. It had been a favorite of his mother's. She used to play it rather well, too, without effort—or so it seemed in memory. Schumann's "Scenes from Childhood." Such simple-sounding tunes, most of them, and so deceptive. These weren't simple at all, but of course the idea was to make them sound as if they were. Simplicity was usually an illusion. He concentrated on the music. He was still at the piano when his mother and Ann returned.

"We could hear you playing when we got off the elevator," his mother said, walking toward him. "Beautiful." She sat down on the end of the bench, in the slanting afternoon light. "I always loved that piece. Let me try it." Andrew made room for her and she began to play the "Träumerei," but stopped. "Well, Horowitz doesn't have anything to worry about from me," she said. "I'm afraid I've gotten awfully rusty." She turned the pages, stopping at "The Child in Slumberland," the next-to-last song.

"Say it in German," Andrew said.

" '*Kind im Einschlummern.*' By the time I got to that, you were supposed to be sleeping. Remember?"

"Yes, I remember. Sometimes I was, even."

She played it through. "That's a little better," she said. "I'm so glad you have your piano. There's nothing more relaxing."

"How was the show?" Andrew asked, getting up from the bench.

"Lots of fun," she said. "Charming. Slight, but charming. But don't stop playing. You haven't played since I've been here, and I'd love to hear you."

"I've played enough. Maybe you should have gone to *Follies*. Depressing, but good."

"It was such a beautiful day," his mother said. "You know, for some reason the air reminded me of the Saturday you and I went to the Island—Easter Even, I think it was—to open the cottage. We opened it early that year. You couldn't have been more than ten. It was a beautiful, warm spring day—so clear, almost balmy—the kind we rarely have up North. Do you remember that?"

"Yes, I remember that day. We had fun. We ate on the porch. You made tuna salad and put those tiny peas in it. That was the only way I liked peas."

"I used to do that for you sometimes. I had to get a vegetable in you somehow. You insisted on rowing the boat, I remember that. One of the Indians got it in the water, but you insisted on rowing yourself."

Andrew chuckled. "I hadn't been doing it very long. Dad never wanted me to, but I liked to do it. It made me feel grown-up."

"We had a lovely time. Just the two of us. Daddy must have been working." She turned to Ann, who had emerged from the bedroom. "He always worried about Tommy on the water. Worried about his driving, too, when he got a little older. His father was a terrible worrier about the boys when they were young."

"Andrew must take after him," Ann said, laughing. "We could use a little light in here." She moved about the apartment, switching on lamps.

"It's light enough," he said. "I like the light in here at this hour." The living-room windows faced east, and the late-afternoon sun always seemed to Andrew to mellow a bit as it passed from the western windows of the dining room and through the open, columned space between to fall on, into, the lucent colors of the rug, igniting them and making them glow like jewels.

She ignored him. "What did you do today? Did you get a lot done?"

"What did I do?" he paused. "Oh, I just sat at my desk and played with my toys—the usual."

"You must have been concentrating," she said. "You didn't even pick up the mail." She turned to his mother. "He's usually standing at the door waiting for it to arrive. There's a letter for you from your Uncle Christian."

"I'll look at it later. Actually, I was working on a movie, writing a movie script."

"You were? Well, that's a switch."

"A porn movie," he whispered. "Want a part?" He thought suddenly of Buck, the black boy at the country club when he was little. Buck was a few years older than he and a whole lot smarter, and he'd told him years ago all about what grown-ups did. Told him pretty graphically, too. Buck knew all about it. Andrew had said he didn't believe it, told him that only Negroes did it, but Buck had enlightened him. He smiled.

"Oh, Andrew," Ann said, "act like a grown-up."

"I am," he said. "We're not talking child's play here. By the way, where's Julia?" He looked at his watch. "It's almost six o'clock."

"She was going to play with her friend Rosie after school. Her mother will be dropping her off shortly. Then we'll have dinner."

"I'm so glad it's only the family tonight," his mother said. "Just the four of us. And after that wonderful dinner last night, and then lunch and tea today, we certainly don't need a lot of food."

"I thought I'd make Welsh rarebit," Ann said. "Does that sound good? We'll have Welsh rarebit and a salad."

"Sounds fine with me," Andrew said. "Nursery food. I love it." Ann looked at him. "Really. I do. And tapioca pudding for dessert?" She didn't respond.

"That sounds perfect," his mother said. "A nice family supper."

"Well, then, perhaps we should have a drink," and Andrew went off to fix them.

"So you're going to Bermuda in a few days," Andrew's mother said as they were finishing their rarebit. "That will be nice for you. It's always nice to have a little holiday by yourselves."

"Actually, it's more work than holiday," Andrew said. "I don't know if I'm looking forward to it or not. I've never been there. I think Julia's looking forward to it, though. Mrs. Bridges is coming to stay with her. Julia loves that. She's got Mrs. Bridges wrapped around her finger."

"Like you had Mrs. Moran," his mother said. "I always suspected she let you get away with a lot when your father and I were away. That's why you were so eager to have us go. It took me a while to figure that out, but I finally did." She laughed. She was sitting across the table from him, Julia beside her, their backs to the windows.

"Do you have Mrs. Bridges wrapped around your finger, Julia?" Ann asked.

"I don't think she'd tell us if she did," Andrew said. "Would you tell us, Julia?"

"I'd rather go to Bermuda," she said. "Why can't I go?"

"You're in school, Julia," Ann said, "and you've just been to London."

"You're a lucky little girl, my dear. You've seen so many places," his mother said, patting her hand.

"But she doesn't care about that. She wants to go to Bermuda. Well, I don't blame you, Julia, but I'm afraid that's not in the cards this time."

"Sometime?"

"Maybe. We'll see."

"I've never been to Bermuda."

"Neither have I. Your grandmother's the only one here who has."

"I'd never been to Bermuda when I was your age, darling," his mother said. "I'd never been anywhere. Bermuda's for honeymooners." She laughed. "You can go when you're on your honeymoon, Julia—but with any luck that will be a while yet."

"We can hope so," Andrew said. "Elbows off the table, sweetheart. That's against the rules." As soon as he'd said it, he wished he hadn't. What the hell difference did it make if she had her elbows on the table? It was one of those rules left over from his childhood—a rule, he realized, that he himself now frequently enjoyed violating, along with most of the adults he'd observed, then and now. Violating the rules imposed in childhood was one of the distinctly pleasurable privileges of adulthood—like making them: "Don't interrupt," "Don't criticize," "Don't do this," "Don't do that." Children had to learn some manners if life was to be bearable, but they also had to learn to criticize if they were to survive. How could children evaluate anything if they didn't first try to criticize it? They had to start somewhere, and where better than with their elders?—there was so much that was wrong. The important thing, he thought, was not to stifle their criticism but to direct it, even encourage it.

"I know, baby," he said, "there are so many rules. Elbows-off-the-table is definitely not one of the major ones. It looks a little nicer, that's all. Think how it would look if all of us sat here with our elbows plunked on the table, flailing our knives and forks. It would be dangerous."

"I don't think it would look so bad," Julia said.

"You shouldn't disagree with your father, Julia," his mother said.

"That's all right," Andrew said. "We disagree all the time. It's just that I'm bigger so I win. Like Dad. And also I like to think that I've learned *something* over the years, so maybe I'm not entirely wrong."

"We'd all like to think that," his mother said.

"Yes," Ann said, "we would—and that's the problem."

"What does that mean?" Andrew asked.

"Andrew's father didn't brook contradiction," his mother said. "Nobody disagreed with him with impunity. But I was very happy with your father, Tommy. We had only one argument in our lives, and we were together a long time."

"Really? One argument in almost fifty years?" Andrew was incredulous. "That's impossible."

"But it's true."

"What was the argument about?"

She laughed. "That's my business." She turned to look about the room. "My, the light is beautiful here at this time of day. Reminds me of Bellevue Avenue."

"Yes, isn't it?" Andrew turned to Julia. "Well, think about the elbows, Julia. Maybe you'll change your mind." The operative rule, of course, was "Do as I say, not as I do." That was the important lesson: that things were not as they seemed, that very often the grown-ups didn't do as they purported to do. "Mother," he said, "that's simply not true. I remember your arguing—more than once."

"You just think you do. We never argued in front of you boys."

"This wasn't in front of me. I was in bed, on the Island. You came home from a party at Mr. Wolfe's, and you and Daddy were arguing."

"Of course we weren't," his mother said.

"Maybe you were arguing about Mr. Wolfe."

"Don't be silly."

"And you had an argument the night the furnace at the plant blew up and those men were killed."

"How could you remember that?"

"How could I not? I *saw* it! From my bedroom window. I saw the fire!" He shaded his eyes. The molten sun was sinking orange behind the buildings across the street, falling into New Jersey, its burning rays slanting into the room. "It flamed like that sunset." He pointed at it. His mother had her back to it. Julia turned to look. The fiery ball, shining on their windows, was reflected in each window across the street—ten, twenty, thirty sunsets—and back again, an endlessly coruscating fire. Ann got up and adjusted the blinds. "Mother, I *heard* the explosion! I was the only one who did. You weren't home. I was the one who *told* you about it!"

"Your father was very upset that night. He felt responsible for those men. It was a terrible thing for him."

"It was worse for the men," Andrew said. "Mother, you can tell me now: did you have something going with Mr. Wolfe?"

"Andrew!" Ann's voice was hushed, little more than a whisper. She looked at him aghast. "Would you like some dessert, Mother? We have fruit and cookies."

His mother turned to Ann. The muscles quivered slightly around her mouth and chin, forming the pattern he recognized. "Thank you," she said, "I always like a cookie."

"Help me clear the table, Julia," Ann said, rising and picking up the plates. "Now, Julia, please."

His mother turned to him. Her chin trembled slightly. Her blue eyes, blurred and magnified behind their distorting lenses, glistened. "I always loved your father, Tommy."

"That wasn't the question."

Ann and Julia returned with a bowl of strawberries, sugar, and the plates; then Ann went back for the cookies. They ate in silence for a time, dipping the berries into their dishes of powdered sugar, dropping the hulls on their plates. Suddenly his mother asked, "Do you remember that book you had, Andrew, about the Sargasso Sea? Christian or Clara gave it to you—one Christmas, I believe. One of them found it in Bermuda. Christian's only trip out of the country—he never did it again." She chuckled. "I guess he didn't like it much; that was years and years ago."

"Yes, I remember." He dipped another strawberry in the sugar and returned it to his plate without eating it. "I loved that book. *Fingerfins: A Tale of the Sargasso Sea*." He picked up the strawberry, looked at it, and put it down again. "I think I still have it. You read it to me the Christmas I had the measles, the Christmas I got the desk. I'll have to read it to Julia." He moved the berry around his plate, toying with it. "Actually, it may be a little young for Julia."

"For God's sake, Andrew," Ann exclaimed, "eat that strawberry!"

"It's amazing—" he said, turning it in his fingers, examining it, "the reddest strawberry I've ever seen."

"Well, now you can visit the Sargasso Sea," his mother said. "Isn't Bermuda in the middle of it?"

"Or on the edge of it, I'm not sure." He ate the fruit. "I suppose we'll find out. I'll have to find the book; I haven't thought of it in years. It's not with the rest of my children's books—those I still have, anyway. They're all in Julia's room, on her shelf. I think I can find it, though." He laughed. "She likes her own books better, but that's all right. She's got to discover her own stories." Andrew knew that he'd kept it, and he knew where it was; he'd seen it, he was sure, at the bottom of the carton he'd opened that day. "I'll go get it," he said, and he went to his office and found the box on the chair where he'd left it, with the thin blue book at the bottom of it. He brought it into the dining room, and opened it—carefully; the book was worn, and its pages were coming loose—and began to read: " 'There is a strange river in the Atlantic Ocean—a stream of water running through the sea just as a real river flows through the land. It begins where the water around the West Indies and in the Gulf of Mexico gets very warm in the southern sunshine. This warm water starts moving northward in a great river sometimes a hundred miles wide. As it flows along the coast of North America, the shape of the land pushes it east across the Atlantic. But some of the stream slowly swings south again, until it winds up at last in the Sargasso Sea.' Yes," he said, "I remember the story. Here's a map. It shows

Bermuda on the edge of the Sargasso." He showed his mother and Ann and Julia the map. "That's where we'll be, baby."

"Read some more," Julia said.

"Later, maybe. We're just finishing dinner. Or you could read it yourself"—he passed it to her—"but handle it carefully. Your father treasures it. Now I have to have some coffee. Or maybe another glass of wine. Yes. Why not another glass of wine?"

Ann laughed. "Are you asking for reasons?"

"No. I know the reasons."

Julia asked if she could be excused. "I want to go read the book," she said.

"I wish you'd play the piano for us," Andrew's mother said to him. "My last night here—it would be so nice. You stopped playing as soon as we came in this afternoon, and I'd like to hear you." She turned, laughing, to Ann. "I want to see if his lessons took. He used to love to play—until he got to be about sixteen. Then he had other things on his mind." She chuckled. "Christian was always very musical too. He had a real talent for it. By the way, are you ever going to read his letter?"

"Yes. Later. You know what it will say: it's just another book report."

"He's fortunate that he likes to read. There's not much else in his life. It's a shame he never bought a piano. I do hope Julia will take lessons. They'll stay with her her whole life. At home, whenever I felt nervous or tense, I'd go to the piano, and in a few minutes whatever'd been bothering me would be gone. It's a great gift, being able to play the piano."

"A great pacifier," Andrew said. Christ! Why be so mean? "Maybe I'll play later, Mother. I can't play when I've had anything to drink. My fingers won't hit the right keys."

"Then I'll play for a while," she said. And she went to the piano while Ann and Andrew cleared the table and took care of the dishes as they listened to his mother's playing, and Julia sat reading in her room.

"I couldn't believe that scene you pulled," Ann finally said to him as they were preparing to leave the kitchen. "What malice! And you talk about my brother!" She shuddered. "You put me in an impossible position, trying to entertain your mother, trying to keep you under control, trying to keep this place running and everyone happy. I don't think you give a thought to me. And what business is it of yours, anyway? It's your mother's private affair."

"Indeed."

"Oh, that wasn't what I meant! Please go into the living room now and play something for her. Do something to make her happy on her last night here. She adores you in spite of yourself."

"I'm sorry. I'll try."

"Try harder than you did at dinner. She's an old woman. You may never see her again."

"I doubt that. But yes, I know."

"And for heaven's sake, what difference does it make now if she did have an affair with someone when you were eight years old?"

"I don't know," he said. He turned his ear for a moment to the music. "I don't know." He stopped—"Weird, isn't it?"—then reached toward her. "Give me a hug? Please? I had an erotically charged childhood. I'm not a well man."

He had made her laugh. "Yes, I know," she said, hugging him. "You told me that this morning. Now let's go into the living room and be nice." She was smiling now, a little warily, and looking into his eyes. "Don't worry about Julia's elbows on the table; worry about your foot in your mouth. And have some heart for your mother."

"I can't. I gave it to you, remember?" He looked at the pendant of clear amber streaked with red hanging from the chain around her neck. "You're wearing it. The heart I gave you in London."

"I'll lend it to you for the rest of the evening. Let's go."

Andrew's mother stopped playing when they came into the living room. "I certainly enjoyed that," she said. "I'm sorry sometimes that I ever got rid of my piano. But there simply wasn't room for it in the apartment, and David enjoys it. I play it at their house now and then. You know, I was astonished at Daisy Meyer—"

"Daisy Curtis," Andrew said.

"Daisy Curtis. She looks scarcely a day older than she did when she left Grande Rivière. And now she's an artist! I guess the Addingtons always had an artistic streak—like my father's side of the family, like the Bigelows. She must take after her father. You wouldn't remember him; he died before you were born. He used to carry his easel out to Boomer Island and paint the loveliest watercolors. As a hobby, of course. One year he did paintings of everyone's cottage and gave them for Christmas. You probably remember ours, Tommy. It used to hang on the wall across from the fireplace."

"Vaguely, I guess. What I mostly remember hanging on the walls were all those animal heads. I used to wonder if they could see us."

His mother laughed. "I never liked them much either. They just came with the territory, it seemed—and they stayed with it, too, thank heavens." Her gaze drifted into the distance, as if she were seeing right then the moose head on the stone wall above the fireplace. She turned back to him. "Daisy said she'd enjoyed seeing you both in London, and that your play was a bigger success than you'd told me. She said it was very exciting, that London was raving about it. You never tell me these things, never even show me a review."

"It's my natural modesty, I guess."

"Well, I wish I'd been there. I love going to the theater in London. Your mother would have been proud."

"If it opens here in the fall—and it looks as if it probably will; Michael thinks so, anyway—you'll have to come out. That would probably be around the time you're heading south."

"I wouldn't miss it, my dear. I hope I'll like it."

"Yes, well, no guarantees," Andrew said.

"So long as I'm not in it."

"Of course you're not in it!" Julia came into the room at that moment, carrying his book. Andrew laughed. "It's all about Julia."

"I'm almost finished," she said. "I got to the part where they captured Fingerfins and everybody is staring at him. Grandma, will you read me the rest of it?"

"Darling, I'd love to," and the two of them sat down at one end of the couch and Andrew's mother began to read—" 'So they put poor Fingerfins into a square aquarium . . .' "—while Andrew and Ann sat in chairs at either end of the couch, lulled by the sounds of her voice, listening to the story: how the artist tried to sketch him, and how they had to shoot the shark that they'd caught with the head of a dolphin for bait but couldn't bring into the boat because he was so big, and how a terrible storm came up, the wind blowing like a hurricane, and a giant wave that might have been King Neptune himself covered the ship with roaring water and washed the aquarium over the side with Fingerfins in it, and he was finally free again and clinging to his little clump of sargasso weed in the raging sea. " 'But the artist who had nicknamed him "Fingerfins" was not sorry to find the little fish had gotten away. His drawings were all done. Months afterwards, at home, he put them in a book called *Fingerfins: A Tale of the Sargasso Sea.*' " Andrew's mother closed the book and looked down at Julia. "Isn't that a lovely story," she said, "and a happy note to end my visit on. I used to read that book to your father, Julia—over and over. I probably had it memorized once."

"That's true," Andrew said. "I bet you read it every day when I had measles. I had to stay in the dark and you rigged up a little lamp so that the light fell only on the book. I couldn't see your face, I remember that. Everything was in shadow but the book. Some of those fish had lights too, as I recall."

"The lantern fish," Julia said. "I just read about them. Daylight hurt their eyes, so they could only come to the surface at night. The women had their lights on top and the men had theirs underneath." She giggled.

Ann rose from her chair. "It's long past your bedtime, Julia. You have school in the morning. Let's go. I'll help you. Kiss your grandmother good night. You'll see her at breakfast, but then she's leaving and you won't see her for a long time."

"I don't want Grandma to go." Julia looked suddenly quite sad.

"Neither do we, Julia," Ann said. "We'll miss her, won't we?"

"I hope you'll come to Grande Rivière this summer," his mother said. "It would be wonderful to have you there."

"We'll see," Andrew said. "It may be a busy summer."

"You could visit us in Maine," Ann said. "Julia and I are going up early, but Andrew will be back and forth and there for most of August. We'd all love it if you would. Julia will find plenty of things for you to read to her. Andrew, why don't you play something for your mother while I get Julia ready for bed?"

"So you're not going to let me out of it. Okay. I'll play something." He kissed Julia good night and went to the piano.

"I wish you'd play *Kinderszenen*," his mother said. "We both loved it so."

Andrew opened the music and played the first piece, and then the second—the "Curious Story." He felt very much out of practice, but he continued playing, warming up to it, until finally he got to the end, *"Der Dichter spricht."* He said it aloud.

" 'The Poet Speaks,' " his mother repeated.

"Yes."

"That was lovely. Thanks for playing for me. It made your mother happy."

"I'm glad. I don't want to hurt you, you know."

"I know."

"But sometimes the poet has to to speak."

"I know that, too."

"Good." He walked over to her chair and bent to kiss her forehead.

"I'm very tired tonight," she said getting up. "I think I'll retire. It's been a long day, and I have a long trip tomorrow— and a little packing to do before I go to bed."

"Do you need any help?"

"No, thank you. I'll be fine."

"Well, good night, then. I'm going to bed shortly myself. We all seem to be going to bed at the children's hour tonight."

"Good night, Tommy my boy."

"Andrew."

She laughed. "Then good night, Andrew my son. Your mother loves you."

"Despite myself?"

"Oh, I think because of yourself." She kissed him, and turned to leave the room.

"Thank you."

She stopped at the entrance and turned again for a moment to face him. "You know, your grandmother used to say, 'If your children never make you cry, they never make you laugh.' "

He watched her leaving, then started to call after her but stopped himself. He heard her go into the kitchen and speak to Ann—Ann often worked at her desk there when he was playing, taking care of business, paying bills—and then tiptoe into Julia's room. He supposed she wanted to check on her, to see that she was sleeping, to kiss her good night. He picked up his book from the couch where they'd left it, and went into his office. The telescope still lay on his desk, the box open on the chair. He set the book down, picked up the box and carried it to his desk. He sat with it in his lap, looking through it. He picked up the dice and shook them, rolling a seven. He rolled them again with the same result. The third time he got still another seven. He shrugged. The dice must be loaded. He wondered why he'd saved them; they hadn't meant anything special to him that he could recall. Maybe they'd reminded him of the dice his brother David used to have, and would never let him touch. In fact, maybe they were his brother's, and not from his Monopoly set at all. He'd probably taken them when David went to war. He returned the book to the bottom of the box, thought better of it, and put it on his shelf. He continued going through the box, pulled out a piece of paper carefully folded in quarters and opened it. It was a poem. Oh, yes. He remembered. It was the poem Mrs. Steer had written out for him one morning after her swim and given him while they were sitting on her dock at the Island. He read the lines:

> *You must turn your mournful ditty*
> *To a merry measure;*
> *I will never come for pity,*
> *I will come for pleasure.*

Well, four lines of verse, anyway. Shelley's, he thought; maybe a variation. Tears had almost filled his eyes when she'd given it to him, he was so stirred by the gesture. He'd told her about a bad dream he'd had, and she'd told him about dreaming when she was a girl of swimming through leather, and said that everyone had bad dreams once in a while. He'd read somewhere that people dream in order to forget. An interesting idea. Mrs. Steer had sensed that something was troubling him that summer. Well, he supposed now that something was, but he hadn't been able to talk about it. It was curious, for someone who grew up to write dialogue for a living, that it had always been easier for him to express what other people, what that mysterious cast of characters who peopled the dense thicket of his imagination, what they were thinking, feeling, and saying than to reveal—if he even knew it—what was on his own mind. Displaced the blame, some-how; shifted the attention. Maybe that was precisely why he'd become a playwright. Sometimes it was even fun, putting words into other people's mouths, and as his father used to say, "You can't beat fun." He put the poem aside and picked up a couple of old postcards, one of them written in his childish hand and sent to his mother when she and his father were out West, telling her he was feeling fine but would feel better if she'd send him a Don Sturdy book. He laughed. The other was from his mother, writ-ten on that same trip. She hoped he could read her handwriting; she'd try to make it clear. She'd found a surprise for him in San Francisco that she thought he'd like, but he'd have to wait until she got home to play with it. He remembered the surprise: a Brownie camera. He'd really had to coax her for it, and when he'd finally gotten it he'd had a lot of fun with it, annoying the grown-ups by making them pose again and again. Then she wrote, "I say 'good night' to you every night after I get in bed, my Tommy boy. I love you." It was postmarked OCT. 25, 1941. He'd been ten years old. He turned it over. The picture was of the Golden Gate Bridge, and the colors were terrible. She'd said the same thing to him recently; apparently she still did it. There was another piece of paper in his box, folded in half. He knew what that was. He'd written on it with the fountain pen his father had given him for his eighth birthday, and what he'd written— the first time he'd ever tried handwriting—was his name, in black ink: *Tommy MacAllister*, with a few blobs of ink around it and some scratches above it where he'd tested the pen. Then, beneath it, his full name: *Andrew Thomas MacAllister*. It was the first time he'd ever used a fountain pen, too, and it looked it; the paper was smudged with his fingerprints. The ink had not faded. There was a line partway across the page, and below it he'd written his full name again. It looked a little better the last time. He looked at the paper, puzzled over it. It wasn't such a peculiar thing to do, he supposed, but strange that he'd saved it. Maybe he'd wanted to remember, though it seemed unlikely he'd forget his name. He set the paper on his desk. Within the box was another box, an old shoe box. The size was on it: 4AAA. The shoes must have be-longed to his mother; no one else had feet that small. He opened it and found, wrapped in the tissue that had once held the shoes —could he still detect the faint lingering smell of leather?—the wooden mask from Mexico that Lucien Wolfe had given him that same summer. It used to hang on his bedroom wall on the Island. Odd that he'd kept it, and not the coins. He looked it over. It was long and narrow, with tiny slits for eyes. He held it to his face. He couldn't see through it. He hadn't been able to see through it then, either; the slits were too narrow. Maybe they should take it to Maine, hang it on the screened porch—the mask was more decorative than useful. He wrapped it in the tissue and put it back in the shoe box. Enough mementos, he thought. And what a mess he'd made of his office, with all this junk strewn around it. He turned to his desk, saw the telescope still resting there. It needed a rest, he thought. He looked across the way and found the apartment. It was dark now. He picked up the telescope and leaned across the desk, straining to point it at the night sky. He couldn't aim it high enough. He jumped up on the desk and opened the window, sat there leaning out, the lens to his eye, hoping to scan the Milky Way or focus on the cold sparkling fire of some ancient, distant star: the clear firm light of Betelgeuse or Polaris, the only two that he easily recognized. The lights rising from the city cast too bright a glow across the night; the stars could not compete. He heard Ann calling him and jumped down, slipping the telescope into his drawer. She came to the door of his office. He leaned against the desk, facing her.

"What on earth are you doing? What's all this mess?"

"Oh, I was just going through some stuff, boxes of papers and things, trying to bring some order to the chaos."

"Isn't it chilly in here with the window open?"

"It seemed stuffy."

"You're not planning to jump out, are you?"

"Not tonight." He laughed. "Why, do I seem suicidal?"

"I was joking," she said. "Your mother's in bed. I'm going myself. Come along soon."

"I will. Good night."

"Good night."

"I'll close the door so I don't disturb you. I'm going to turn the radio on. I want some music. See you shortly." He quietly shut the door, switched on the radio, and sat down at his desk. He took the telescope out of the drawer, saw the cigarettes, and lit one. The room was chilly. He didn't want to shut the window, didn't want to sit in a smoke-filled room. He pulled his old sweater out of the file cabinet and put it on, then turned the radio down low; he couldn't turn it off. He looked again at the dark windows of the apartment across the street. Had he imagined the whole thing? And what was so awful about it, anyway? Dogs in the park happily did it all the time, and nobody thought much about it, least of all the dogs. Well, some people averted their eyes. Of course, dogs shit in front of Gristede's, too; people, at least, were beginning to think about their doing that. He supposed if dogs made movies, they wouldn't be visual at all, simply a succession of aromas wafting through the dark to set their noses twitching, humans scarcely able to detect a scent. He imagined a theater full of dogs and people, the dogs groveling with desire and the people sitting bewildered, superior, archly amused. Sin comes in through the nose. You had to have the nose for it, of course, like those people who blend perfumes or appraise wines. Except for touch, he supposed, smell was the most primitive sense, the first to develop, almost vestigial now to the dominance of sight, the last to emerge, the richest, the most sophisticated, and the most inflammatory. Sin comes in through the eye. Then we reach for it. There was a lot to be said for touch, but films hadn't yet achieved it, nor had the theater, though it occasionally tried—when the actors urged the audience onto the stage at the end of *Hair*, for instance: a little daring, in a Broadway sort of way, a little titillating, but still safe enough for the matinée ladies from Larchmont. The ladies from Larchmont wouldn't have approved of the matinée he'd seen today, those naked gladiators tangling in the ring. He thought of the Living Theater's Dionysian group-gropes in Brooklyn, actors and audience thrashing wildly about the hall and the stage, grunting like pigs, shrieking like banshees, and calling the confusion *Paradise Now*. But the Living Theater was self-destructing. The shock of the body. Broke down the distance. The whole point *was* the distance, the barrier. The immediacy, the ineffable poignancy of art depended on it: the proscenium arch, where the private fantasies of the audience met, mingled, and more or less safely grappled with the fantasy being portrayed, the dangerous fantasy of the artist. Art was always controlled violence, even the stillness of Vermeer's. Look at the Greeks, at their tragedies, their myths. Leda and the swan? See, but do not touch. You'll get burned if you do. In the case of Leda, raped. Funny that he'd written "*Do not touch*" in his clumsy hand at the back of *Fingerfins*. At the time, it had seemed the grown-up thing to do, he supposed, if a little prissy; he didn't remember doing it. The rule had been a favorite of librarians and other adults. See, but do not touch. The unattainable object of desire; the self and the other—not that you were supposed to touch yourself either, except when unavoidable. Reality was always so much less vivid, so much less compelling than the fantasies we wove around it, blended into it. The reality was, there was the self, and then there was the other. The dance grasped that; so did the dancers, perpetuating the illusion that perfection of form exists in light and motion. The dance was the most physical of the arts, the most sensual, the most erotic: a glorious celebration of the body at the same time that it denied it, denied its limitations, denied its possession. See, but do not touch. The body in its transcendence sublimated itself, subjected, submitted itself, to the incredible demands of the art—not altogether unlike the movie he'd witnessed that day; he'd be curious to see the edited version, the version he was meant to see. Dichotomies do not exist in nature, a professor he'd once had was fond of reiterating. Ah, but they do. There is the self, and there is the other: *the* original dichotomy, the first flaw in the scheme of things, the original sin—God's, of course; He'd made it: the original event from which all dichotomies flowed. But dance was so ephemeral, each performance unique, as evanescent as music in the air, as words on the stage—or on the page, for that matter. That was its poignancy and its beauty, the brief shimmering beauty of the butterfly, like that numinous moment he'd witnessed at the end of a jungle trail in Cambodia years before. You don't see the butterfly's brilliance, feel its slow laboring, in the chrysalis, any more than at Lincoln Center you saw the swollen feet or heard the cries of pain of the dancers. He'd stood in the wings once, at the New York City. He'd heard the exhausted cries, seen the wincing pain when the dancers—ethereal creatures—landed there—*thump!* Like that: *thump!* "*Brightness falls from the air.*" It wasn't pretty at all. "*Queens die young and fair.*" And yet . . . there were those rare heightened moments, in art, in life, when everything seemed condensed, compressed, sharp, intensely focused, and, in a flash or slowly, the self fused with the other: the other as self. The obscure object of desire. Sometimes skiing was like that, Andrew thought, when you were speeding down the moun-

tain and the light was flat, and the only sound was the *whishhh* of
skis on snow and the only light was white and the earth became
the air; the air, the earth. Falling in love was like that: the long
slow grinding of plates, a sharp certain shift, and suddenly a rift
in the fundament and you were falling weightless through air and
it all made total, dizzying, marvelous, scary sense, sense that was
beyond sense: meta-sense. He gave a little laugh. Non-sense?
Sometimes, whenever he felt he was grasping something, he'd
lose it. Gone. Vanished. *Poof!* Like that. Like God. He supposed
a religious experience was like that, too: transcending without,
sadly, transfiguring, trapped as we are in the Incarnation. That,
Andrew thought, was truly the profound primal mystery, the
central fact, and the terrifying splendid message of Christianity:
the Word made flesh. Some flesh! He looked across the way; the
windows were still dark. Almost all the windows were now, at
this hour. It must be late; he didn't look at the clock. Entangled
in the Incarnation: he pondered that idea, that event where all
dichotomies began, and ended. He thought of those elegant
carved figures coupling so gracefully, so endlessly on the Hindu
temple in India that he'd seen only in pictures. He'd like to see
the real thing someday. He'd have to control himself. He'd heard
that story—Pliny's anecdote—about the young man so aroused
by the Cnidian *Venus* of Praxiteles that he'd shot all over it; left a
permanent stain. Well, that's art, as Michael would say. Maybe
after the fellow had gotten that out of the way he could look at
the statue a little differently. First things first; we're all biology's
victims. The kinetic comes before the aesthetic. Art may arouse
desire, but eventually it has to satisfy it on some other plane.
Transmute it, maybe. Render it, the way fat is rendered in the
fire—the refiner's fire. Then the fat is thrown away. Andrew
wasn't sure his filmmaker understood that. Yes, someday he'd
have to go to India. But not now. Now he had to clean up his
desk and go to bed. He picked up David Roper's letter and read
it. It said what he'd thought it said, feared it would say. But he
decided to put it out of his mind. He picked up the various things
he'd pulled out of his box and returned them to it, carefully
folding the poem Mrs. Steer had given him and the paper that
he'd written his name on so many years before, in such an awkward, childish hand. He picked up the telescope. He started to
put it on his bookshelf, changed his mind, set it on his desk. He

lit a cigarette, thinking about it, not thinking about it. *My God!—death is like that!* Must be. Finally he picked up the telescope, wrapped it gently in the scrap of paisley, and returned it to the box. He looked out the window for a time, smoking his cigarette. Then he returned the carton to his closet. In a few days, he knew, he would be smoking again.

"Your shoes need shining, my dear," Andrew's mother said as they were pulling out of the garage on their way to the airport. "I hope you'll take care of that. Your father would never tolerate shoes that weren't polished. It would be nice if you'd get a hair-cut, too. Oh! And don't forget to read Christian's letter. I'm sorry I didn't think of it when we were in the apartment. I'm sure he intended me to hear it."

"Oh, I'm sorry. I forgot all about it. And yes, my shoes. Well, there were lots of things Dad couldn't tolerate." Andrew stopped for the light and glanced down at his feet. "I'll have them shined, though." He smiled. "I don't know about the haircut." He looked over at the corner near his building. "I see the shoeshine man is back at his stand. I'll stop on my way home from the airport."

Tiny the shoeshine man arrived as regularly as the green every spring when the weather warmed up, and set up his stand on the corner by Andrew's building. This spring, though, he was late. He was usually back at work by the middle of April, and it was already the sixth of May. Andrew had wondered where he'd been. He liked to stop there, enjoyed talking to him. Everyone called him Tiny; it was the only name Andrew knew. Tiny was very small—frail, almost. He was a fixture of the corner, like the newsstand, and he did know how to polish shoes, going at his work with a kind of concentration and crisp dispatch that was a pleasure to watch. When Andrew returned from his mother's uneventful farewell, he paid him a visit.

"You're back in the nick of time, Tiny. Where've you been?"

"Back home, Mr. Mac. I been back home."

"Where's that?"

"Outside Sumter, South Carolina."

"I thought you were a New Yorker, Tiny."

"Nope. New York's just where I live. Sumter's home. These shoes need work, Mr. Mac."

Andrew laughed. "Mr. Tiny, you sound like my father. My

mother just told me my father would say my shoes are a mess."
It had, in fact, been virtually the last thing she'd said before she
boarded the plane: "Read Christian's letter. Don't forget to have
your shoes shined. Remember your father. I love you." Then
she'd hugged him—"Have a wonderful time in Bermuda; I think
you need a rest"—and hurried off, jaunty and straight and determined as ever, turning at the gate for a final wave. "I told her
you'd fix them up, Tiny." He noticed the pack of cigarettes in
Tiny's shirt pocket.

"I'll fix 'em, but your momma's right—they're a mess. You
oughtn't be walking around in shoes like that, Mr. Mac. Not right
for a gentleman like yourself."

"Huh! I'm afraid I'm not much of a gentleman, Tiny. Say,
would you give me one of your cigarettes?"

Tiny took the pack from his pocket, shook one out, and held
the match for him. "Didn't think you smoked, Mr. Mac. My
daddy never let us smoke in the house. 'It's a city habit,' he'd
say."

"I don't. Just once in a while. What were you doing in Sumter?"

"Takin' care of my father. Somebody got to do it. Like somebody got to take care of these shoes of yours." He whipped the
saddle soap into a lather and began scrubbing at the shoes.

"Was he sick?"

"He was dyin'. Livin' with my sister, but she got children to
take care of. Besides, she's workin'. He couldn't get out of bed,
you know? Nope, he couldn't get out of bed."

"I'm sorry." Tiny continued scrubbing, then rubbed the
lather off, using a little swab to get it out of the space between
the soles and the shoe. Andrew could feel the tickling at the edges
of his soles.

"Somebody had to do it. Somebody had to carry him to the
bathroom." Tiny continued working, dabbing polish on the
shoes. He stopped, looked up. "A person . . . you know, if you
can't do for your own kind, then you ain't . . ." His voice faded.
He went back to the shoes. Andrew could feel the leather softening. He stopped again. "Then you ain't . . ." Andrew sat there
looking at him, leaning toward him, riveted by his words, his
voice, his touch. "Then when he got real bad, I couldn't carry
him no more. They took him to the hospital and he died."

"Oh, Tiny, I'm sorry. I'm very sorry."

"He was born on the farm, and he wanted to die on the farm. Never been out of Sumter County in his whole life—except once, to Columbia for the state fair. He wouldn't have known what to make of this place. 'What's in the city?' he'd ask me. 'Nothin' but trouble.' That's what he'd say. 'Whiskey, bad women, tobacco. That's trouble.' " He was brushing vigorously now.

"He had a point there."

"Nothin' in Sumter, either. No work. No money. Just ten acres of soybeans and 'taters now. Ain't no livin' in that. Work, is all." He finished up the shoes, whipping a rag across them so they gleamed. He tapped his foot. "There. That's better," he said, looking at his work.

"Lots better," Andrew said. "Thank you, Tiny."

"You say 'hello' to your little girl, Mr. Mac. You tell her Tiny's askin' after her. You take good care of her, Mr. Mac. She's a mighty fine little girl. Smarter than both of us."

"You're probably right on that point, Tiny. I'll tell her you asked about her. We're going away on Saturday, but she'll be here. You look after her for me, okay? Keep an eye on her. Don't let her get into trouble."

"I wouldn't let no trouble touch her, Mr. Mac. Wouldn't let no trouble touch her, don't you fret."

"I'll see you when I get back. We'll only be gone a few days. And I'll try to take better care of my shoes."

Tiny laughed. "You bring your shoes to Tiny, Mr. Mac. Tiny'll take care of those shoes."

"I'll do that. I'll be sure to do that. And Tiny, I'm sorry about your father. I know what it's like, and I'm sorry." Andrew got up and shook his hand. He always shook Tiny's hand; it seemed the least he could do. "And thank you for the cigarette."

"Weren't nothin'," he said. "Nothin' at all. You have a good trip, Mr. Mac."

"Thanks. I'll try."

Andrew returned to his apartment. Mrs. Bridges was cleaning, and Ann had left for the day to work on one of her projects. He went to his office and sat down to toy with an idea for another play, a play about families, maybe, or actors acting in a play. He needed another play, he felt, but so far he had just the germ of an idea. It was all very unclear. He didn't seem to be getting anywhere with it, so he browsed through his bookshelves in a desultory kind of way. Sometimes that helped. Sometimes he found an idea in the most surprising places—even, occasionally, in a comic strip, or in a popular song that was playing on the radio while he drove—some idea or line or fragment of a line that helped his own thoughts coalesce. He took his ideas wherever he found them, grateful and unquestioning. He pulled a book from the shelf and began to leaf through it. *Hamlet's Enemy*, it was called, by Theodore Lidz. Interesting enough, he supposed. Quite interesting, he realized, reading on, in its thoughts about trust in the cardinal human relationships and what happens when that trust is destroyed, but it didn't do anything for him at the moment. He set the book on his desk to look at later, and continued his browsing. One of these days, he'd have to get his books organized. He took another from the shelf: selections from Gramsci's prison notebooks. He scanned the pages. They weren't meant for scanning; the Sardinian hunchback didn't write the most transparent prose in the world. Suddenly a sentence struck him. He read it, read it again, then decided to copy it into one of his notebooks: "The crisis consists precisely in the fact that the old is dying and the new cannot be born; in this interregnum a great variety of morbid symptoms appears." He looked at the sentence in his handwriting in his notebook. It gave him a little tingle on his skin. He supposed that was why he'd transcribed it; tingling was a good sign. This was definitely an idea, but it didn't seem to generate any further ideas of his own, so he left his office and walked around the apartment, musing. He went into the kitchen and spoke a few words to Mrs. Bridges. He found Christian's letter still unopened on the table in the foyer. He'd forgotten all about it. Nobody'd mentioned it again, and he'd simply forgotten. He was sorry; his mother would have liked to hear his uncle's news—not that Christian ever had any news; his letters were largely book reports or catalogues of recent acquisitions. He opened it. Well, this was news. In the letter Christian said that Dennis had helped him get the secretary ready for shipping, and that it had gone out by van on Friday. He'd decided he was through with it, and he wanted Andrew to have it now. Andrew read the letter again, bemused, amazed, a little ashamed. Christian loved that desk. He didn't have much else. Andrew left the letter on the table for Ann, and then walked into the living room and sat down at the piano to try to work through the *Inventions*.

The night before he and Ann left for Bermuda, Andrew told Julia another episode in their story.

"Well, let me see," he began. "When we left our fearless trio, Ralph had just escaped from the clutches of the Dowager Duchess of Dork and was reunited with his friends and comrades, the fetching Emily Roo and Anthony Armadillo, who, as we know, had come originally from Mexico. Perhaps—who can tell?—Anthony will take his friends to Mexico someday, show them the grisly Aztec temples." Andrew shuddered. "However, it's not on the route to Australia, thank God; not this time—barring, of course, the intrusion of mysterious chance. For now, our threesome is happily ensconced once again in stateroom nine on the *China Hand*, steaming slowly, steadily, through the waning storm into calm tropical seas and the port of Bombay, India's western gateway and its richest city—like New York, only it looks better. Smells better, too.

"Knowest thou the land where lemons bloom, and dully gleam the golden oranges? So Bombay, a magical city, a city of temples and towers, soft green hills and rustling palms and everywhere the magnificent, flamboyantly flaming poinciana tree. Hear the play of fountains in the sultry afternoon, the twitter of birds, the sleepy buzz of the occasional odd insect, and, interestingly enough, the gentle lowing of the cows who meander the streets, because in India the cow is highly revered, sacred, you might say. They don't eat meat in India, you know; it's Ralph's kind of place. You do remember that he was a vegetarian?"

"Yes, Daddy."

"He thought he would feel safe there; he was looking forward to a pleasant interlude as a tourist in a new land. He didn't reckon with the ferocious mongoose, or with the feared and wily snake charmers—the *saperas*, the *madaris*, as they are called in India—who roam the streets, flute in hand, ready to charm the most recalcitrant cobra. The snake charmers were ubiquitous, and there were a lot of snakes, too. As snake charmers, they were much more effective than the Dowager Duchess, who foolishly believed she could charm a snake but ended up seducing herself

—with Ralph's help, of course, although she didn't realize that; didn't even realize she'd been charmed. Well, Ralph was a *little* charmed himself, but he saved his scaly self by concentrating his mind on his planned escape. When we left the Duchess and her son the Duke in stateroom six, she was dancing, I believe, to 'Begin the Beguine,' having swathed the torpid Duke in her veils like a butterfly in its cocoon, a newborn in its caul."

"What do you mean, 'call'?"

"No, not that kind of call. *Caul.* It's spelled differently: c-a-*u*-l. It's a membrane, a kind of veil, that covers the heads of some babies when they're born. It's supposed to be a sign of luck, a sign of supernatural powers, I think. Born under the sign of the caul, they used to say."

"Was I?"

"No, baby. But that's all right; neither was I. You can still be lucky. Back to the story."

"Daddy, have you ever been to Bombay?"

"No, Julia."

"How do you know what it's like?"

"I don't really. I'm just imagining what it might look like, what it *ought* to look like."

"You mean you're making it up?"

"Yes. I'm making it up."

"Oh." She sounded disappointed.

"But it sounds like a pretty place, don't you think? Like Mandalay. I've never been there, either. That's in Burma, on the other side of India." He picked up his pace. "Or we could make it Ceylon: elephants and spices, and everywhere the fragrance of jasmine, tea, and coconuts. It sounds a lot like Ceylon, actually, and that's on their route. Yes, maybe they should have gone to Ceylon."

"How can they do that? They're in Bombay."

"Well, we could go back and revise it."

"Revise it?"

"Change it."

"*Daddy*, you're *ruining* the story! You can't just go back and change everything."

"Okay, sorry. I'll continue. As the grand ship steamed majestically into the harbor, our three intrepid travelers were standing on deck, watching the city slowly reveal itself in all its mysterious splendor. The smell of oranges and lemons wafted through the gentle morning air, already thick with the sweetness of frangipani, yellow oleander, jasmine, and champa: the whole munificent tropical bouquet. It was a heady incense, almost intoxicating, combined as it was with the fragrant smoke that rose day and night from the burning incense of the many shrines and holy temples that dotted the city. The people of Bombay have very sensitive noses, and they like to keep their noses happy. By and large, they are a gentle people, soft as the air: a city of Ferdinands, like Ferdinand the Bull, who was always sniffing the blossoms of the cork tree back in Spain. Ferdinand the Bull does not appear in this story, Julia; I just used him to illustrate the point."

"Daddy, I wish you'd get to the story." She snuggled down under her covers, eager and impatient.

"I'm sorry. I'm in my baroque period."

"Sounds more like rococo to me," Ann said, appearing at the door, laughing. "Daisy Curtis is on the phone."

"Why don't you talk to her?" Andrew said. "I'm in the middle of Julia's story."

"I think she wants to talk to you, Andrew."

"Then I'll have to call her back, okay?"

"When you finish, I'd like you to help me arrange the foyer. We have to move a couple of pictures and figure out what to do with the table, now that Christian's secretary is here." It had arrived that day.

"Okay. Later. Now, Julia, where were we? Oh, yes, Ralph and Emily and Anthony were standing on the deck of the *China Hand*, preparing to disembark. The ship was going to be in port for only the day, before stealing off again, a white vessel darkly gleaming in the dark middle of the night. But a day would give them a little time to see something of the city, and better to see something than nothing at all. As they were standing on the deck, sniffing the delicious richness of jasmine and incense, the pungent odors of fat frying and food cooking, and gazing in astonishment at the fabulous sights, they were careful to keep a safe distance between themselves and the Dowager Duchess, now wearing her hat of many veils, and her son the Duke, who was looking a bit peaked this morning, a bit pale. They decided it would be pru-

dent to allow them to leave the ship first, considering what a
dangerous passion the Duchess seemed to have for Ralph. She
was waiting impatiently now at the gangway, eager to see what
strange creatures she might find in the bazaars of Bombay: something to stuff, perhaps, and take back to the Great Hall of Dorkminster—after she'd devoured the tender meat, of course. The
Duke was thinking about having a lemonade, maybe with a mar-
aschino cherry in it, at the Sea Lounge of the Taj Mahal Hotel,
which is a splendid old hotel on the water, and, it has to be said,
more Ralph's idea of a good time, too. Suddenly the gangway
was lowered, and the Dowager Duchess shoved ahead of everyone. She was, after all, a Duchess, and she thought herself entitled to all the rank and privileges thereof. She and the Duke
scurried off into the hustle and the bustle, the hurly and the
burly, the sights and the sounds of strange Bombay. 'Boy!' she
shrieked. 'Boy!' She seemed to be calling for a driver. Of course,
the Duchess called all Indians 'boy,' regardless of their age or
rank. She would even call the Prime Minister 'boy,' should she
happen to meet such a distinguished person. Very British, our
Duchess. She and the Duke were followed shortly afterward by
Ralph, the loyal, steadfast Anthony, and the graceful Emily, now
festooned with garlands of marigolds. That's a pretty custom in
India: garlands of marigolds were everywhere, adorning the necks
of oxen on holy days, of which there were many and this happened to be one, offered to the gods in their temples, and, nicely
enough, to arriving visitors as well—a sign of welcome. Emily
had never looked lovelier. It was harder to get a garland around
Anthony's neck, and harder still around Ralph's, but the trick
was accomplished somehow; Indians can be very clever, as we
shall see. And you should remember, Julia, that *by and large* they
seemed a gentle people; there's a bad apple in every barrel, you
know.

"For Bombay was not all that it seemed, not exactly as it first
appeared to be. Behind the broad boulevards, behind the splendid façades and the glorious monuments, and down the dark
alleys, hidden in secret nooks and crannies behind the smoking
temples, was another Bombay: a city of violent pestilence and
plague, of strange songs and even stranger mysteries, of secret
rites unknown in staid London or even in Egypt, Ralph's native

land and certainly no stranger to strangeness. Of course, such things were totally unheard of in Australia, the object of Emily's desire, her lovely, placid island home."

"Is Australia an island, Daddy?"

"Yes, dear, but a very big one. You'd never think it if you saw it. It's an island so big that they call it a continent. Back to Bombay: the people weren't as soft and gentle as they had appeared to be from the ship, either. They were, in fact, quite odd. Here was a swarthy fakir of sinister mien—m-i-e-n: that's the way someone looks—disappearing into an alley with his bed of nails on his back. On a tiny, crowded square five dancing women danced to the music of instruments never seen or heard in our own familiar New York. As they weaved round and round and in and out, their colorful, diaphanous veils swirled about them, the coins they wore like earrings in their nostrils jingled and the rings on their fingers jingled too, like tiny castanets. Entrancing, Ralph thought; thoroughly enchanting. Hypnotic, you might say. And there was a man in a loincloth, lying quietly on a bed of glowing coals! Another was swallowing fire, and still another was piercing his cheeks with a blade. No blood, no burn—amazing! In the center of it all stood a very skinny man on one foot, stark naked, his other leg bent at the knee, like a stork, unnoticing and—if you can believe it—apparently unnoticed, in a kind of Yogic trance. Oh, Bombay was a *very* strange place! Our trio stood huddled together, all agog. Too strange, too strange. Hot as it was, Anthony decided for reasons of comfort and safety that he would be more secure if he were peering from Emily's pouch, so he climbed in. It was warm, all right. Ralph arranged himself around her neck, boa fashion, his colorful coat of scales blending attractively with her many garlands of marigolds. Emily could move at a great rate, you know, and bound through the most crowded of bazaars, should it be necessary. It might be. Best get to Australia soon, Ralph thought. Though he was not without defenses, this place might be over his head. He felt responsible, being their guide, but he also felt rather sleepy.

"Suddenly, from behind, they heard a soft, mellifluous voice. 'Sirs and gracious madam,' the voice said, 'please to allow me to accompany you through the haunting splendors of my beautiful seaside city, to guide you through my house of mysteries dark and strange.' Emily turned abruptly, and necessarily Anthony and Ralph with her. There stood a man in an astonishingly white robe, considering the dirt surrounding them, and an equally white turban. 'I know them all,' he added. 'Most certainly you will need a guide, strangers like yourselves in my very foreign land.' He smiled. He was suave and smooth, slim, rather attractive, almost fair. 'Let my introduce myself. I am he who is called Hashish. I deal in dreams.'

" 'What an odd thing to say, young man,' Emily said. 'What sort of dreams do you deal in?'

" 'Pipe dreams?' Ralph asked.

" 'Oh, very fine dreams, very fine dreams, indeed,' the man replied. 'The finest. Let me take you to a shop of essences.'

" 'Shop of essences?' Emily asked.

" 'Oh, you know, Emily,' Ralph said. 'Don't you remember Cairo? There's one on every corner. In your country they call them perfumes. Joy, Arpège, Fruits de Nuit. It's all right.'

"What goes with our Ralph?" Andrew asked. "Is he intoxicated by the gyrations of the dancers, the fumes of frangipani and incense hanging heavy in the air? I am a little concerned about him."

"Go on," Julia said.

" 'Are they high in cost?' Emily asked, in her more formal, more British manner.

" 'Oh, most assuredly. Very high caste, very high caste indeed,' Hashish replied.

" 'Then I am afraid, sir, that you are sniffing up the wrong tree. We are simple travelers, weary from our journey, and we find ourselves now in straitened circumstances. We have many miles to go before we reach our destination, and money, alas, is not easily come by. We have nothing to spend on souvenirs, no matter how tempting the price, how marvelous the goods.'

" 'Ho, ho,' Hashish exclaimed, but rather mirthlessly. 'Ho, ho! In my country, when we speak of *caste*, we pronounce it *cost*. It is the station in life to which a man is born. Most assuredly'— he laughed heartily now—'I would not take you—fine, gentle things like yourselves, and obviously several cuts above this greasy crowd—to a shop for persons—excuse me, creatures—of low station. No, no, no. But as to the cost: my dear friends, the cost is nothing. Nothing. And I am sure my friend Ravi, who is naturally of the highest caste, will offer you a cooling libation for your trouble.'

" 'Lemonade, maybe?' Ralph asked, stretching his neck a little.

" 'Ah, you are familiar with our *nimbu pani*?'

" 'No,' Ralph said, 'merely thirsty.'

" 'It is made from the finest, sweetest, freshest limes—and a few other magical ingredients. Thrown in only to bring out the exquisite flavor, of course, to give it a little fillip. No need to list them. I shall certainly see that Ravi prepares you a *nimbu pani* beyond compare, for his are like none other's. The drink they call the *nimbu pani* in the Sea Lounge of the Taj Hotel? Ach! Pfui! The water of the streets, compared with Ravi's, and not worthy of the noble name.'

" 'I don't know, sir,' Emily said. 'We have little time. We are eager to see the sights of the city.'

" 'But I told you, fair madam, *I*, Hashish, will show you the sights, sights you would never otherwise behold. Come with me now. And your name, please, madam?'

" 'Miss Roo,' Emily replied. 'Emily Roo. Miss Roo will do.'

" 'And this cunning creature coiled so bewitchingly about your neck like a boa? Yet surely no boa, Miss Roo. A cobra, perhaps?'

" 'Ralph,' he said. 'Just Ralph.' Ralph felt sad. Sometimes he longed for a last name like everybody else. 'Ralph will suffice.'

"As if reading his mind, Emily said, 'Ralph Richardson,' giving him the first name that came into her head. 'And here, tucked in my pouch, is Mr. Richardson's cousin, Anthony Armadillo. And now, kind Hashish, we must be off. Ta-ta. Ciao. Shukran, 'afwan. Au revoir. Sayonara. In other words, Hashish, goodbye.' Emily, you see, did not trust Hashish. Sometimes, Julia, Emily is right.

"But Ralph was intrigued. 'Oh, let's give it a shot,' he said. 'What have we got to lose?'

" 'Plenty,' Emily replied, but slowly, reluctantly, she agreed to follow the smooth Hashish through the streets of beggars and strange dreams, past more dancing women and fakirs everywhere doing the weird things that fakirs do: lying on their beds of nails, chewing burning coals, standing naked on one foot, and so on.

The steadfast Anthony was a little frightened, and burrowed deeper into Emily's pouch, but Ralph was quite fascinated, stretching his neck to see the passing sights, flicking his tongue with avid interest, and arousing, it must be admitted, a little curiosity, a little fear himself. Never forget: he is a cobra, and cobras can strike. Even Ralph. Down the winding alleys they went, under ancient arches, through the narrow gateways, until they arrived—at last—at the shop of essences. The cunning Ravi greeted them effusively, ushering them into the courtyard, fluffing pillows, insisting they rest. He snapped his fingers and three musicians appeared and began playing in the corner, on the other side of the fountain. Five dancing animals followed, swathed in gossamer silk and dancing Indian dances. He snapped his fingers again to produce a huge tray laden with fruit—such fruits as Emily had never seen—and eventually, as had been promised, three frosty silver cups engraved with gloriously entwined figures from the *Kama Sutra* and filled with the cooling, fragrant, and delicious *nimbu pani*. Ravi did know how to squeeze a lime; they all agreed on that."

"What's the *Kama Sutra*, Daddy?"

"The *Kama Sutra*? Oh, for heaven's sake! How did I get into that? It's a long Indian poem, one of their classics. Like our *Canterbury Tales*, or *Beowulf*, or something. It just popped into my head, that's all."

"What's it about?"

"I don't really know. I've never read it. I could have chosen something else. Shall we make it the *Bhagavad-Gita*? That's a sacred Hindu text. Maybe more appropriate. I've never read that, either."

"Daddy! Come *on*! It's not fair to keep trying to change the story."

"Okay. So there they were, examining the cups with their artful, graceful scenes from some stranger, more distant world, nibbling strange fruits, listening to strange tunes, sipping their strange drinks—and growing just slightly drowsy. Just slightly, now. Nothing to be concerned about, Ralph thought, passing his forked tongue over his dry little lips. Snakes have very tiny lips, Julia. It was hot, after all; still morning but already growing very hot. Definitely a somnolent sort of day, and they were all feeling a little torpid as Hashish passed a jeweled bowl of pistachios and litchi nuts and the aromatic fruit of the durian tree, urging them to taste of these finer, even more exquisite pleasures of the house. The durian, he said, was a rarefied taste, but once acquired it was like none other, and nothing else would satisfy it. When they had tasted—the durian must indeed be an acquired taste, they decided, but no doubt they were learning—a servant appeared, bearing a magnificent Damascene dish of rosewater and lemons, with a matching ewer of the same fluid to pour over their fingertips or the equivalent, and cool scented towels to brush their lips. Then, only then, did Ravi produce his ravishing essences, one after another, passing them under their noses with a subtle flourish, filling the air with fragrance. Ah, India. We shall not see its like again. Ralph stretched out on the edge of the fountain, basking in the burning sun, sniffing the narcotic air. Snakes like sun, Julia, even when it's really hot. It relaxes them, makes them sleepy. Anthony burrowed into a cushion, and Emily was languidly leaning against the cushions on the long divan that filled one wall of the courtyard and curved around the corner to fill part of another, like the letter L. A lazy day in old Bombay. Home was never like this; nor was the *China Hand*, for that matter. India was a sensual assault, filling their ears with strange sounds, their nostrils with the fumes of unfamiliar flowers, their mouths with the juices of strange fruit, their eyes with wonder, and caressing their bodies with the unguent air. Indeed a feast for the senses; indescribably delicious. Even the vigilant Emily succumbed to the silken pleasures of a passing day in Bombay, and the most vigilant Ralph was stretched out limp with pleasure and delight beside the splashing fountain, a ewer of rosewater by his side. Anthony—dear Anthony—appeared to be sound asleep and snoring. Only Ravi and the smooth Hashish did not rest. Hustle, bustle; hurry, scurry. More *nimbu pani* was poured, more essences wafted through the shaded air. Time passed. Strange cigarettes were proffered from a satinwood box. 'Thank you, no, my dear Ravi. I don't do drugs.'

" 'But Miss Roo—may I call you Emily?—it is I, Hashish. I am not offering you *drugs*,' Hashish said; 'not your loathsome nicotine, or worse. You are not in Australia now, or vile Egypt, or even viler London. Not—God help us—New York! This is India. There are no *drugs* in India, the land of jasmine, of almonds, and of honey.'

" 'Never been to London,' Emily replied, taking the cigarette and examining it. It was long and thin and encased in the thinnest beaten silver foil. 'Very pretty,' she said. 'Oh, Ralph. Have you ever been to London?'

" 'No, Emily. Aleppo once, but never London. London is too cold.'

" 'Oh, what the hell.' Emily shrugged and accepted the flame from Ravi, who was hovering near. 'In for a dime, in for a dollar. You're only young once.' Hashish had moved on with his satin-wood box to Ralph, and because Ralph found it difficult to hold a cigarette, being so sleepy and his tail so limp—his tail, you know, functioned more or less as a grasping tool—Hashish held the slim silver tube to his lips while Ralph sucked in the heady fumes. Ralph figured it was all right. After all, Emily was doing it, and he sometimes relied on her to lead him in such matters, even though he, Ralph, was their stalwart guide. He did not notice, for a time, the strange misshapen flute made of a gourd and a bamboo stem and partially concealed in the robe of Hash-ish. 'More of that potion, please. My lips are very dry.' *Nimbu pani* splashed into his cup, poured by the skilled hand of Hashish. 'The fluid of the gods, worthy of the Pharaoh,' Ralph said, sigh-ing in the shimmering light, the slanting light of a fading Bombay afternoon. He cast his eyes toward Emily, and smiled dreamily. Emily smiled dreamily back. Ralph had a very pretty, a very sweet smile, Emily thought, and Ralph thought the same of Emily. Then Hashish slowly removed the flute from his robe, raised it to his lips, and began to weave back and forth, back and forth, playing his eerie melody as the other musicians quietly stole away and the five dancing animals now moved to another, different tune.

"Could one of those animals be a mongoose, the cobra's an-cient, dreaded enemy? Could it be? Ralph asked himself, but drowsily. Could *all* of them be? No, it was not possible. They were too pretty, and such good dancers, besides. One of them, though, had a wart on the end of her nose, and a mole on her cheek that sprouted long hairs. Where had he seen that mole before? No matter. 'Hashish,' Ralph asked, his voice coming from far, far away, 'what is the name of that fetching creature, the dancer in the sari of saffron silk, with the wart on the end of her nose and the mole sprouting hairs?'

" 'She is called Veronica,' Hashish replied in his soft, melli-fluous voice, scarcely interrupting his playing, 'Veronica the ra-diant, Veronica the fair.'

" 'She reminds me of a nasty old aunt I had once,' Ralph said, 'a biter if ever there was one, and venomous as a snake.' He smiled. 'Of course, she *was* a snake. Genus is destiny, as one of the great thinkers of my kind has written.' He looked again to-ward Emily, who seemed much more fair than Veronica, much more radiant, but Emily was talking quietly to Ravi and did not see him."

"Daddy," Julia said, "I'm getting scared."

"So am I," Andrew replied. "The light was fading now, and servants brought in pots of smoking incense, and more servants carried flaming torches, which they placed in sconces on the walls of the courtyard. Hashish continued playing in the flickering light; Anthony continued his soft snoring and Emily her dream-ing, while Ravi floated about in the deepening night, doing this and that, that and this, as the eerie melody played on, floating in patches in the narcotic air, and the dancing animals danced, and Ralph, poor Ralph, slipped, dying, into his trance. Oh, Julia, if only Hashish would play a little Bach! But he was not playing Bach. Slowly Ralph began to move. His little head, lying so quietly at the edge of the fountain, rose ever so gradually from the stones, and his little snake's eyes met and fixed on the beady eyes of Hashish, who did not stop his playing but instead quick-ened the pace. He had, it must now be clear—though it was not entirely clear to Ralph, so bewitched was he by the eerie tune, the beady eyes of Hashish—fallen into the insidious clutches of a charmer of snakes! A *sapera*! And beneath their saris of glowing colors, the lovely dancing creatures were not lovely at all but vicious mongooses, each and every one! And there were five of them! The bewitched Ralph, the dreaming Emily, and the still snoring Anthony were hopelessly outnumbered! Oh, frightful thing! Oh, terrible calamity! The danger was grave, and the white ship would soon be sailing."

"Andrew, you're scaring poor Julia to death!" He jumped. It was Ann. "I've been standing at the door listening for the last couple of minutes. That story's not baroque—it's bizarre. Stop it now. I'll put Julia to bed, and then I want you to help me."

"No, Mommy! Daddy has to finish the story. He can't leave it like this. You're going to Bermuda tomorrow!"

"I'll finish it quickly," Andrew said. He turned to Ann. "That's a promise. It'll only be a few more minutes. I want to finish it too, you know. I'll make it nice."

"Then call me when you're finished," she said, leaving the doorway, "and please make it soon. I'll tuck you in, Julia."

"Are you frightened, darling?" Andrew asked, turning to Julia.

"A little," she said. "It's a scary story."

"It *is* a scary story," Andrew agreed. "It scares me too. But we'll get them out of it. Everything will turn out all right. That's the thing about stories: everything always turns out all right."

"Not always. Remember *Charlotte's Web*? Charlotte spun her last web for Wilbur and died." Tears welled in Julia's eyes.

"Well, that's true. But it turned out the way it had to turn out, and that made it right, somehow. You understand?"

She lay there for some moments, snuggled in her blankets, not speaking. Finally she said, "Yes, Daddy, I think I understand. Tell the rest of the story."

"Okay. But Julia?"

"Yes."

"We have to go through a bad patch before everything comes out all right. Are you ready?"

"Yes."

"And Julia, remember that Ralph was not actually dying. He was just dead to the world, in a trance of his own."

"Okay."

"But of course, he was in grave danger. It is very dangerous to sink into a trance, a trance so deep that the world around you fades and vanishes. And that is what is happening to Ralph. The light, the sounds, the tastes and smells of the house of essences have cast their spell. Hashish holds Ralph in thrall. Slowly, slowly he rises from the stones, his hooded head and body seeming not to depend on the earth at all but to float in the air like a puppet on a string, weaving rhythmically back and forth, back and forth to the strange narcotic music of Hashish's flute. Ravi scurries quietly about, marshaling the five dancers, who have shed their gossamer robes and are now revealed not as lithe, lovely creatures at all but as five vicious mongooses in all their hideous horror. Oblivious to the danger, Emily reclines dreamily against the cushions, her limpid eyes drooping. Anthony has crawled out from under his cushion and is snuggling up to her. He climbs into her pouch again and falls back to sleep, his darling armadillo head resting against her downy kangaroo body, like a mother and a child, an armadillo and his beloved kangaroo, unaware of the dire situation that envelops them. Suddenly, one mongoose—Veronica, it is—bares her fangs with ravenous desire, and snarls, not loudly but just loudly enough to jar Ralph the slightest bit from his trance, and for a fraction of a second his veiled eyes flick from Hashish and the flute he continues to play, to the somnolent Emily with Anthony in her pouch, to the hideous mongoose dancers. That fraction of a second is enough. The veils fall in a flash from his eyes. He gives the tiniest little twitch, so tiny it is not seen by the evil Hashish or the wicked Ravi, who is busy trying to keep the mongooses under control, anyway. You see, Hashish and Ravi do not want to kill little Ralph. Far worse. They want to capture him, destroy him, hold him forever in thrall. Ralph gazes on the lovely Emily, beautiful and fair as Dante's Beatrice, and the darling Anthony snuggled so comfortably there, and he realizes in one splendid clarifying moment that he must save his friends and save himself as well. The situation is dire, perhaps beyond his powers. But he must make the effort. His mind is clear now, sharp as icy water. With a tremendous effort of will he instantly puffs his head up to his fullest, most terrifying glory—and he *strikes*! The cowardly Hashish screams and drops his flute. The mongooses rush to attack, tripping Ravi in the charge, and in the confusion they turn on him, their cruel master, tearing at his robes, overturning his trays of essences, the trays and bowls of fruit, the ewers of rosewater. Hashish, the cringing coward, is near faint with fear, but finally turns and flees the courtyard, turban askew, his white robe flapping around him. Ralph speeds straight to Emily, slaps her with his tail—slap! slap! slap!—three times to waken her, springs to her neck, and spurs her on. Out of the courtyard they charge, into the darkened street, dark as a pocket, as fast as Emily's bounding legs can carry them, which is very, very fast indeed, past—would you believe? —the Dowager Duchess of Dork in her hat of many veils who lurks waiting outside the house of essences. Waiting for what?

Waiting for Ralph, of course. She had engaged Hashish to en-snare poor Ralph for her trophy room in Dorkminster Hall, leaving her son, the Duke, to sip his *nimbu pani* in the Sea Lounge of the Taj Mahal Hotel. Ha! The perfidious Hashish has betrayed her, taken her coins of gold but intending to keep Ralph a captive forever in his own dark house of essences, taking him out now and then to demonstrate his evil prowess as a *sapera*, a charmer of cobras. With merely a blithe wave in the Duchess's direction, the trio race toward the harbor, taking a wrong turn here and there but always heading into the fresh breeze from the sea, until finally they reach the shore. Oh, no! The white ship gleaming like a ghost on the dark water is moving! They have missed the boat! But wait! Snakes are excellent and swift swimmers—although kangaroos don't take so readily to water and armadillos detest it. Clever Ralph quickly comes up with a solution. Emily will lie on her back in the water so that her pouch is in the air—nobody wants Anthony to drown—Ralph will curl his tail around Emily's neck, and just to be safe she will hold the end of it in her mouth, taking care not to bite, and Ralph, his head up high, will streak triumphant toward the ship, drawing his friends behind him. Quick as a flash they are in the water, Ralph swimming with all his might to overtake the swiftly moving ship, moving faster now, out of the harbor and toward the open sea. Once the great ship reaches the vast ocean, things will be very difficult indeed. Faster and faster he swims, Emily and Anthony behind him, Emily kicking her feet as fast as she can to help, until, just as they begin to feel the great surge of the sea, he sinks his teeth into a line left trailing from the ship—thanks to the carelessness of a drunken deckhand. Slithering up a line is no problem for Ralph. He tells Emily to hold tight to the line, and to clamp her teeth into the end of it. He slithers up to the main deck, finds the rope ladder used in emergencies, pushes it with all his might to the rail, and drops it over. Emily climbs up, exhausted, Anthony in her pouch. 'Time to get out, Anthony,' Emily says. 'I am very tired. We must all make it to stateroom nine on our own.' And together the three of them slithered, crawled, and hopped, each according to his or her fashion, to their cabin, where Emily fell into bed, Anthony onto his cushion, and Ralph sought the peace and safety of his dear wicker basket, the basket he called home. And they fell sound asleep and slept the night away as the ship sailed south through calm seas, bringing them ever so slightly closer to Australia, Emily's beloved homeland and their ultimate destination.

"And guess who missed the boat? The Duchess. But the Duke didn't seem to mind; he assumed his not entirely dear mother was sipping a pink gin in the ship's lounge as he too slept peacefully in his cabin, dreaming spicy dreams about the tea and spice plantations of Malangprabang, the delicious *nimbu pani* from the Taj Hotel gurgling happily in his tummy."

Julia looked sleepy. "That was nice, Daddy. Thank you."

"You're welcome, Julia. Thank *you*. You're a good listener. That was a long story. I'm worn out myself."

"Daddy?"

"Yes?"

"Please, don't go to Bermuda tomorrow. I don't want you to go to Bermuda tomorrow."

"I have to, angel. Everything will be all right—don't you worry. We won't be gone long, only a few days. And Mommy and I will find a surprise for you, some strange and wonderful thing that you can find only in Bermuda."

"What? What can you find only in Bermuda?"

"I don't know, but there must be something. Good night, baby." He kissed her. "I love you. I'll send your mother in to tuck you in."

Andrew moved the pictures that night, and together they found a place for the table and settled the foyer again. The secretary looked handsome there, and in the morning Julia found the two secret compartments beside the pigeonholes and appropriated them for her own. Everyone agreed that it was a fine piece of furniture—"Not," Andrew said, "that we needed another one."

"Well, it does make the foyer look more comfortable," Ann said. Then she laughed. "Start working on the Chinese rug."

Ann had not seemed especially eager to go to Bermuda. She was tired of traveling, having returned from Miami not long before and London shortly before that, she had things of her own she ought to be doing, and she didn't ordinarily enjoy events connected with his work—the people, she thought, were too theatrical and talked of little else besides themselves—but he had prevailed; a man cannot for long remain content in his own room, no matter how comfortable. "It's scarcely costing us anything. Sam Walcott is picking up the tab for the flight and the hotel," he'd said, "Mrs. Bridges will stay with Julia, and we'll have fun. You'll need a rest after my mother's visit. I won't really be working. We'll have plenty of time to play. Wouldn't it be great to lie on a beach beside the sea? Besides, you like the Walcotts."

"And what's left of the Rockefeller grant is burning a hole in your pocket," she added, laughing; but they had finally agreed that it seemed a reasonable time and certainly a good opportunity for them to get away by themselves—a little honeymoon, as it were, on the traditional honeymoon isle. Ann packed a new evening dress and assorted other finery—she liked stylish clothes and took considerable satisfaction in her appearance, however much she felt she ought to be above such ephemera—and they prepared to embark, aloof from and a little contemptuous of this world of things and the things of the world with which they surrounded themselves. They were a lot alike in some ways.

Their departure that Saturday morning was more confused than even their haphazard attitude toward time had accustomed them to. They'd all overslept. Ann felt slightly sick. He'd dropped a glass in the bathroom and it shattered all over the floor. There was trouble on the subway, so Mrs. Bridges was late. Julia seemed fretful. He'd mislaid a book he wanted to read. Ann reminded him that he hadn't returned Daisy Curtis's phone call, but after picking up the phone and starting to dial he'd decided there wasn't time now. Finally they closed their bags and Andrew carried them to the door. Frank took them down in the elevator, telling Julia—she and Mrs. Bridges were going down to wave them off—that it was too early for a treat, but maybe he'd have something for her later, and Andrew carried their bags to the gate.

"Here comes Tiny," Andrew said, as Henry the doorman flagged a cab and Tiny left his stand and walked toward them. "Well, hello there, Mr. Tiny. Are you coming to see us off?"

"I had to see this little girl," he said, "tell her that Tiny'd look after her." He bobbed his head toward Ann. "I told Mr. Mac that I wouldn't let no trouble touch this little girl. I'll be watching out for her, don't you fret. You don't need to fret about Miss Julia with Tiny holding the corner."

Ann and Andrew laughed. "Thanks, Tiny," Ann said. "We won't worry as long as you're here."

"I still wish you weren't going," Julia said.

"We have to, darling," Andrew said. "It won't be for long. You'll have a heap of fun. But remember to behave. Henry and Frank and Tiny and Mrs. Bridges—they'll all be watching out for you." He hugged her. "You'll be a girl well guarded."

"Maybe Frank will have a surprise for you this afternoon," Ann said. "I bet he will. That would be fun."

"Will you send me postcards?"

"Of course, sweetheart," Ann said. "We'll send you postcards every day. But they may take a few days to arrive." She squeezed her hand.

"And we'll have a surprise for you when we get back," Andrew said. "Then you can come with me to see Tiny and you two can tell me all about what happened while we were away." Sometimes Julia liked to sit with him while Tiny shined his shoes. She liked Tiny; they all did.

Henry had found them a cab, put their luggage in the trunk, and was holding the door open. Ann had a few final instructions for Mrs. Bridges, they all shook hands, and shook hands with Henry and Tiny too, kissed Julia, and after a final flurry of handshakes and happy kisses and goodbye hugs, they sallied forth waving and smiling, full of ardor and hubris, and confident that nothing could really disturb the natural order of their days, least of all a holiday in Bermuda. "All we need is confetti," Andrew said, taking Ann's hand and squeezing it.

"I'm glad I decided to go," she said, squeezing him back and moving a little closer toward him. "I'm looking forward to seeing you again."

"Me too." He tapped her wedding ring with his. He hadn't done that in a long time. She looked at him and laughed, returning the signal. As they were leaving the park, he glanced at his watch. "It's awfully late."

It was one of those crystalline May mornings in New York, all the more dazzling for their rarity. They missed their scheduled flight from Kennedy—the taxi driver maintained a very leisurely pace across Manhattan that Saturday morning—and had to take a helicopter to Newark for a flight that would get them to Bermuda in time for dinner. But it was only money, in a sense not really their money, and it didn't bother them much. "We'll let it be a Rockefeller expense," Andrew said, laughing; "we certainly can't ask Sam Walcott to pay for it." They enjoyed the flight above the sparkling, sunlit city, and the little misadventure would give them something to dine out on that night. And of course they made it in time for dinner. They always did.

BERMUDA IN THE SARGASSO SEA

Bermuda is not one but approximately one hundred forty-five separate islands located in the midst of the Sargasso Sea, an immense, slowly moving and relatively warm eddy within the currents of the North Atlantic gyre. Still by comparison, the Sargasso Sea is a discrete body of water formed and enclosed by the clockwise flow of the swifter waters of the Gulf Stream on the west, the North Atlantic Drift and the Canary Current on the east. Its borders, therefore, are water and water only. This ever-growing, elliptical sea extends southward from the lower tip of Greenland to the latitude of Santiago, Cuba, covering the deepest part of the Western North Atlantic Basin (5,000 to 23,000 feet at its maxi-

mum), and continues to widen as the continental land masses framing the Atlantic continue their slow, inexorable drift apart. The expansion of the Atlantic and the Sargasso within it is scarcely perceptible, of course, but during the course of a man's lifetime it amounts to approximately his height.

The sea, the surface of which consists of a lens-shaped mass of warmer water floating on the cold ocean depths where the eels of the North Atlantic breed, is characterized by the abundance of brown seaweed (gulfweed, or sargasso weed, from which the sea has taken its name) borne up by small translucent amber floats, or bladders, that resemble berries. This sargasso weed (Sargassum) *is pelagic, passing its entire life cycle on the open seas. It sometimes forms windrows and very large rafts that can extend from horizon to horizon. These flotillas of* Sargassum *harbor a unique sea life, although the Sargasso Sea itself is a biological desert and the plankton that is a basic food supply for fish is sparse in comparison with richer coastal and upwelling waters.*

Such great quantities of sargasso weed deceived early explorers sailing through the horse latitudes (a belt of high barometric pressure, calm water and light winds thirty to thirty-five degrees North) into thinking they were near land when in fact they were many hundreds of miles from shore. Fueled by returning seamen's tales and a dearth of empirical evidence, legends grew and flourished: of vessels lost forever, ensnared in huge, impenetrable masses of floating weed; of mariners driven mad from salt water and perishing from lack of food; of strange, inhuman cries rending the night (probably the voice of the cahow, or Bermuda petrel, a small sea bird which breeds on the islands and feeds on the Sargasso).

Of the "dreadful coast" of the Bermudas itself, a contemporary account (Howe's Annals) *of the shipwreck of the* Sea Venture *in 1609 says the islands "were of all nations said and supposed to be enchanted and inhabited with witches and devils, which grew by reason of accustomed monstrous thunder, storm, and tempest, near unto those islands. Also for that the whole coast is so wondrous dangerous of rocks that few can approach them but with unspeakable hazard of shipwreck." When the exhausted voyagers finally made it to shore, the reality proved altogether different. The soil and water were "most sweet and delicate." The survivors ventured farther into the island for food, "which being never yet inhabited by any people, was overgrown with woods, and the woods replenished with wild swine, which swine as it is very probable swam thither out of some shipwreck. They found also great multitude of fowl of sundry kinds, being then in a manner very tame. They found some fruit, as mulberries, pears, and palmytoes [palmettos], with stately cedar trees. And in the sea, and in the rocks, great plenty of most pleasant and wholesome fish."* The foundering of the Sea Venture, *which led to the English settlement of Bermuda, caused a sensation when news of it reached England a year later, and Howe's account of it and his descripton of "The Bermodes" is thought to have provided some of the inspiration for Shakespeare's last comedy,* The Tempest.

Yet still today legends persist of a mysterious, doom-ridden Bermuda Triangle where ships and planes may suddenly disappear without warning or explanation. The triangle, with Bermuda its northernmost point and extending in a line from Miami to beyond Puerto Rico on the south, covers part of the Sargasso Sea. As with most such legends, rational explanations can be offered, and fact readily unsnarled from myth. Although sailing ships may have been briefly becalmed, no ship was ever frozen in the weeds, which are easily pushed aside. Vessels have disappeared, however, in enormously powerful water spouts, sometimes but certainly uncommonly as much as five miles in diameter, which have been seen to lift a thirty-foot yacht out of the water. These spouts are caused by a sharp, critical disparity between the temperature of the air and the temperature of the water, and a correspondingly sudden drop in barometric pressure. Small ones, thirty to forty feet wide, are commonly seen by voyagers. The same thermal energy produces tornadoes on land. The phenomenon is more dangerous at sea, however, if less frequently encountered by man, because of the greater density and hence greater power of the water. As to the mysterious disappearance of aircraft in the Bermuda Triangle, the planes most likely encountered flocks of migrating birds, their numbers in the millions, flying from the Canadian Maritimes, New England and the Mid-Atlantic states to their winter feeding grounds in South America. A collision of a plane with such vast numbers of birds can cause severe and immediate damage, even incapacitating the aircraft as hundreds are sucked into the jet engines. Inexperienced navigators, too, may be confused by the unusual compass variation between true North and magnetic North in the area, which can be as much as fifteen degrees, depending on the season. Knowledgeable Bermuda sailors approaching the is-

lands navigate by the stars because of the unreliability of compass readings there.

The Bermuda islands are centered sixty-four degrees forty-five minutes East, thirty-two degrees twenty minutes North, occupying a fishhook-shaped speck of twenty-one square miles on the sea's vast expanse. Only about twenty of these islands are inhabited, however, and the seven main islands commonly thought of as "Bermuda" are connected by bridges and causeways, giving them the appearance of one continuous strip of land extending twenty-two miles end to end but only two and a half miles at its widest point. The sea is scarcely more than a mile from any spot on Bermuda. About the size of Manhattan, the Bermudas lie isolated on the vast ocean, the only bits of land to disturb the surface of the North Atlantic between the Azores and the Canaries far to the east, and Cape Hatteras, the closest point on the North American continent, five hundred seventy miles to the west. New York is seven hundred eighty miles away and London over three thousand.

The islands are actually the protruding peaks of a long extinct undersea volcano. Three such volcanic cones lie in a southwest to northeast line within a space of twenty miles, but only the southern rim of the most northerly, Mount Bermuda, breaks the water to form the single zone of dry land in the entire Sargasso Sea. The Bermuda Rise, as it is known, began in a climactic upheaval on the ocean floor one hundred million years ago, erupting with unimaginable force to form, in the course of time, the gentle, rolling islands we know today, the highest point of which is a mere 259 feet above sea level. (The possibility of renewed volcanic activity is extremely remote, however; the floor under the Sargasso Sea is geologically stable and has been for eons, although active volcanoes do line the Mid-Atlantic Ridge on the sea's eastern margin.)

Thus these lonely islands are volcanic in origin, although not in surface composition. Ocean waves and rain eroded the exposed cone of the volcano, washing volcanic sand down into the sea where it formed a platform just beneath the water's surface. In warm periods, coral grew and flourished on this platform, which also served as a collection ground for calciferous mollusk shells washed from the shore. Glacial cycles of low sea level alternating with warmer periods of high sea level created sand from the shells and coral rock. The sand was blown into dunes by the wind and over time was solidified by *the rain into aeolian limestone, consisting largely of particles of shells and old coral rock, before the sea rose again and the entire protracted process was repeated time after distant time, building the islands over the course of many eons.*

Aeolian limestone forms the cap of Bermuda today and is widely used as building material there. The original volcanic rock that is the base of the islands lies far below the surface of the sea. The topographical features of Bermuda, including its many fascinating caves and strange natural rock arches, were formed by humic acid from dying vegetation percolating into the stone and dissolving some of the lime.

The coral reef that surrounds Bermuda is the northernmost in the world, and one of the most lush. It teems with a great variety of fish; sea fans and brain corals may reach ten feet across. There are no mammals native to Bermuda and one native reptile: the lizard. There are no poisonous insects or snakes. There are no rivers or streams, and wells must be drilled horizontally to tap fresh water because the surface stone is so porous that rainwater flows through it and out to the sea. There has never been a frost in Bermuda since official weather records have been kept. The climate is sub-tropical. The best beaches are on the south shore, which is more mature in terms of geological time, but the swimmer should be wary of the occasional rip tide, which can be dangerous. The capital of Bermuda and its largest city is Hamilton. Because of its mild climate and beautiful sand beaches, tourism is the chief industry of Bermuda, although many flowers, including the Easter lilies for which the islands are famous, are grown for export. The people (population 53,000) are largely of English, Portuguese and African descent, Negroes being in the majority.

" 'Ware the lizard lieth lurking in the grass,' " Andrew said, finishing the article he'd been reading on the flight, and handing it to Ann. He loved her in that blue linen dress, pearls glowing against it. She looked so beautiful: like a girl still, but enhanced now by a woman's full register.

"Lizard?"

"It says there that the lizard is the only reptile native to Bermuda. Read the article. It's interesting. I had it copied from a kind of encyclopedia at the library while you were away. We're going to be sitting on top of an ancient volcano."

"Are you sure you really want to go here?" Ann asked, taking his hand and beginning to read. "It could blow."

"It won't. It's extinct. The only thing we have to worry about is the birds, but it's not fall, so they won't be migrating. Oh, yes, and the compass. It does strange things around Bermuda, but I guess I'll let the pilot worry about that. Read it. You'll understand." He continued holding her hand while she read, looking out the window of the plane and down at the tiny white clouds, fluffy as little pillows, and far below the brilliant, incredibly brilliant, blue sea shining in the sunlight. He loved the way light played on water and water returned it in a million coruscating beams. He'd grown up on the water. He was a water person. "I love the sea," he sighed, mostly to himself, and there below him he saw the reef, dark green and brown in the blue sea, and as the plane descended farther, the islands themselves, dotted with white roofs and looking very flat on the water.

The sun was intense and the air humid, but the breeze was cooling and fresh as they rode, windows down, in the taxi toward their hotel. Andrew was still holding Ann's hand lightly in his own. It seemed a languid afternoon, a lazy afternoon, meant for a long slow drink on a shaded terrace above the sea, and then a nap, as if they had passed through time and the hour no longer mattered. He was sleepy in a pleasant sort of way. He watched the narrow road loop and turn, passing now through arches of trees so thick the sunlight could not penetrate—the driver said they were poincianas—and then so close to the white stone walls and lush hedges of oleander and hibiscus that he could have reached out and brushed them with his hand, reached out and plucked a blossom. At times it seemed to Andrew as if he were going through a dark woods, a dark and lovely woods, before the road took a sharp climb and emerged abruptly as a breathtaking corniche, splendid in the sunlight, with sudden, dazzling views of the sea below. *"Brightness falls from the air"*: the line sang in his head. It was a long ride to the gates of their hotel—a sprawling, vaguely pink and quietly luxurious place—and when they arrived they went directly to their room and had two Tom Collinses sent up. The drink struck them as funny—neither of them had had a Tom Collins in years—but right. They sat on their balcony for a few minutes, sipping their drinks, taking in the lush garden view and, off there in the distance, the twinkling, sunlit sea. They continued sipping them as they settled into the room, soon moving them to the table beside one of the two huge beds—"big enough for an army," Andrew said as they lay down upon it, hands entwined, and began in a leisurely sort of way to kiss and fondle one another, and eventually to make love in their lovely yellow room, the curtains blowing gently in the breeze. Reprievèd, Andrew thought, reprievèd. He smiled and drifted easily into sleep.

That evening they had dinner with the Walcotts. The Walcotts were somewhat older than themselves, funny, attractive, but, Ann thought, a little on the silly side. They loved to dance. In New York they were always up for an evening in the Café Carlyle listening to Bobby Short; they knew all the songs, and all the people, too. Sam was a highly successful producer, and producers, particularly good ones, came in handy. Molly was a striking woman, tall, patrician, with thick black hair and remarkable cornflower eyes, and more thoughtful than she first appeared to be, or, for that matter, believed herself to be. When she wasn't playing tennis or decorating furniture with découpage or taking care of Sam, she designed clothes and jewelry which were sold, from time to time, in places like Bendel's. She was good at it, but didn't pursue that career with much vigor. What she was really good at was découpage, a minor art, perhaps, but a lovely one. Andrew had seen several objects she'd decorated, including a beautiful screen covered with exotic tropical birds and then layer after painstaking layer of varnish—it had taken her months—but she didn't seem to have much confidence in the results, or even in the worth of the pursuit, dismissing it as a hobby, as if it were equivalent to collecting teacups. Andrew thought the découpage was worth a lot more than the clothes and the jewelry, and he would have liked to have something she'd made, but for obscure reasons of her own she couldn't bring herself to sell any of it, and she'd never offered to give him a piece, either. He wished she had, but more he wished she could believe that what she did was at least worth doing. She came from one of those inbred Boston families with more than a trace of talent in its genes, but with more than a trace of madness, too. Molly seemed fearful of both, and at fifty and beautiful still, a little restless. Her mother, it was said, had tried everything once and, liking it all, most things more than once. Mad as a hatter now, she had to be tended by nurses. Sam was avuncular, garrulous, generous; a wonderful storyteller. The fact that he was an important producer might have made him more attractive in Andrew's eyes, although he didn't really think so: he liked him. Of course Andrew was always on the lookout for someone like Sam, and he hoped that Sam was on the lookout for someone like him; *41 East 73rd* still lacked a producer in New York. And he could enjoy an evening with Bobby Short, too. Sam's generosity seemed boundless. He always insisted on pay-ing wherever they went, just as he was paying for their Bermuda holiday, saying he could charge it off to one production or an-other—"feeding the talent," as he put it.

Both the Walcotts had charm and good manners, qualities Andrew had once dismissed as unimportant but which he now found redeeming. They made everything easier in a world where so much was hard, not the least of which was sitting through dinners with boorish egotists, and the Walcotts were certainly not that. Andrew felt he had endured more than his share of such dinners, and so had Ann, egotism being a condition of survival in the theater and boorishness a common affliction. The only prob-lem with an evening with the Walcotts was not that they both loved a party but that when they partied the party never ended, and to spend a few days in their company, as Andrew and Ann were about to do, was to come to feel like Scott Fitzgerald at four in the morning, when the party had been over for years. Except for the fact that they worked, and worked hard, the Walcotts did sometimes seem like a couple from a Fitzgerald novel. It was the look they cultivated, but it was only a look. Andrew knew he'd never hear that they'd been fished out of the fountain in front of the Plaza at the end of one of the madcap evenings of their lives.

Sam prided himself on knowing the best places in whatever corner of the world he found himself. In Los Angeles he stayed at the Bel Air, nicely removed from the flashier hotels in Beverly Hills to the east but at least as luxurious. In London he tended to favor Claridge's. In New York he and Molly lived in a spectacular apartment on Beekman Place, overlooking the river, although they preferred their rambling house in Connecticut, a relatively modest structure on an immodest piece of land, with a profusion of flowers and a bountiful vegetable garden, a spring-fed pond but no pool, and a tennis court that seemed always to be filled with the laughter of their daughters and their daughters' friends. It was there that Molly had her studio. And this night in Bermuda, Sam had found a magnificent restaurant on a spectacular rocky perch above the sea, where the four of them dined on the terrace and laughed at Sam's stories. He knew all the gossip—the inside skinny, as he called it—about the people people gossip about. It was the gossip that Ann found a little silly, interesting up to a point, maybe, but for her the point was soon reached. Also, Sam consulted an astrologer before committing himself to a production or setting the opening day. Andrew rather liked that; it was somehow endearing and human, a tiny crack in a seemingly invulnerable façade. Besides, maybe it worked. *Something* certainly worked for him. "The theater," he liked to say, quoting Robert Anderson, "is a place where you can make a killing but not a living." He'd made a killing.

"You're lucky," Sam said, after Andrew and Ann had recounted, with some dramatic embellishment, the saga of their journey. "We're all lucky to have arrived at all. We're in the Bermuda Triangle, you know. Ships, planes—they just vanish. Gone. Zip. No trace. No distress calls, either, a lot of the time."

"Oh, come on, Sam," Ann said. "It's the birds. Those planes flew into the autumn migration and the birds clogged their engines. I just read about it."

"Sure it's the birds," Sam said. "It takes a hell of an albatross to drop a plane, kiddo. I've read about it too. And those giant whirlpools like underwater cyclones? A big freighter disappeared a few years ago, and then that ocean racer vanished a little later. I follow these things. I like to know where danger lurks."

"You can't be too careful," Andrew said.

"But Sam, ships do sometimes sink."

"Without a trace?"

"Well, they run into storms. They spring leaks. And there are those waterspouts. They're just like tornadoes, only over water. They're caused by a difference in temperature between the air and the water."

"Ann, for a nice Catholic girl, and so beautiful, too, you're entirely too rational." Sam laughed, and squeezed her hand.

"One of us has to be," Andrew said. And yes, he thought, isn't she beautiful? Especially beautiful tonight, her pale hair illuminated against the twilight; her face, her throat, her pearls glowing in the mellow flame of the huge hurricane lamp burning on their table. Ann smiled and picked up a flower, one of the small magenta orchids above each plate, and tucked it into his mother's diamond arrow, his wedding gift to her, that sparkled in that delicious hollow near her shoulder, beneath her collarbone, before her breast began its soft rise. Her dress was the color of rich cream, a soft creamy silk with a rosy tinge as if a vial of blood had been poured into the vat of cream, suffusing it with the faintest blush, like the luster of certain special peonies. The silk curved and flowed over her body, moving softly as she breathed, as the blood flowed. He wanted to touch his lips to her, enfold her lightly in his arms like the air that embraced her. He touched his hand for a moment to her thigh, feeling the cool silk and the warmth emanating from within. She glanced toward him, smiling, and reached beneath the table to squeeze his hand as she turned her face back to Sam. He wanted suddenly to ravish her, and he felt, in the sudden fullness of his feelings, strangely like crying.

"But Sam," Ann said, a teasing smile playing across her face, "I do allow for the work of the devil. From time to time, of course —not all the time. The nuns used to warn us against him. He goes to the Protestant boys' school."

"What would a bad Jewish boy from Brooklyn know about that?" Sam said, and everyone laughed. A sudden puff of air ruffled the edge of the tablecloth, and the candle flickered in its globe. "There he is now. They always said this place was the devil's isle."

"Sam, you're entirely too weird," Molly said. "Sometimes, Ann, I think he believes it. I need a drink, dear. I think we all do." And Sam beckoned the waiter and ordered another round of daiquiris, which they sipped in silence for a time as the twilight sank quickly into starlit night above them, the sea lapped easy at the shore, and the breeze that had been playing fitfully in the casuarina trees slowly faded and died. The flame that burned within the shining glass on their table, illuminating it and their faces around it, the other flames lighting the tables and faces around them, the lanterns marking the edges of the terrace: all glowed soft and steady in the softly beaded air. It was a fluid night, luminous and still.

"Prospero's magic isle," Molly said, quietly breaking the hush, "where bones are coral and pearls are eyes, and

"Nothing of him that doth fade
But doth suffer a sea change
Into something rich and strange.

What a magical moment! What a perfect, magical night! Shakespeare had it right."

They all agreed that he did, and then they turned to the menus. As they were ordering, Andrew noticed a young couple sitting side by side at a nearby table, against the edge of the terrace. They seemed very attractive, he thought, and very young; full of delight in each other, like honeymooners. There was something touching about them, something sweet and almost . . . almost innocent, he supposed. They must be honeymooners. The young man was wearing a dark summer suit that had the shapeless cut but good fabric of Brooks Brothers, and a paisley tie—rather like the paisley shawl Ann had put over her shoulders earlier and that now hung prettily from the back of her chair. Andrew could see, when the young man studied the menu in his hands, that just the right amount of immaculate cuff was showing beneath the sleeves of his jacket. He was trying to appear very grown-up. He looked, really, like a student from the Fifties, as if the turbulence of the last decade had passed him utterly by. He was dark, though she was fair—rather awkward-looking in a pleasing sort of way; not so good-looking as he, but still quite pretty enough in her pretty summer dress that reminded Andrew of one Ann used to have: black cotton piped in the color she called bone, and the girl wore shoes that matched. Ann had had a pair very much like them, but without the little straps. Andrew smiled.

The waiter served their plates. As they were eating, Sam said, "There's a Russian who says that these disturbances on the sea around here are caused by forces of the sun and the moon. Their gravitational pull draws the molten rock beneath the ocean floor."

"Tides under the earth?" Andrew asked. "In the magma?"

"Well, there are tides on the ocean. Why not tides under it? The rock is liquid, and it's ionized. When it flows, the compasses and gyroscopes go crazy. They do go crazy around here, you know. That's when you have these sudden violent storms, mysterious calms, and all the rest."

"Sam, dear, we all know who's a little crazy." Molly rolled her eyes. "The next thing you know, Ann, he'll be asking us for our signs. Tell us your sign, darling," she said to her husband. "It may explain something." Everyone laughed, Sam included.

"You're making fun of me, Molly. You'd think you were a Virgo, instead of a mixed-up Gemini."

"No, Sam," Ann said, "I'm the Virgo."

"Yes, but probably your moon's in Pisces. There's got to be something to stir the waters."

"Andrew's the Pisces." Ann looked at him and laughed. "He's a slippery fish."

"That explains it," Andrew said, laughing with her, pressing his hand against her leg, his foot against her shoe. "Lord knows where my moon is."

"Speaking of the moon," Sam said, "that Russian scientist all of you are mocking says that the disturbances are much more common when the moon is either new or full and closest to the earth. Its gravitation pull is strongest then."

"I guess that's indisputable," Andrew said. "The tides are always highest in Maine during a full moon."

"Tell me," Sam said, momentarily diverted, "when is Aldrich showing up? I thought he'd be here tonight. We should talk."

"I don't know," Andrew said. "When I last spoke to him, he hadn't made up his mind. You know Michael: he'll breeze in at the last minute."

"And with some pretty young thing on his arm," Molly added, taking the orchid from her place and tucking it into her hair.

"That too," Andrew said. "He does like young things."

"Nothing wrong with youth," Sam said. "Except that they don't know anything yet. Too soon old, and too late smart, as the Pennsylvania Dutch say."

" *'Young we loved each other and were ignorant,'* " Andrew murmured. "As the poet said." He observed his young couple again. They had been lingering over their wine, apparently; their food had just arrived and they were beginning to eat. He was picking at his meal, but she ate with gusto, her face turned slightly toward him. She had very white teeth. She looked thoroughly in love—and seemed very hungry; he, his fork ignored in his hand, looked bewitched, enraptured. As she ate, Andrew noticed, she was stroking his thigh with her free hand, slowly back and forth. He had a grin on his face, a sort of bemused, foolish grin, as if he couldn't quite believe what was happening down there on his leg but he certainly didn't want it to stop. No wonder he wasn't eating. Andrew laughed to himself.

"But Michael's no youth," Ann said, putting down her fork. "Sam, this fish is marvelous—fresh enough to leap off the plate. I'm sorry I can't finish it. I wish I could take the rest of it back to the hotel for breakfast, but I'm afraid it might not keep until morning. Thank you, Sam. You always find a wonderful spot."

"You could take the fish," Andrew said. "There's a refrigerator in the room."

"No matter. I'll leave it." They had all finished their meal now, and coffee was being served. No one wanted dessert, but Sam insisted they try the island liqueur, Bermuda Gold, a sweet but not too overwhelming concoction made of a local fruit— loquats, the waiter said—and tasting of apricots.

"We can always find another fish," Sam said. "The reefs around Bermuda are full of them. Farther out, it's supposed to be a desert, most of the life concentrated in the weeds. All kinds of strange fish live there"—he gestured toward the dark water, Andrew following with his eyes—"fish not found anywhere else. There's a whole world of its own in the Sargasso Sea—little creatures working, feeding, living on those weeds. And hanging on, I hope, for dear life." He laughed. "Because if they fall off, that's it."

"Downed by the moon in the Bermuda Triangle?" Andrew asked, smiling, teasing him.

Sam laughed. "Of course. That's got to be it. In fact, most of them aren't true swimmers. They need the weeds. You know— like us."

"We were just reading about it on the plane," Andrew said. "The library copied an article for me. I had a book about it when I was a kid, too. We dug it out when my mother was visiting, and she read it to Julia."

"I'm sorry we couldn't make your party," Molly said. "I'd have liked to meet your mother."

"I'm sorry you couldn't make it too," Ann said. "It was a last-minute thing, very spur-of-the-moment. We were lucky anybody made it."

"I suppose that's one way to look at it," Andrew said. "It was a fairly wild party. That crazy Hope Harvey brought her crazier therapist, the dining room was given over to the radical caucus, dope was smoked. And my mother rose graciously above it all— apparently she didn't notice the drugs. Yes, all fairly crazy. Michael saved it."

"I thought you were going to credit me with that," Ann said. "Certainly it wasn't Andrew's mother's usual crowd. In retrospect, not quite the group I would have chosen for her—or for anyone else, as far as that goes. But you may have another chance to meet her, Sam. She'll be out again in the fall, if Andrew's play opens."

"We'll work on that," he said.

"That would be nice." Andrew hoped he sounded sufficiently casual. A fading pianist in the corner by the bar had begun to play the sort of sophisticated show tunes played in places like the Carlyle: the old, familiar songs—Porter, Gershwin, Sondheim— cool, witty, a graceful whiff of nostalgia and harmless irony, coupled with a lot of flirtatious innuendo directed toward the blue-haired ladies in their pink and lime-green dresses sitting with their madras husbands, all clustered around the tables near the piano. He sang a little less well than he played, but his phrasing was good, and the music drifted pleasantly over the terrace. Andrew took a drink of the liqueur, glancing across at his young couple once again. He wanted to check on them, to see that they were all right. They had finished their meal—or at least, she had; he'd scarcely touched his plate. He had the same delightfully mindless smile on his face, and her hand still moved back and forth on his leg, her fingers curling around his thigh, as they followed a rhythm of their own, oblivious to the music. Andrew wanted to go over and hug them, send them home to bed; they couldn't keep that up forever.

"One of the curious things about the Sargasso Sea," Sam said, "is that all the eels of the North Atlantic—millions of them— leave the freshwater and travel thousands of miles to one of the cold layers deep in the sea to breed. No one knows exactly where. No light ever reaches it. They know they're there, but not one has ever been seen. Not a single one. They think they die there after they spawn."

"How do they know they're there?" Ann asked.

"They've found larvae near the surface. Eventually they get caught up in the Atlantic currents; the larvae change into little eels and they swim back to freshwater. Can you imagine what it's like down there in the dark? A tangle of copulating eels? Sort of" —he looked around the room and laughed—"like Bermuda. Look at them. We're surrounded by honeymooners in heat." There were indeed several couples who seemed at least as hungry for each other as for the food on their plates; Andrew's young friends were not alone, although they might as well have been. He thought of the eels breeding there in the cold, lightless abyss of the sea, and he wondered if maybe his couple left the lights on when they made love.

Molly looked around the room, then began softly to recite:

"O weep, child, weep, O weep away the stain,
Lost innocence who wished your lover dead,
Weep for the lives your wishes never led."

Andrew looked at her, startled. She turned those remarkable eyes on him and smiled. "I noticed them too." She nodded toward the couple. "The lines are Auden's. About the patron saint of music. Andrew, let's dance." She turned to the others. "It would be fun to dance, don't you think?"

"But there's no dance floor," Ann said.

"Oh, what difference does it make, my dear? We'll create our own." She stood up. "Andrew?" Molly extended her hand. "Would you?"

"My pleasure," he said, rising, and together they moved to an open space near their table and danced to the Cole Porter tune the pianist was playing, Sam and Ann following after a bit. Soon they were joined by another couple—two of the honeymooners —and he and Molly returned to the table. Andrew watched the pianist. He was handsome in a theatrical sort of way. Probably he'd been very good-looking once: an unsuccessful actor, maybe a model. Now his hair was thinning and his face was gaunt. Andrew wondered if he wore makeup. He didn't look healthy. His accent was studied, and he was quite cynically flirting with the older ladies, who seemed to love it. It was harmless enough, Andrew supposed, and it brought him tips. Andrew imagined that he traveled around the world entertaining on cruise ships, pausing for a time at one resort or another to sing for his supper. There was an army of people like that. A terrible life. " *'Almost we made it, but almost that's all,'* " he was singing; " *'almost we had it'* "—Andrew stopped listening, watched Ann and Sam glide about the small space near their table. She was a beautiful dancer, a natural dancer. Music seemed her element, and her yellow hair, her flowing dress, her laughing face and body floated with it. She looked fresh as the flower on her shoulder—splendid, really. He turned to Molly. "Shall we cut in?"

"Sam is having so much fun. It seems a shame to spoil it. She's a beautiful girl, Andrew. You're lucky."

"Yes," Andrew replied, "I've heard that before." He laughed. "Everybody tells me that. They all sound surprised. How did I ever persuade such a splendid creature to marry me?"

"That wasn't what I said. You're not exactly the runt of the litter, you know. I'm sure lots of girls would have snatched you up. Why, if I'd been a few years younger, I might have done it myself."

Andrew laughed. "Be careful. I always liked older women."

"Michael says you still do."

"What do you mean?"

"Don't be so serious. I was joking. I think you're lucky you've got Ann. And vice versa. Both of you could have done worse." She paused. "Of course, it's never too late."

"Never too late?"

She looked at him. "To do worse, my dear."

"Oh. I suppose not." He thought for a second. "But I certainly hope not." Another couple had joined the others on their little dance floor now, a couple Andrew thought looked vaguely familiar; but then, a lot of people did. He was always encountering strangers on the street, people he might have passed a hundred or a thousand times, and thinking that he ought to recognize, that he must know them, when it was simply that he'd passed them many times and their faces had become familiar. "The restaurant is probably thoroughly alarmed at our rowdy table's turning their dignified terrace into an impromptu nightclub, but let's cut in anyway." And they did.

They danced for a few minutes as the pianist played on, playing to them now, but eventually the glow began to fade and Andrew started feeling a little self-conscious. "It must have been the Bermuda Gold," he whispered in Ann's ear, "but it's wearing off and I'm feeling a little foolish out here. Let's sit down." Laughing and happy and a little breathless, they returned to the table. Before leaving, Sam insisted they have another drink, on the terrace, under the starlight. The pianist was taking a break, the only music now the chirping of the tree frogs. Andrew's young couple had already gone. A little later, they left too, passing out of the restaurant along a gravel path edged by low stone walls and overhung by huge hedges of hibiscus: a kind of narrow allée lined with torches that flamed in the darkness, giving off an acrid smoke. Andrew hadn't noticed them when they'd arrived. Of course, it was daylight then; they wouldn't have been lit.

"Very pretty," Sam said, "but it stinks like hell. Let's top the evening off with a walk on the beach." They all got into the car Sam had somehow secured—autos were hard to come by in Bermuda—and drove to a spot nearby, making their way down the sandy path, their shoes in their hands, to walk the margin of the shore, the cooling wavelets rippling at their ankles. Andrew loved the feel of the wet sand beneath his feet, between his toes. He noticed a glow on the horizon and slowly at first, then suddenly, the huge moon heaved loose from the black water, and climbing into the sky revealed the dark looming shadows out there to be natural columns of rock rising from the susurrant sea, protecting the edges of their little bay from the water's surge. Behind them, twinkling in the distance far above, they could see the lights of the terrace where they'd dined.

"The moon must be full," Andrew said.

"Almost," Sam said. "It'll be full on Monday." Then he mentioned one last and indisputable phenomenon of the Bermuda Triangle: "It's one of the two places on earth where the compass points to true North instead of magnetic North"—which struck Andrew, for no particular reason, as eerie. He stepped back from the waves that lapped the sand, pulling Ann with him. He felt momentarily tired.

As they were driving back to their hotel, the road silver in the moonlight, Sam suggested a nightcap but Andrew was afraid that one nightcap would shortly turn into another, and then another, and he begged off. They were tired from their crazy flight, he said. Then he laughed. "And Sam, I've got to think about this play, figure out how I'm going to sell you on it." He laughed again. "I've got to sing for my supper too." Besides, he could see that Ann was growing restless.

His real desires, though, were more pressing, and more devious. They made love that night, as they had made love that afternoon, slowly, luxuriously. If the moon was causing strange tidal forces in the area, Andrew thought they seemed in his case to be largely internal. He felt a heightening of energy and a thickening desire on this fragile coral isle, and he was intoxicated again, not with the liquor they'd drunk that night, but with Ann. Her familiar body, the curve of her belly like a sheaf of wheat, seemed as strange and exotic to him now as it had when he'd first discovered it and begun to explore its delicious mysteries. He loved a woman's body, loved this woman's particulate body: the cool silk of her breasts, the tiny network of veins on her eyelids, the nape of her neck with its feathery hairs like down, the softness of her throat. Hers was a body Andrew knew as no other. He knew it, he thought, as well as he knew his own—how it tasted, how it flowed, its mysterious tides and cycles—and her self as well. He felt like a boy again, and he was filled with wonder that she could affect him so strongly after all these years. She too seemed stirred, her blood intensified in the tropic night. Bathed in the moonlight that flowed soft as the air through the shimmering curtains of their room, they forgot about the Walcotts, about the spinning world out there, and focused instead on the great salt sea of one another. Eventually, ardor sated, they drifted into easy sleep, as delicately entwined as the commensal creatures that live in the floating weeds on the still Sargasso Sea, amidst the Atlantic's swirling currents.

Andrew woke up slow and happy, a gentle surfacing in the yellow room, sunlight filtering through the gauzy curtains, a chameleon clinging to the wall next to the doors that opened to the balcony. He thought of a line he had read somewhere—"After thirty a man never wakes to the prospect of happiness"—and how grim it was, and how false. He felt a kind of liquid contentment and warmth beside Ann's sleeping body that seemed happy enough to him. Her moist, regular breathing touched his hand.

She smelled of yeast and flowers. Her yellow hair gleamed in the soft light. Ann was one of the few people Andrew had ever seen who looked as beautiful sleeping as waking. Her features, rinsed of cares, assumed a lovely smoothness. He kissed the edge of her breast, the back of her shoulder, the hair above her ear. Then he got up, and trying not to disturb the chameleon—he liked chameleons: harmless, curious creatures whose color cunningly reflected their surroundings—he closed the heavier curtains so the light wouldn't waken Ann. He decided to go out for a run, to explore the terrain on this unfamiliar island, on this fresh new day that made him feel renewed, restored. He smiled as he was getting into his running gear, and sang the little tune from *The Threepenny Opera* that had been playing lately in his head: "*Reprievèd, reprievèd.*" He looked through the desk for some paper to write a note to Ann, found some postcards, and wrote one to Julia: "*Dear Julia, Mommy is sleeping, Ralph and Emily and Anthony are safe at sea, steaming happily toward Ceylon—this place looks a little like Bombay, I think: lots of flowers—and I am going out for a run. Your Daddy loves you.*" Then he wrote a note to Ann to explain his absence and to tell her that he'd be back in an hour for breakfast. Maybe she'd like to order it? He left the note on the bed, and quietly closed the door to the room. They could eat on the balcony, he thought, looking out over the gardens and the golf course to the coral bluffs and the gentle sea beyond, translucent now in the morning light, green as an emerald near the shore and so intensely blue beyond it.

When Andrew asked the clerk behind the desk to mail his card, the man asked if he'd like his messages. Messages? No, Andrew said; he'd pick them up later. He frowned. Should he send a postcard to Daisy Curtis, to apologize for not returning her call? He supposed he ought to, explain that he'd been rushing off to Bermuda at the time. He asked the man for another card and a pen—he remembered her address—and sent it off. Then he went out for his run.

From the balcony, the route to the water had seemed simple and clear. It was not so clear on the ground. As he was considering his path, an enormous toad leapt suddenly out of the shrubbery. Andrew jumped. It was the biggest toad he'd ever seen. He'd heard toads were venomous here, that they could paralyze a dog. He decided to avoid the toad—no reason to test the story

—and the hotel's main roadway as well; the path he chose was enclosed by trees and shrubs, passing—it was apparent only from the soft *thwock!* of balls hitting clay—the far side of the tennis courts. The island seemed gentle enough, though not so lush as some more tropical islands—almost dry, actually, but tempered by the softness of the air, the yellow light, and the hibiscus blossoms speckling his path. It was curious how much yellow there was here: the hibiscus, an unknown succulent in exotic, splendid flower, the pale crushed rock, the chameleon in their room, the room itself. Places have their own colors, Andrew thought; Bermuda's were yellow and green, with an occasional splash of pink from a wild rose or some other, more exotic plant whose name he did not know.

The hibiscus way soon joined another to emerge at the gates of the hotel directly onto the corniche, with its sudden, startlingly intimate glimpses of lovely hidden coves and then of the great ocean's vast expanse. Fragrant trails edged with bay laurel and sea grape, flowering succulents, and tiny wild roses led off the highway into the sandy bluffs above the sea, the sea whose waters reached into the limestone itself to form the succession of coves —some small and secret, some with a broad expanse of beach— between the descending fingers of rock. It was indeed beautiful —exhilarating—to run along the ridge in the sparkling light and the salt air, though slippery underfoot and occasionally treacherous because of the twists and turns, the sudden ups and downs the narrow trail took. Andrew stopped for a moment on one of those little rises to admire far below a sparkling, jewel-like cove not yet—if ever? could it possibly be?—dotted with bathers, and out there in the distance the slowly twisting great Sargasso Sea. He was surprised that no one seemed to have claimed such a pristine spot, and on an impulse, he scrambled down the bluff to become a part of it. Once there, he could not resist. The place could not be seen from the highway, the protected beach looked totally deserted, and standing on the little promontory, he stripped off his shoes and running shorts and dived naked from the rocky ledge into the sea.

He swam out to a natural stone arch that marked the western extremity of his cove; he had already begun thinking of it as his cove, his by right of sole possession. The waves crested and broke there, and though the surf was light, the sea swirled around and under the arch less gently than it had appeared from shore; he had to make an effort to keep from being tossed against it. The rocks were rough, encrusted with coral, and the water around them full of brilliantly colored darting fish. He stayed there only briefly, bobbing in the waves, and then swam quickly back to the beach. He did not like to be in the ocean alone, having almost drowned in it once; he hadn't come to Bermuda to drown. He clambered up the ledge where he'd left his clothes and carried them to the sandy beach to dry off in the sun, in comfort; it wasn't easy sitting on the rocks. The cove and the beach itself were tiny, the space so small it could scarcely have contained more than a dozen people, and seemed as idyllic, as unreal, as a photograph in a tourist brochure. Feeling a little unreal himself in that enchanted setting, he sat for a while naked in the warming sun and felt the drying salt tingle his skin, watched the waves lap at the shore, the sandpipers dart back and forth in the wash. The song from *The Threepenny Opera* drifted through his head. He wondered, idly, if there were sharks out there. Of course there must be, somewhere out there; it was a big sea, after all. Warmed to drowsiness, he felt slow to move, torpid; almost—he chuckled to himself—paralyzed, but deliciously. Finally, reluctantly, he got into his shorts and shoes and began climbing back up the ridge when a voice, seemingly from nowhere, startled, shocked him from his reverie.

"Welcome to Bermuda, Mr. MacAllister. Nice dive."

Andrew jumped. He recognized the voice, of course; not instantly, but virtually so. He stopped, turned, looked, and there to his left and slightly downward, in a tiny sunlit sandy hollow edged with laurel so that it was almost hidden from his path, was David Roper, leaning back on his elbows, looking up at him and laughing. He seemed such a natural part of the setting, like the chameleon on the bedroom wall, that Andrew would scarcely have noticed him if he hadn't moved. "Nice dive, Andrew," he repeated, sitting up, adjusting his brown racing trunks. "You looked good. Water must be your element."

"Well, thanks," Andrew finally said.

"That's all right." He laughed again, and nodded toward his trunks. "Usually I wear a swimsuit, however."

"You took me by surprise."

"I could say the same. I figured I'd find you soon enough, but

I didn't expect to see you playing porpoise on my beach this morning."

"Your beach? I thought it was mine. I thought I was alone." He looked back toward it. He was vain enough to be flattered that his dive had seemed worth remarking—in fact, he rather prided himself on his skill in the water—and modest enough to be embarrassed that his body's naked, mindless delight in the sun and the sea had been observed. He was a little annoyed, too, that the cove he had thought was his alone was not. "Yes, you wrote that you were coming. I expected you'd turn up eventually."

"You didn't respond to my letter. I was afraid your agent might not have forwarded it."

"Oh, she couldn't have known. You didn't put your name on the envelope."

"Would she have thrown it out if I had? I wasn't saying that I thought she screened your mail."

"No, no. Of course not. I'm sorry. I didn't mean it the way it sounded." Then what else could he have meant? Andrew asked himself, a little shocked by what he'd blurted out. "Anyway, I didn't have time to reply. It arrived just the other day. Besides, it didn't require a response."

"You could have said 'Come ahead, I'll be glad to see you.' " He beckoned Andrew into his nook. "I am. I'm glad to see you."

"I guess I could have. But you wouldn't have received it in any event." He looked at him. "You've already got a little tan."

"Protective coloration." David laughed. "I tan not well but easily. I got here four days ago and discovered this place the next day, and you're the first person aside from myself to have dived off that rock. I like that. In fact, you're the only person I've seen here. Most people want company, I guess. I suppose they're afraid of the ocean, afraid to swim alone."

"They're wise to be afraid of the ocean. It's a little less gentle out there than it looks from shore. It can surprise you."

"Yes, I've noticed that, and I saw that you noticed it too, out there by the arch. But you look like a good swimmer."

"Thank you."

"Aren't you going to sit down?"

"I will. Thanks. In a minute."

"You arrived yesterday."

"How do you know that?"

"I called around to various hotels and learned where you were going to be staying, and when."

"You should be a reporter."

"Or a detective. Please," David said, "sit down. You can relax. It's nice here. A great little nook." He shifted a little to make room for him, though there was scarcely a place to shift. "I left a message for you at the hotel early this morning."

Andrew stood gazing again on the empty scene he had just left, then down at the slender body of David Roper glistening in the sunlight like some figure from a Grecian frieze; like one of those figures in the Elgin Marbles looking blandly toward the tumult of the procession. The morning sun caught the filaments of his hair—the curls on his head, the almost adolescent down tremulous as antennae on his arms and legs—and bathed him in a kind of shimmering radiance, as if light were emanating from him as well: the light, he suddenly thought, in Rilke's archaic Apollo, "*suffused with brilliance from inside.*" The sonnet, its dreadful closing line, flashed briefly to his mind again. "What did the message say?"

"It told you where to find me."

"Oh." Andrew sat down cross-legged in the space David had made.

"You didn't expect to see me again, did you?"

"When I got your letter, I thought I'd probably see you again."

"Were you surprised by my letter?"

"Not entirely. Daisy Curtis told me she'd heard from you and that you were coming to the States. I was surprised when you said you were stopping over in Bermuda."

"Were you pleased? Don't answer that; I will: not entirely."

Oh, *say* it. Andrew thought. He looked directly at David's face. "The last time I saw you, it seemed very strange to me, very disturbing. I was frightened. I wasn't entirely sure I wanted to see you again."

"That's better. Thank you." David paused. "Really, I appreciate your saying that." He paused again, looking out to sea, and then back at him. "I'm a decent man, you know, and I'm not stupid."

"I know." They sat for a moment in silence. Andrew looked over at him. He smiled. "It's good to see you."

"I've been sketching. Would you like to see what I've done?" David reached behind him for a sketch pad tucked into the laurel. Andrew hadn't noticed it before. He opened the pad and leafed through three or four drawings in pencil, various views of the empty cove but all from the perspective of his little niche above it. "When I saw you swimming and then sitting on the beach, I realized what was lacking: a human figure." He turned another page, to a sketch of a man leaning back on his left arm, his right resting on his knee, his gaze fixed on the sea. "But I'm not going to put him on the beach." He turned another page. "I sat him on that ledge you dived from." There was the same figure, smaller now and sitting on a shirt or cloth of some kind on the rocky ledge, his arms clasped loosely around his legs, his head resting dreamily on his knees. He could have been sleeping. It felt very odd for Andrew to look at that dreaming figure on the rocky ledge, the arch floating calmly in the distance, like a real thing. It made his flesh move.

"It looks"—he paused, searching for the word—"archetypal."

"It's not an archetype, it's a specific. It's you."

"A pretty idealized me," Andrew said, giving him a skeptical look.

"Not so very. I'll probably make a watercolor from it, to try to catch the light. I like to work in watercolors. I'm not yet sure about the scale, though—how large to make the figure in relation to all the rest. Do you like the sketch?"

"I'd have to say yes. Yes, I like it. But it's strange." He laughed. "I'm glad you let him sit on something. Those rocks are hard." Andrew looked at David Roper again. He seemed no more than twenty-five or so, perhaps younger, though Andrew had never been very good at estimating ages. He never felt entirely sure of his own, since his chronological age seemed quite different from his mental age. "How old are you, David?"

"I'm thirty-one."

"You're so slim. I thought you were much younger. You could be ten years younger!"

"That's just the way you see me. I don't look twenty-one. And you? How old are you?"

"I'm forty."

"You'd never know it."

Andrew laughed. "Are you referring to my looks or my behavior? Don't answer. Yes, I like your sketch. It makes me think of Thomas Eakins. Or of a painting I saw in Paris once. I don't remember the artist."

"What was it?"

"Just a young man sitting on a rock beside the sea. A lot younger man than I, that's for sure. The figure in your sketch looks a lot younger, too."

"That's the way you strike me. Maybe the way you are." He laughed. "You know: essence, not existence."

"I'd like them to coincide, to be what I am. It's nice to be young, but I want to be my age."

"Forty is not very old."

"I used to think so."

"So did I. So did everybody, when everybody was eight."

"Why eight?"

"When they were kids, then."

"Well, at forty, I think thirty-one is young. It's not bad to be thirty-one. It was good for me, anyway. It was quite a happy year." It was the year that Julia was born. Yes, it had been a very happy year. It seemed a long time ago, now, and yet at other times it seemed as close as yesterday.

"And this year?"

"Oh, it's happy too."

"It ought to be. Your play is a great success in London. Doesn't that please you?"

"Of course. And I hope it's a success in New York."

"When will it open?"

"I don't know yet. I don't know yet if it will. But the prospect is looking better."

"Not that it's a happy play. Funny, but not happy."

"We've been through that before. I don't want to talk about the play. Really. The play's the play, my life's my life. Don't you sometimes not want to talk about your work? Well, I'm the same way."

"I don't mind talking about it. I just draw what I see. That seems simple enough."

"I do the same thing. I write what I see, or try to. It doesn't seem exactly simple, though. Of course, what I see in my mind doesn't necessarily correspond to what's there on the rock, you know? I'm not constrained by—what was it Joyce said?—the ineluctable modality of the visible? You must know that. But still the visible has got to be contended with. That's the problem. I never sat on that ledge, for instance."

"No, but you should have."

"For the composition."

"Yes."

"The imagination isn't the reality, my friend. Life isn't art."

David laughed. "Maybe it should be. I could sketch it nicely. It would be so much prettier."

"Sometimes more satisfying, maybe; more beautiful, more . . . more *right*. But only sometimes. No, certainly not necessarily prettier."

"Okay, better, more pleasing, then; more gratifying."

"Yes. More gratifying. The beauty is in the order, in the form the content takes—capturing the moving form in stillness." He thought for a moment. "No. Capturing the movement in the stillness of form." He paused again. "Maybe both. Stopping the flow, anyway, so we can see it for a minute. Like the Elgin Marbles." Andrew's gaze drifted off toward the sea, the blurred line of whiteness shimmering on the horizon. All forms were fluent. He could feel his mind thickening in the beads of light, in the diaphanous air: like clotted cream. "Nothing incongruent." Suddenly he laughed. "No ugly bumps and angles. No scars, no mars. No wrong turns, either. None of that. It's the best of all possible worlds."

"Now you're not talking about art, Andrew. You're talking pretty pictures. You're talking about fantasy."

Andrew laughed again, and shook his head vigorously back and forth as if he were struggling to waken. "I'm confusing illusion with hallucination. Sometimes it's easy for me to slip from one to the other. They're related."

"Yes, but how? That's the question."

"And it would take a long time to answer it, if it can be answered. If I could answer it. The one takes work and talent. Control. You control the illusion. The hallucination controls you."

"You'd probably know more about that than I," David said. "You're the thinker. You're the word person. Let's talk about the real world. How about breakfast?"

Andrew closed his eyes. "Oh, Jesus," he whispered. He stood

up. "I've got to get out of here. I'm supposed to be having breakfast with Ann back at the hotel. She's probably ordered it. *Shit!*
Do you have a watch? No, I don't suppose you do. I said I'd be
back in an hour. It's got to be a lot more than an hour." Andrew
started out of the hollow.

"I'm sorry," David said, rising and picking up the pair of
shorts he'd been using to sit on. "I didn't mean to keep you. I just
liked talking to you, seeing you here, like this. The hotel didn't
tell me your wife would be with you." He pulled the shorts on
over his swim trunks and slipped the sketch pad into his pack.

"You didn't keep me. It's not your fault. But I can't talk any
longer. I don't know how far I ran, but I've got to get running
now. The real world calls—you know?"

"I'll take you there. I've got a moped. It won't take long."

"There's not room on a moped."

"Sure there is. Come on." As they walked up the slope, a man
was laboriously making his way down the opposite ledge, a beach
umbrella under his arm, a cooler and a radio in his hands. He
was followed a moment or two later by a woman struggling with
two collapsible backrests, a big beach bag, and two young children. "Someone's discovered our cove," David said. "Too bad."

"Don't bother driving me to the entrance," Andrew said when
they pulled up to the gates of the hotel. "I'll get off right here.
Where are you staying?"

"I told you on the message. I've got some friends in London
who have a house not far from here. They come for August, and
usually rent it out from Easter until then. But it's vacant now for
a couple of weeks, so they offered it to me. They like my work.
Nice of them, heh? That's one reason I decided to stop here. I
thought I'd do some sketching—and when I asked your agent for
your address in New York and she coolly told me you were going
to be in Bermuda, I thought, well, then I'd see you too, that it
would be easier than in New York." He looked at the handlebars,
turning them back and forth, then pointed the wheel toward
Andrew and looked up. "If I were being really truthful, I would
have put the second reason first."

"Oh."

"She didn't give me your address."

"Pamela's very protective. But it's in the phone book."

"I drew you a map so you'd know where to find me. It's in an envelope at the desk. There's a telephone number, too. I've got the house to myself—drop by. I've been here a few days. I've seen a lot. Let me be your guide. I'd like to be your guide."

"That would be nice."

"Yes," David said, as if the matter were settled, "I'll be your guide." He smiled. "Your Virgil."

"I don't think I need a Virgil. I'm not planning a tour of the Inferno."

"I didn't mean that." He paused. "You know, I'm glad we found each other like this. Thanks. It seems"—he looked suddenly into Andrew's eyes—"right. I'm sorry we couldn't have had breakfast. I would have fixed it for you."

"Yes. I'd better take care of that now. Goodbye."

David opened the throttle of the moped. "See you at the beach," he shouted above the roar, and he drove off, waving.

"Hey, thanks," Andrew called after him, but David could not have heard. He turned and ran up the drive, breaking into a sprint as he approached the hotel. Breathless, he asked the desk clerk for his messages.

"There are none, sir," he said.

"There *are* none? There's got to be a message. Someone here asked me earlier if I wanted them."

Another attendant came to the desk. "There was only one, sir. Mrs. MacAllister picked it up a while ago."

This place was big on *sirs*; quite a change from Manhattan, Andrew thought. "What time is it, please?"

"It's quarter past eleven, sir. The clock is right here." He pointed to a big clock on the wall behind the desk.

Andrew ran to the elevator and directly to their room. No key. He knocked on the door. No sound. He knocked again, louder. He waited. "Ann," he called out. "Ann?" No answer. Oh, shit, shit, shit! He looked about, saw a maid at the end of the corridor. "Please," he said, "could you let me into my room? I went out for a run and forgot the key." She selected a key from her chain and opened the door. The room was empty. He walked quickly to the balcony. The doors were open, and on the table there, set for two, was breakfast, one of them still under its warming lid but thoroughly cold now, the other partially eaten. "Oh, shit, shit, shit!" He said it aloud, softly, and went into the room and sat down on the bed, the one that was made, across from the bed they'd slept in. The maid hadn't cleaned the room yet. The dress Ann had worn the night before was laid out across the unmade bed, beside one of the hotel's laundry bags, with a note on top. Andrew walked over to it, picked it up and read it. It was for the maid. *"Could you ask the laundry to try to get the saltwater stains out of the skirt? Please be careful—the fabric is delicate."* Andrew looked down at the hem. There was a rippling pale brown line along the bottom of the skirt, like a wave of iodine, with some spatters farther up. She must have gotten the dress wet wading in the sea the night before. The stains looked permanent to him. It was one of his favorite dresses. It reminded him, he suddenly realized, of the dress she'd had on their honeymoon, and that had gotten ruined wading in the sea at Key Biscayne years before. Peau d'ange, that was it. Angel's skin, light as air, over a layer of stronger stuff. She'd looked like an angel, too, a playful angel. Her hair was so blond then; still was, but now she had to help it along a little. Christ! She would be *furious*! He could hardly blame her. He would have been in a screaming rage, himself. He got up and walked into the bathroom. There was a note taped to the mirror. He smiled at the tape. She never traveled without a collection of useful items—Scotch tape, Band-Aids, a flashlight, insect repellent, and so on. She'd waited for an hour, the note said, then had her breakfast and gone out for a walk. It was signed with her initial: A. Her handwriting, Andrew thought, still bore traces of her convent school. He heard the door open, and looked over to see Ann standing at the bathroom doorway.

"Where have you been?" Her face was flushed. "Where *have* you been? I waited for hours. It's almost noon!"

"I went out for a run. I'm sorry. I got lost. I didn't have my watch. I didn't know what time it was."

"Got lost! Didn't know what time it was?" Her voice softened. "Oh, Andrew. What a dope you are." She looked away from him, toward the balcony. "This was supposed to be another honeymoon."

"Don't be angry. Please. Don't be angry."

"I'm not angry." She turned to face him. "I'm worried, that's all. I was worried sick." He could see tears welling in her eyes.

"Oh, no," Andrew said, going over to her, taking her in his arms. "Oh, please, no. Don't cry."

"I sat out there on the balcony, trying to eat my breakfast. It was cold by the time I decided to go ahead without you."

"I'm sorry. I was running and I came upon this beautiful cove and . . . and . . . and I just went for a swim. I couldn't help it." He smiled and kissed her cheek, trying to coax her out of it. "Forces beyond my control." He bowed his head a little and raised his eyes to her. He gave her a look like an errant child's, half smile, half pout. "The sea cast a spell on me."

She cocked her head back and shot him a skeptical glance, as if she were in fact looking at an errant child. "I don't think it was the sea. I think you just wanted to go swimming and did it. I think you just decided that I could wait. But I didn't."

"Let's sit down," Andrew said. "I'll tell you what! We'll have iced coffee. I'll make it. There must be some ice in the refrigerator." He got the tray of ice, led her to the balcony, and emptied the water from the goblets into the pitcher on the table, filling them with ice and coffee. She reached for the cream. "No, let me," he said. "I'm fixing it for you—just the way you like it: this much cream"—he poured it into her glass—"and two lumps of sugar." He stirred it and buttered a croissant. "Would you like this?"

"No, thanks."

"If I put some jam on it?"

She laughed. "No, not even if you put some jam on it."

"Then I guess I'll have to eat it myself." He put an ice cube in his warm orange juice and drank it, then took a bite of the croissant. He reached across the table for her hand. "You looked so beautiful last night. We had fun, didn't we?"

"Yes. I get tired of the Walcotts, but it was fun. He's a good dancer."

"I'm sorry you stained your dress. I love that dress. I hope they can clean it." He took another bite of the croissant. "You know what we should do this afternoon? We should go to the cove I discovered. It really is beautiful. Like a jewel, and so tiny, and utterly deserted. And out on the water there's this strange rock formation, a natural arch, with a whole lot of beautiful fish swimming around it. We'll get some snorkeling gear and go over there." He stopped. "Hell!"

"What's wrong?"

"I just realized it's not deserted. When I was leaving, a couple with two kids was heading for it. They had a radio, too. Ugh! Well, maybe they'll have left. I'll tell you what. We'll have lunch at the hotel—at their beach club. We haven't seen that yet. It's probably nice. And you must be hungry. I'll take a quick shower, and you could get our gear together, and then we'll go down to the beach for lunch. Okay?"

She looked at him and shook her head, laughing in a mystified kind of way. "You're talking a mile a minute! You are a funny boy, a funny, strange boy. But okay, yes. We're in Bermuda, after all. There's not much here besides the beach, as far as I can tell. Unless you want to play golf." She looked beyond the gardens to the golf course, and laughed, teasing him. "I don't suppose you want to play golf?"

"Oh, yes, sure. I'd *love* to play golf. I spent so many happy childhood hours on the golf course. Please! We ought to go to the beach. I'll be just a minute," Andrew said, heading for the shower. "Sing something for me. You know I can't sing. You can do my singing for me while I'm in the shower." As he turned on the water, he heard her start to hum. "What's the tune?" he called to her.

" 'Smoke Gets in Your Eyes.' " And she began to sing.

*"They asked me how I knew
My true love was true . . ."*

Good, he thought. She was singing. She's all right. He hurried with his shower, deciding to shave there to save time. When she passed the bathroom door, he could hear patches of her melody above the sound of the water. It was a lovely tune, he thought, and he began to hum it himself. He didn't remember the words. When he got out of the shower, Ann was sitting on the balcony, waiting. He dressed quickly.

"I picked up a message for you when I went out for my walk," she said as he was pulling on his shirt. "I forgot to give it to you. It's on the desk." He glanced over at the envelope. "Aren't you going to open it?"

"It can't make a difference now. Let's go to lunch. Did you pack my book?"

"Yes, I put it in the bag." She walked over to the desk and

handed him the message. "For heaven's sake, open it. It might be important."

"I don't *want* any messages."

"You can't avoid them. Don't be silly—just open it. Or do you want me to?" He opened the envelope and glanced at it. "Who's it from?" she asked.

"It's from David Roper."

"Who's that?"

"A guy from London."

"I don't remember any David Roper. Who is he?"

"He was at the Huntingtons' party."

"Well, who was he? There were a lot of people at the Huntingtons' party."

"I don't know how to describe him. He came with Patrick Rysdale."

"Do you mean that boy who wanted to talk to you about your play? The one with the critic?"

"Yes."

"What on earth does he want? Why is he sending you messages in Bermuda?"

"He's here visiting. I guess I forgot to tell you. There was a letter from him in that packet from Pamela. I didn't see it until after our party. We were so busy, I just didn't think to mention it. He said he was coming to the States—to Washington and New York. He wants to see Daisy Curtis. He's an artist, you know. He's interested in her work. Didn't you hear her say she'd heard from him?"

"No."

"You must have been somewhere else, I guess. Taking care of the conservative contingent while I tried to confine the revolution to the dining room."

"So what's he doing in Bermuda?"

"Visiting some friends. Pamela told him we were going to be here. That's how he knew. That's why he sent the note."

"Are you going to tell me what it says?"

"Here, read it. It just says where he's staying, with a map and a phone number." He picked up the bag she'd packed and opened the door. "Can't we go to the beach now?"

She read the note. "He wants to see you. He wants to continue the conversation."

"Yes."

"What conversation?"

"About the play, I guess." He took her hand and led her from the room.

"You talk with whom you want, but I'd rather not see him."

"We don't have to. It's not important." He followed her onto the elevator and they rode down in silence.

"Do we know those people?" Andrew asked Ann as he picked at his seafood salad under the green umbrella lined with pink, at their table on the terrace overlooking the beach and the sea. He indicated an attractive young woman with a man about his own age sitting a few tables away.

"Not that I know of," she said. "I'm sure I've never laid eyes on them."

"I thought they were looking at us as we came in. They were at the restaurant last night. They looked vaguely familiar to me then, too."

"Go over and say hello if you'd like. Then you'd know."

"I'd be embarrassed. Probably I'm just imagining it." He put down his fork. "You know, it's really stifling under this umbrella." The sun was at its height, and although the umbrella blocked its rays, it admitted its heat and trapped it there, making an effective oven of the space above their table. "You could roast a pig." He wiped the sweat from his forehead and adjusted his sunglasses, which kept slipping on his nose. He could see from the sporadic movement of the pennant by the stairway that there was a breeze, but their corner of the terrace was protected from it. He gazed down at the beach, at the lines of figures stretched out on rows of reclining chairs like docile prisoners in a luxurious Auschwitz. "It's probably cooler on the beach. At least we could go in the water. Maybe we can get a cabaña. Let's go down and join the prisoners."

"Prisoners?"

"They just look so . . . *lined up*, like automatons under the control of the warden. See! There's the warden up there on his stand. They're all under surveillance."

"I believe we call him the lifeguard, darling."

"It's depressing. There's scarcely a chair out of place. *Move that chair, buster, and you're a dead man!*"

"And you want to go down and mess things up a bit?"

Andrew laughed. "Yes. They need some disorder on the beach, don't you think?"

"I thought you wanted to show me the cove you found this morning. That sounds more interesting than lying in a row of lounge chairs."

"We could do that. It would be a long walk, though. We'd probably have to go back to the hotel and rent mopeds."

"That might be fun."

"Yes. Maybe we should do it later—it's so hot. Here they'll serve us a drink, at least. Also, I told you some people were arriving as I left. It wouldn't be the same. Why don't we stay here for a while? Let's go down." Andrew signed the check, and as they rose from the table he nodded to the couple he thought looked familiar. They returned his nod in a friendly way but otherwise gave no sign of recognition, and Andrew and Ann made their way down the stone stairway that curved to the beach. They signed up for a cabaña and changed into their swimsuits, and Andrew went immediately into the water. It was cool there, and very calm. The sea was virtually empty. The hotel's beach was safer than the empty cove he'd been in this morning, he supposed, and certainly larger, but this tamed and manicured and unfortunately rather crowded spot was not nearly so dramatic or so beautiful as his cove: a few rocks at the far end, the restaurant perched at the other; no fish, no weeds. From the water he looked back toward the restaurant far above. Figures dotted the terrace. He could see the waiters scurrying about, and now and then someone leaving or arriving. The flaps of the umbrellas fluttered in the occasional puff of air, revealing the pink underside. He looked back to the beach, littered with bathers who were not bathing but baking in the sun, awash in protective lotions, light reflecting from their dark glasses, their oiled brown bodies. He missed the arch he'd swum to earlier, missed the pristine quality, the silence of his cove. He felt suddenly lonely out there, and he waved to Ann, beckoning her into the water. They played in the water for a bit, then returned to their chaises. "Back to prison," Andrew said, laughing, waving at Molly Walcott, who was making her way along the lines of chairs toward them.

"You were smart to avoid the nightcap last night," she said, sitting down on the end of his chaise. "I woke up at dawn feeling like a dog's mouth. Sam's found someone to play tennis with. Give me a cigarette, would you, darling? Oh, I forgot: you're not smoking."

"I'll get some," Andrew said, trying to attract the attention of one of the beach attendants.

"Chesterfields, please," Molly said. Her voice was husky, as if she'd smoked too many of them.

"Would you like something to drink? A beer? A lemonade?"

"I think something preposterous would be fun. How about a Singapore Sling? I don't even remember what they are, but they're supposed to be a specialty of the place. Don't tell anyone in New York that you heard me ask for one."

Andrew laughed. "What would you like, Ann?"

"Oh, why not? I'll have the same. Experiment. It's a holiday, after all."

The waiter approached, and Andrew ordered the cigarettes, the drinks for the women and, after some consideration, a lemonade for himself. He asked for a beach chair for Molly, but none was available. "That's all right," he said. "There's plenty of room."

"We can snuggle," Molly said. "I'm dying to see your play, Andrew. Did Sam tell you that we're going to London next week?"

"No, he didn't. Are you really?"

"He probably wanted to tell you himself. You know how he is. He likes to hold his cards. But we're going primarily so he can see the play. He loved the reading a couple of weeks ago, and he's looking for a property."

"That's great. That's just great! I hope he likes the production." He laughed. "Should I check with his astrologer, to see if it's an auspicious time?"

"I don't think you have to worry about that, darling. For you, all times are auspicious. You're the couple on the wedding cake, you know. We all say that."

" '*Ware the lizard lieth lurking in the grass*,' " Andrew said.

"Whatever are you talking about?"

"That's just one of his lines," Ann said. "He read that lizards are the only reptiles native to Bermuda. It's affected him."

"You know how I am: nervous."

"But it didn't say they were poisonous. They're probably

sweet little lizards. There was a chameleon in our room this morning."

"Yes, I saw it," Andrew said. "I like chameleons."

"But there is something slightly creepy about them," Molly said, "changing their colors all the time."

"They don't have to worry much here," Ann said. "The basic scheme seems to be pink, green, and yellow. They've probably lost their ability to do much else."

"But there's every color in the rainbow out there in the water," Molly said. "And of course, the sargasso weed is brown. Have you two been snorkeling?"

"Not yet."

"Well you must go. The fish are beautiful. A myriad of them. We could all go together tomorrow. Rent some equipment, maybe go out in a boat. Make a picnic of it. There's supposed to be a captain with a good boat, one with a glass bottom. Sam knows his name."

"That would be fun. I'd love to do it," Andrew said.

"I'm leery of those cruises," Ann said. "They're usually a rip-off."

"Well, we could try it. Let's."

"I'll ask Sam to book us. Maybe he could charter it. We'll do it tomorrow." The waiter arrived with their drinks and the cigarettes; he helped Andrew adjust the umbrella so they would be shaded, and the three of them lounged on their chaises and watched the sunbathers, the occasional swimmer, and the changing light on the sea. " *'Kennst du das Land,'* " Molly murmured, half-singing the lines; " *'Knowest thou the land where lemons bloom, where in the dark leaves the golden oranges glow, a soft wind hovers from the sky, the myrtle is still, and tall the laurel stands? There, there I would go,* O mein Geliebter—*O my beloved—with thee!'* Goethe may have been thinking of Italy, but he might just as well have had Bermuda in mind. What a lovely, lazy afternoon! I spent years studying German, and it was worth it for those few lines— about all I remember now."

"I love the sound of the language," Andrew said, squinting his eyes at the horizon. "I wish I knew the sense. Then maybe I could understand Rilke better." Suddenly he turned back. "Molly, why don't you make a découpage of pieces of classical sculpture? Just fragments: a piece of an arm, part of a shoulder, and so on. As if you'd been sifting through the wreckage, through the ruins. I think it would be interesting—like pieces of a jigsaw puzzle."

"I suppose it could be. Yes, I can see that. But right now I'm doing things with shells. Why don't we walk along the beach and see what we find?"

"I'd love to," Ann said. "I have a limited tolerance for beach chairs."

"And I for shelling," Andrew said. "The sun and the sea are making me sleepy. I think I'll just lie here and tolerate it." He laughed. "Maybe even give in to it. I was up early this morning. If that fails, I'll read."

"What are you reading?" Molly asked.

Ann pulled his book from her bag. "*The Greeks and the Irrational*," she said. "Andrew's getting back to his basics."

"Well, Dionysus, you know, is the patron of the theater. I'd like to do a play," he said, "but so far all I see is the backdrop. The Elgin Marbles. Make a nice set."

"You could call it *Museum Pieces*," Molly said.

"Now I have the set and the title. I need just a little action and dialogue. MacAllister's my name, ecstasy's my game. Put on a mask, and be what you're not." He paused. "Or at least, other than what you are. Nothing to it." He laughed. "Wouldn't it be nice if it were that simple?"

"Sweetheart, you really ought to settle down to one play and write it." Ann turned to Molly. "He's had about ten different ideas in the last month—ever since we came back from London —everything from a play cast entirely with children to an expedition to the South Pole without a woman in it." She laughed. "Hopeless! A dearth of ideas is not his problem."

"I learn by going where I have to go. Enjoy your walk. I'll be here."

"He'll be dreaming when we get back," Ann said. "I know it."

"I wake to sleep, and take my waking slow, girls. I'm dreaming now. This whole place is like a dream. See you later," he said as they walked off. He picked up his book, opened it at random, read a sentence: "To resist Dionysus is to repress the elemental in one's own nature; the punishment is the sudden complete collapse of the inward dykes when the elemental breaks through perforce and civilization vanishes." He put down the book—too enchanted an afternoon for such heavy, dismal stuff—and noticed out of the corner of his eye that Molly had left her cigarettes. He didn't know how she could tolerate Chesterfields—like smoking straw, or gravel. He scanned the sea, and saw nothing but a couple of bathers sitting in the sand at the edge of it, the waves lapping at their bodies. An older woman in a black swimsuit, who had been sunning on a nearby lounge though she was already the color of coffee, got up and strode to the water, plunged in, and began a slow, rigid crawl back and forth the length of the beach, taking care to keep her head above the water. She did this five times, then returned to her place in the line and turned her other side to the sun. Andrew shook his head and picked up his book again, opening it to another place. "Plato tells us in the *Ion* that οἱ κορυβαντιῶντες 'have a sharp ear for one tune only, the one which belongs to the god by whom they are possessed, and to that tune they respond freely with gesture and speech, while they ignore all others.' " He leafed through the pages, wishing he knew Greek. "There must have been a time when the maenads or thyiads or βάκχαι really became for a few hours or days what their name implies—wild women whose human personality has been temporarily replaced by another." He set the book aside and looked out to sea again. It was empty now. Heat shimmered in waves above the sand. He was grateful for the shade of the umbrella. He lowered the back of his lounge chair, and slumberous, drifted off.

He awoke to the jiggling of the umbrella, caroming shards of light, and Ann standing above him. "Wake up, darling. I've got some nice people I want you to meet."

He rubbed his eyes, and shaded them with his hand. He looked toward her. "I must have been dreaming," he said, his voice full of sleep. "I'm groggy. What did you say?"

"I said I've got some people I want you to meet. A surprise." She shook the umbrella again. He sat up and saw Molly talking with a man and a woman, two other men who seemed to be part of the group standing a short distance behind.

"I'm too sleepy to meet people," he muttered. "Who are they?" The light had blinded his eyes.

"They're the couple you thought you recognized, and probably you did. You must have seen them on the street. We virtually live on top of one another in New York. Molly and I started talking to them when we were walking on the beach. They're very attractive. You'll like them. Wake up and see."

Slowly Andrew rose from his seat and walked over to Molly and the couple. "I understand we're neighbors," he said, introducing himself. "Sorry I'm so groggy. I was sleeping. I must have been sound asleep. This heat will do it, and the sea air."

"Yes," the woman said—a young woman, pretty in an Ivory Soap sort of way; no, more like the woman on the Breck shampoo bottle. "Rick and I live right across the street from you."

"For God's sake! What a suprise. Somehow, you don't expect to come to Bermuda and meet a neighbor from New York. You were at the restaurant last night, too. Yes, I thought you looked familiar."

"You started the dancing," she said. "I wanted to ask you to dance, but Rick wouldn't let me. He said you'd think I was too forward." She giggled. "He's always curbing my natural impulses."

Andrew laughed. "I shouldn't let him do that, if I were you."

"I noticed that you didn't."

"I didn't?"

"Curb your natural impulses."

"Oh, you noticed that, did you? I suppose it was fairly bold of us to turn that elegant place into a wild dance hall—but before I fell asleep on the beach I was reading that it's unwise to resist the Dionysian. So we did the right thing."

She glanced over at the book lying opened on the table. "You're reading one of my favorite books! *The Greeks and the Irrational*. Rick made us read it in his drama course."

"You teach, Rick?"

"Yes, at Columbia. Comparative lit."

"He was tough, but"—she laughed—"I softened him up." She walked over to the table and picked up the book, looking at his place in it. "You've been reading about the dancing women— the maenads, Dionysus' followers."

"I wasn't really reading it. I leafed through it for a minute and promptly nodded off. It's a little heavy for the beach."

"It says here, 'he that knows the Power of the Dance dwells in God.' Ancient Mohammedan sage." She laughed again.

"Let me see," Andrew said. She handed him the book,

pointed to the place. "But right after that it says, 'the Power of the Dance is a dangerous power. Like other forms of self-surrender, it is easier to begin than to stop.' " He laughed. "Well, I've known that all along."

"Why were you reading this?" Rick asked.

"I've gotten interested in the Greeks. I have this idea for a play, but so far I've only got the backdrop—the Elgin Marbles. I guess I was hoping some ideas would come to me, some stunning synthesis of order and ecstasy. Or at least the imposition of form. Something Apollonian. Instead, I got Dionysus. What brings you to Bermuda?"

"We've been working hard," he said. "I've gotten interested in film, and we were doing an experimental thing that we just finished. I'm calling it *As You Like It*, with apologies to Shakespeare. Anyway, after that I decided we needed a rest. You write plays?"

"Yes."

Molly approached with the two men. "Andrew wrote *Riverhead*, among several other things, and he's got what we hear is a smashing new one playing in London now." She introduced the men.

"Oh, yes," Rick said. "I thought your name sounded familiar." He smiled. "We should collaborate. Have you ever written a film?"

"No, but I've thought about it."

"There's nothing he doesn't think about," Ann said.

"This place would make a great setting," Rick said. "Call it *The Bermuda Triangle*. A cast of honeymooners."

"These people have been helping us look for shells," Molly said. "They've all got an eye for it, but we didn't have much luck."

"I found a few things," Ann said. "Nothing very impressive and nothing whole. It did give me an idea, though—something for Julia. She loves shells. You know how she's always picking them up. I'll go into Hamilton tomorrow. There must be a shell shop there."

"It doesn't seem quite fair to buy it," Andrew said.

"I can tell her we found it on the beach. She'll never know the difference."

"But I will," Andrew said. "Anyway, aren't we going snorkeling tomorrow?"

"I'll get up early."

"Would you like to come with us?" Molly asked of the new people. "My husband is going to charter a boat." She laughed. "He doesn't know that yet, but he will—as soon as I get him off the tennis court."

"I'd love to," the girl said. She turned to the men. "Wouldn't you?" Everyone agreed. "I'd love to go dancing tonight, too. Are you up for that? You're all terrific dancers. We'll show these people how to have fun. It's too stodgy here."

"Rattle their cages, you mean?"

"Exactly," she said. "You've got the idea, Andrew." After establishing where to reach their new acquaintances, Molly went back to the hotel to find Sam, and Andrew and Ann returned with her. Ann was very tired, and wanted a nap.

Michael had shown up that afternoon with not one but two women, sisters, of Greek and Lebanese descent, and stunningly beautiful, dusky and opulent. While Ann and Molly were resting, and the sisters were off exploring the beach club, Sam and Michael and Andrew strolled around the hotel's ample grounds, talking. Sam liked to do business on the move. He was definitely looking for a property, he was definitely excited about *41 East 73rd*, he had a line on a couple of theaters, one on Broadway and one off, he knew Michael was the right director for it: it just hinged on the casting—"that's a month, two at the most"—and his impression of the London production, of course. He'd like to get Larry Evans. "He's good, he shows up sober, and he doesn't carry his brains between his legs. I've never known him to have a tantrum. For an actor that's saying a lot." If they could use the same set designer, well then it would take only about six weeks to build the sets and the whole thing could open in October or early November. He'd decide what theater would be right for it when he saw it at the Royal Court.

"So it's a deal?" Michael asked.

"Almost a deal," Sam replied. "But almost-a-deal is a good enough deal for me. I've broken out the champagne for less. We'll all meet at eight, in the bar. I'm ready to celebrate."

"You're the producer," Michael said.

"That's right, and I'm going to produce a hell of a party tonight. Dress for it."

And they did. Ann was still sleeping when Andrew returned to the room. He called for some tea, and when it arrived he poured a cup and carried it to her bed. "Wake up, darling." He gently shook her shoulder. "I've got terrific news. I'm almost sure that Sam is going to do the play. It just depends on the casting and his look at the London production. We're going to celebrate tonight!"

"That's wonderful, darling." She thought for a moment. She always woke up instantly and fully. "Andrew, are you sure you're not being premature?"

"It was his idea. He said he'd pulled out the champagne for less, and I guess he's pulling it out tonight. He said to dress for it."

"I'll dress for you." She took his hand and kissed the back of it, then sat up. "I'm thrilled for you. But I won't be *totally* thrilled until the deal is delivered. I've heard producers make promises before. I don't want you to be disappointed."

"Sam is different."

"They're all different"—she laughed—"yet they're all the same. So are you, my dear."

"Which?"

"Both, you silly innocent." She got up. "Well, let me bathe. I think I'll take my tea like a lady, while I'm lying in the tub. I feel like a nice, leisurely soak. When I come out, you won't recognize me."

"Don't do anything too radical. I like to be surprised, but not alarmed."

"Have I ever alarmed you?"

"I'm not sure—but please don't start now. It's a delicate time." While he was waiting to take his shower, Andrew poured himself a cup of tea, then decided against it and fixed himself a gin and tonic from the little bar the hotel had cleverly supplied to increase its revenues. He noticed the envelope from David Roper lying on the desk. He picked it up and read the message again, then put it in his bag. He never traveled without that bag of books and papers, and often he never did anything with it either; but the presence of the bag made him feel more secure. He carried it to the balcony with his drink and sat there waiting, his legs stretched out, feeling himself grow heavy in the slanting light. He slowly ceased resisting, gave in to the gravity that tugged at his tremulous lids, then swiftly pulled them down, shuttering his eyes. He felt neither asleep nor awake but in some kind of quiescent state between, neither pleasant nor unpleasant, aware of the world around him and at the same time distant from it, when he was startled by a light or a motion. It was Ann, swathed in an enormous white towel with a smaller one wrapped around her head, passing across the room in a cloud of scented vapor. "I must have been dreaming," he said. "Am I still?" Lightly tanned from the beach, and glowing from her bath, she moved in radiance amidst the dimness of the room, as if she had caught some of that Bermuda sun and were slowly, very slowly, exuding it. From the light on the balcony, she struck him suddenly as exotic as a creature from the East. "I told you I didn't want to be alarmed," he said, entering the room, drawn toward her, astonished by her. "Where are the pipes and timbrels? You should be accompanied by music. 'Enters, stage center, sinuously from her bath and accompanied by maidservants and a band of musicians . . .' "

"Andrew," she exclaimed, "you are such a nut! What role have you assigned me now? Susanna?"

"Oh, I think not Susanna." He stopped, looking at her. "Astarte, maybe."

"Astarte?"

"She's a primitive Venus. Drop the towel—I'll check it out." She walked back into the bathroom, ignoring him. He called after her, "I'm not sure you're that primitive, but you're not a tame Roman Venus, either. More Greek, I think—the Archaic Age." She came out again, still wrapped in the towel. "Yes, I think the wild Aphrodite, with perhaps a touch of Athena's glory. Cleverly disguised as a pretty maid of Athens. *'Maid of Athens, ere we part, Give, o, give me back my heart!'* "

She looked at him, rolled her eyes, and chuckled again, shaking her head. "Why, are you going somewhere?"

He laughed. "Just to the showers." He drained his glass, tossed his clothes on the dressing-room floor and bounded into the bathroom, stepping happily into the shower, feeling the water pour over him. He shaved again; it was a special occasion, after all. He was feeling excited, keyed up. He'd have to remember not to drink too much. He didn't want to make an ass of himself. He wanted to be in control of the situation, not have the situation take control of him. Drinking a lot didn't help. There had been a time, when he was younger, that if he drank too much he simply got sleepy; it didn't work that way now, not until after the damage was done.

When he had finished, Ann was already dressed and sitting on the balcony. The last rays of the setting sun caught in her hair. He stood in the doorway, watching her. "Jesus! You look on fire. Stand up. I want to see you." She rose from the chair, her dress, stark lustrous black, falling straight to the floor around her. He stared at her, awed. "You see, I was right," he finally said. "You are a goddess. Now in all her glory."

"I don't want to be a goddess."

"Why not?" He walked toward her, clutching his towel around him. "It's fun to be a goddess before the trembling mortals. I adore goddesses."

"Would you fasten my pearls?"

"I adore you, anyway."

"Andrew, I don't *want* to be adored. We adore God, we venerate the saints, and we love one another—one of the lessons we learned in school." She laughed. "Oops! I almost forgot: we shun the devil."

"But I didn't go to your school."

She handed him the pearls. "Wind them twice, would you?" She turned her back toward him. "I'd just like you to love me. Just me." She laughed again. "Simple, adorable me. The girl who used to grow flowers around her heart."

"But angel, I do." He kissed the back of her neck and felt, suddenly, helpless. His fingers tangled in the necklace; he couldn't seem to work the clasp. "But you just said I wasn't supposed to adore you. If you're adorable, how can I not?"

"It was just an expression, for heaven's sake. What are you doing with my beads? What's taking so long?"

"I'm having trouble with the clasp." He unwound them and started over.

"You know, Andrew," she said, resignation in her voice, "sometimes I think you don't see me at all but some figment of your imagination."

He sighed. "A beautiful figment, my fair, my black Aphrodite. Stand still; I'm trying to fasten these damned beads." He fumbled with the clasp. "There! Why didn't you just slip them over your head?"

"I wanted to double them. I can't do it then."

"No, they'll look better long." She turned to face him. "Yes, they do. What's that in your hair?"

"The arrow you gave me." She laughed brightly. "If I must be a goddess, I've got to have a diadem. Do you like it?"

"My mother's arrow."

"My arrow, darling. And see? I'm wearing the buckles, too, the buckles she gave me." She raised her skirt a little and extended her foot, revealing a black silk shoe with the silver buckle sparkling on it. "I like them."

"They look nice."

"You'd better get dressed. We're supposed to be meeting the Walcotts right now." She picked up a fringed silk shawl of her mother's and laid it beside her evening bag on the spare bed. It was softest pink, like the inside of a shell.

"I'll just be a minute," he said, leaving the balcony and going into the dressing room. "Hell!" he muttered, and returned immediately to pick up his bag. He found a place for it on a shelf in the closet, then dressed quickly, and hand in hand they left their room to join the Walcotts in the bar. The group from New York was already there, and soon they were joined by Michael and the sisters ripe as olives, Marika and Yasmine. They had a leisurely drink together before dividing up for the ride to the restaurant, ordering taxis because there wasn't room for all of them in Sam's car. As they were standing in clusters under the portico, waiting for the taxis to arrive, Andrew nodded in the direction of the sisters, who were talking with Ann. "Well, you've got balls, Michael, I have to admit that. What's more, they're truly beautiful. Are you doing threesomes now?"

"It's a thought," Michael replied, a wicked grin on his face. "Never say never, but the fact is Marika won't travel without Yasmine. It was a question of both or none, and you know me: none wouldn't do."

Marika moved away and began talking to Rick and Sam. "They seem to have separated now and be doing all right. Just who needs the protection here?"

"There's always safety in numbers," Michael said, "but who

wants safety? Risk your ass, I say. Speaking of numbers, Andrew my boy, where did you find your intriguing foursome?"

"Ann and Molly picked them up on the beach. You know how it is: they wander off to find some shells and come back with a collection. The people seem interesting, though. Rick teaches comparative lit at Columbia, and I guess Ruth snagged the teacher. She's sweet. Full of enthusiasm. It was her idea that we go dancing tonight."

"She looks sweet, all right. Where do they come from?"

"They live right near us in New York. Odd. I'd seen them here earlier and I kept thinking I somehow knew them. I'd just seen them around the neighborhood, I guess."

"What about the two guys?"

"I don't know. They don't talk much, do they? Shy like you, probably. One's a student; I don't know about the older one. Rick and Ruth seem to be the couple, but it looks to me as if Rick's got them all under his thumb. He's definitely the one in charge."

"Do you think the two guys are a couple too?"

"Beats me—I can't figure it out. I'm sure your dusky Levantines with their shaking tambourines—excuse me, I'm practicing spontaneous rhyme—I'm sure they'll bring them out, if they need it."

"Too bad Daisy Curtis isn't here. She'd bring them out, one way or another—right? And we could use another woman, just to even things up."

"Or mess them up. Aren't two enough for you?"

"I was thinking of you, of course. Here come the cabs. Let's go."

They all piled into the various cars and followed Sam, who had taken Ann, Ruth, Marika, and the older of the two young men with him. As usual, Sam had found another extraordinary spot—this one with a real dance band that looked and sounded as if it had come straight from the Thirties, along with the mirrored globe that was slowly turning above their heads, below the stars; or perhaps the intervening decades had simply passed Bermuda by—but not as usual, he hadn't been able to charter the boat for the next day, so they were going Tuesday instead. "Sorry I couldn't manage it tomorrow," he said when they'd finished their meal, "but I've found a great boat and we'll have it to ourselves."

"Oh, goody!" Ruth said, clapping her hands. Somehow the innocent, silly exclamation fell naturally from her lips, and brought a smile to Andrew's face. There was something beguiling about Ruth, something delightfully spontaneous and artless. "I can hardly wait. I love to snorkel, and what a luxury to have a boat of our own. And what luck to have run into you people! You're all really fun."

She was very pretty, too. "Let's dance," Andrew said to her, putting down the champagne that Sam had insisted they have. "I'm feeling Bacchic." He led her onto the floor. "The god will be served." He took her in his arms and turned her slowly to the music, beginning to the get the feel of her.

"Or you will."

"Would you like to explain yourself?"

"Well, you know, haven't you read *The Bacchae?* Some of those Dionysian revels got a little violent."

"Violent?" He was warming up to her movements now, and danced a little more freely.

"When Pentheus tried to stop them, they tore him up with their bare hands. His own mother did it. You should have taken Rick's course." He raised her hand and twirled her around— "Then you'd know; he's a good teacher"—and around again. "Pentheus defied the god, you see, and the god brought him down." She was back in his arms now, gliding easily to the music. "Ripped that poor boy right apart! They were going to eat him. It's a bloody play. I'd like to see it performed. Can you imagine what it would be like when his mother brings his head in on the end of a stick?"

"Please, we're dancing. This is supposed to be a party."

She looked at him and laughed. "It *is* a party. It's a great party —a pre-celebration celebration, Sam says. You must be excited. It must be thrilling to see your own play on the stage in New York, your name in lights. I wish they'd play something fast."

"Ruth, my name won't be in lights." He twirled her again. "Isn't this fast enough? I don't have that kind of name. I'm not Neil Simon."

"Well, you never know. I've never danced with a famous person before."

"You're not dancing with one now, sweetheart. Try Sam.

He's the closest thing to a famous person around here." He looked down at her, drifting slower now to the tune. "You *are* a terrific dancer. You make me look better than I am."

"Are you looking down my dress?"

"What?"

"I said, Are you looking down my dress?"

"It's hard to avoid."

She giggled. "Stop it. People will notice. Your wife likes me. I don't want her to get the wrong idea."

"Maybe you should try a brassiere sometime. Just for fun. Then if some strange man happens to look down your dress . . ."

"Yes?"

"Well, he wouldn't see anything. He'd just see your brassiere."

"That wouldn't be very exciting, would it?"

"I think maybe we'll return to the table," Andrew said. "As the poet put it,

"Look homeward, Angel, now, and melt with ruth:
And, O ye dolphins, waft the hapless youth!"

"I don't get it."

"Isn't your name Ruth?"

"That makes you the hapless youth? You're kind of old to be a hapless youth."

"I hadn't thought of it in quite that way." He held the chair for her, and sat down in his own. "Hello, everybody."

"You two cut quite a figure out there," Molly said. "We've been admiring your energy."

"It's the band," Andrew said. "They're good." He raised his glass—"To the music!"—and drained it. Sam refilled the glass before the waiter could get to it.

"Out there he said it was me. Now he says it's the music."

"I think I'll find out which it was," Michael said. "Would you like to dance?"

"I didn't want to stop," she said, laughing gaily and rising again from the table."

Sam went off to dance with Yasmine, and the older of the two extra men—his name was Jack; the other was Kevin—took Molly. Rick spoke to the rest of them. "They had this dancing madness at the end of the Middle Ages. Saint John's dance, they called it, or Saint Vitus's, because it seemed to break out around their festivals. It started out with one or two people and spread like wildfire. Highly infectious. They believed the saints caused the dancing, and their supplication could cure it."

"The cure was the disease, the disease the cure," Andrew said. "Interesting."

"It was a kind of spontaneous mass hysteria, and it swept through Europe on and off for about three hundred years." Rick spoke matter-of-factly, without any particular expression, as if he were reciting notes from an old lecture. "Seemingly rational people dropped everything and ran off, possessed. An epidemic of dancing. It pops up periodically through the ages. Those dance marathons in the Thirties, for instance—a modified form."

"Sam should be here," Andrew said. "He loves this stuff."

"Possessed by what?" Marika asked.

"By an excess of the divine. The divine turns demonic."

"The other side of Apollo's sweet song," Andrew said.

"Yes," Rick said. "The Thracian women tore his son Orpheus to pieces, you know, after he'd played with them and then neglected them."

"You're talking about my ancestors!" Marika exclaimed in mock horror.

Rick laughed. "They were dancing to a different drum."

"That's for sure," Andrew said. "At least we can hope so. I thought Apollo's motto was 'Nothing in excess.' "

"It was also 'Know thyself.' That's what I try to teach my little band here." He nodded to Kevin. "Right, Kevin?"

"Rick knows a lot," Kevin said. It was virtually the first thing Andrew had heard him say. "He made us learn about those snake-handlers in Kentucky, the people who pass rattlers around in church. They work up to it by dancing and speaking in tongues. They do it for their Pentecostal God."

"Are you a student of Rick's?" Ann asked.

"Well, not exactly. I've never had a course with him. I go to Brooklyn College; but I've done some work for him, and if you work for him he makes you learn things."

Rick laughed. "I'm a teacher. I can't help myself. I've always been interested in folklore and myth, and the common thread that runs through different literatures, different cultures—from the most primitive to the most sophisticated. The Kentucky snake-handlers, for instance—"

"Hardly sophisticated," Ann said.

"No, they're not. They're very simple people, whose practice is more ancient than they know. They think they're following the Gospel—'They shall take up serpents'—whereas in fact they're following an earlier, more primitive god: Dionysus, although they'd send one of their snakes after me if they heard me say it."

Andrew laughed. "Fortunately there are no snakes in Bermuda, just lizards. But how so? How are they following Dionysus?"

"Dionysus sometimes manifests himself in the form of a snake, and the maenads—his dancing followers, the ones who destroyed Orpheus—snatched them up in their ecstasy. They do the very same thing. I suppose there's some suggestion of the motion of a snake in certain dance movements." He turned to Ann. "Shall we try it?"

Ann laughed. "Not if we're going to imitate snakes."

"We can do better than that," Rick said as he led her from the table to the floor. Andrew noticed that the young couple he'd been watching the night before had found this place too, and were dancing dreamily, a little stiffly, to the music. They looked so innocent and clean, still so engrossed in one another, enchanted by one another, that it brought a smile to his lips. It was quite wonderful to be young and in love; it made everything seem so fresh, like the first time. He wondered if he and Ann had looked like that once. He watched her dance with Rick. "I think he's trying to demonstrate his lecture."

"Rick is real interested in all that stuff," Kevin said. "He's sort of psychic. He was born under the sign of the caul, you know?"

"I've heard of such things."

"I believe in those things," Marika said. "Be careful. They're still very real where my family comes from."

"Well, Rick really is—what's that word?—charismatic, that's it. He's sort of a prophet."

"He's the piper? Remember, Kevin," Andrew said, "you've got to pay the piper."

"You know that saying you mentioned, 'Nothing in excess'? Rick talked about that, too. He says that it contradicts 'Know thyself,' and that the only way to know yourself is to let yourself go. He said that's what the saints did."

"The saints? I'll have to ask him about that, but in the meantime, Marika should be dancing. Now if you're not going to ask her, I am," and Andrew walked over to her chair and took her hand and they began to dance. She was an effortless, natural dancer, and they moved easily together under the mirrored globe that scattered light like broken glass around them, and as the moon began to rise caught those beams too, in an eerie blend of earthly and unearthly light. It was another extraordinary night, soft and luminous, and fragrant with the scent of flowers floating like music through the air. They were dancing near Ann and Rick now. Ann tossed her head back, the pearls swung around her, and her arrow released a shower of sparkling darts. "Stop it," he called to her as they danced for a moment side by side, "you're piercing my heart." She shot a smile toward him and flung back her head in soundless laughter, and Rick led her into a series of graceful, swift arabesques before they all came to a stop with the orchestra and walked off the floor together.

"My dress wasn't made for this kind of dancing," Ann said, lifting her skirt and glancing at it. "I'm afraid I've lengthened the slit. I'm still breathless." She turned to Rick. "Andrew's mother told me not to wear hobble skirts. I should have listened."

"I don't think she meant a dress like that," Andrew said.

"I've altered it now, in any case. That was exhilarating. Rick, you're a marvelous dancer."

"We're all dancing fools," Marika said. "Someone must have slipped something into the champagne."

"Madder music, stronger wine!" It was Ruth, returning to her seat.

"I think the orchestra's taking a time-out," Sam said, "but stronger wine is no problem." He beckoned the waiter, asked him to fill their glasses, and told him to keep the buckets filled too.

Andrew excused himself, and on his way to the men's room he stopped at the bar, gave the bartender some money, and asked him to send a bottle of the same wine to the young couple he'd been observing with benevolent envy and delight. "Just tell them it came from someone who wishes them well," he said, "and don't point out the source. Did I give you enough?"

"Yes, sir."

"Here's another five," he said, laughing. "Hush money."

On his way back to the table he passed Michael going to the men's room. "Did you see those jugs?" Michael asked. "Well, of course you did. Who could miss them? Sweet as melons, I'll bet. If Marika weren't here, I'd be all over her."

"I didn't know that would stop you."

"I'll discuss it with Marika."

"Maybe she comes with company."

"Well, you're cute, sweetheart. Want to join us? I forgot—you like older women. We could ask Molly and take the show on the road."

"Jesus!" Andrew shook his head. "What a mind you've got. It's a national treasure."

" 'Nothing human is alien to me': Terence, Roman playwright, not like you."

" 'Nothing in excess,' baby: Apollo, Greek god, unlike you."

" 'Know thyself.' Same god"—and Michael went on his way, laughing.

Another glass of champagne, Andrew thought, returning to the table, and he might be up for anything. He should definitely not have had that gin and tonic in the hotel room. And then there was the drink in the bar, and at least one drink before dinner, too. He couldn't drink like this. Yasmine was sitting in his place, and he sat down next to Rick. "Kevin said you had some theory about the saints, that the saints let themselves go?"

"Imaginatively speaking," Rick said. "I was talking about the codes they use to describe their raptures. Basically they had a very erotic idea of God, and their mystical language was obviously sexual. Have you read their writings—Saint Catherine, the two Theresas, Saint John of the Cross? What they're really talking about is plain as the nose on your face. The Church had to clean up a lot of that stuff so the faithful wouldn't get bad thoughts, and in fact they don't encourage people to read them without a spiritual director, an interpreter, at the ready. But I think the saints themselves knew full well what they were doing. They got off on God. In some cases, literally, I'll bet." He smiled. "You've heard the expression—perhaps you've even used it—'Holy fuck'? Well, that says it."

"Diabolical fellow, aren't you? Surely there's a little more to it than that."

"Is there anything else—really?" Rick took the bottle of champagne from its bucket and filled his glass. "The opium of the people. Have some."

Andrew laughed, and Ruth pulled up a chair between them. "Give me a cigarette, would you, Rick? I wish we had some dope. Bermuda is so uptight, but you can't tell me somebody around here doesn't have a line on some."

"I'll see what I can do," Rick said, passing her the cigarettes. "One of the beach attendants would probably know where to get it, maybe the bartender."

"Rick wouldn't let us bring any in. He was afraid we'd get stopped at Customs." She took a cigarette from the pack and looked at Andrew, waiting. He picked up a book of matches from the table, lit her cigarette, and watched her tilt her head back and slowly inhale, watched the smoke pour from her mouth. "When I was a kid, I always wanted to be able to blow smoke through my nose. I thought that was the height of sophistication."

"That's funny," Andrew said. "So did I. That and blowing smoke rings."

"Would you like a cigarette?"

"No, thanks. I don't smoke." His eyes moved about the room. He found his young couple, toasting each other, it appeared, with his champagne. It made him happy that he'd sent it.

"Never?" She inhaled again, and lowered her arm to the table. The smoke floated in a lazy plume from her hand to her face. The orchestra had resumed its playing, and various members of their party were drifting toward the floor, Kevin toward the bar, leaving the three of them alone.

"Well, I used to, but not anymore. Hardly ever." He paused, looking at her, at her dress the color of peaches, at the cigarette lightly grasped in her polished fingers. "But maybe"—he took it from her—"I'd have a puff of yours"—and quickly inhaled the smoke. He started to return it to her hand, but put it in the ashtray instead. "Thanks."

"Are you a Yankees fan?" Rick asked him.

"Not really. I don't follow baseball much. You should talk to Michael about it. He gets violent about the Yankees." Molly had left her cigarettes on the table. He reached over and took one, held it without lighting it. "Strange bunch to get violent about, if you ask me. Do you follow the team?"

"I compare it to the dance: highly codified, highly stylized, an all-male democratic ballet controlled by a tyrant-coach with three central figures: the pitcher, the batter, and to a lesser degree, the catcher. As innocent as Eden."

"Innocent?"

"Harmless. Unthreatening. A fantasy, of course, a safe, acceptable fantasy for boys, and one that players and fans—the dumbest, beer-swilling jerk from the Bronx—can easily participate in, without fear or censure."

"Rick has a theory about everything," Ruth said. She struck a match and extended the flame toward him. "Aren't you going to light your cigarette?"

"I hadn't thought about it," he said, laughing, accepting her light. "Thanks. What's so democratic about it?"

"Every member of the *corps* is allowed his moment of glory. Everyone comes up to bat and then all the attention is focused on him and his magic stick."

Andrew took a puff on the cigarette, shuddered, and stubbed it out. "I hate Chesterfields."

"Have one of these," Ruth said.

"No, thanks. Maybe later."

"Football is just bloody warfare. Have you read Huizinga on game-playing? *Homo ludens?*"

"No."

"It's a very dense, closely argued theoretical work on the philosophy of play—"

"You'll be sorry if you get him started on that," Ruth said. "The next thing you know, he'll want you to join the team. He can be very persuasive."

"I'm not much of a ballplayer," Andrew said. "A miserable game of tennis is about all I can manage."

"Oh, Rick doesn't play *those* games," Ruth said. "He just talks about them."

"Ruth was speaking loosely," Rick said. "What she meant was that she'd like you to join our group."

"But you've joined ours. We're already a group." Andrew reached over and took one of the cigarettes Ruth had offered. He slipped it into his pocket, with some matches.

"You should come over to see us—Rick and Kevin and Jack

and me. Rick has rented a house in Sandys. It's very private. He's gotten this film bug, and he's thinking of making a movie here."

"You could make a great movie in these coves," Rick said. "Some of them are totally deserted, if you can believe it, and the light is perfect."

"That's right, you said you'd made a film. *As You Like It.*" Andrew looked up at the sky, at the moon looming huge above them. He shook his head vigorously back and forth.

"You have a good memory," Rick said.

"You mentioned it on the beach this afternoon." He shook his head again. "I think I'm getting drunk. Excuse me"—he got up from the table—"I'm going over there and breathe in the sea"— and he walked to the stairs that led to a parapet, climbed the few steps, and stood leaning with his hands against the stones, looking toward the water darkly glistening, flat in the moonlight. The nightclub was built on a hilltop in the middle of the island, and the sea must have been half a mile away. Closer, he could see the approaching lights of a moped, followed by an auto passing on the road below, and tiny dots twinkling starlike from the occasional house; then, beyond the darkness of the land, the strange whiteness of moonlight streaking the water. He shook his head hard, and turned his back to the sea to look at the place he'd left, sunk like the crater of a small volcano into a kind of hollow in the rock—to protect it from the wind, stronger, he supposed, at this mild elevation. He smiled with amazement, with a kind of mad, wry amusement. Lunatic! *Of course it couldn't be.* He felt for the cigarette in his pocket, took it out and lit it, breathing in. The smoke made him dizzy. It must be late—he didn't bother to look at his watch—but the band was still playing and the dance floor was moving, a few couples still coming and going from the tables clustered close around it. He didn't see his young couple; they must have left. His own table was empty; most of the tables were now. The place was emptying. Ann was dancing with Rick again, then Jack. Michael cut in and Sam followed, laughing. Ann was easy to spot; the arrow sparkled in her hair and the pearls gleamed against the blackness of her dress. She looked to be having a great time. They all did. Michael cut in on Kevin, who had gotten to his feet at last to dance with Marika. Suddenly Michael was dancing with Marika and Yasmine too, and Ruth was dancing with Kevin, who reached for Jack and pulled him into their group. Ruth and Kevin and Jack. He gave a dry little laugh and shook his head, incredulous. *It couldn't possibly be!* He stubbed out his cigarette on the parapet and dropped it into the darkness. Everyone seemed to be dancing with everyone else, even Molly in her dress the color of cornflowers, who had joined Sam and Ann and now Rick. He turned back to the sea again, shimmering molten silver where the moonlight broke the blackness. *As You Like It*, indeed. The deliveryman and her husband; the man in the baseball cap. The New York Yankees cap! It was preposterous. He looked back to the floor. Ann and Ruth were waving at him, beckoning him to come. He stood there, grimly looking: the mirrored globe turning slowly beneath the moon, shooting its rays back into the darkness; Ann sparkling with lights; Ruth bleached white as chalk in the moonlight. She grabbed a tambourine from the orchestra and rushed toward him. "What a way to celebrate the Sabbath! Kevin scored three joints." Ruth pushed the glowing tube at him. "Have a hit."

"You're not smoking those on the dance floor!"

"Of course we are. We've got the floor to ourselves. No one is noticing but the band, and they're all stoned. Sam has dropped so much money in this place tonight, they'd let us do anything. Come on!"

He sucked on the joint, held in the smoke until he was forced to expel it. "Ruth, exactly where do you live?"

"I told you. Directly across the street from your apartment."

"What floor?"

"The fourteenth."

"The fourteenth?"

"Well, it's actually the thirteenth, but they call it the fourteenth. There's no thirteenth floor in our building, and Rick would never live on it if there was. Why all the questions? Come on."

"I could look in your windows." He smiled at her.

She laughed. "I suppose you could. We'll have to remember to pull the shades." She raised her tambourine to the night and shaking it pulled him down the steps to join the wildly surging figures on the floor. "Join the dance," she shouted. "Orchestra! Step up the beat! Yaiieee!" He stood there hesitant for a moment, churning, dumb with despair and desire, then grimly abandoned himself to the frenzied dance.

"Fun, fun, fun!" Ann tossed her head back, her pearls swinging around her neck, her feet glittering with tiny lights. She drew him and Kevin toward her, Jack behind her. Someone in the band tossed her a tambourine, and suddenly all the women had them and everyone was dancing in a line that curled and wound behind Ruth now, before the order broke and they all shook to another, wilder tune, laughing, shouting, madly dancing, joints passing freely between the dancers and the frantically playing band. Ann snatched a sort of pompon from one of the musicians, shook it in the air, and they all fell into place behind her, hands entwined, tambourines rattling, their cries piercing the night as she weaved around the floor, releasing his hand now and reaching for Marika's and Marika's for Molly's, and soon the six men were dancing in the center of the five circling women when Ann lowered her wand, Sam shouted, "Where is it written that only the young must dance?" and to the cheers of the crowd he wriggled under it, followed by Jack and Michael and Kevin and Andrew as the baton inched lower and lower; and suddenly they had all broken up again—Sam running to the table with his billfold out, then to the band, showering money—and the men and the women whirling and writhing, in a line now on the floor, now moving toward the exit, following Ann and her baton, her shaking tambourine, as the band played "When the Saints Go Marching In" and their flushed and laughing troupe sang "When the Saints Go Marching Out," into the moonlit Bermuda night.

"Well!" Ann exclaimed, tossing her stick aside. She smoothed back her hair, and removed the arrow. "Well!" Laughing, she tried to catch her breath as the line broke up and they began slowly walking up the path to Sam's car and the waiting taxis.

"Look!" Sam was pointing to something beside their path. They all turned. "One of the wonders of Bermuda: a night-blooming cereus!" The flower glowed white as the moon outside, a brilliant, intense yellow within, so magnificent and strange and richly fragrant that it seemed to come not from the earth at all but from some other marvelous, alien world. "It won't last beyond the dawn," he said.

Ann banged her toe getting into the car, and by the time she reached the hotel she was limping. When they got to their room, Andrew took off her shoe and examined her toe. "Even the Queen of the Night has to pick up her feet," he said. "I wonder if you broke it. It's turning purple."

"I'm sure it's just bruised," she said, rising, pulling off her other shoe, then her dress, and tossing it on the chair. "Oh, Lord, I forgot to leave the tambourine!" She picked it up and rattled it again. "Shall we dance?"

"You're still limping."

"I'll worry about it in the morning. I have something else on my mind now." She was still flushed with excitement.

"What's that?"

"You. I want you. I want to make love."

"I'm sorry." He felt a sudden desperate sinking in his stomach. "I'm sick." And he rushed into the bathroom and threw up. When he came out, pale and shaking, the room was lit only by the moon rushing like the air through the gauzy curtains, falling on the tambourine, the pearls, glinting off the stones of her arrow on the table, in the jeweled buckles of her shoes askew on the floor. Ann was already asleep.

Andrew opened his eyes. Sunlight streamed through the curtains. He looked around the room. It looked like Newark after the riots. He glanced at Ann. She was still sleeping. He carefully left the bed and went into the bathroom. He brushed his teeth, and looked at himself in the mirror. He looked alive. He didn't even feel so bad, which was amazing. He drank two glasses of water and stepped into the shower. He took a very long shower, and when he had finished he felt quite refreshed and ready for breakfast. He put on his robe and walked back into the room. The disarray hadn't magically disappeared. He began to pick things up, hanging up Ann's dress, checking to see where she'd torn the seam. It looked as if it could easily be fixed. He put her pearls away, took the buckles off her shoes, put the buckles in a drawer and her shoes in the closet. He put her arrow in the drawer too. Oh, God, there was the tambourine! He didn't know what to do with that, so he took it to the balcony, trying to keep it from rattling, and set it in the corner on the floor. He stuffed their soiled clothes into the laundry bag—he certainly couldn't wear that shirt a second day; it looked as if he'd taken a bath in it

—and hung up his own things. Ann was beginning to stir. He picked up the telephone and ordered breakfast.

"Please don't do that," she said.

"Do what?"

"Mention food." She was curled up in the bed, her head buried in the pillow, not moving. "I feel sick."

"Hung over?"

"Just sick."

"Maybe you'll feel better when you eat something."

"I told you not to talk about it."

"Okay, sorry. But breakfast is coming anyway. You can go into the bathroom. I'll have it put on the balcony. You won't need to see it."

"Please be quiet."

"Dance the tune, you pay the piper," he said, going to the balcony to wait for breakfast. He shouldn't have said that; maybe she hadn't heard. He saw her get up, move limping to a chair and sit hunched on the edge of it, elbows on her knees, hands supporting her head. She looked miserable, and he was about to see if he could comfort her when she rushed to the bathroom and slammed the door. He went in and stood outside the door, heard her vomit. "Are you all right, angel? Can I do anything?"

"I'm all right. I'll be out in a minute."

He heard a knock on the door and let the waiter in, directing him to leave the trays on the balcony, telling him he'd set them up. "No, no," Andrew said. "That's all right." He hurried him toward the door, and returned to the balcony to set the table for breakfast.

"Suddenly I'm ravenous," Ann said, coming out of the bathroom in her robe and sitting down at the table. "What's for breakfast?"

"You must be feeling better. But you're still limping."

"That's nothing," she said, glancing at her foot. "I felt fine as soon as I threw up."

"Perhaps it was something you ate?" She gave him a skeptical look. "Or maybe drank?"

"I didn't have that much to drink. I don't think I drank as much as you did, in fact. I don't know what it was, but I feel fine now. Better than fine. I feel wonderful, ready for anything!" She bit into an English muffin. "I had a good time last night."

"It was crazed."

"Well, I guess it did get a bit wild, but I'd hardly call it *crazed*. I thought those people were very nice."

"You did? Which people?"

"Rick and Ruth and Kevin and Jack. Who did you think?"

"You might have meant Marika and Yasmine."

"Well, I didn't. I meant the people Molly and I met on the beach. They were more interesting than Michael's new girlfriends—or whatever they are."

"You liked them?"

"Yes, didn't you? You certainly seemed to be enjoying them. Of course, you seemed to be enjoying the others, too." She was eating her eggs now. Andrew watched her, fascinated. It was amazing how she could eat with such gusto, when just minutes before she wouldn't tolerate the mention of food. "Funny they should turn out to live across the street. We ought to have them to dinner sometime."

"Do you really think so?"

"Well, yes; why not?"

"What would we serve—raw meat?"

"Really, Andrew. What's the matter with you? Rick and Ruth are good company. Certainly entertaining, and intelligent, too. I'd think you'd like them. Anyway, I'm glad I met them."

"They may not be what they seem."

"Are you trying to tell me something, in your usual roundabout way?" She finished her English muffin.

"I don't think so."

"You don't *think* so? You're certainly peculiar this morning. What a good breakfast! Yes, I thought all of them were quite nice. Kevin and Jack seemed a little quiet, I guess—especially Kevin—but it's hard for anyone else to get in a word around theater people. They're all such egomaniacs."

"Yes, they were quiet. Until the end. They're theater people too, you know—more or less."

"Nobody was quiet at the end. I haven't danced like that in a long time. I didn't know I had it in me."

"Neither did I."

"You didn't?" She laughed. "Well, I like to surprise you now and then. It's good for you." She laughed. "I'm not what I seem."

"You looked beautiful."

"Thank you. You looked pretty good yourself out there on the floor"—she gave a throaty little chuckle—"good enough to eat." She'd finished her eggs, and was taking another English muffin from the basket. "Yes, good enough to eat." She smiled. "Would you pass me the jam, please?" He passed her three little pots. "Nice. A choice." She raised her eyes to him, a teasing smile playing across her face. "You still do." He laughed. She opened the raspberry and sniffed it. "Smells good. I'll save the marmalade for you." She glanced at his plate. "You're not eating. I can't believe it—I'm still hungry."

"The demon must have been exorcised."

"What?"

"Nothing. Would you like my eggs?"

"Don't you want them?"

"I'm not very hungry." He took a perfunctory bite of his muffin and put it down. "Here, take them." He passed her his plate. "I just want some juice and coffee."

"Eat your muffin, at least. You'll need your energy."

"I'll eat it."

"You do seem a little subdued this morning, darling. Are you feeling a trifle ragged, maybe?" She laughed. " 'Ragged, but right,' as the song goes?" She hummed the tune. " '*I just called up to tell you that I'm ragged but right*.' "

"Let me look at your toe." He rose from the chair and crouched before her, lifting her foot to his knee. It was badly bruised, mottled and purple. "That does not look good," he said. "It's really swollen. Is it the little one?"

"Yes."

"Does it hurt?" He pressed it lightly with his finger.

"Ouch! Of course it hurts—if you jab it!"

"Let me get some ice." He grabbed a washcloth from the bathroom and filled it with ice. He pressed it to her toe. She winced. "You've got to have this taken care of. I'll bet it's broken. We'll find a doctor in Hamilton. The hotel will know of one."

"I don't want to go to a doctor. It'll be fine."

"It's not fine now, and you don't want to make it worse. I'll call the desk." He went to the telephone to see what he could do, and in a few minutes he'd found a doctor who agreed to see her at noon. "It's getting close to eleven already," he said to her. "We'll have to hurry. I don't know how long it'll take us to get to Hamilton. I'll get you some aspirin. It'll help the swelling."

"Damn! I don't want to go to Hamilton. I'd rather stay here." He returned with the aspirin. "I'd rather"—she hobbled over and sat on his lap, ruffling his hair with her fingers—"make love. My foot isn't involved in that."

"Oh?"

"What do you mean, '*Oh?*'—you silly!" She nibbled his ear, then spotted the tambourine in the corner, and looked down at him. "What's my tambourine doing there?"

"I had to put it somewhere."

"Hand it to me, would you? I think I'll keep it. A souvenir. Who knows, it might come in handy." She shook it, gave him a sidewise glance.

"It sounds like a rattlesnake."

"No, it doesn't. It sounds nice. What *is* the matter with you this morning? Julia'd love it." She set it on the table, then looked at her toe, felt it, tried to wiggle it and winced again. "I suppose I ought to have it looked at, though. Well, maybe we can find something for Julia while we're in town. Then that would be taken care of."

"Ann, take your aspirin. It'll reduce the inflammation."

"Oh, have some fun! All you want to think about is my foot." She kissed his forehead. "There are better things to think about."

He laughed. "Get up," he said, pushing her off his lap and handing her a glass of water. "Swallow those pills. Do as the doctor tells you."

"That's not what the doctor ordered."

"It's what this doctor ordered. I'm going to get dressed. You'd better do the same. By the way," Andrew asked, leaving the balcony, "do you want to have your dress fixed?"

"What's wrong with it?"

"Last night—you ripped the seam."

"Oh." She came into the room, went to the closet, and examined it. "No, I don't think so. I like it with a longer slit. It's a lot better for dancing. I'll take care of it myself when we get home. Besides"—she looked at him—"don't you think it's sexier this way?"

"I guess maybe it is," he said. "You'd better get dressed."

"Rick liked it."

"And he said you ought to be in the movies, right?"

"How did you know that?" She stepped into her skirt.

"He's made one. He's thinking about another. I figured he must have told you that. In fact, weren't you there when he mentioned it? Did he tell you anything about his movies?"

"No, not really. Just the title. Something from Shakespeare. *All's Well That Ends Well*? No. It's *As You Like It*. I gather they're rather avant-garde."

"When you introduced me to him on the beach yesterday, he said we should collaborate."

"Really?"

"Not because I know anything about movies; because I'm a dramatist."

"Maybe you should. You said the other day you were thinking about a movie script."

"I did? Oh." He remembered it. "That was a joke. Are you ready? Let's go."

They ran into Molly in the lobby. "Sam just rang your room," she said. "He's looking for you, Andrew."

"What did I do now?" What ever had made him put it that way? he asked himself; he felt absurd. But he'd said it with a little laugh, so he hoped he hadn't sounded too foolish.

"What did you *do*? Did you do something we ought to know about? Tell us, darling. You'll feel better."

He laughed again. "I was joking. I was afraid maybe I got a little wild last night."

"*You* got a little wild last night? Lovey, we *all* got a little wild last night. Myself included. Even Ann." Ann laughed with her. "Your wife is not quite so Junior League as she looks."

"She's not a member."

"I know, sweetie. Why would anyone want to be? It was just a way of speaking. And Sam, the dancing fool! He's feeling a bit sheepish today, I think—as well he might."

"Sam promised he'd produce a hell of a party," Andrew said, "and he certainly did. He's unquestionably a terrific host. And you're pretty terrific, yourself."

"You did your part, my dears. Both of you. You're such great fun, and wonderful dancers. And Ann and I produced the mystery guests. What did you think of them?"

"They're really exceptionally nice," Ann said, "and they certainly livened up the party. What good dancers!"

"This little dancer has done something to her toe," Andrew said, pointing to Ann's foot. "Broken it, I think. I'm about to take her into Hamilton to see a doctor."

"Oh, dear! I thought I noticed you limping, Ann. You should get off it. Let's sit down." Molly walked over to a couch. "You should see an orthopedic man. Who are you going to?"

"Someone the hotel recommended," Ann said. "I don't suppose he's a specialist, but I think most anyone can bind up a toe, if it needs it. I could do it myself, I'm sure, but Andrew insists on a doctor."

"Do you have time for coffee?"

"Actually, no," Andrew said. "We're in rather a rush. I don't know how long it takes to get into Hamilton, and the appointment's in an hour."

"Why don't I drive you in, Ann? We could make a little shopping trip out of it, if you feel up to that. Then Sam could talk to Andrew while we're gone. I'll just leave a note for him— or Andrew, you can tell him. If Sam finds out about your toe, Ann, he's liable to have you in the hospital. He's really a Jewish mother, you know. I want to get him some Cuban cigars, anyway, and perhaps something for the children."

"Oh, that's not necessary," Andrew said. "You don't want to spend your day in Hamilton."

"Nonsense. I'd like to. I have to go in sometime, and today seems as good a day as any. We'll find some wonderful spot for lunch. And now we do have time for coffee. I've got to have another cup. I've had a bit of a struggle getting started this morning. Ann, why don't you elevate that foot?" She pulled a chair closer so Ann could raise it.

Andrew called for a pot of coffee. "So what did *you* think of the mystery guests, Molly?"

"Entertaining. Unusually good-looking, all of them. Fun. Infectious. But a bit odd—an odd group." She rummaged in her bag and took out a pack of cigarettes.

"Odd?" Andrew asked. "In what way?"

"Oh, I don't know. Not the sort of people you usually meet in resorts like Bermuda. Maybe on some Greek island. Mykonos.

A place like that. Do you have a light? I can't seem to find my matches."

He found some matches on a nearby table and lit her cigarette, watched her inhale. "How do you mean?"

"Bermuda is so straight, so . . . *bourgeois*. A sedate little haven for captains of industry, and honeymooners who couldn't care less. Five days is *it* for me. Look at the people around us. Everybody's got blue hair and pink dresses and arthritis. Not our friends' kind of crowd, I should imagine. Not my kind of crowd, either—nor yours, as far as that goes. Don't you agree?"

"They do seem a little more wild than that. Yes, I agree." He laughed suddenly. "Maybe those others aren't affected by the crazy compass here. They've got magnetic immunity or something." He paused. "I'm not sure that Rick and company are our kind of crowd either."

"Andrew's being very dignified this morning," Ann said. "Even the slightest bit stuffy. They're very nice, and they certainly were fun last night. If that's what the compass here does, I like it. I'm glad I'm not immune."

"Actually, I thought Rick seemed rather pedantic at times," Molly said, "but I can imagine he's an effective teacher—all that lore he's full of. In any event, you meet people at these places, you're flung together for the time, and you never see them again, despite assurances to the contrary."

"Since they live just across the street," Ann said, "I'm going to have them to dinner one evening—so perhaps you will see them again. A little Bermuda reunion. We could dance. That would be fun."

"If your foot is okay," Andrew said.

"Are you really? Well, it should be interesting, to see them on their home turf, to see if they're different. As we all know, people behave differently when they're away from the constraints of home."

"Andrew, my foot will be fine." Ann brightened. "We'll see them tomorrow, anyway, on the boat. I'm looking forward to it. When are we meeting?"

"I hope you'll be able to go."

"Andrew!" Ann shook her head, half exasperated, half perplexed. "Of course I'll be able to go. At the very worst I've just broken my toe in a very minor way. I'm sure all it needs is some tape. When did you say we're meeting, Molly?"

"I think Sam said at nine thirty, in the lobby. The boat is docked at a marina near Somerset Bridge. He's engaged it for ten. We'll have to get word to them. Ruth gave me their number. *That* girl is a pistol! Lord!"

"Isn't she," Ann said. "A bundle of energy. And so pretty, quite sweet-looking."

"Almost," Andrew said. "Sweet like a volcano."

Molly laughed. "Sarah Lawrence blows off in Bermuda."

"Blows up Bermuda, I think," Andrew said. "Maybe both. But she went to Columbia, or Barnard."

"She looks like Sarah Lawrence. A voluptuous Sarah Lawrence. Little Miss Boobs."

Andrew looked off across the lobby. "Once I thought she looked like a Wellesley girl, maybe Bennington."

"Well, she does, in a way," Molly said. "Those girls all have something in common. It's their rich daddies, I think. One thing I do know is that I'm too old to smoke marijuana. I don't know what seized me. That was the third time in my life."

"Really? A few years ago, when I first discovered it, I thought it was the solution to the problems of the human race. I thought if Lyndon Johnson took a toke, the war would be over. I've since changed my mind. He might have nuked them. I guess that would have ended the war, all right." He laughed. "I felt as if I'd been nuked last night."

Molly chuckled. "We were *all* nuked last night. You don't smoke that stuff often, do you? Does he, Ann? It's not good."

"What stuff?"

"Funny stuff, dear. The stuff we're talking about. Your basic controlled substance."

"No," Ann said. "He had his mild pot period a few years back, when everyone was discovering it. It had the most wonderful effect on him then. He'd get these laughing highs. Now it doesn't make him laugh, and it seems to leave him depressed."

"Are you depressed this morning, Andrew? You shouldn't be. Oh, there's Sam, trying to find me. Sometimes I wonder how the poor thing makes it across the street." She rose and called to him.

"He may have trouble crossing the street," Andrew said, "but he certainly knows how to make it down Broadway."

"Yes, thank God." She turned to Sam as he approached. "Darling, won't you sit down for a minute? I'm taking Ann into Hamilton in the car. We think she's broken her toe—but don't worry; everything will be all right. You and Andrew and Michael can talk while we're gone."

Sam looked at Ann's foot, fussing over it, insisting she keep it elevated. "You're making me feel I'm ready for traction," Ann said. "Really, Sam, it looks worse than it feels."

"I told you he'd be calling for an ambulance," Molly said. "Oh, Sam, you're such a Jewish mother! That's why I love you, angel." She kissed him on the cheek. "Isn't he wonderful?" she asked, of no one in particular. "He's just a softy underneath it all."

When he had finished examining Ann and they were settling down to their coffee, Sam asked if anyone had seen Michael. "I was going to call his room but I was afraid who might answer."

"You could try the sisters' room," Andrew said. "I guess that's assuming the sisters are sharing a room. A mistaken assumption, I'm sure."

"I might get all three of them."

Andrew laughed. "Anything is possible."

"You know, I quite liked Michael's girls," Molly said, "better than most of his women, and certainly better than his last wife—but then, I have a weakness for Levantines. How else could I have gotten mixed up with Sam?"

"I liked them too," Andrew said. "I'm fearless. I'll call." But before he could pick up a house phone, Michael appeared, alone.

"Speak of the devil," Ann said.

"Michael's not the devil," Andrew said. "Michael's my friend. Right, Michael?"

"Good morning, everybody—what there is left of it. Has everyone had breakfast?" Michael looked at them. "Well, yes, I suppose everyone has had breakfast." He noticed Ann's foot on the chair. "What's wrong with your leg, Ann?"

"I stubbed my toe last night getting into the car. It's nothing, really. Molly's driving me into Hamilton in a few minutes to see a doctor—at everyone's insistence. Are you just getting up, Michael?"

"After a night like that? Of course I'm just getting up. How you two ladies ever linked up with Dionysus and his merry band I'll never know. What's their story?"

"He teaches comparative lit at Columbia and he's making movies."

"Yes," Michael said, "I know—but what's the *real* story? He's not exactly your typical professor, and the nightclub last night is definitely not your ordinary classroom. Harvard was never like that. Maybe Columbia's changed since the revolution."

"Everything's changed since then." Andrew turned to Molly and Ann. "You two have got to get going. You'll miss your appointment." He picked up her cigarettes. "Don't forget these."

"I wonder if Marika and Yasmine would like to go with us," Molly said, returning the cigarettes to her bag. "They're quite special, Michael."

"They're coming along now," Michael said. "Why don't you ask them?" In a few minutes, the four women had left for Hamilton, and Sam and Michael and Andrew found a table in the shaded lanai near the pool.

"I've got some very good backers lined up for the show," Sam said. "We've got to arrange a reading for them and it has to take place as soon as I get back from London, which will be the end of next week. Oddly enough, they want to know something about the play before they throw money at it. I talked to my secretary this morning. She's sending them the London reviews and some cost estimates that I pulled out of my ass, but I want you both to work on Larry Evans. We've got to get him for the lead. He's a name, there's an audience out there that wants to see him, and the backers want their money back. They're funny that way. We'll make the reading very casual, maybe at my place. We don't want anybody to lose face. We'll make it look as if it just kind of"—he paused, shrugged—"happened. Everybody knows it doesn't just happen, but it's important to keep up the bullshit. Christ! You stay in the theater long enough and the *Bar Mitzvah* boy turns Japanese." He mused for a moment, cracking his knuckles. "Maybe we could do the reading at Larry's. Backers are basically star-fuckers. Does he have enough room? Does he live like a human being or an animal? Have you ever seen his place?"

"He's got room," Michael said, "but I think it would be better at your place or Andrew's. That way he wouldn't even have to take part, unless he should suddenly feel the Muse's call. He could just sort of 'appear,' you know? I'll work on Evans. So will Andrew. We both threw him some softballs at Andrew's dinner last week. Now we'll play hard. Why don't you just give him a casual call when you get to New York? If he knows you're serious, Sam, he'll be interested." He laughed—"You give good phone"—and Sam and Andrew laughed too. "It's a great role, for Christ's sake! He ought to be begging for it!"

"He will be. I'll call him, maybe suggest a drink. And Andrew, I want you to be prepared to talk about your play with these guys. You wrote it, you've got to sell it, kid. I know you hate to get your hands dirty, but you're not an innocent bystander in all this. You're guilty as shit."

"Guilty?" Andrew felt himself bristle, and then begin to flush. "What did I do now?"

"*Not* now. You've already done it. That play didn't write itself. *You* wrote the fucking thing! Sometimes you act as if you didn't have anything to do with it—but sweetheart, your hands are already dirty. You got to get them dirtier. You're not the only one with an investment in this. We've all got something at stake, and we don't want to lose it. We're talking hard sell that looks as smooth as Ruthie's little tush." He cracked his knuckles again. "By God, that girl could break balls! We'll get around to her in a minute. We're not talking about breaking balls at the reading, of course. We're just talking about twisting an arm or two, and so sweetly they'll never know they've been twisted until they get home and discover their wallets are missing. No *goyisher kopf*, Andrew—think like a Jew. Understand?"

Andrew couldn't help himself: he laughed. Sam liked to stud his speech with his grandmother's Yiddish when he was talking theater business—especially if the recipient didn't happen to be Jewish and most especially if he was but preferred to overlook it. "Throws them off their guard," he liked to say. "They want to think because I have a name like Walcott and married a *shiksa* and can walk through the Knickerbocker Club without the chandeliers crashing to the floor, that I forgot I was a Jew. That tells them."

"Okay," Andrew said, "I get it. Guilty as charged. I'll grit my teeth and think of something."

"Give them your best Gentile charm. They love that, especially if they think they've got something you'd give your left nut for." He looked him in the eye, unsmiling, then slowly spoke. "And Andrew, you would."

"He'd never miss it," Michael said.

"But don't be so goddamned *goy* that you're hiding behind the couch!"

Andrew laughed again. He really did like Sam. "Okay. I promise not to hide behind the couch. I won't even escape to the bathroom. As I once told Michael, I'll give my best impersonation of myself."

"You know, fellows, when I asked you to meet with me here in Bermuda, *Forty-one East* hadn't opened in London. I had nothing to go on but an early script, and the belief I've had in your work—your work, Andrew, and your work, Michael—since I saw Andrew's first play at that dump that was so far off Broadway it might as well have been in New Jersey, before it settled into the Manhattan Theater Club. *Riverhead.* I must have been fascinated by Gentile folkways. Once they seemed as crazy to me as five nights in a Turkish harem. Still do, sometimes. Probably I was trying to figure out my wife." He laughed. "Still am. You may have had some lean years since, Andrew, but you've got a great one coming up. I know it. It's already started. And now that we've talked enough business so I can write off this road show, let's get to the good parts. Michael, what in the fuck are you doing with *two* women, these two gorgeous *shiksas*? I even like them! And they're smart!"

"Ask him that question," Andrew said, "and you'll get a pageant. Sorry to steal your line, Sam. I had to. It's too good." He turned to Michael. "Well? We're waiting. Let's hear it."

"You think I've got too much of a good thing?" Michael asked. "Everything in excess. It's my new motto."

"What's so new about it?"

"You're right.

"More happy love! more happy, happy love!
  For ever warm and still to be enjoy'd,
    For ever panting, and for ever young . . .

Nothing new about it at all. It's as old as that Grecian urn. Older."

"Let's hear the rest of the stanza, Michael."

"It doesn't apply."

"The fuck it doesn't," Sam said, and began to recite it:

"All breathing human passion far above,
That leaves a heart high-sorrowful and cloy'd,
A burning forehead, and a parching tongue.

You guys think Sam Walcott can't quote Keats? He wasn't talking about *people*; he was talking about figures on a fucking vase! That last line is the operative one. It's especially poignant today."

"Sort of the way I feel," Andrew said. "Well, Michael, what is their story? Marika told me she does documentaries."

"She does. She took a group of Greek immigrants in Queens and went back to the island they came from, traced their roots, followed their children, recorded the changes. The film won a prize at the Edinburgh festival. It's scheduled for public television next season. She's serious."

"She may be. Are you?"

"And the other one?" Sam asked.

"Yasmine's a designer. Clothes once, now interiors."

"Sets?"

"Restaurants."

"That's a set. Funny she didn't mention it to me."

"Probably she was afraid you'd think she wanted something."

"That didn't stop Ruthie. She wants something."

"She wants your balls," Andrew said.

"Among other things." Michael laughed. "I'd let her play with mine for a while."

"She might not give them back," Andrew said.

"Well, if you want to lose yours, Michael," Sam said, "fine. Mine stay where they are."

"She's pretty powerful. Built like a brick shithouse, as they say. Andrew noticed that. Right, Randy?"

"Who didn't?" Sam asked. "I had to pull her nipples out of my nose."

"What was your head doing down there?" Michael asked.

"It wasn't my head, pal. That was right where it always is: firmly attached. It was her boobs. She practically shoved them in my face."

"Ann thinks she's nice." Andrew smiled, and shook his head. Sometimes Ann quite bewildered him. He remembered his mother's believing, when he was in high school, that his wildest girlfriend was the nicest, and the first girl he'd ever had a really heavy crush on was "fast." She was the daughter of a barber, who acted as if a chaste good-night kiss or two were something recklessly approaching an orgy. For that one, any subtle shift of attention below the neck was tantamount to rape. She thought she might have a vocation as a nun. Andrew eventually had agreed. He still remembered the linoleum on her living-room floor; he'd spent a lot of time with both feet planted firmly on it as he sat on her couch, imagining what forbidden mysteries perched hidden under her sweater, what that provocative gentle roundness might feel like bare—wondering, as far as that went, what it might feel like clothed. He never found out, and he never even dared to imagine what any other part of her might feel like. He supposed his mother didn't think nice people had linoleum on their floors. And the other one didn't. She'd had a nice Persian rug that she liked to grapple on, hoarsely panting, uttering little moans, biting his neck. She was a biter, that one. It was no problem getting her sweater off, or her brassiere either, except for the hooks. Of course she wouldn't go "all the way," as she put it. She was outraged when he rather aggressively suggested it one afternoon after school, there on the rug in her mother's empty house. She was saving that, and probably, Andrew thought now, she had kept it for another six months at least—but an occasional hand job didn't count. She was good at making distinctions—a lot of girls were then—and crazy as a loon, too. His mother had loved her. Ann had been good at making distinctions too, distinctions that used to mystify him when he first met her, then thought he understood for a while, and that now were beginning to mystify him again. Before they were married, her mother had told him she was a "nice" girl; Andrew had agreed. "Sometimes my wife's judgment is off," he said.

"We have proof of that," Michael said. "Look who she married."

"Well," Sam said, "we're seeing them tomorrow, anyway. I guess we got a reprieve today."

"In the nick of time," Andrew said. "It was a hard day's night."

"They're a strange bunch," Sam said. "I can't quite figure them out. I don't think I entirely trust them, although I certainly put myself at their mercy last night. I'll be more careful tomorrow. None of that dope. Christ! I *never* smoke that shit. My kids would be shocked. Sex, drugs, and rock 'n' roll!" He shook his head, then laughed. "They think they're the only ones who can get high and make fools of themselves."

"I guess we proved them wrong," Michael said.

"Rick tells me he's made a movie," Sam said.

"Everybody thinks he can make a movie these days," Michael said. "I'd be curious to see his. Ruth is in it."

"They're all in it," Andrew said.

"How do you know that?"

"I've seen it."

"What were you doing—looking through their windows?"

"What makes you say that?"

"You live across the street, and I know what you're like. I should tell your mother. 'Tommy,' she'd say, 'come in here this very minute. I have something to say to you. Your room is being moved to the cellar, where your mind is. The windows will be boarded up.' "

"Actually, I wrote the script, dildo-head. Go jerk off."

"Well, sewer-brain, tell us about it."

"Would you two assholes not get started on this shit? When you go into your little-boy routines, it's too much for a grown man to bear. That place you grew up in must have been a zoo. Especially with you two chimpanzees in it. And I thought Jews were crazy! Waiter," he called, "bring these animals a bunch of bananas. It's time for their feeding." The waiter looked a little puzzled, but he brought the bananas at once. "I'm glad to see I've got some clout with some people."

"You've got plenty of clout with me, Sammy." Michael peeled his banana. "Just what the doctor ordered. But Sam, I didn't grow up there, only summered there."

Andrew cleared his throat. "What I meant was, Rick has asked me to collaborate with him, maybe write a script for his next movie. Perhaps you'd like a part. He could make you a star, if you lost about twenty pounds. Twenty years, too."

"Are you crazy? You can't do that," Michael said. "You've

got better things to do than play with some English teacher's home movies."

"He teaches comparative lit. I'm not going to."

"Either of you up for tennis?" Sam asked.

"I'm up for a nap, myself," Andrew said. "I woke up early, and suddenly I'm very tired. It's so hot." He wiped his brow with his napkin.

"You're sweating," Sam said. "In fact, you're dripping. It's not that hot. Do you have a fever?" He reached over and felt Andrew's forehead. "Are you sure you're feeling all right?"

"Yes. I'm fine. Just tired."

"I'll play with you, Sam," Michael said. "I've got the afternoon off."

"We've all got the afternoon off, and I guess we need it. Why don't you go lie down, Andrew? You do look a little tired. You've got to take care of yourself. For your own sake. I think you should see my doctor when you get back to New York. He's the best. I'll have my secretary set up an appointment. Maybe you need some vitamin shots or something. I want you to stay well."

"Really, I'm fine. Just suddenly sleepy. It's nothing to worry about."

"Yeh, well, I worry about it anyway. Go rest now. We'll meet around eight thirty for dinner. An early night. I know a quiet spot that's good. We'll feed you chicken soup."

Andrew laughed and got up from the table. "Oops! Forgot my banana. Thanks, Sam. See you guys later." He picked up the banana, peeling it as he walked toward the lobby. When he got there, he asked the man behind the desk for a postcard. *Dear Julia,* he wrote: *Our fearless trio are steaming full speed ahead toward adventures yet unknown but to be revealed when your mother and I get home. We're going out on a boat tomorrow, into the Sargasso Sea, looking for Fingerfins. Won't that be fun? Mind the store. Love and a bundle of hugs, Daddy.* He gave the card to the clerk, asked him to stamp it —"Airmail, please"—and finished the banana. He thought the clerk looked at him a little strangely. It must have been the banana. The jerk! Hadn't he ever seen a man eating a banana before? "Could you dispose of this, please?" He handed him the peel and walked to the elevators, then changed his mind and went to the newsstand. The clerk peered at him from behind an array of sun lotions and oils. "Could I have a pack of cigarettes, please?"

"What kind, sir?"

"What kind? Oh, any old kind; I don't care."

"Winstons, perhaps?"

"Dunhills, I guess. They should be cheap here."

"Cheap, sir?"

"Well, this is a British colony, isn't it?" When he got to the room, he set the cigarettes on the table and took off his clothes. He closed the curtains and lay there on the bed in the gauzy light, not sleeping, not thinking, feeling his heart beating. After a while he got up and took a shower and shaved. He wrapped himself in a towel and returned to the room, sitting in a chair this time. He looked at the cigarettes on the table by his side. He opened the pack, lit one, and smoked it, watching the tendrils of smoke curl in the stillness of the room. He finished the cigarette and continued to sit there in the chair, his legs stretched out before him, his head flung back, his eyes focused on nothing but the soft light that suffused the yellow room.

It was hot in the room. He must have drifted off. He looked at his watch. It was just past one. He couldn't have drifted off for long. He got up and went to the bathroom, decided to get dressed. He'd go out for a walk. He put on a pair of shorts and his running shoes—maybe he'd run a little; they were comfortable for walking, in any case—and returned to the room. He saw the cigarettes on the table and picked them up, went to the closet and pulled his bag off the shelf, put the cigarettes in it. He went back for matches. Maybe he'd find a pleasant spot, some grassy dune above the sea, and read. He threw in his book; then, as if an afterthought, his swim trunks. You never knew. He might go swimming, test the Sargasso Sea. He guessed he'd already tested it. Yesterday. He noticed David Roper's message in the pocket of his bag. Maybe he'd walk that way, drop by, see if he was in. He didn't want to telephone, didn't want to commit himself. He pulled the note out of the bag, looked at the map David had drawn. Not far, obviously. He put the note back in its envelope and the envelope in the bag, then decided to close the doors to the balcony so the room would be cool when Ann returned. He picked up his bag and left the room and the hotel.

It was hot, the hottest day since they'd arrived in Bermuda. He should have worn a hat. He didn't know that he'd brought one from New York. Probably not. At least he had his sunglasses. He ambled along. He wanted to think, didn't want to think, didn't know *what* to think. What did he want to think about, anyway—the play? No. He'd written the play. He was tired of the play, though he couldn't say that. It was important to him, but it was done. The work was done. Of course, if it opened in the fall there would be a lot more work, but not yet. He would have a month or two to relax, puddle around with his next project, the Elgin Marbles, maybe—after he'd sold himself to the backers. Mustn't forget them. He needed those backers. He needed this play, as Sam had said. He couldn't live on air, after all, and his hands were already dirty, as Sam had also said. *How do you plead? Guilty as charged, Your Honor.* What was so guilty about him, for Christ's sake? He hadn't done anything. He thought of Daisy. Well, nothing much, anyway. Practically everybody had done something like that. It was no big deal. He'd have to remember that: it was no big deal. Just astonishing, that's all, a little crazy. More than a little! And in retrospect, a little frightening—he'd been so . . . out of himself, so . . . *seized*, as if he'd been operating on automatic pilot, responding to, controlled by urgent signals other than his own. The past floats up within us, he thought, until we give it proper burial: a line he'd read somewhere; maybe a line he'd written. It was peculiar, at any rate, and peculiar that he couldn't seem to let her alone—writing her that note, the postcard yesterday. Yes, that was peculiar too. He could have let that event in the Huntingtons' library simply pass; their paths had rarely crossed, after all. At the same time, he couldn't let her near. It was as if he had to keep her in sight, like a dangerous fish. He'd hardly been infatuated; more mesmerized than anything. He didn't know what he'd been, what he'd felt, and he didn't want to think about it, either; didn't know how. He pulled out David Roper's map and looked at it, checked his position. He was walking along a path above the sea, the highway curved and rolling to his right. He was heading into the sun; he must be heading west. The sea was to his left. He turned to face it. A thousand, a million, a billion—an infinite number of tiny mirrors shot back at him like diamonds' fire. He put his hand to his head. It was very hot. Piercing. He felt like sitting down, but he didn't see any particular place to sit, any place that seemed to invite him. The grasses were prickly. Probably there were snakes. He forgot: there were no snakes in Bermuda. He pulled himself on. He saw a lizard scuttle out of his way. He'd been baking in the sun, Andrew supposed, and he'd surprised him. "That's all right, little lizard," he said aloud. "I won't hurt you. I didn't mean to scare you." He laughed. What was he doing, talking to lizards? Lord! What would he be talking to next? The toads? Plenty of toads to talk to here; the place was full of them. The trees? That laurel bush over there? He was glad he'd thought to take his swimsuit; he'd probably need to cool down. He did feel a little ragged this day; not smooth at all. It had been a fairly wild weekend, of course. His shoulder gave an involuntary twitch. Yes, that was just how he felt. Spastic. His shoulder knew it before he did. Interesting. The body had its own secrets, its own ineluctable rhythms. It went placidly on about its business, sometimes, it seemed, quite independent of the life its occupant lived, or wished to live. It was just *there*: gurgling, flowing, digesting, metabolizing, excreting: all on its own, like those poor brain-dead victims they keep alive year after year. *A splendid machine for staying alive under the most hostile conditions, the animal body's major product is shit, its minor products sweat, saliva, and urine, and, in the course of the lifetime of the male, untold billions of microscopic but vital spermatozoa conveyed by the seminal fluid; in the female, a predetermined, fixed number of ova, which, if not fertilized, are carried away by a bloody discharge. Although nature is profligate with the spermatogenetic male, it is highly economical with the ovulatory female. The total number of ova in a woman's body, could each be fertilized, would populate a village, while the number of spermatozoa in a single ejaculation could in theory father a good-sized city, the number generated by one male in his lifetime spawn the entire present population of the earth. These natural processes are beyond the creature's control.* Amazing! That must be where the energy went. Suddenly he realized he'd been thinking about the body in the same tones that that article he'd read had spoken of Bermuda: a new and mildly interesting territory to be visited briefly, its origins noted and major attractions admired, a few snapshots taken, here and there a shocker. See, but do not touch. To put it grossly, the body is a machine that shits and fucks, or tries to. That's the base of it. Literally. He smiled, puzzled by himself, disgusted. Still, it was fantastic. Untold billions! No wonder men died younger than women. He was, he realized, leaving certain other organs out of it. The human brain, for instance, with its tortuous folds wherein the mind, mired in that body, goes about its strange and risky business, occasionally floating free. Frightening. Dichotomies do not exist in nature; not in the single organism, anyway, no matter how complex. Mind is minding, as a professor he'd once had, a cultural determinist, used to say—over and over and over again: the mind is simply a function of the brain, as producing bile is a function of the liver, sperm of the testes. But that doesn't say much, does it? Or account for those accidents, those free-floating variations, the quirks and kinks that make the difference. The professor, though, had had an answer for everything. Andrew shuddered. *Sanity is to insanity as the shell is to the egg.* A fascinating idea, if alarming. He heard the sounds of pebbles crackling under his feet, felt his head pounding in the heat. Keep that shell intact! He imagined the inchoate plasm, waiting, churning within it. An incipient chicken whose destiny is to lay another egg. Or if a cock, more likely reach its apotheosis in a masterly chicken Kiev. Listen to him. Apotheosis! Masterly chicken Kiev! Now he was thinking like one of those overwrought food writers—ravishing sauces, blissful rémoulades, seductive thises and provocative thats. They wrote about food as if it were sex. It's not. It's just food. Raw material for the shit factory. Sometimes it's good, sometimes it's bad. Eating it is a pleasure, of course. Wasn't it Woody Allen who'd said that even if sex was bad it was still pretty good? If you're really hungry, food is like that too. A starving man wouldn't sneer at garbage; he'd find a succulent little something in the mess.

Andrew walked on. So what about those people? Well, we all lead the lives we're programmed to lead—always taking into account the small but critical magnetic impulses that modify the course from True North, or toward it. And how funny that Ann, who prided herself on her discernment and who also took a rather firm stand on certain matters of behavior—she seemed to find Sarah Spenser's taking up grenades less disturbing than her throwing away her brassiere, and maybe, in the long run, she was right; Sarah would eventually put down her weapons if she didn't blow herself up, but she'd never have quite the same attitude of necessity toward a piece of underclothing—how funny that Ann had actively *liked* them. How could he tell her? *Well, Ann, your wretched husband just happened to be looking out the window the day you and your mother-in-law went to* No, No, Nanette *and our neighbors, the nice new friends you'd like to have to dinner, were making a fuck movie. Yes, actually fucking—all three of them: quite an energetic little group, with Rick directing. Another Rick Reynolds production, brought to you by Ivory Soap. Why Ivory Soap? Well, they looked clean, and of course they'd want to be, all things considered. Isn't that amusing? Oh, it's not? I ought to have my mouth washed out with soap? Make it Ivory, please; so pure it floats. But Ann, sin comes in through the eye, not the mouth—unless you're really getting down to it. What shall we do about that? My eyes are very important to my work. It would be a pity to lose them.* Oh for Christ's sake, he thought: control yourself! The situation was actually pretty funny; ludicrous, in fact. And he rather liked them, too, if the truth were known. Well, perhaps *liked* wasn't the precise word; more probably he was fascinated by them. Who wouldn't be? A secret maker of skin flicks who taught comparative literature at Columbia? A porn star who read Euripides and *remembered* it? It's a free country, of course. She could read whatever she wanted. Nobody said you had to be dumb to fuck. Doing it on film was another matter, however, every vulnerable orifice exposed to the public's probing eyes. And those guys so shy and quiet—except for their cocks' and balls' going blindly about their usual business—enacting some forbidden private fantasy for the world to see. They might as well have been doing it in the Colosseum. *Kevin's sweating like a bull in mating season. Now he's ahead by a nose! Jack's dragging a little, holding up the rear, and Ruth—that little filly—looks a little feverish but she's panting doggedly on. Atta girl, Ruthie!* Maybe it wasn't even their fantasy. Just a couple of actors out for hire. Look, Ma, no hands! Innocent as the devil. It had to be *somebody's* fantasy, though. He wondered how many people in the world were into threesomes. No need to take in the whole world: how about just Bermuda? Staid old Bermuda. Forget New York. That figure might astound him. *One of the Mayor's significant accomplishments has been to reduce the number of sexual acts with three or more participants by one-sixteenth of one percent. The number of reported incidents of oral and anal sodomy among heterosexual, homosexual, and bisexual combinations of two or more presumably consenting adults was reduced by three-tenths of one percent. The number of orgasmic females declined by an unknown factor that is believed to correspond roughly to a similar decrease in the number of other-assisted male ejaculations. The proximate cause of this encourag-*

*ing decline in the index of Gross Sexual Depravity (GSD) is attributed to
the closing of an obscure apartment on Manhattan's West Side under a
rent-control statute defining an eligible household and an ordinance re-
stricting business activity in covered buildings. Although the incidence of
solitary masturbation could not be determined, the Archdiocese of New
York nonetheless strongly endorses the Mayor in his current campaign for
re-election, despite his questionable views on abortion.*

Andrew sat down, dizzy. He had to get himself together, get
off this lunatic train of thought. The sea had lost all color in the
brilliant sun. He shook his head and looked again. It shimmered
still, a sheet of quicksilver. On the shore the heat rose in waves
from the sand. He opened his bag, noticed the cigarettes, pulled
out David Roper's map. He was virtually there, he realized.
Maybe David would have some lemons. He'd love a lemonade.
He returned the map to his bag and saw the cigarettes again. No,
he would not have one. He got up and resumed his walk, leaving
the path for the highway, the spectacular corniche, and shortly
took a smaller road off it, lined with thick hedges and curving up
a hill. Within a hundred yards or so he reached the stone gate-
posts of—the plaque indicated—the *Jardin des Délices*. The iron
gates, wrought in fanciful arabesques, were open, and he passed
easily through into a winding drive overhung with hibiscus. The
air was fresh, and scented with flowers. Somewhere a wind chime
tinkled. He slowly made his way up the drive toward the pretty
shuttered villa at its end.

The house was not large, but no bungalow either: stucco,
painted a very pale creamy pink, almost white now in the intense
sunlight, and set a little back behind a stuccoed wall that extended
beyond the house to enclose, it appeared, a garden. Surrounded
by shrubs and flowers, its shutters closed against the heat, the
house squatted silent and glistening at the top of the hill,
strangely still amidst the twittering of birds and the occasional
drone of a honeybee. Andrew paused for a moment, dumb like a
dog before it, looking at it, taking it in. Dumb like a dog! Why
was he always thinking of Rilke? He felt a mild irritation. This
hill was not the Mont Sainte-Victoire, although the house could
have been in the South of France, in Greece, in some Mediterranean land. His sunglasses slipped on the bridge of his nose; a
bead of sweat ran down it. He brushed it away. He walked a few
more steps in the direction of the doorway. The door itself looked

solid and firmly shut. A very serious door. But toward the end of
the wall there was another, smaller door, ajar, leading into the
garden. He walked tentatively toward it, avoiding the house, and
touched the tips of his fingers lightly to it. The door swung
noiselessly open, startling him. He stood there, staring at, not
entering, the luxurious, verdant garden. It felt Mediterranean
too, and to the right, at its end, a small pool, six feet wide maybe,
but thirty or forty feet long, ran almost the width of the garden.
It was opaque, more a reflecting pool than a swimming pool, and
centered on its farther edge, a small stone dolphin, archaic-look-
ing, leisurely spouting a stream of water. He heard the gurgling
of the water, the lazy twittering of the birds. Opposite him the
wall lowered and was broken by a series of graceful iron gates
opening to reveal the now intense blue sea billowing in the distance below. Two lounges, a few chairs and small tables were
dotted about the middle of the garden, between the house and
the pool. The furniture was covered in a blue cloth almost as
electric in color as the sea. A white towel, brilliant in the sunlight
and startling against the blue, splashed across one of the lounges.
On the table beside it, a book lay opened, facing downward, a
sketch pad and pencil on the paving stones below it. To the left,
louvered doors, flung wide, beckoned into the house itself. He
could hear music playing softly within—Paul Simon: "Me and
Julio down by the Schoolyard." The music stopped. No other
house, no other sign of human occupation could be seen. The
Jardin des Délices could not have seemed more isolated if it had
stood alone on an island in the middle of the sea. He walked into
the garden. It was cooler there.

He stood a few moments. He could still turn around, he
thought, turn and leave. He heard a familiar voice calling
his name. "Andrew!" David Roper, shirtless, tanned, smiling,
was bounding out of the dim interior of the house. "I've been
waiting for you." He hurried toward him, burst suddenly into
a broader smile, opening his arms. He looked so young standing
there, his arms like that. "Welcome to the *Jardin des Délices*,
Mr. MacAllister." David glanced at him to see if his remark,
his form of address, had registered. "I'm happy you've made
it."

"The door was open," Andrew said. "I just walked in."

"That's what you were supposed to do," he said, walking over to the door and shutting it. "Psychic door." He shrugged, amusement in his eyes. "It knew you were coming. But now that you're here"—he laughed—"don't stay at the gate. Come in a little farther. It won't hurt. I don't bite. I'm delighted to see you. Really." He reached for Andrew's hand and drew him in. The light was softer there. "Here, let me take your bag." He took it from his shoulder and gestured toward one of the lounge chairs. He smelled of coconut. "Please, won't you sit down? I was just thinking of having something to drink. What would you like?"

"Would you have some lemonade, by any chance? I'm parched."

"By chance, I would. The last of the lemons, in fact—from that tree right there." He pointed toward a glossy thick green tree in the corner near the gate. "Would you like anything in it? Gin? Vodka? They keep a well-stocked bar."

"I don't think so, thanks. They keep a pretty fair garden, too." His gaze took it in. "This place is . . . well, special. Really. Clearly you've got the right friends."

"Fantastic, heh? They're good friends to have, that's a fact, and very generous. I couldn't believe my luck. Let me get your lemonade. I'll be right back." He looked at him. "You could sit down and relax. You look hot. Or jump in the pool, if you'd like. There's no one here. That would cool you off. I'll get you a towel." He moved one of the reclining chairs out of the sunlight into the dappled shade, and set Andrew's bag near it.

"I'll sit down in a minute. I'd like to look around the garden." David disappeared into the house, reappearing a moment later with a towel. He set it on a table and disappeared again. Andrew moved here and there, seeing, not seeing. He peered into the pool. It must be lined with some black material, he thought, because to look into it gave an impression of infinite depth, though he didn't suppose the thing could be more than four feet deep, maybe five. What would be the point? He wondered if there were fish in it; he looked closely, but his eyes couldn't penetrate the surface, gleaming like a piece of coal at the sun's present declination. He bent down and put his hand in the cool water, stirring it, spreading his fingers, seeing them waver there in the moving, watery light, strangely disembodied against the clear blackness of the depth. He pulled off his shoes and socks and standing beside the pool, dipped one foot, then the other in the water. It felt silky, cool and tingling to his foot; probably it was rainwater. He concentrated on his foot shimmering beneath the surface, broken askew from his body by the angle that the light struck and entered the water: an optical illusion caused by the bending of the rays as they passed from the density of the air to the greater density of the liquid. That must have mystified primitive people. They couldn't have known about physical laws, about refraction. It did look a little weird. A fish darted toward him. He raised his foot from the water, shook it, and walked over to the gates that opened to the sea. He stood leaning against the wall, looking. The hill fell away before him. There was nothing to see but the tops of trees and sky and the southward-stretching sea. He stared at it, into its blueness. The shoreless Sargasso Sea. How odd to think of a sea without a shore, a sea bounded only by water. In his mind he heard Lotte Lenya's voice singing. *"Ja, das Meer ist blau, so blau."* He picked up the tune, sang the last line under his breath: " *'das Meer ist blau-au.'* " Blue, and so calm, too; flat as glass. Curious that it had looked quicksilver to him earlier. The sun was at a more oblique angle now; that must explain it. He left the gate and sat down, not on the chaise that David had moved for him but in one of the armchairs in the shaded garden. In a moment he got up and changed to the chaise in the sun. He wanted sunlight; he wanted rest. He took off his shirt, picked up the towel that had been flung there—it smelled of coconut oil— and set them both on the table. Then he lay back feeling the warmth suffuse him, heard the birds idly singing, the water splashing softly in the pool, and closed his eyes to wait for his lemonade.

"I went to the cove this morning," David said, rousing him from his reverie. His back was to the sun, and its rays formed a kind of aura around his head. He had put on a shirt. "I thought I might find you there, but no. The place was deserted. No bathers, no radios; nothing but the sun, the sea, and me."

"It must have been nice," Andrew said. "No, I didn't go. I couldn't go this morning."

"That's too bad. But then you could come here this afternoon, so that's good." He set two glasses and a pitcher of lemonade on the table.

"The light does strange things here."

"It does? Everything looks normal to me."

"Well, when I put my foot in the water it made it look as if it were an object separate from my leg, and when I looked at the sea a few minutes ago, it looked a different color than it did when I was walking above it, and just now when I opened my eyes and saw you standing there with the lemonade, I couldn't see your face, just the light around your head." He laughed. "So it does strange things." He looked at him. "I know it's crazy. Don't bother to confirm it."

David shrugged. "Okay."

"Like a solar eclipse."

"That would make me the moon."

Andrew laughed. "Yeh, well, you do seem a little loony."

"*I* seem a little loony?"

"Maybe it's my glasses." He took them off and set them on the table. "Nobody's perfect. Why don't you sit down? You're making me nervous." He laughed again. The light made him squint. A drop of perspiration rolled into his eye, stinging it. He tried to blink it away, and rubbed the sweat from his brow. "How long are you going to be here?"

"Another week, maybe." David poured the lemonade and sat down on the end of Andrew's chaise. "You've already gotten some sun."

"Like you, I tan quickly." Andrew laughed again. "Protective coloration. I'm a chameleon. We chameleons adapt." He took a drink of his lemonade. It was delicious. He finished the glass.

"That was quick."

"You squeeze a good lemon, and I was thirsty. I've been walking in the midday sun. You know, 'Mad dogs and Englishmen.' It does something to a person."

David refilled his glass. "If you're going to lie in the sun you'll need some lotion. I'll get it. You don't want to get burned. The sun is intense." He went into the house and returned in a moment with the lotion. "Here," he said, handing it to Andrew and sitting back down. "Smear some of this on yourself." He lifted the book from the table and took a pack of cigarettes from under it. Rothmans, Andrew noticed. "Would you like a cigarette?"

"No, thanks." Andrew, rubbing the oil on his shoulders and chest, gestured toward his bag. "I brought my own." He reached for the bag. The smell of coconut oil filled his nostrils. "Perhaps you'd like one. They're your favored brand." He handed him the pack.

"You remembered."

"Yes."

"Thank you, I will." He took a cigarette and set the pack on the table. "Aren't you having one?"

"Not right now." David lit his cigarette, then moved to the other chaise, stretching out on it, gazing toward the pool. Andrew watched him smoke in silence for a time. Only his arm moved, slowly raising the cigarette to his lips and back to his side, then after a time back to his lips again. The motion was smooth, hypnotic. Finally Andrew pulled his eyes away. He felt heavy, as if his body were growing more and more dense, and to raise his arm would be a defiance of the tug of gravity. He decided to test it and reached for the cigarettes on the table. His arm worked. It was easy. He took a cigarette and held it without lighting it.

"You're not saying much." The words hung in the distance, floating slowly to Andrew's ears. David continued to look toward the pool.

"No." Andrew was silent again. Then: "What are those fish in the pool?"

"Small tropical river fish. Pretty, aren't they? They're curious little things—always investigating me when I swim." He turned his head toward Andrew. "Why did you come here?"

"Because you asked me."

"Do you always do everything you're asked? You must get into a lot of trouble." He struck a match and extended the flame toward Andrew.

"Not always." Andrew drew on the cigarette.

"You don't always do everything you're asked, or you don't always get into a lot of trouble?"

Andrew laughed. "Both."

"You've scarcely looked at me."

"No." Andrew paused. "I guess not."

"Why not?"

Andrew looked toward the gate that he'd entered, the lemon tree. He didn't say anything.

"Why not?" David asked again.

"Actually, I have," Andrew said, still staring at the gate. "You're wearing khaki shorts, a blue shirt, and no shoes. Your shirt matches your eyes. So you see, I looked at you."

"Well, that's a relief!" David laughed. "The man does see! I think you need something to cheer you up. I'll be right back," David said. "I'm getting you some trouble."

"No, don't! I don't want any." Andrew felt panicked. "Please," he said, "give me your hand." He reached toward it.

"Why—" David asked, teasing him, "do you read palms?"

"I wish," Andrew said, looking away, taking his hand away. "I've got to get out of the sun. Would you like to switch places?" He got up, taking his shirt from the table. He slipped it on.

"Sure." David moved into the sun. "Would you hand me the oil?" He took off his shirt, poured some oil into his palm and rubbed it on his body, making it glisten in the light. Then he kicked the chaise a little closer and lay down, turning to face him, his hand supporting his chin. With his free hand, he reached across the space for Andrew's. "It's all right," he said, serious now. "I don't read palms either." He rubbed the back of Andrew's hand with his thumb, casually, easily. Andrew gazed off toward the sea, then to the corner of the garden, near the pool. "Just as well, I think. I'm happy you've come back."

"Back?" The sound of his own voice surprised him.

"Here, then. I'm glad you've come here, even if you won't look at me. I'm happy you're here."

"Yes." Andrew glanced quickly at David, baking there, his body glistening, then away, back toward the sea. The sun's warmth washed over him; the thick sweet waves of coconut oil struck his nostrils. He focused on the sea, but the afterimage shimmered in his eye. He looked at the wall. It seemed to be shading into a deeper pink. Light plays funny tricks.

"Why are you shaking?"

"I'm not shaking," Andrew said.

"And my name isn't David, either. I'll be right back." He got up, lifting Andrew's hand and setting it on his chest, patted it; then released it and walked quickly into the house. He was back in a moment with a little box, a Chinese box, it appeared. He opened it, took out some cigarette papers, and rolled a joint. He tilted the box, tapped it, squinted into it. "Might as well roll another," he said—"finish it off. It's the last of that bag, but there's more where it came from."

"You got it here?"

"Yes. I wouldn't try to sneak it in through Customs. There's plenty available. It comes from the West Indies, I think. Jamaica." When he had finished, he took the joint and moved to Andrew's chaise. "Shall I light it? You'd feel more relaxed."

"I guess so." Suddenly he reached for his cigarettes. "No, not for me. I think I'll smoke one of these instead."

David held the light to Andrew's cigarette, then lit the joint and sucked in the smoke, expelled it, coughing. "It's a little rough," he said, "but it's good."

Andrew laughed. He set his cigarette in the ashtray and handed David his glass. "Have some lemonade. That might help." Then he took the joint from David's fingers and quickly inhaled the pungent smoke, holding it in as long as he could, feeling the smoke rush to his head, filling it like a great billowy cloud. He choked, sat abruptly up, and pushed the smoke from his lungs, doubling over in a spasm of coughing. He reached for David's knee to steady himself, trying to stop the coughing, aware of the oil smooth and slippery beneath his palm. David handed him the glass.

"Speak too soon, you pay the piper—or something like that. Are you all right?"

"Yes," Andrew said, swallowing the lemonade, recovering.

"That'll teach you to laugh at me. The first toke is always the hardest." He took another and easily exhaled it. "See? Smooth as silk. You shouldn't hold it in so long. Just take it in slow"—he took a little puff—"and let it out easy"—he exhaled it, passing Andrew the joint. "No problem."

"No problem"—Andrew took another toke—"except that it makes me feel like a helium balloon. Lighter than air." He exhaled easily this time, and took another small puff, then set the joint on the ashtray. His cigarette was still burning. He stubbed it out, raised his knees and wrapped his arms around them. Suddenly he felt chilly, and his throat was very dry.

"Come here," David said, taking his arm and pulling him lightly toward him. "You're shaking again." He picked up the joint and held it to Andrew's lips, waiting for him to inhale; then to his own, finishing it. He wrapped his arms around him. "You know something?" Andrew looked up. David looked him in the eye. "You want me to do this."

Andrew pulled back, curling up a little on the chaise, his head in his arms. "No," he said.

David lay down beside him, took his fingers and rubbed their tips with his own. "Yes, I think you do. You're just afraid. Don't be afraid of me. There's nothing to be afraid of." He brushed the back of Andrew's hand with his lips, turned it over and brushed the palm. He held it against his chest. "Push me away if you'd like." Andrew didn't move. David cradled Andrew's head in his arm, stroking his hair, toying with his ear, grazing the nape of his neck and softly rubbing the fine hairs there. "But why would you want to do that?" He turned Andrew's head toward him and lightly kissed him on the mouth—his lips were very soft—then again, and flicked his tongue quickly across his lips, catlike, pushing them a little open. Andrew heard the air leave his body in a soft guttural groan. His nostrils were overwhelmed with the sweet heavy smell of coconut. He put his hand to David's shoulder, his head, and kissed him. It wasn't any different. Curious, he kissed him again, harder. No, it wasn't. What was different was that the body was firmer, leaner. He touched his chest. There was no soft cushion of flesh there. He ran his finger along the crease where David's upper arm met his body, and felt the smooth muscle, the hairs at the edge of his armpit. He touched his tongue to the shoulder, tentatively, then the sinew of the neck and the vulnerable place below the jaw. He felt himself billowing, floating, sinking. He moved to David's chest, felt the plate of his breast smooth and hard as an apple, touched his nipple, licked it, tasting it, tasting coconut. He raised David's arm and kissed his armpit, licked it smooth. He looked down at him. "You asked for this, you bastard!" His voice was raspy. He bit his arm, harder than he'd intended, on the muscle. David gave a little cry. He ran his hand over his shoulder and down his back, feeling the ridges of his spine where it curved inward, then out again, scraping hard with his knuckles. He opened his hand taut and pressed his palm across his buttock, small and firm—yes, different—and curled it around his narrow hip. David grabbed his arm. "Let's go. It'll be more comfortable," he said, his voice thick, taking

Andrew's hand and leading him quickly through the louvered doors into the interior of the house, dark suddenly as smoked glass after the brilliant sunlight, through a large room and up a flight of stairs into a bedroom, where without releasing his hand he threw back the sheet from the bed and tumbled onto it, pulling Andrew after him.

"Oh, God," Andrew moaned, falling, his voice scarcely a whisper. He burrowed into him, escaping, not seeing, wanting only to cover him, to be covered by him, to consume him. "Oh, no," he moaned again, eager, dismayed, as David put his hand on the band of Andrew's running shorts and tugged them down, pulling off his own at the same time. Andrew jerked out of them, out of his shirt, muttering, voiceless. How can I be doing this? he thought, doing it, licking the tender flesh inside the elbow, reaching for the foot, scuttling down to nibble and lick at the tendons of the knee, at the soft back of the knee, the tender hollow of the inner thigh, as David—*Jesus!*—flung him back and crouched over him, holding his balls, licking them, sucking them, his hands, his tongue all over him. A thought flashed dimly through a crack in Andrew's mind: So this is what it is to make love to a man—and vanished. He raised his head and saw David's half-closed eyes fixed intently on his cock, watched him take it into his mouth. *Andrew wanted to fuck him!* He felt suddenly, briefly sick. How could he want to do such a thing, how could he *imagine* doing such a thing; but he did. He was stoned. Yes, he was stoned, but he knew what he was doing. His hands felt for David's head—like a blind man's. His eyes narrowed, unfocused, scarcely seeing. Sin comes in through the eye, and then we reach for it. He lapped him as a cat laps cream, as David had lapped him, covering his cool fluid body with his rough animal tongue. The memory of a marble floated up to him. *Say it!* He clenched his jaw, turned David's head roughly toward him, and looked him in the eye. "I'm stoned, but I know what I'm doing."

"You sure do," David said. "I want you to fuck me."

"No! I can't," he said. "I can't do that," he whispered. But he did. He fucked him like a dog, turned him and fucked him face to face. It didn't feel any different—the fact registered with astonishment in some thick drugged depth of his brain—it was just like a woman, except there was a cock to hang on to, and balls to cushion and protect. Suddenly Andrew cried out, coming, and collapsed over him, crumbled on him, eventually slipped off him and fell asleep by his side, his arm flung across his chest.

He woke up slowly, on his side, a body curled around him, an arm resting on his hip, fingers grazing his abdomen. He jerked, and shot suddenly up, his eyes open wide. He looked down. *Who is this? Who is this woman?* He shook his head, looked again. He saw who it was. *Oh, Jesus!* He must be crazy. He fell back on the pillow, turned on his side again, away from him, felt David's fingers on his ear, a finger tracing its shell, running along the lobe and under it to the hairline of his neck. He shivered, lay there frozen, tensed, struggling to shake off the drug, shut off sensation. He may have known what he was doing, but still he had been stoned. He tried to concentrate his mind. It was difficult, like cracking clouds, an occasional patch of breaking blue. He made an effort to speak, but uttered only a guttural. He sank paralyzed, inert. David's fingers traced his spine; his hand touched his penis, lifted it, gently cradled his balls. Andrew could feel his penis swelling, and suddenly David's—hard now, pushing against him. He felt David's hand between his legs. He couldn't seem to move, couldn't seem to talk. He heard the sound of David's voice, smooth, lulling, through a cloud. He tried to focus on it. It was quiet, level, scarcely inflected. "Don't move," David said, "just relax. I'm going to fuck you now."

"No."

"You won't mind. Stay where you are, on your side." He could feel David's fingers fumbling with him, with his anus now, trying to open him, to wedge into him.

"No," Andrew said, his mouth half open to the pillow. The pillow was wet with his spit. "Please, no." He could hardly talk. He seemed able neither to close his jaw nor open it. Saliva dribbled from the corner of his mouth. David pressed into him. "Stop. It hurts."

"Only for a second." His voice was soft, like a mother talking to a baby. "Only at first."

"No!"

"There!"

Shocked, his eyes opening wider, Andrew gasped, felt himself opened, entered, something slipping deep inside him. Panic shot through him. He groaned, heard the voice of David. "Help me. Slide onto your stomach. Easy now." David pressed him over with his hand, guiding him, and then he began to move, slowly, smoothly, as Andrew—unbelieving, incredulous, stunned, aghast—buried his face in the pillow, his eyes fixed and frozen on its whiteness, and felt the spittle run from his mouth, felt enormity filling him, splitting him. He grunted. He bit the pillow, heard David utter a sudden sharp cry, felt him thrust faster, his body heave and gradually stop. A terrifying hot fullness suffused him, a burning, tingling numbness in the warm dark secret core of his body as he again fell into a kind of dumb, now grateful sleep.

He woke with a start for the second time. This time he knew where he was, whom he was with. He eased himself up. He could still feel the fullness, the heat deep inside him. David was lying on his side, his mouth partly open, his face toward him, asleep. Quietly Andrew got out of the bed. He looked down at David naked, vulnerable on the rumpled sheets. He was, Andrew could see, a fine man, snug and smooth as a boy, so calm and innocent in repose. He wanted to weep. He bent and touched his fingers to David's hair, his forehead, his arm, his beardless cheek. He couldn't be thirty-one. Andrew felt very cool, very distant, very objective. He knew what he had done; he couldn't quite believe that he'd done it. The strangeness inside him, though, told him he had to believe it. He began slowly to look for his clothes, felt a sudden, overwhelming urge to defecate. He found the bathroom, and did. He returned to the bedroom. He hadn't really seen it before. The windows overlooked the empty garden and the sea. He gazed down at where they had been, at the towels, the shirt, the lotion, the various signs of their passage there, and then out to the sea. He picked up his clothes and carried them to the garden. The house seemed a very deep pink now. He walked to the pool, dropped his clothes beside his shoes and socks, and eased himself into the water. He grasped the side of the pool with one hand and let his body float free for a time, let the water wash it, the fish investigate it, and then he swam its length. He bumped into the side of the pool, hard. There were no markers, the bottom was black; it was confusing. He straightened his course and began to swim laps, vigorously, concentrating on his stroke, on his breathing, on his counting. He liked to swim laps; he always counted them. There was a pleasure in monotony, and he found the dull regularity of the laps very soothing. He stopped when he saw David's legs looming above him at the edge of the pool.

"Hello."

"Hello."

"Mind if I join you?"

"Come ahead. I'm getting out, though. Would you hand me a towel?" He hoisted himself out of the pool, sat huddled on the edge of it, feeling small and naked. David came back with the towel and put it around his shoulders, standing behind him, rubbing them. "You don't seem so nervous now," he said.

"I think I'm beyond nervous," Andrew replied. "I'm afraid it's awfully late. I've got to get back."

"I'll give you a ride, if you'll just let me take a dip—rinse off."

"Thanks. I'd appreciate it." David jumped into the pool. Andrew dried himself off in the dissolving light, watching him bob for a moment in the water, then swim two laps. Andrew wrapped the towel around himself and went to pick up David's. In the distance, a wind chime tinkled. The house, he noticed, was no longer pink but drained of color in the fading light. When he returned with the towel, David was climbing out of the pool, his face concentrated, water falling in sheets from his body. His body shone, glistened in the twilight. He should paint him, Andrew thought, catch him in just that precise moment: one leg crooked on the edge of the pool, the other still in it, his arms rigid for the hoist, and the falling sheets of silver water. Yes, a splendid animal. A pity he couldn't paint; then anyone might understand. Andrew handed him the towel, stepped into his shorts and shirt, his socks and shoes, and waited for David to dress.

As they were getting onto the moped, David said, "If I'd known this, I would never have let you get away in London."

"If I'd known this," Andrew replied, "I might never have gone."

"Don't say that," David said. "Besides, you're a great success there."

"Let's hurry, my friend. I'm expected for dinner. I'm probably late." He hadn't looked at his watch, didn't want to. It was still in his pocket.

"You've never done this before, have you?"

"No."

"Thank you."

"You're welcome." What was this mad conversation, this insane politeness? Suddenly he wanted to scream! *No, of course I've
never done this before! I have never imagined doing this before! I'm a
married man, you idiot, with a child! Do you think I'm out offering my
ass every night to any passing dildo? Do you think I'm sucking cock in
Bloomingdale's men's room of an afternoon? Lurking around Times
Square for some hustler to fuck? Getting blown in the steam room at the
Y? Why, of course. I'm known all up and down Broadway. Any minute
now they'll put my name in lights. 'Randy Andy Rides Again!'* Instead
he said, "Thank *you*," and he meant that, too. *Thank him? Thank
him for sticking his dick up my ass?* No, just thank him; and after all,
what had *he* done? The same. He shuddered to think what he had
done. Was there anything now that he hadn't done? Probably.
He thought of his actor friends. Yes, in fact. He didn't want to
think about it.

David was singing, the same song he'd heard playing in the
house when he arrived:

> *"Well I'm on my way,*
> *I don't know where I'm going,*
> *I'm on my way I'm taking my time . . ."*

He hummed a few bars, then sang again:

> *". . . me and Julio*
> *Down by the schoolyard,*
> *Me and Julio down by the schoolyard.*

You've made me happy," he said, "but I'm afraid the reverse isn't
true." He started the motor. "Hold on."

Andrew felt a sudden thickening in his throat and a rush of
tenderness toward him, toward this flesh, this boy, this young
extraordinary David intensified by breathing. "It's all right," he
said, his hands on David's hips, the side of his face pressed against
his back as they roared off down the drive.

David turned his head toward him. "What did you say?" he
shouted.

"I said"—Andrew spoke directly into his ear—"that it's all
right. Don't worry." They were on the corniche now. The sea
was gray in the twilight. A faint glow appeared on the horizon;

then suddenly a huge orange ball surged out of the sea and hovered there for a moment, before it began to rise in the sky. "My God," Andrew murmured, "look at that moon!" David veered off the highway, onto an overlook. A toad jumped out of the way; another one lay squashed on the road. This place was hazardous for toads. He stopped. "What are you doing?" Andrew said.

"I wanted you to see the moon rise. It's full tonight."

"Yes, I know." He must be late. What would he say? He'd think of something. He got off the moped, walked to the edge, and stood there, his hands on the stone barrier, watching the rising moon, paler now in the still pale sky. Like a wraith. "David, how old are you? Not thirty-one. You can't be more than twenty-six. Really."

He laughed. "What would you like me to be? Give me an age. Twenty-six? Twenty-seven? Twenty-nine?" He put his hand on Andrew's shoulder. "Forty-two?"

"The age you are."

David paused. "I'm twenty-eight. I'm sorry. I didn't mean anything. I wanted to seem older, that's all."

"You thought I'd feel better?"

"I suppose so. I knew how old you were. I looked it up before I came here. I know a lot about you: when you were born, where, when you were married, your wife's maiden name, your mother's, when your daughter was born, the list of your colleges"—he laughed—"almost as long as the list of your plays. It's all there, in the book. Easy to find. Except for your address. It doesn't give that, just your agent's."

"But it doesn't tell you much, does it?" Andrew turned to him. "You knew how old I was when you asked me?"

"Yes."

"You were testing me."

"I suppose so."

"Well, I'm glad I passed." He'd meant it wryly; probably it didn't come across that way.

David laughed. "I hope I did. Would you like proof? I'd show you my passport but it's back at the house."

Andrew's heart sank. "Shit! So is my bag." He patted his pocket, felt his watch. "And my sunglasses."

"Come on. We'll go back."

Andrew pulled the watch out of his pocket, afraid to look at it, looked at it. "We can't. There's no time." He felt panicked. "I'm supposed to be meeting some people in the lobby this very minute. Shit!"

"I'll drop them by your hotel later, if you'd like."

"Would you? I'm sorry. I can't leave my bag for long. Let's go." He muttered to himself: "What the fuck am I going to say?" He jumped onto the moped and held tight to David's waist as they sped toward the hotel. "Go on up the drive," he shouted to him. "I don't have time to walk it."

When they pulled up to the entrance, Ann and Molly and Sam, Michael, Marika, and Yasmine were standing there, Sam's car at the curb. "Christ!" Andrew exclaimed, leaping off, "I'm sorry."

"Where have you been?" Ann asked. She looked so pretty, Andrew thought. Oh, Christ, she looked so pretty in her pretty summer dress! "Where on earth have you been? We've all been worried. I just left a note for you at the desk, telling you where to join us."

"I'm sorry," Andrew said again. "I went out for a run late this afternoon and ran into David on the beach. We had a drink." David was still astride the moped. "Ann, you remember David Roper—from London?"

"Yes," she said. "How do you do?"

"Is your toe all right?"

"Yes, fine."

"It's broken," Molly said.

"But nothing major," Ann said. "The doctor just taped it up."

Andrew looked at her, glanced down to her feet. She was wearing sneakers. He touched her hand. "I'm sorry."

"We weren't going to send a posse," Michael said. "I told them that we should go on without you. See"—he turned to the group—"didn't I say he always turns up intact sooner or later?"

Andrew introduced David to the rest of them.

"And more or less," Michael added, an aside to him. He turned to David. "Yes, we've met. I remember. You're the artist, interested in the Greeks."

Andrew explained to Sam and Molly: "David's a friend of one of the London critics. We all met him there, after the opening. He's stopping over in Bermuda on his way to the States."

"You stay friends with that critic," Sam said. "Those London reviews were fantastic. Which critic?"

Molly interrupted. "We can't just stand here talking, boys. We're already late for dinner. Why don't you come out on the boat with us tomorrow—David? It is David, right? Continue the conversation there. We're taking off at ten from the Somerset Bridge."

"Oh, I couldn't do that," David said.

"Nonsense!" Sam exclaimed. "Of course you can. It's a big boat."

"And a big group," Michael said.

"Bring your swimsuit," Molly called to him, her hand on the door to the car. It was dark now.

"And be there a little early," Sam said, opening the door for Ann and Yasmine.

"Well, thank you, then," David said. "I'd love to. I won't hold you up any longer. Thanks for the drink, Andrew. Good-bye," and he sped off.

"I'll run up and change," Andrew said. "It'll just take me a second."

"We're going on ahead to secure the table," Molly said. "We can't all fit in one car, anyway."

As he was going into the hotel, Andrew heard Michael say to her, "I'll wait for him—just to make sure he doesn't get lost again."

"Too late for that," Andrew said, but of course Michael couldn't hear. "Christ!" he muttered, running for the elevator. "Christ!"

"I don't like him," Michael said when Andrew jumped breathless into the front seat of the waiting taxi. "You shouldn't mess with him."

"Hello, Marika. Hope I didn't hold you up."

"I made Michael let me come with you," she said. "The taxi just arrived. We've only been waiting a minute."

Andrew slammed the door. "What's your friend talking about?"

"I'm not talking *what*, I'm talking *who*. And who do you think? You know who I'm talking about."

"The case is objective. Use *whom*." He shook his head.

"Sometimes, Michael, you are truly crazy." Andrew looked back at Marika. "How was the shopping? Is there anything interesting in Hamilton? I'd liked to have seen it."

"I was thinking more in the accusative, actually—but thanks for the grammar lesson." Michael shook his head slowly back and forth, staring out the window of the car. "We'll talk about it later. I just don't understand it."

"Behave yourself, Michael," Marika said with a laugh. "I *like* Andrew." She turned to him. "Oh, you know, there were lots of shops. Sweaters, woolens, and Spode. They're very big on Spode here. Great if teacups turn you on."

"It's the outpost-of-empire mentality, I suppose."

"Yes. They're actually more English than the Queen."

"The Queen's a Kraut," Michael said, turning back to Marika.

"What did I just say? They're more English than the Queen."

Andrew laughed. "She's got you there, Michael. You know, Marika, Michael's a total realist, except in certain special areas of his own."

Michael burst into laughter. "That's the game *you* play, my friend." He patted Marika's leg. "Andrew's always shoving off his own particular quirks onto me. We call it 'Let's Pretend Michael's—whatever.' He gets to fill in the blank. It makes him feel better."

"Well, we didn't stay long," she said. "There's really not much to do in Hamilton unless you're a truly dedicated consumer, and there were too many of them for my taste. For all our tastes. Ann had to wait awhile at the doctor's. He insisted on an X-ray. Then we had lunch and looked around, bought a few things. We must have been back on the beach by three thirty, I suppose. We hoped you'd join us."

"You got back early!" He'd blurted it out, then quickly struggled to recall Marika's work. Oh, yes: films. Documentaries. It was coming back to him. "How's the movie business?" he asked.

"Not great. I'm thinking of getting out of it."

"Really? Why? You're good at it. Your film on the Greek immigrants in Queens won a prize, didn't it?"

"But documentaries cost too much, funding is scarce, and there's no money to be made from them. That's why I'm thinking of getting out of it. Three excellent reasons." She laughed. "I'm tired of begging at the door of every foundation in town."

"I have an idea for you. Do one on the Parthenon sculptures. The shots would be spectacular. The British Museum, Greece, the Acropolis. The Louvre, too. They've got some choice pieces there." He liked Marika. "And there's a small museum in Illinois —at the university in Urbana, I think—with a complete set of plaster castings of the frieze." He laughed. "What luck! You'd get to go to Urbana. Isn't that odd? That they should be in Urbana?"

"Well, yes, it is odd," Marika said.

"God knows how they ended up there. They were made by a French consul in Athens when the figures were still on the monument, before Lord Elgin carted most of them off." He was talking very rapidly. "The interesting thing about them is that they show how well preserved the sculptures were just two hundred years ago, and how much they've deteriorated since, particularly the ones that remained in Greece—ruined by the air of Athens. It's corrosive. The ones in the museum are pretty much the way they were. Elgin may have gotten them under questionable circumstances, but at least he saved them."

"Doing a film like that would cost a fortune!"

Andrew was growing excited by the idea. He tried to slow down. "Yes, but the Greek government would probably give you some money, or at least air fare, maybe accommodations, and that would amount to quite a lot. They've been trying to get the Elgin Marbles back from Britain ever since they arrived there. Throw a little propaganda into it—you know, liberation theology." He laughed brightly. "They'll love it. It's a great idea. I'll help you. And besides, don't you speak the language?"

"Yes, I do."

"So, you see? It's all set. *Voilà!* The movie's all but made. It would be a help to me, too—help me get my thoughts in some coherent form."

"That *would* be a help," Michael said, laughing easily at last, "a help to us all. We seem to have arrived. Would you like to pay the driver?"

"We're here? That was quick." Andrew was surprised. He looked out the window. "So we are. I'd love to." He pulled out his billfold, paid the driver, jumped out and bowed deeply as he opened the back door—"After you, m'sieur, madame"—and extended his hand to Marika. "I'm thinking about a new play, you see, using the Elgin Marbles as a backdrop. Molly gave me the title: *Museum Pieces*. Do you like it?"

"Provocative title," Marika said. "What's the play about?"

"He doesn't know yet," Michael said.

"That's why I need your help." With Marika on Andrew's arm, they passed a crude piece of stone that was intended to look like an oversized eagle and entered the restaurant, quickly descended a steep flight of stairs which Andrew negotiated without falling—he noted the fact with dull surprise—and joined the rest of their group. The restaurant was a cozy place and quiet, typically Italian, without, for a change, a view of the sea or, for that matter, a view at all, which was just as well, Andrew thought; he'd seen enough.

Dinner was good: he was hungry; uneventful, for which he was grateful: a few details about the shopping trip to Hamilton, a little more conversation about the New York theater in general and Andrew's play in particular, talk of the expedition the next day to the nearby reefs and the Sargasso Sea, gossip about this one and that. Sam told some mildly funny stories about an elderly friend of Molly's mother who'd neither eaten nor heard of lasagne —"Why should I, my dear? I've never had an Italian chef"—and her great-uncle Danny who used to walk to the bank every morning to withdraw a dollar and return in the afternoon to deposit the change—"he didn't want to lose the interest"—and who stood up to recite Shelley's "Ode to a Skylark" at her father's funeral but was ushered quickly out—"before he could take off his clothes," Sam said. "Daft, the lot of them. They needed a good shot of Jewish blood—didn't you, my *bubeleh*? Do you want to hear about her *meshuggeneh* mother? There's a case!"

"No, we don't," Molly said. She smiled, but didn't seem terribly amused. Her family's thoroughly Boston madness—it was certainly more than eccentricity—delighted Sam, but the reminder disturbed Molly. She was smoking a lot. Beneath her breezy assurance, there was something mysterious about her, something vulnerable, almost frail. Sam turned to Ann and Michael and began to regale them with stories. Molly turned to Andrew. "Tell me," she said, "where'd you go for your drink? Any place I should know about?"

"No," he said. "No place special. In Somerset. A little café sort of place, on the harbor."

"You walked a long way!"

"Yes, well, I didn't walk. When I ran into that fellow, he had his moped. The drawbridge was up on the way back. That's why I was late." He looked at Molly's Chesterfields lying on the table. He slipped one out of the pack, saw that she'd noticed. "Do you mind?"

"Of course not, but I didn't—"

"Shhh." He rolled his eyes at her and squeezed her hand; whispering, made a joke of it: "Don't say a word." He lit the cigarette and pushed his chair back a little from the table, trying to keep the cigarette discreetly out of sight. He turned to Marika, drawing her into the conversation, dredging up whatever questions he could, making an effort to amuse her. He said something; he heard her laugh. Soon he had the three women—Yasmine had joined their conversation now—laughing and talking. He took another of Molly's cigarettes, wishing she smoked something a little less offensive than Chesterfields, glancing toward Ann out of the corner of his eye. She didn't seem to be noticing him. He lit the cigarette. He learned a lot about restaurant design, and told Yasmine about Molly's découpage, and soon the women were all chatting animatedly about their work. Andrew felt like an impresario, directing the dance, and then the dinner ended— early, thank God. All of them were tired, and Sam insisted they be fresh for the next day. Andrew picked up the check. "You're paying for everything else, Sam. I want to do this," and after a small argument, he did. He was, after all, beginning to see a little money from London, enough to get them through the summer, probably, without recourse to one bank or another, and he was anticipating some more in the fall. Might as well spend it now, he thought. Why depart from custom?

"We'll all meet tomorrow at the bridge," Sam said, "and then this road show will end."

"Why don't we just meet in the lobby and go together?" Michael asked. They were climbing the stairs.

"I've got some errands to do beforehand, got to lay in a few supplies. We wouldn't want the ship to run short, and we've got quite a crew now. I forget how many I told the captain to expect, but not as many as we've got. No, it would be easier if we all met at the dock." They were leaving the restaurant, passing the lump of an eagle, entering the resonant night drumming with animal cries and whispers. "Quite a racket," Sam said. "Them babies ain't no nightingales." He looked at the sky. "The moon"—he pointed—"look at it! Unreal!" They all tilted their heads to the sky. The luminous disk hung full and cool and distant, and almost directly overhead. Motes of silver fell from the sky, drowning the stars, filling the darkness, flooding the path to the car, bathing the gravel in a cool, unflickering tungsten light. Andrew could see their shadows moving beneath it. "It's full tonight," Sam said. "Better be careful."

"Nothing to worry about," Andrew said; "the damage has already been done."

"The damage has been done?" Ann looked at him.

"I meant last night, when we were dancing. It was just a joke."

As they were walking to their room, Ann said, "You were hungry tonight."

"Yes."

"I was watching. You ate like a horse."

He realized, suddenly, that he hadn't had any lunch, and hadn't thought of it until that moment. "I sent Julia a postcard this morning."

"She'll never get it before we return," Ann said.

"I suppose not, but I wanted to do it anyway."

She broke into a slow smile. She seemed for a moment happy. "Actually, I sent her one too. From Hamilton. She'll be getting lots of mail from us after we return."

"You looked so pretty tonight—like a schoolgirl in your summer dress"—he gestured toward her feet, and smiled—"these sneakers. Do you think your foot is all right? You're not limping as much as you were."

"It's not bothering me," she said. "The doctor said it would be fine in a few days." The smile had faded from her face. "Andrew, why were you smoking tonight?"

"Smoking?"

"Surely you're not going to try to lie about it. Yes, smoking. You took at least one of Molly's cigarettes. I didn't bother to count. And you must have forgotten to empty the ashtray when you left the room today."

"I don't know," he said. "I don't know."

"You had to have bought cigarettes. Where are they?"

"I threw them away."

He opened the door to their room, saw his bag on the luggage rack—David had returned it; the bell captain must have sent it up—and beyond, through the gauzy curtains to the balcony, something gleaming on the table. "What's that?"

"It's a surprise I found for Julia. A shell. I think it's beautiful."

"She's not old enough." He pushed the curtains aside and walked out to look at it. It was a huge white serrated mollusk, striated, its valves clamped almost shut. It looked very old, like something from an ancient, a primordial sea.

"It's a kind of clam," Ann said.

He returned to the room. "Where on earth did you find it?"

"In a little shop in Hamilton. I didn't see anything else like it."

"I can believe it. I've never seen anything like it either."

"Isn't it nice?"

"I'm not sure 'nice' is the operative word. It's awesome, at any rate. It's got to be ten inches long, maybe longer. That's one big mother! I knew I shouldn't have let you go into Hamilton alone." He was trying to make her smile again.

"I was fine," she said. "More likely, I shouldn't have left you on your own. I felt lonely today." She was taking off her pretty flowered earrings, the only jewelry she was wearing, setting them on the table beside her jewelry pouch, the tambourine. She must have moved it from the balcony. Her hands fluttered across the pearls that trailed from the bag. "I still do."

"I'm sorry," he said. "I'm very sorry."

"It's as if you're somewhere else." She looked suddenly very tired. "But you seemed to be having a good time at dinner."

"Oh?"

"Well, you certainly had Molly and Michael's girls laughing. There were peals of laughter from your little group."

"I felt like a high-wire act on a high-tension wire." He snapped it out, wished he hadn't. "Didn't you have a good time?"

"Not particularly. Sam tried, but his stories wear a little thin on me. They're both *your* friends, after all."

"I thought you liked them." He was resigned.

"I get tired of them." She walked into the dressing area and began to get ready for bed. "Sam thinks you look tired," she said.

"He says you don't act it, but he thinks you are. He suggested we stay on a couple of days. He said he'd pay for it."

He's a kind man, Andrew thought. "Would you like to?"

"I don't know yet." Andrew heard her go into the bathroom and close the door. He picked up his bag to put it away. He glanced inside. There was a note on top. *"You didn't need this"*—a drawing of a pair of swim trunks—*"but you might need these"*—another drawing, of a box of Dunhills. *"I enjoyed the drink. Anytime."* He crumpled the note and rummaged through the bag, saw his sunglasses, his book, and the other things, the cigarettes in one of the pockets on the side. He took them out and threw them in the wastebasket, then the note, then went to the table and found a couple of tourist brochures under Ann's tambourine. He dropped them carefully on top of the cigarettes and the note, and waited for Ann to come out of the bathroom. "I'm going to sleep," she said. "I'm very tired."

"I won't bother you. I'll be out of the bathroom in a minute. I'm tired too." Sam was right, he thought: he was tired. He hung up his clothes. He noticed that Ann's dress had been returned from the laundry, the dress she'd worn Saturday night when they'd gone walking on the sand, in the sea. He examined it. There was still the trace of a stain, like a wave, running along the hemline. He didn't suppose anyone would ever notice. When he got into the bathroom, he decided to take a shower. He took a long shower, and when he came out and went to the bedroom, Ann appeared to be asleep. He put on his pajama bottoms and climbed gently into bed beside her, touched her hip with his hand, turned on his side, and closed his eyes, trying to ignore the faint tingling, the vague terrifying fullness or emptiness, he wasn't sure, that lingered deep inside.

When he awoke—had he been asleep? he didn't know—he awoke to the faintest *ping!* in his ears; not a ring exactly, but a kind of thin, fading strum on the tympanum, as if at some great distance a string had been plucked and set off there a single tonal vibration. Did he imagine it, or had he actually heard it? He opened his eyes: the moon was bright; he heard it still, but receding now. They'd forgotten to close the heavy curtains. In the morning the room would be flooded with sunlight. He turned.

The ping vanished. Ann seemed sound asleep. He curled up around her, hugging her to him, feeling her settle back, deeper into the spoon of his body. He brushed the wispy tendrils of her hair from his face. He began to drift off again, fitfully. He moved his arm. The pillow was hot. Once he became aware of it, he couldn't get it out of his mind. He turned once more, trying to make himself comfortable. He was facing the balcony again. He should close the curtains. Ann's body shifted with him, stuck to him. It was too hot. He pushed against her with his hips, moving her back. He had no room. He lay there on the edge of the bed in the close still air, his head resting on his fist, looking out toward the balcony, through the filmy curtains, to the night bathed in whiteness, the mysterious shapes and shadows. Moonlight struck the shell, white as chalk, white as bones. Suddenly he felt panicked, felt a momentary keen fear that something was wrong at home, that Julia was not all right, that she had hurt herself in some way. It was preposterous. Mrs. Bridges would certainly have telephoned. He couldn't call New York now. It was the middle of the night. They'd think he was crazy. They shouldn't have left her. She was their only child, the only one. It was a heavy responsibility for a child, to be the only one. He was sorry about that. He longed to see her. He would see her soon. He moved his hand away from his head, shifted toward his stomach, and rested his cheek on the sheet at the edge of the bed. It was cooler there. His knee extended over the edge. He pulled his arm out, fumbled on the table for his watch—he'd been in bed not half an hour!—and rested his hand on the floor, pushing against it. He raised his head and looked at Ann again. She sighed, turned, sinking into a deeper sleep. She looked so placid, so *full*. He might as well get up; he couldn't sleep, though he felt drugged. Drugged, but wired. Had he imagined the whole thing? There was, as Dr. Rip-off had told him years before, a part of his experience that seemed to elude him—the only intriguing observation Dr. Rip-off had ever made. He arose gingerly, putting on his watch, and silently made his way to the refrigerator. He felt the tiny pinprick of strangeness. Desire itself was neutral, he told himself. But desire didn't exist in a void. Nature abhors a vacuum. He supposed it was its trajectory, carrying the charge, that disturbed. He took a glass, one of those small bottles of whisky the hotel had provided, and an ice tray from the refrigerator and carried them to the balcony. He went back for soda, thought to pick up his bag, hesitated, then retrieved the cigarettes from the wastebasket and tucked them into his bag and took it to the balcony too, closing the gauzy curtains behind him and sliding the door almost shut. He leaned against the rail, looking over the edge, into the dark gardens below, up toward the fairways, beyond to the trees, their tops limned with silver, and the platinum sea—all eerie in the moonlight; then sat down at the table, pushed the shell aside, took three cubes of ice from the tray, opened the whisky, and poured himself a drink. He sat looking at the amber fluid, pale under the moon's peculiar nacreous light: moonlight lacked those fiery rays that released the world's full warmth and richness. He didn't move the glass. He thought of the event that had happened that day. Of course, he'd thought of little else since he'd climbed the hill—was it that very day? yes: to the *Jardin des Délices. Event?* It was not a random occurrence he'd happened by accident to witness. There was a person connected with that event. Two people, actually: participants. One of them seemed to be himself. He must remember that desire itself was always neutral. He thought of the other, of what he'd done with him. More precisely, what had been done to him by—he had trouble getting his mind around the name—yes, David. A splendid name. For that matter, a splendid animal, David. Kind. Tender. He could hardly forget what had happened; he could still feel it, the faintest heat in his core, that peculiar gathering fullness or emptiness as if something had shifted deep inside and things had not yet settled into place, leaving his thickening innards still fluid, shimmering, an occasional clot or void. Frightening. Shifts in the magma under the sea. Oh, yes, there's always an explanation: plate tectonics. The surface, though, remained unbroken, as undisturbed as ever; the smooth saline sea adjusted, covering every gash and fault. *Thalassa.* The Greeks had a word for it. The very word had a healing sound. *Thalassa. Thalassa mou, sas agapo.* Byron might have said it. He pulled a chair toward him and put his feet up on it, glanced at his bag. He reached for it, setting it in his lap, and began to fumble through the contents: his sunglasses, his swimsuit, the book he was reading; and tucked into a pocket on the side, the map showing the way to the *Jardin des Délices.* He looked at his drink, at the sweat on the glass, at the cubes of ice polished to the sheen of oil in the moonlight. One of the cubes cracked—loud in the stillness—and settled in the glass. He hadn't yet tasted it. He took a sip; didn't like the taste. The cigarettes were in his bag too, under the same flap with the message. He pulled out the box and set it on the table. He tried to recall the talk at dinner, but he couldn't remember it. There *was* an area of his experience that eluded him. *Gemina teguntur lumina nocte.* He couldn't see it. He'd made them laugh, though. He remembered that—that, and the stupid Roman eagle in a niche outside the door of the restaurant. Why that should remain etched in his mind was a mystery. He got up, stole into the room, and went to the wastebasket, rummaged there for David's crumpled note and returned with it to his seat. He smoothed the paper on the table. If he'd strained, it might have been possible to read it in the moonlight. No, it was too dark to see. He didn't need to read it. He knew what it said. He reached for the box of cigarettes, took one, looked in his bag for matches, and lit it. His hand shook. He took another sip of his drink, the ice crackling in the glass, and inhaled deeply on the cigarette, its tip glowing red, the only color in that chiaroscuro hour of whiteness and shadow. He peered through the glass and the scrim of the curtains to see if he'd disturbed her. He saw pearls flowing from the mouth of the little bag, the metal disks of the tambourine gleaming quiet in the moonlight. Ann. He thought he could make out her still form under the whiteness of the sheet, but that was all. The form might have been a doll. He leaned back in his chair, staring into the ceiling. He moved his chair farther out; he wanted the sky above him. He reached for his sunglasses and put them on, and plunged into darkness. How peculiar to be sitting there in the middle of the night in sunglasses! He shook his head in wonder, thought of Catullus again: "*My eyes are covered by a double night.*" It sounded better in Latin: harder; worse. Odd that Catullus too had heard a ringing in his ears. He took the sunglasses off, put out his cigarette, and in a moment lit another. He suffered from the Protestant equation between behavior and belief. That must be it. He felt himself screaming, but of course he heard no sound. Sodomy was quite common in sixteenth-century Florence, it is said. Look at Cellini, father and pederast. They hadn't mentioned that in art history. His *Ganymede* was simply a sculpture, an allegory of the superiority of heavenly love—certainly not one of his pretty assistants! There were so many things they didn't tell

in school. He should have been Italian. So David. Yes. He looked
at the note, smoothed it again, dropping ashes. He blew them
off, over the balcony. The fairways looked so mysterious, so
quiet in the pearly light. So he'd done something with a
man. More than that. What? Insistent: *What?* He felt the slow
sink of dismay: what he had allowed, permitted—*wanted?*—
David to do. Yes, of course he'd wanted it. Otherwise it
wouldn't have happened. *The dread desire.* He felt something
move inside him, something slide again. All forms are fluent.
Emerson knew. No. Stop. Think of something else. Think of a
poem.

> *A shudder in the loins engenders there*
> *The broken wall, the burning roof and tower*
> *And Agamemnon dead.*

Not that poem. *And I, Tiresias, am alone escaped to tell thee.* Tiresias, who knew what the other felt, what the other wanted. Not
even the sagacious seer—sewer?—of Vienna had known the answer to that. That dark, mysterious desire. Deeper than mysterious. Dark as tar. The primary opposition: the man and the
woman, the one and the other. Tiresias, throbbing between two
lives, reversing the polarities, the blind seer of Thebes foresuffer-
ing all: he alone knew the awful diapason of desire. He had seen
snakes coupling. Twice. And been transformed. Twice. Andrew
trembled. The gaping, yawning enormity of it. It made that guy
Ann had told him about on the plane coming back from London
—Frank Potter, that's the one—look like a bizarre, pathetic fool,
a eunuch. He shook his head, bemused: Ann had *admired* him!
The fellow was writing a book. He'd have to watch for it, get it
for her. "*Merry Christmas, Ann. Love, Francesca.*" Well, forget
Frank Potter. Forget Tiresias. Forget the heated Catullus, con-
sumed by his ardor for the lascivious, faithless Lesbia on the one
hand, the tender youth Juventius on the other. Forget the mur-
derous, insatiable Cellini. Did he know where he was? He didn't
live in sixteenth-century Florence; ancient Greece or Rome,
either. He would need all his powers. He took a drink. That
wouldn't help. Just get it right in his head; the form would come
sometime. Maybe. He closed his eyes and took a deep slow
breath; then another, three times in all, draining his mind. He let

his eyelids slowly part, focusing on nothing, sensing the moonlight falling like bright silver rain on the water beyond the darkness. His lids drifted open, independent of his will. He moved
his arm, touched his leg, his clavicle—felt his finger scraping
there—reached for a cigarette, and lit it. His mind resumed its
wayward course. The structure of desire. The desire of desire: to
be what one is not. To possess what one does not. Did he know
who he was? He watched the smoke from his cigarette idly float
in the currents of air. He finished it, watched its coals expire in
the ashtray. He fumbled with the box, decided to light another.
He felt his mind swing toward its focus again. The cigarette was
bringing him in touch—or was it? Yes, that's better. Of course,
it was easier for a woman. *C'est plus facile ouvrir la bouche que tendre
le bras.* He smiled secretly: maybe more fun, too—not that a
woman would be likely to admit it. When Tiresias told that to
Hera, that she got nine or ten times more pleasure than Zeus, she
was enraged, blinded him on the spot. But Zeus, kind father of
them all, gave him second sight and made the darkness of his
doom much lighter. Still, he'd lost a lot. Curious, this obscure
duality, polarity, of desire. There is the one, and there is the
other. All forms are *not* fluent! Except at the beginning. *In the
beginning was the Word. Logos.* The fertilizing word. *Logos sperma-
tokos.* That was it! That was the crux. Desire's fatal arc. And then
—*voilà!*—mired in the Incarnation, in the marble and the mud:
the polarities. The structure. The double helix of desire. He
shook his head vigorously. Christ, did he think he was Greek?
Well, he had acted it. No need to pursue that. In fact, there was.
There was a need. He was making this event in time so abstract,
when in fact it had been utterly, immediately, overwhelmingly
there the afternoon of May tenth, nineteen hundred and seventy-
one, at a specific latitude and longitude on the island of Bermuda
on the watery planet Earth. He trembled, saw the moon reflected
on the sea, and put on his sunglasses again. Too bright, he said
to himself, emitting a dry puff of a laugh, too bright. Sometimes
his knowledge—not knowledge at all, but the random informa-
tion of an *idiot savant*—exceeded his grasp of it. He was not, after
all, talking about dead Italian sculptors, or dead Roman poets, or
characters who had never lived at all except in myth and drama
and someone's—someone's?—fierce imagination. He was talking
about the proximate cause, one particular person, David Roper,

age twenty-eight—the age he'd been when, so full of love, he'd married; David Roper, resident of London, putative artist, whom he had followed like a dog to a house in Bermuda and there had had knowledge of the same David Roper; who had then opened him, filled him, and left his mark, an indelible, shuddering sign. He was talking about *himself*! He wanted to escape that self. He shivered, burst into sudden sharp laughter, glanced quickly into the room to see if he'd been heard. No, he was safe. *Guilty, Your Honor. It's all true. Sex is indeed knowledge. A terrible knowledge. Ask Tiresias. And look what it got him. The gift of blindness.* It couldn't be true! His stomach suddenly sank—whoosh!—his breath stopped, and his head began suddenly, voluptuously, to spin. Crazy! More then crazy; mad. He clutched his drink to steady himself, and turned to look again through the glass, through the curtains, to his wife's sleeping form. He couldn't make it out. Was he still wearing his sunglasses? He touched his head. They were so light, he'd scarcely noticed. He took them off. The light was striking the glass of the door at the wrong angle now, making it a mirror to the moon. Oh, it couldn't be true! The feeling in his body's tremulous core denied the denial. He dismissed it. He had to see him again, to believe it. He'd forgotten for a moment: he would see him again. Tomorrow. They were *all* going out on that blasted boat, into the Sargasso Sea. Could he get out of it? Could he survive it? Of course he could survive it. Somehow. He had to see him again. What was it they said? Oh, yes: seeing is believing. Sometimes. But he had to see him again. He lit another cigarette, turned his eyes to the sea. It looked so still, with the moon like a knife on the water. Sam had said—part of his lore— that if you're ever caught in a waterspout, you should cut it with a silver knife. Maybe he would bring one. There is a world out there so much larger than this, he thought. Larger than the work he did, the plays he'd written. Some of them—the first, he supposed; this last, people told him—were good, good of their kind. He was no longer interested in their kind. He wanted to go beyond that, dredge deeper than that. He wanted to plunge to his extreme limits, plumb those limits, and he wanted to come back. It might not be possible. Either to go, or then to come back. He should never leave. It was too late: he'd already left, started the dive. The dive into the *dreck*. He had no choice now but to continue. Forms were dissolving. Words were too crude, but for him there was nothing else. Numbers were not his medium, nor colors, nor clay, nor stone, nor tones on a scale. He needed another language, but he had only one. If words were inadequate, he would have to twist them to his own design to make them adequate.

He struggled from his chair; took the cigarettes from the table and, leaning over the edge of the balcony, looking into the garden, watched them slip from his hand into the darkness below. Then he took David's note and his message and tore them into small pieces, letting them flutter like confetti into the night. He glanced at the moon, still bright in the sky, and parted the curtains, passing into the room. He slipped Ann's pearls—his mother's pearls, which had been his grandmother's, of whom, really, he knew nothing—into the pouch and closed it. He carried the ashtray to the bathroom and switched on the lights, blinding himself. He quickly turned them off. He was more comfortable in the dark. He flushed the cigarette stubs down the toilet, cleaned the ashtray and took it into the room, padded toward the balcony and opened the door wide. It made a noise. He turned. Ann bolted upright in the bed, her eyes gleaming white in the moonlight. "It's all right," he whispered. "I was just closing the curtains." She fell back abruptly. Probably she had never really wakened. He closed the heavy curtains, shutting out the light, and like a blind man felt his way to the bed, got into it, and caromed toward sleep as Ann shifted and settled around him, her breath warm on his shoulder.

In the morning the feeling inside him was gone, but the taste of cigarettes lingered in his mouth, on his burning tongue.

The white vessel swayed easily, gracefully on the swelling tide, sparkling in the sunlight, and the group gathering at the dock that morning waiting to board it was all gaiety and laughter and anticipation. It was going to be a big group, too, an even dozen now that David had been added, the women outnumbering the men by two—without counting the captain and his small crew. But it was a big boat—at least eighty or ninety feet long—considerably larger than Andrew had expected, and could easily have accommodated a dozen or so more. He and Ann and Yasmine were the first to arrive—a startling break from custom. They had shared a taxi, Michael and Marika following in one of their own. When they got there, snorkeling equipment and diving gear and crates of provisions were still being hauled on deck and stowed away.

"It looks as if we've got enough here to survive for a month," Michael said, looking at the fruits and cheeses, the beer and wine and who knew what else being carried aboard.

"What's Sam got on his mind, for God's sake? A trip to Portugal?"

"Maybe we're being kidnapped," Yasmine said.

Andrew walked over to the gangway and checked the bags. "You know Sam: if he does something, he does it all the way. I mean, somebody might have a sudden craving for an artichoke. What if he couldn't supply one? The whole thing might be ruined for want of a simple artichoke."

"Yes, well, let's just hope the compass behaves itself. I don't want any funny stuff today."

"Hell!" Andrew exclaimed. "I forgot the knife."

"The knife?" Ann asked.

"You remember. If you're caught in a waterspout you're supposed to cut it with a silver knife. They do have waterspouts around here."

"Yes," she said, "and if you see a shark you're supposed to punch it in the nose. Please"—she laughed—"let's not hear any more foolishness about the Bermuda Triangle." She turned at the sound of a car pulling off the highway and heading toward the dock. "Here comes Sam. Don't get him started on the subject. He'll insist we make voodoo dolls or something." She looked at the crates stacked up beside the ship. "Probably the captain is just stocking the boat for the week. He must have other charters. This stuff can't be intended only for us."

"I don't know," Michael said. "Andrew looks hungry."

Sam and Molly stepped from the loaded car, Sam pulling a roll of crepe paper from a bulging bag. He waved it at them. "I've got streamers, kids. We're going to make this a real *bon voyage*—worthy of the Cunard Line." He motioned toward the vessel. "Pretty little thing, isn't she?" One of the crew members appeared and began to unload the car.

"*Little?*" Yasmine asked. "Not so little, Sam. It's a lot fancier than I'm used to—big enough for Niarchos! It's even carrying a launch."

"The launch has a glass bottom," Sam said, "so we can see the fish and the coral. We'll all go out in it later."

Ann looked at the launch hanging from its davits in the stern. "It can't possibly hold us all."

"We'll break up into smaller groups," Sam said.

"This is wonderful!" Marika laughed with delight. "Crazy, but wonderful. It does feel as if we're embarking on a real voyage. We're going to have a wonderful time."

"Where's the band?" Michael asked.

"By God, I knew I forgot something!" Sam looked just the smallest bit crestfallen, as if for a fraction of a second he thought he really ought to have hired a band to send them off. "Well, we'll just have to supply our own. We'll sing, lads—'Auld Lang Syne,' as the ship puts out to sea. Maybe the captain has a bugle or something—"

"A pipe to pipe us aboard!" Yasmine said. "That's what we need."

"We'll see. You stay here—all of you. I've got some business to attend to," and he danced off like an eager child, full of excitement for the coming show. He got the fellow who'd unloaded the car to help him, and by the time Rick and his group arrived in their taxi, soon followed by David on his moped, the vessel was festooned with streamers and they were ready to board.

"You're just in time," Michael said, turning to Rick and Kevin; Ruth and Jack were still at the taxi, organizing their gear. "The curtain's about to go up." Two cameras hung from Rick's neck, and Kevin, a pair of those annoying mirrored sunglasses concealing his eyes, was carrying a small movie camera and a bag of equipment. "Are you planning to make a movie of this?"

Rick reached into a back pocket and pulled out his New York Yankees cap. He laughed. "I brought my director's cap, just in case. I never shoot without it." He put it on his head. "I never know when I might get some footage I could cut in. It's all material. Nobody minds, do they?"

"Yes," Andrew said, but mildly.

Ann shot him a look. "Of course we don't mind," she said.

Rick raised one of his still cameras and pointed it at her. "Stick with me, baby, and I'll make you a star." He laughed; she smiled; he snapped the shutter.

"She doesn't want to be a star," Andrew said.

"Of course she does. I can see it gleaming there, just under the surface. The camera will bring it out."

"I think it already is," Michael said. "It's already out."

"I can speak for myself, boys, thank you."

Andrew left. He walked over to the gangway, called up to Sam: "Can I do anything to help?"

"You stay right where you are. This is my production. Send Molly up here. I need her. You get back there and entertain the group. That's your job. Get them warmed up for the curtain."

Ruth and Jack approached the gangway, dropping their gear beside it. "Wow! Look at that!" Ruth exclaimed. "What fun! What fun! I feel ready for anything."

"That's our Ruth," Jack said, shaking his head in mock wonder, "always fresh as a daisy in the morning, no matter the rigors of the night."

Andrew was surprised; Jack had seemed so quiet. "You can't beat fun, as my father used to say." Andrew laughed. "And she looks fresh as a daisy, too. Or at least a buttercup." It sometimes astonished him how he could respond to circumstances, carry on the show.

"You look *fantastic*!" Ruth threw her arms around him and exuberantly kissed him on the mouth. He looked at her, startled. "What have you been *doing*?" She pulled back, her hands on his shoulders, looking at him. "It's not fair!" She called to Ann. "Andrew looks good enough to eat."

"Depends on your appetite, I guess," Michael said, turning to Ruth and Jack, greeting them, shaking hands with David, who had just approached.

David. It had not been twenty-four hours since he'd seen him; scarcely more than twelve. Andrew remembered, and his stomach dropped. He saw the white towel tossed so casually on the lounge chair in the empty garden, the white towel intense and shining in the sunlight; heard the dolphin's splashing, the crisp rattle of the lemon tree. David spoke. He moved toward him. The light glinted on his hair. Andrew saw the vulnerable sleeping boy, warm and breathing against the cool rumpled whiteness of the sheets; saw the body as he would have painted it, caught in that moment of its climb from the pool. He felt flushed, clammy, and looked away, then back. He walked toward him, heard his voice speak. "Hello, David. Glad you could make it." It seemed unnaturally loud, beyond his control. Perhaps he was losing his mind.

"Hi. Isn't it a great morning?"

"Have you met Rick and his merry pranksters?"

Ruth burst into laughter, joined by Rick and Kevin. David smiled a little sheepishly. "Well, yes, we have met, actually."

"You'll never guess where," Ruth said.

Sam blew on a whistle. "All ashore that's going ashore," he shouted, "and all that's sailing, haul yourselves up here." He whistled again, a sharp, earsplitting call—"All aboard! Last call!" —and they picked up their gear and moved toward the gangway.

"Off to the mines, men," Michael said, scurrying them along; "there'll be no strike today."

"Tell you later," Ruth whispered to Andrew as they filed up the gangway and onto the afterdeck, dropping their gear and moving along the ship toward the bow. The engines coughed; two deckhands slipped the moorings and leapt aboard, another cranking up the anchor with the windlass; the ship gave a little shudder and suddenly eased from the dock, floating free. Sam tossed rolls of streamers at the members of his party, and laughing and cheering, they hurled them into the bright transparent morning, watched them float and ripple there before they fluttered slowly toward the shore. The vessel seemed for a moment to drift like a chip on the electric sea; then, pennants flying, streamers trailing, and the group on the forecastle singing now " *'Should auld acquaintance be forgot, and never brought to mind,'* " gathered control and sailed into the harbor, toward the mouth of the harbor, and picking up speed, the reefs and the open sea beyond.

Marika laughed, brushed her hair from her eyes. "I feel I'm on the *QE Two.*" She squeezed Andrew's arm. "A first for me. Those people on the dock must think we're mad!"

"They wouldn't be wrong," Andrew said, smiling at her. Then he headed toward the stern, breathing deeply of the salted air. He stood there alone for a moment, gathering himself, and watched the soft hills and shore recede, as if his eyes were a camera and the camera were dollying inexorably back—by powers of ten, he thought, powers of ten.

"What are you doing, standing here by yourself? You ought to be facing the sea, not the shore." The voice was Ruth's. "Come on, mopey. Join the party."

"All right, my dear." He turned. "You asked for it." He took her hand and placed it on his arm. "Let's go. I shall set my face like flint, as Saint Paul tells us," and laughing now, they strode off arm in arm, bumping into David Roper on the way.

"I was afraid you were trying to escape," David said, taking Ruth's other arm in his own. "I was coming back for you."

"Which one of us?" Ruth asked.

"Well, both of you, of course."

She laughed. "But I found him first."

"Obviously neither of us was going very far," Andrew said. "The boat's not *that* big."

"You could have fallen overboard," Ruth said.

"Not yet," Andrew replied. "Anyway, I'm a good swimmer."

"That's good. So am I. Let's go to the other side."

"You got a lifesaving certificate, Ruth?"

"Who needs the certificate? I know what I'm good at." They passed around the stern and stood against the starboard rail.

"I'm sure you do."

"You want a demonstration?"

"That won't be necessary. I believe you."

"I'll show you later, when we're in the water." She leaned against the rail. "My famous hammerlock."

"You do that. Only that's not a lifesaving hold, it's a wrestling grip."

"Same thing."

"I hope not. Let's go back to the party."

"You didn't ask how we met David," Ruth said.

"I guess I didn't. Well, how?"

She reached into her bag. "This seems like a quiet spot. Care for a little smoke?" She pulled out a joint. "I'm important to the story."

"I never smoke before lunch."

"That's too bad. Maybe you'll change your mind."

"Do you think we should be doing this here?" David asked. "Sam might not like it."

"No," Andrew said, "I don't."

"Sam won't mind a bit," Ruth said, ignoring him, lighting up, taking two hits, and passing the joint to David, who took a small puff and passed it on to Andrew.

"No, thanks," he said, handing it back to Ruth.

"Would you like one of these instead?" David offered him a Dunhill.

Andrew looked at it, started to shake his head, hesitated, took it. "Thanks," he said. David struck a flame. Andrew stared at it, leaned toward it lighting his cigarette, then squinted at the shore, faint in the distance. "Well"—he turned toward her—"what's the story?"

"It's so funny!" Ruth exclaimed. "We met at the soccer stadium!" She burst into laughter, took another hit—"Wow! Where did they grow this weed?"—and fell into uncontrolled giggling. "I can't stop! I'm getting an instant laughing high." She inhaled again. "Wow!"

"Were you playing or watching?" Andrew asked.

Ruth looked at him, trying to gain control of herself, failed. "In a minute." She looked away. "You're so funny, it's serious." She was convulsed again. "I meant, you're so serious, it's funny." She shook her head. "God! I'd better watch this stuff. What's the matter with you, David? Why aren't you laughing?"

"Different strokes for different folks," Andrew said. "Do you think one of you could tell the story, or shall I leave to let you get a grip on yourself?"

"No, I can do it. Well, you know Kevin scored those joints at that place we went dancing and then Rick persuaded someone in the band to sell him a nickel bag, but we finished it up yesterday. The guy told us, though, that we could get some more around Horseshoe Beach. So we stopped there this morning."

"Were you there, David?" David shook his head.

"No, he wasn't there. But this beach attendant was. Her name is Rita. She rents snorkeling gear and stuff. Anyway, Rick asked her if there was much of a drug problem on the island. She looked a little mellow, you know? Stoned, in other words."

"Already?"

"Yes, already. Not everybody has your crazy rules. It's nice to get a little buzz on in the morning. Helps a person face the day. Anyway, Rita said in this very casual kind of way, 'Not much of a problem,' but she gave him kind of a funny look. Then

Rick asked her, very seriously, 'Rita, if you were looking for a drug problem, where do you think you might find it?' He was so funny, and he looked so, you know, *serious*. Like you."

"Sounds like a riot," Andrew said.

"Well, it *was* funny. Want another hit, David?"

"No, thanks."

"Andrew? No, I don't suppose you do. You were a lot looser the other night." She had another toke.

"I'm always tight in the morning. The day wears down my resistance." He drew on his cigarette; felt like a spring.

"That's a relief. I can hardly wait." She looked at him. "Yes, you are fairly crazy at night. Me, I'm crazy twenty-four hours a day, but I can pass when I want to." She eyed the joint in her hand. "Enough of that for now." She carefully extinguished it, slipped it into an empty film canister, and returned it to her bag. "That is potent herb. The tourist ads in *The New Yorker* don't tell you about all of Bermuda's fabulous attractions!"

"Probably they couldn't handle the stampede. So, as you were saying."

"Oh, yes. Well. 'You looking for a problem?' Rita asked. 'We might be,' Rick said, still totally serious. She reached under the counter, said, 'Here, take this,' and handed him a joint. Well, we lit it and smoked it right there, the five of us—Rita too. It was too early for anybody to be around. We had a fucking *ball*! 'Any more where that came from?' Rick asked. 'Oh,' she said, 'you're looking for a *big* problem.' Rick said yes, and she told us to go up to the soccer field at the top of the hill and mosey around the clubhouse. She said we'd find the problem. We found the problem, all right—it would be hard to miss—and we found David, too. That's where we met, over the nickel bags. Fan-fucking-*tastic*! But he'd been there before. And then he pulled up behind us at the dock! What a shock. I can tell you, Rita was right: drugs are no problem in Bermuda."

"No problem to get, anyway," Andrew said. He looked at his cigarette, took a final puff, and flipped it over the rail. "So what's the good news?"

"Tell you later, Andy. David's not talking much." She poked him. "What's the matter, Davy?"

Andrew interrupted. "Listen, I don't know about you two, but I've got to get back to the group."

"I should too," David said. "I'm the interloper here."

"So he does talk. He and Jack—the quiet types. You got to watch 'em. Well, I suppose I might as well go along with you. You try to have a little fun with a couple of guys, and look what happens. I'll have to work on you later."

Andrew laughed. "You do that, Ruth."

"He's a tough nut to crack," David said.

"Oh, you've noticed that, have you?" Ruth took their arms. "You just wait. I'm sure it can be done." She straightened her shoulders. "Well, time to be a lady. I'll do my Wellesley impersonation. It's very good."

"Let's go forward," Andrew said, and they returned to the party, gathered now in the bow.

Andrew went over to Ann and sat down beside her. He sniffed the air. "This boat smells like one gigantic coconut. The fumes are so thick you could cut them with a knife." He shuddered.

"The sun is intense. Nobody wants to get a burn." She'd changed to her swimsuit and was lying on a deck chair, drinking tea. "You'd better put some lotion on too, unless you're going to stay in your clothes."

"I think I will for a while."

"You know, darling, I've been thinking. You ought to work on Sam and Michael to find some roles for these people. At least give them a chance. Rick tells me they're quite good. I don't know about the men, but Ruth certainly has something."

He laughed. "You think so? I hope it's not contagious."

"If it is, I trust you haven't caught it." She laughed gaily, teasing him.

"I was thinking of you."

"I wish you could be serious."

"Darling, I'm always serious," he said. "You look pretty this morning. Fra Angelico. No, Botticelli. The celestial Venus. Anyway, I thought they were busy. They're already involved in a movie, aren't they? Let me get a cup of coffee. Where do you find it?"

"It's in the lounge." She gestured toward it.

He walked into the lounge, looked around, noticed a pack of cigarettes on a table. He poured himself a cup of coffee, decided to skip the Danish. He went over to the table, stood there sipping his coffee, leafing through a magazine. Finally he shook two cigarettes from the pack and put them in his pocket, found some matches. The name of the ship was on them: *Bermuda Queen*. He hadn't noticed that before. He returned to Ann. "Sam's thought of everything," he said. "Not only coffee, but pastries, yet. What'll he do for lunch?"

"The captain and his boys are going to spear some fish. He always does it for his charters. It's his specialty. Kevin wants to join them, but Molly and I"—Molly was approaching with Michael—"aren't sure Kevin knows what he's doing." She laughed. "We think he just wants to play with a spear gun, and Rick wants to shoot the action—isn't that what you think, Michael?" Michael shrugged. "Tell me, do you think Kevin's one of the boys?" She raised her eyebrows knowingly.

"One of the what?"

"Oh, I just thought he might be, you know, one of the boys. He's too good-looking to be true."

"Do you mean, is he a faggot? I haven't a clue," Michael said.

"He's certainly a boy, though. Look at him." Molly chuckled. "What a pose!" Kevin was leaning back against the windlass, his head tossed back, eyes half-closed, a sultry pout on his face, a hand resting lightly on his open thigh, a little cap and the twin black mirrors of his glasses on the deck beside him: so casual, so self-conscious, trying to appear grown-up and hard and knowing, and succeeding in part. Really, though, he was a child still; alarmingly young, Andrew thought.

"I thought he was trying to do a little number on Yasmine; but Ann, if you're really curious, you could follow it home and see what it eats."

"Michael!" Molly laughed.

"She asked."

"You *are* outrageous. He's just young, he knows he's stunning, he knows other people know it, and he loves it."

What a frightening, ignorant age, Andrew thought, gazing at the boy in his sleek black trunks; a perilous condition: poised in fierce, sullen defiance between the terrible innocence of the child-king and the relentless abrading world. "You think he's stunning?" he asked. "I think he seems rather sad."

"Pretty, maybe. Pretty is more accurate."

"Yes. There's something unformed about him. Almost petulant. You can see it around the mouth. I think he's one of those people who looks better at first sight than second."

"Well," Michael said, "if he's got the brains in his head that he's got between his legs, he'll be fine. Hey, Kevin! Come on over here. Ann wants to talk to you."

"Michael!"

"She's afraid you'll burn. Here." He picked up the bottle of tanning oil and squirted it at Kevin's chest. "Rub it in. Draw up a chair. Join the party. Let's get the rest of them." Michael beckoned the others clustered here and there. "Gather around, everybody. We're going to have an emergency drill."

"We are?" Ann asked.

"I always like to keep an eye out for the life preservers," Michael said.

"Where are they?" Marika asked, looking around.

"They're in that box over there by the bridge," Michael said. "See the sign? A dozen of them. Enough for us all."

"Let's not forget the crew," Molly said.

"There's another box in the stern," Andrew said. "Where's Sam?"

"He's playing captain." Molly pointed toward the flying bridge and Sam behind the wheel, the captain at his side.

"I'm going to get into my swimsuit. Be right back." Andrew picked up his bag and carried it to one of the cabins. When he had changed, he transferred the cigarettes to his shirt pocket and went up top. "How do you get to be the captain, Sam?" he asked.

"He's paying for it," the captain said. He was a man in his forties, probably, but looking younger. "The boss always gets to guide the ship."

Sam introduced them. "Want to try it?" he asked.

"Is it okay?"

"Sure it's okay. It's easy. Fun, too. Try it." Sam handed him the helm.

"I've never done this before, not on a thing like this. Is this ship yours? Are you the owner?"

"No," the captain said, "she belongs to a rock star." He named a famous musician. "He keeps it here, hardly ever shows up. Keep an eye on the compass, now. You want to maintain the course, about one hundred ninety degrees. Everything is just what you'd expect. If you want to move to port, turn the wheel that way. If you want to head to starboard, turn it the other. See those two buoys way out there? They're marking the inner reef. We want to go between them, but keep close to the port marker. There's an old wreck to starboard. When we get beyond the first reef, then you'll have to keep a sharp eye on the compass—things look different on the open sea, and they're deceiving. No landmarks, only the compass to guide you. Or the stars."

Andrew took the wheel, tentatively. "Do you want me to steer it through the reef?"

"Sure. You can do it. Just remember what I told you." He called down to one of the crew, who ran to the bow and leaned over, peering into the water. "Those glasses he's got on, they're Polaroid. They let him see into the water better." They were approaching quickly now. "The ship's doing fourteen knots. Let's cut it back a little." The captain reached for the throttles and slowed the engines.

The boy on the bow called up to him. "Coral head! Five degrees off port. Thirty feet."

"Move it a little to starboard, five degrees or so." Andrew turned the wheel. Nothing happened. He turned it farther and the boat began to veer to the right. "A little too much," the captain said. "It takes a while to turn a ship this size. She's sensitive, but she doesn't respond instantly. Make a correction to port." Andrew turned the wheel, and the boat slowly glided into position. "That's right. Perfect. We'll be passing over the reef in a minute. See it? The darker water?" Andrew looked, nodding. They were gliding over it now. The boy on the prow scanned the water, signaling toward port. Andrew adjusted the course.

"All clear," the boy shouted, and went below.

"Okay, let's open 'er up. Both engines. You can do it. Hands on the throttles and pull. That'll empty the forecastle, give it a little spray. You'll see your friends heading aft in a minute."

Andrew pulled on the throttles. The engines pitched higher, settling into a powerful hum. "Get it up to twenty knots or so," the captain said, "and correct the course to a hundred sixty-five, south-southeast." Andrew followed his directions. "There! Easy, wasn't it? We'll make a sailor of you yet. And see?" He pointed toward the deck. "Your friends are starting to move. They'll like it better aft."

Andrew looked. The wind was stiffer now, blowing spray

across the bow. He watched them slowly pick up their things and move toward the stern. Ann's hair was blowing hard in the wind, and Rick clutched the baseball cap to his head. "I was a sailor once," Andrew said, "but I spent all my time in the engine room. On the dog watch. Never saw a thing on deck." He laughed. "Unreal." Yes, unreal. The marvelous unreality of motion, all things relative to speed and distance, an occasional pause for the hurly-burly of the shore and then the safe refuge of the ship grinding continuously on, remote and inviolate through the water. A world both safe and secret, a child's world of hide-and-seek: a boy's world, not a man's. A different language was spoken there. He looked again at the figures scurrying from the bow. Not here, though. His world had pursued him. He was not home free. What was that line from *The Tempest*? "*Hell is empty, and all the devils are here.*" That was it. Andrew smiled, shook himself from his reverie, and turned back to the captain. "This is great! Thanks."

"You know the saying, 'True Virgins Make Dull Company'?"

"I can't say that I do," Andrew said, "but I don't think there's any need to worry about being bored here."

The captain laughed. "No," he said, "it's a seaman's rule for setting a course. True is the course you want to set. Virgins stands for the variation adjustment. Make is magnetic; Dull, deviation, and Company is the compass. But it doesn't hold true for this area. You get within two hundred miles of Bermuda and the compass wobbles like a drunken sailor, so we navigate by the stars."

"What did I tell you?" Sam said. "It's the Bermuda Triangle."

"You don't need to worry today," the captain said. "We're not going that far—just to the outer reef. Even if we were, the stars work just fine."

"I'd like to go into the Sargasso Sea," Andrew said. "I've always wanted to see it."

"You're in it. Just look in any direction."

"But I want to know it. I want to see these masses of floating weeds they talk about. I want to feel that I'm there."

"It's funny around here," the captain said. "Sometimes you won't see any sargasso weed for days, and other times you can't seem to see anything but. I'll see if I can find a patch for you— after lunch. We'll take a little turn beyond the reef. I'm going down to the bridge now. Better switch controls. But anytime either of you want to take over, let me know. Join me whenever you want. I'll show you the charts and the radar, and the instruments we use, if you're really interested."

"Thanks," Sam said, "we will."

"Sam, this is *great!*" Andrew stood facing the wind and the sea. He felt exhilarated. "It's wonderful. Thanks a lot. You are a truly great guy. Chartering this incredible yacht!" He shook his head, laughing. "Only you. Actually, it's just the sort of thing I'd do if I could afford it. I've always admired people who can bring off mad, flamboyant gestures." He sat down and put his legs up on the bench facing him, relishing the thought. "I love it! That must be why we get along so well. I admire your spontaneous craziness, and your willingness to act on it. Not to mention how well you carry it off. The world needs someone like you—someone with the means to do it."

"Speaking of craziness," Sam said, "I've been wanting to talk to you."

"Oh?"

"You seem tired to me. You don't act it, and you don't really look it, except now and then. But I think you are. I think you need a rest. I spoke to Ann yesterday. I'd like you two to stay on here for a few days. Stay for the weekend, if you'd like. As my guests."

"Sam, I can't do that."

Sam dismissed the protest with a wave of his hand. "No problem. Of course you can. I've made more money in the theater than I ever dreamed of having. You know that."

"Yes, and you spend more than anybody'd ever dream of spending—most of it on other people. Ann told me you'd spoken to her. I really appreciate it—you're a generous, kind man, and a rare one, a special one, but I don't know that we can do it. Among other things, we have a child at home."

"That's not a problem. That's why we have telephones."

"I'd like to do it. I'll see what Ann says."

"If she doesn't want to stay, you could always stay on by yourself for a few days. That might do you a lot of good. Get away from your work. Get away from Ann for a while." Sam laughed. "It would probably do her a lot of good too. Imagine having you as your cross!"

Andrew laughed. "She's not a Catholic for nothing. 'Offer it up,' I keep telling her, but I don't know that she listens." Suddenly he remembered, and his gut sank.

"What's the matter? Why the frown all of a sudden?"

"It's too complicated," Andrew said. He gazed out to sea. There was a haze on the water. The light was diaphanous now. He shaded his eyes. "I'd like to stay, but I don't know that I can." He felt suddenly tired. Sam was right. "No, I'm almost sure that I can't." He took a deep breath and smiled at him. "I'm a working boy, after all."

"You do as Sam tells you. You're like a son to me, Andrew. Never had one of my own, you know. And you need a father to guide you."

Andrew thought of his own father: stern, demanding, impossible to satisfy until Andrew had gotten married and then, suddenly, his father was a different man for a while. Until he saw *Riverhead*. Andrew was swimming in a different pond. His father had scarcely mentioned it, though its success had pleased him. He'd liked the success, been impressed by the money it had brought him, but Andrew knew he'd hated the vehicle. More than hated it: loathed it; despised it. But he'd never said. Only "I see," in that cold tone he sometimes had, cold as space. "I see," and the light glinted from his glasses. Not that Andrew's mother had been thrilled by it. But nobody had ever talked about it. There were certain things—most things—his family didn't talk about. That old WASP rectitude. God, he hated that! Lies, all of it. Most of it. Much of it. Some of it. When Andrew looked back now, he wondered that he'd had the nerve to do that play. It had taken him a long time to do another, and then he hadn't liked it. After his father died, Andrew had had a dream. In the dream his father was dead but not dead, lying on a sofa in his bedroom in the house on Bellevue Avenue in Grand Rivière. He was wearing his glasses, and he'd read a play Andrew was working on, the best he had ever done, though the play itself existed only in the dream and Andrew, however hard and painfully he labored, could never recall it. He wasn't even working on a play at the time, being in the slough of his dry spell after *Riverhead*. Ann, against all the rules, had given his father the manuscript; it was in a box beside him. He'd turned his head to Andrew, peered at him through the lenses that beamed like headlights, and said,

"This is shit," in a tone of utter contempt. He was dead, but he knew. And Andrew had heard his father say "shit" only once in his life. But he must have said it at work, at the plant. He must have had a life as a man. Andrew knew he did. He had wakened wondering if someone had placed his father's glasses on him in the coffin. It was a terrible dream. He realized he knew very little about his father, about his father's life, his boyhood and man-hood. That familiar figure, as familiar as the furniture in the house, seemed only a figure to him now: the puzzling tyrant king of his boyhood, the benign despot of his first married years. He'd known the right way to row a boat in the current, the correct route from the Island to the shore, and he knew how to keep the fires constantly burning in the furnaces at the plant. From his bedroom Andrew could see their flames reflecting in the sky at night, every night, year in, year out. His father had taken him—he was Tommy then—to the furnace room once; it had looked awesome, like something out of the *Inferno*, only he didn't know about Dante in those years. His father had let him fuel the fires —amazing!—and then, full of enthusiasm from the experience and awed by the power he'd displayed, he'd told his father he wanted to grow up to be a chemical engineer, but his father had doubted that he was smart enough. Maybe he hadn't been; one of the furnaces blew up a few weeks later, and three men were killed. His father had loved Ann, though—he'd had his gentler moments—and he'd seemed relieved when Andrew married and was saved from what he'd thought was the rootless bohemian life of a dropout in New York, even though at the time Andrew had held a marginally respectable job writing headlines for the *Daily News*. Ann was a proper wife, and pretty besides. Now, maybe, he'd get a proper job. Instead, he'd written *Riverhead*. Andrew shook his head, roughly, shaking the memories. He looked at Sam, felt an almost tearful rush of gratitude and love. He laughed with relief. "You're not old enough," he said.

"I'm fifty-eight, kiddo. That's old enough. How old are you? Thirty-seven? Thirty-eight? I'm plenty old enough."

"No kidding! I didn't realize you were that old." He was recovering now. "You look so young. Both of you."

"Molly's only fifty. I got her before she knew any better."

"Well, I'm forty."

"That's okay. I'm still old enough to be your father. I started early—the best time to start." He rose from the bench. "Anyway, Andrew, promise to think about it."

"I will."

"Heading below?"

Andrew got up, then changed his mind. "I think I'll stay up here for a minute. To think about it." When Sam had gone, he lay down on the bench, turned on his side, and curled up as best he could, trying to think of nothing, to banish all ghosts, the living as well as the dead. It seemed a safe place. He felt safe there. Sometimes, though, his judgment was off. He moved his hand, felt the cigarettes in his pocket. He sat up, leaned back against his arm, looked down. No one was on the forward deck now; they must all be in the stern. Occasionally he could hear the sound of voices, and a sharp, staccato burst of laughter. He pulled out one of the cigarettes and lit it, smoked it there in his safe place. How could he possibly stay? He'd like to. A free week in the sun? Who wouldn't like to! With Ann? He had no answer. Alone? That was too frightening. In his present state, what might he do? *Ann, you have to understand: I was pursued by a gang of porno stars. Unfortunately, I was captured. Yes. They tortured me, Ann. It was terrible! You'll never know what I've been through, the things they made me do. Incredible! Interesting, however. Mildly. Be an angel, Ann. You know the poem? "Look homeward, angel, now, and melt with ruth"?* Ruth. That was her name. And then there was David. Andrew was at once fascinated, startled, and repelled; his body was continually surprising him, horrifying him. Terrifying him. He'd thought he was long through being taken unaware by his other, murkier self. He had to think about it; there was too much to think about. He couldn't do it. It was beyond him. He felt trembly, sick. He took the other cigarette and the matches and tucked them between the cushions. He might want to come back later. He should be joining the group; didn't want to; decided he must. In a minute. The cigarette had made him dizzy. He lay back down, feeling the air wash over him, the sun sink into him. He took off his shirt, decided to smoke the other cigarette—to be rid of it. He heard laughter. It was such a nice party—or it should have been, could have been. It sounded as if they were having a good time. Of course he could laugh too—with the best of them. It didn't mean a thing. He finished the cigarette. What to do with the butts? He could hide them under the cushion. Oh, come on!

He wasn't a child sticking his chewing gum under the table, for God's sake! He opened a drawer, rummaging for something to put them in. There was an old can—a tuna fish can, it looked like —clearly used for an ashtray. Surprising to find such a homely receptacle on such a splendid boat. He dropped them into it, shut the drawer, and returned to his bench. He'd cool down, count his breaths for a while, from one to ten, one to ten, begin again; then he'd go back to the group. He closed his eyes and began to count. Not too fast; he didn't want to hyperventilate. He listened to his breathing becoming regular, felt the steady rising and falling of his ribs, was lulled. He heard footsteps approaching. He didn't know who it was, didn't want to know. He'd pretend he was sleeping. He turned to face the back of the bench and closed his eyes. It was Ann; he could smell her. He continued counting. She sat down next to him and rested her hand on his shoulder. She leaned over and kissed his head, reached for his hand tucked under his chin, giving it a gentle shake.

"You're not sleeping, baby. What are you doing? Hiding?" She spoke very softly, kissed him again. Her hair fell into his face.

"Yes," he whispered.

"From what?"

"I don't know. I'm tired. Sam was right."

"No, actually, darling, I think Ruth was right. You do look pretty good. I don't know what Sam was talking about." She felt his back. "You're burning. Put your shirt on."

"In a minute. He offered to put us up here through the weekend. Would you like to?"

"I know he did—I told you, remember?—but we can't do that. We have Julia to think of."

"We could telephone."

"No. We told Mrs. Bridges we'd be back tomorrow evening. She has her own plans, I'm sure. They're both expecting us. I don't want to disappoint Julia. I'm sure she's eagerly awaiting another installment in your story."

"So am I. I'd like to know what happens next."

"Don't you know?"

"I'm continually being surprised."

"If you really do feel tired, you could stay on without me. It's not as if you'd be lonely. There's plenty of company. Ruth and

Rick and the rest are going to be here through the week, I believe
—they're going to be doing some shooting; you could watch, it
might be fun—and your friend from London will be here too,
won't he? It would be all right with me if you stayed over a few
days."

He shivered. "I couldn't stay without you."

"Why not?" She ruffled his hair. "Aren't you old enough?"

He closed his eyes, burrowing into the cushion. "You guessed
it. I'm not old enough to play with the big kids. I'm not allowed
to play their games."

"I thought you liked them."

"Not very much."

"You like David Roper."

"He's all right, I guess."

"Why don't you turn around and face me? It's hard to understand you when you're talking into the cushion. He certainly likes
you."

"That's nice."

"He's been looking all over for you, but he didn't know where
to find you."

"How do you know that?"

"He keeps getting up and wandering off, then comes back in
a minute or two. He looks a little lost, as if he's searching for
something. No one else is missing. It must be you. You're the
only one here he knows, after all, and you're ignoring him."

"He knows you. And Michael, too."

"Hardly."

"Well, he's a grown-up. I'm sure he can make out on his
own."

"Barely."

"Barely what?"

"Barely a grown-up. And he's mesmerized by us. It's rather
sweet, really—like a puppy dog. Aren't you going to turn around
so I can see you? And put on your shirt." He turned. She looked
into his eyes. "What's wrong, darling?"

"Nothing. He's not mesmerized by me. That's ridiculous."

"It's because of you that he's on this little trip, after all. You
could at least do your duty to your guest. Act like a big playwright." She chuckled. "Remember, you're a new voice in the
theater."

"But I'm not. I'm an old voice." He sighed. "I'm no voice at all."

"Pretend. And let's not feel too sorry for ourselves."

"I'm going through puberty. It's hard when your voice is changing."

"What's it changing to this time? And will you *please* put on your shirt before you're completely broiled?" She tucked it around his shoulders.

"I don't know." He fixed his eyes on her leg. "You look a little burned yourself. How did you know where to find me?"

"I figured you'd be at the highest point. When you're hiding, you always go as far up as you can. Apparently David doesn't know that." She smiled. "You must have spent a lot of time in the attic when you were little."

Andrew smiled—a tentative half-smile. "Not so much."

"In a tree?"

"Only when I was trying to fly."

"I know something is wrong, darling. Tell me. You'll feel better if you tell me."

"Nothing's wrong. I don't know." The smile vanished.

"Look at me." He stared at her chin. "Tell me."

"Why do you keep harping on it? If I knew what was wrong, I'd be sure to tell you. You'd be the first to know." He tried to sit up, but she was blocking his way. "Excuse me, would you move? I want to sit up now."

She didn't move. "I would be the first to know, darling, but not because you'd tell me. Because I know you."

"Then you must know me better than I know myself"—he was becoming irritated now—"because there's nothing wrong. Please, let me get up."

"I sometimes think I do. At least, I can tell when something's bothering you, which is more than you can admit to." She paused, looked into his face. "You know something? I miss you, too. I miss my Tommy boy." She began to croon in a plaintive singsong: "Oh, Tommy, Tommy, where have you been? Tommy, Tommy, where are you going? Where are you now, my Tommy boy?"

"Where I am right now is on this bench, and I'm trying to get off it." She moved, and he sat up. "Please don't call me that." He shifted to the edge of the seat. "Don't you think we should find out what's going on below? Rick may be wanting to start a movie or something. He can't start without you—you're the star."

She laughed. "Not yet."

"Oh, that's right: but he's going to make you one."

"We can go down now, but I want you to know something: I don't want to stay on in Bermuda. I want to go home. I'm serious. I want to live a normal life. This is not a normal life for me."

"You shouldn't have married somebody in the theater."

"You weren't in the theater when I married you. You were a needy headline writer. Almost normal."

"Headline writers aren't normal. You should see some of them! Neither are theater people. 'I am not what I am'—*Twelfth Night*."

"I'm beginning to see that." She paused, staring at him. "Then what are you?"

"You tell me. Oh, look"—he rose abruptly to his feet—"aren't you having a good time? This is a fantastic boat."

"The boat isn't the problem."

"You like the Rick brigade."

"He pays attention to me. It's flattering to have someone pay attention to you. I wish you paid a little more."

"Oh, I see: *I'm* the problem. Chester Huntington paid attention to you, too—the old fart."

She ignored him. "And there's something very spontaneous —delightful and sweet—about Ruth."

"Delightful and sweet? Not exactly the words I'd have chosen. She must be a great actress."

"I don't believe it's an act."

"Sweet as a porno star, I'd say. She must be doing her Wellesley number on you. I'll bet she'd take on the whole boat in a heartbeat, crew included. Another Sam Walcott production, directed by Rick What's-his-name, with script by that precocious old voice in the American theater Andrew MacAllister and featuring the legendary Ruth Let-Every-Orifice-Be-Plundered Revere and that rising star on the peter meter, the one and only Annie MacAllister, the playwright's wife. And a cast of animals, of course."

"Are you losing your mind?"

"I think so."

"I think so too. I'm going back to the party. You do as you wish." She looked angry and alarmed.

He reached for her. "Come here. Please? I'm sorry." He put his arms around her, tried to kiss her. He could hardly blame her. "I'll get myself together. Please? I really am sorry. Don't leave me now, like this."

"I don't want to hug you now. I came up here to hug you, but I don't want to hug you now. And you've been smoking again. I can smell it. Where are the cigarettes?" She looked at him, then quickly away. "Oh, what difference does it make!" She pulled away. "If you're going to smoke, you might as well do it in front of me. Just so you don't make an utter fool of yourself. I'm leaving now. If anybody asks for you, I'll send them up here."

"I'm coming with you. Wait for me." But she had already turned and didn't seem to hear him.

"We'll be at the reef in a few minutes," Sam was saying when Andrew appeared moments later in the stern. "Then we'll anchor. The captain's going to spear lunch while we do a little exploring. The launch can take six of us. You can swim or dive from there, if you want, or from the boat. Either way. Everybody ready?" Hands pawed through the snorkeling gear. They began handing masks and flippers from one to another, trying them on for size, blowing through the breathing tubes. It was curious: these New Yorkers who could probably count on one hand the times they'd been forced to venture uneasily onto the concrete earth of the Bronx or Queens instead of speeding across it to Connecticut or the airport, now eagerly preparing to dive into a world surely more alien and perilous than those habitats of mankind. "Anyone here who's never snorkeled before?" Everyone had, though Kevin and Jack had done it only once, and that the day before. "The important thing is to keep the tube straight up, and when you dive blow out before you breathe in, unless your lungs like water. The captain'll give us all a little lesson, anyway, and one of the crew will be watching from the deck, another on the launch."

"It looks like an awfully big ocean when you can't see the shore," Jack said.

"My sentiments exactly," Molly said. "There's something very reassuring about the sight of a beach."

"What about sharks?" Yasmine asked.

"Yes, what about them?"

"Oh, you just punch them in the nose," Andrew said. "Simple as anything. Right, Ann?" A chain clattered and the anchor broke the water.

"I may curl up on deck with my book and a gin and tonic," Molly said. "Nobody's *required* to do this, Sam. Anyone want to get quietly plastered with me?"

The captain had joined them now. "The chances of our running into a shark are practically zero," he said. "There hasn't been an attack in these waters in years."

"Well," Molly said, "in that case, maybe I'll try the glass-bottomed boat."

"When was the last time?" Michael asked. "I read somewhere —not in any of the official guidebooks—that somebody's been attacked by a shark every fifteen or twenty years. If it happened last year, maybe I'd feel safer. Better odds."

There was a ripple of laughter. Kevin, who'd been playing with his cap on the end of a spear—Andrew recognized the cap: a Greek seaman's, he could see now—looked for a moment as if he'd like to take Molly up on her offer, but after a brief wrestle with the odds decided he'd rather risk a shark than appear less than the total man. He put on his sunglasses. "I'm not afraid of sharks," he said.

"Well, that's stupid," Andrew said. "Any rational man is afraid of sharks." Kevin's black mirrored lenses turned toward him. Andrew hated those glasses, impenetrable pools aggressively shooting back his own twin reflections. "I mean, *I* am." He felt a little ashamed. "You should be too, Kevin. It can be a mean world down there."

"Sorry, Andy." Kevin set down the spear and put the little cap on his head.

"Please don't call me that. It makes me feel like a character in a bad movie. A Mickey Rooney movie." What was the matter with him? How was Kevin to know his every little quirk?

"Okay." Kevin looked a little surprised, a little taken aback. Andrew felt more ashamed.

"That's all right. It's just one of my peculiarities. Hardly your problem."

"He's very sensitive about his names, Kevin," Ann said. "We

all run into trouble from time to time." Andrew wanted to go to sleep. He hadn't had enough sleep last night.

Michael began to sing:

> *"Oh, the shark has pretty teeth, dear,*
> *And he shows them pearly white . . .*
> *When the shark bites with his teeth, dear . . ."*

The captain seemed mildly annoyed. "You're not going to *see* a shark; forget about having one chew you up. It never happens here. These waters are benign. There's not enough for sharks to eat in these parts. They like more fertile seas." He laughed—a little demonically, Andrew thought. "They're all chomping tourists in Florida." Probably the questions were always the same. He must get sick of them, and of the boatloads of people whose idea of water was something that occasionally provided a fish and filled the pool or lapped prettily at the shore—pounding surf at the most. Picturesque. The ocean was a different world. Andrew scanned the horizon. Water was all he could see.

"This sea isn't fertile?" Ruth asked. "I thought it was going to supply our lunch."

"The Sargasso Sea is practically a desert," the captain said, "and like the Sahara, life is sparse, but what there is of it is clustered around the reefs and highly visible. These reefs are the oases of the sea."

"The guy's a poet," Michael muttered under his breath.

"He's said it all before," Andrew muttered back.

"Plenty here for lunch," the captain continued. "You'll see. The reef is teeming with life. You'll never see anything like it. The vertical visibility is fantastic. For some reason, it's a lot better than the horizontal, but that only matters if you're scuba diving. I guess we won't be doing any of that today."

"I'd like to do that," Andrew said.

"Ever done it?"

Andrew laughed. "No."

"Well, if you're going to be around, call me up. I'll give you a couple of lessons."

"I don't expect to be around," Andrew said. "We're probably leaving tomorrow."

"But we're still debating that. Right, Andrew?"

"Yes, Sam. We're still debating it."

"Probably Andrew should stay on a few days," Ann said, "but I've got to get back."

"Might you stay on?" David asked. "I'd enjoy that. I'd like the company." He turned to him. "You know there's plenty of room in my house. You'd be welcome. No need to pay for a hotel."

"Oh, why don't you?" Ruth said. "Stay with us. That would be fun! Help us with our movie. Rick would love it. We'd all love it."

"I'm not much of an actor," Andrew said.

"You wouldn't have to act in it. You'd write the script! Oh, if you wanted, Rick would probably give you a part." She laughed. "You look pretty good in a swimsuit." She turned her head to his ear and lowered her voice. "Not that you'd need it."

"So it's settled then?" David asked. "I won't have to wait until I get to New York to see you again?"

"No, it's not settled."

"Rick, you've already started shooting and you don't have a script?" Michael asked.

"Rick's very modern," Ruth said, her voice suddenly affected and grand. "He belongs to the *auteur* school of the cinema." She sniffed. "Very hoity-toity. He works out the script as we go." She turned to David. "I didn't know you were coming to New York."

"In a couple of weeks, I think. After I visit Washington."

"We just started yesterday," Rick said—"taking advantage of the beach. Great light here. We'll shoot the interiors later. You see, my films are rather improvisational. I have a general idea of what we want to do, we talk about it a little, and then we just shoot—see how it goes. I get some interesting surprises that way. I've been heavily influenced by Artaud and Grotowski and also Judith Malina. You know, the Living Theater."

"Yes," Andrew said, shifting his attention. "*Paradise Now.*"

"And *Dionysus in '69.*"

"I'd forgotten that one."

"Just as well," Michael said. "Have you had any screenings of your film?"

"*As You Like It*? No, it's in the can but I haven't let it out yet." He laughed.

"Too hot to handle?"

Ruth laughed. "You betcha! Right on the nose, Michael." Kevin glanced toward her, touched his hand to his cap in a kind of desultory salute, a trace of a smirk on his face. She grabbed the cap and put it on her head. "Where are you staying in New York?" she asked David.

"I don't know yet," he replied.

"You'd be welcome to stay with us," Ruth said. "We've got room. It might be a little crowded, but cozy. And certainly cheap. Hotels in New York aren't."

"I thought I could find something somewhere in Manhattan."

"Some dump, maybe. Stay with us."

"I'd be curious to see this film, Rick," Sam said.

"I'd *love* to see it," Ann said. "Why don't you arrange a screening for us when we get back to New York? Here you've got all these people in the business. Take advantage of them. They could be helpful."

"The theater business and the film business are poles apart," Andrew said.

"Oh, not that far, surely? You needn't have an official screening, Rick, just a private little showing for us," Ann said. "You could do it in our apartment. You must have a projector. It would be fun."

"Wouldn't it," Andrew said. "Excuse me. I'll be right back." Ann amazed him. His Fra Angelico! His Botticelli wife! And what about her husband? he asked himself. Hieronymus Bosch? Francis Bacon? He went into the lounge, saw the cigarettes were still on the table, took one, and went to the bathroom. No, he didn't have to smoke it there. He returned to the group and asked David for a light.

"Are you really going to stay on?" David asked him.

"No, I don't think I possibly can." Andrew glanced toward him, and quickly away. "I don't do well away from home."

"I'm sorry."

"Yes, I am too."

"You're not angry with me, are you?"

"Of course not. I have no reason to be angry with you." He stopped, looked across the deck, saw himself and David reflected in Kevin's impenetrable anthracite lenses, their two images twinned and doubled. "Not that anybody needs reasons." He laughed. "I'm angry at those glasses. I hate them. Don't you?" Actually, he wanted to break them. "No, my friend, I'm not angry with you." Well, he'd had to see him again, and now he'd seen him. "Bear with me." He didn't know what to do about it, didn't know what he wanted to do about it, what he could do about it. It was preposterous on the face of it. He rubbed his forehead. Preposterous? It was *mad*! He felt dizzy again, felt himself sliding. It was so utterly unlike him. Wasn't it? He felt something flutter, like wings, in the emptiness deep inside. That wasn't his desire at all! He shuddered. The blood drained in a rush from his head. He grasped the rail to steady himself. The lost object of desire. But what had he lost, and when? Andrew moved to touch David's arm, started to speak, recovered, stopped. He walked slowly away, picked up a mask and fitted it to his face, biting down on the mouthpiece.

David walked over to Ann. "Have you seen Mrs. Curtis since London?"

"We saw her last week in New York."

"Too bad she's not here," Michael said. "The party would be complete." Andrew looked at him though the mask. "What I meant, shithead"—Michael spoke out of the side of his mouth— "was that all your obsessions would be on board. On second thought, it's a good thing she's not. The collective weight might sink the ship."

Andrew released the breathing tube—"Thanks"—and took off the goggles.

The launch had been lowered now, and Ruth and Ann were climbing down. Rick was busying himself with his cameras, testing the light, checking his lenses. "Women and children first," Michael said.

"We're not abandoning ship," Sam responded. "We're just taking a little run over the reef for a look into the deep." He directed Kevin and Yasmine toward the ladder, and followed them down himself. "Room for one more," Sam shouted. "Who's coming?" Suddenly Rick stopped playing with his cameras and jumped into the boat, giving the launch a shove away from the ship. It started slowly off. Kevin had abandoned the spear; that was good. Andrew thought it more likely he'd spear himself or one of them than a fish. He watched them line up on either side of the window at the bottom of the boat and sit huddled there, peering down into the water, intent.

Andrew turned to Michael. "I think I'll abandon it, though." He walked to the end of the ship, stood poised there for a moment, and dived off the side, into the clear blue sea.

"Nice dive," Ruth shouted from the launch. She was still wearing Kevin's cap. "Just holler when you need my hammer-lock."

"I don't need it yet," Andrew called back. "Hey, Kevin, let her practice on you." He swam to the side of the ship, reaching for the ladder, and shouted to Michael. "Throw me my mask, will you? And some flippers? I think I'll do a little exploring on my own."

It was David who responded, tossing him the things and diving in with his own. "Never swim in the ocean alone," he said, coming up, shaking the spray from his head, treading water.

"Aren't you going to wait and go out on the boat?" Andrew was clinging to the ladder with one hand, holding his flippers with the other, the goggles and breathing tube hanging from his neck.

"I'm happy doing this."

"I'd like to ask you to stay with us in New York, but you know it's not possible." He put on his flippers.

"No. I know it's not."

"I'm going to swim now." Andrew fixed the mask to his face, blew through the tube, took a breath, and choked. "Nice try," he said, gasping. "I should have listened to the lesson." David laughed. "I'll do better this time." He cleared the breathing tube, clamped it tightly between his jaws, and leaving David behind, swam slowly off, the air at his back and the sea at his belly, a strange new denizen of that margin between two opposing elements. He adjusted his breathing tube, his connection to the familiar, sustaining world he knew, and peered through the mask that admitted him to the other he did not. Sea fans wavered in the easy currents. An exotically colored sea anemone reached toward him. Mysterious fronds and tendrils brushed against his slowly moving legs. He saw a fish, then another, suddenly a myriad of brilliant, magical creatures darting before him, below him, around him—within reach of his fingers, it seemed, but the underwater world was illusive. The light was different there. He heard David call something; the voice was faint, distant, and he couldn't distinguish the words. He swam on, his ears filled with the soft rustling of the sea, his eyes with the fantastic shapes of coral, the colors so surreal, the shimmering watery light, and the unfamiliar creatures moving there before his pearled eyes. A world of marvels and incredible life, fascinating, rich, and strange, hypnotically beautiful. An entire other living world sustained by the vast whelming slough of the sea, visible to him only through goggles with breathing tubes, and no more accessible than the moon or Mars. It amazed him. He watched the bubbles flowing between his fingers, the beads of light clinging to his hands and arms, his legs, his body. He felt magical, transformed. He swam on, heard a melody in his mind:

> *Full fathom five thy father lies;*
> *Of his bones are coral made;*
> *Those are pearls that were his eyes:*
> *Nothing of him that doth fade*
> *But doth suffer a sea change*
> *Into something rich and strange.*

He looked at his arms, each hair beaded with amazing, aqueous transforming light. Oh, he was a water person, born in a water sign. It was his element. He glowed like a fish as he moved easily through the water. A coral cavern slowly opened below him. He could dive into it, for a moment. It would be possible. He gulped deeply of the air and forced himself down, grasping at a coral limb. It was sharp. He kicked with his flippers, struggling to go deeper, pushing himself off from the coral, and down toward the dappled cavern; deeper still, to make water his domain, fighting against his natural buoyancy, the limitations of his lungs. He thought of the Hart Crane line *"uneaten of the earth or aught earth holds"* and stared into the deep. It was true: the water was amazingly clear, transparent as old glass, and the light caused only the smallest distortion. But was something there? The brilliantly colored fish—cheerful things—swam quickly about. No, something else. He looked, strained to see, almost weightless in this other world where gravity seemed suspended, seemed, in fact, to work on him the other way, urging him up, not down. Yes, there was something, something below him, lurking in the crevice. He peered, his lungs aching: a great unmoving fish—he might have touched it!—pewter in the wavering light, an awesome thing, hanging there suspended in its element. Truly an awesome, terrible thing. He could see its mouth, its teeth. There was no question but that this was not a benign fish. He did not know what it was, but it was not benign. Benign fish did not look like that, gleam with that intensity, that flat, deadly color of cooling lead. Its teeth were made for shredding. He bolted, tried frantically to rise to the surface, kicking hard, and broke the water, shot out of it gasping and choking into a clump of weeds. He brushed them from his face, couldn't see the boat, couldn't see anything but the swelling sea and, looking down, the giant hypnotic creature rising slowly, effortlessly, gracefully from the depths, moving without a ripple, as indifferent as God. Andrew felt paralyzed, felt as if the sea were leather. He tried to swim, but where? Where was the ship? The launch? The currents had carried him farther than he'd realized. He tore off the mask, looked frantically about, still saw nothing but the clump of weeds floating in the trough of the swell, the sun beating down, and the endlessly heaving, all-engulfing sea. He felt the fish moving close behind him, casual and indifferent. Oh, where was he? Lost in the weeds. Lost in the weeds but swimming. Nothing was fixed, nothing solid. *Thalassa. Thalassa mou, sas agapo.* Ah, Julia, look at your father now. He shuddered, sensed the nearness of the creature. A rising swell carried him up, up, and there—far off, it seemed—the white ship rode on the water; he could not see the launch. He began swimming for it, watched it disappear as he sank, his heart sinking, in the trough, appear again as he rose buoyant on the trembling surge and kicking still—as steadily, as evenly as possible so as not to disturb the water, the fish in the water—he moved, inch, it seemed, by excruciating inch, toward it, followed ever so closely by his companion of the deep whose element it truly was. Yes, the currents had carried him far, but slowly, so slowly, they were carrying him back. He was swimming hard, drawing closer now, felt a nudge against his leg, swam faster, almost there, saw the ladder, lunged for it, seized it, and in one continuous motion—he hadn't known he had the strength —flung himself gasping from the sea. He clung there on the ladder, looking down, saw the creature bump the ship.

"What's wrong?" He turned. The captain was leaning above him.

"Look!" He pointed, his chest heaving. "Look!"

"It's a giant barracuda! That's surprising. I wonder what he's doing around here. Unusual to find a predator like that in this desert. Must be a rogue." Andrew started to shake, violently. "What's the matter?" He stared at the fish, couldn't talk. "Oh, he won't bother you. Here, let me give you a hand." The captain reached for his arm and pulled him aboard. "Where'd you find him?"

"Out there," Andrew said, pointing, shaking still.

"They're nothing to worry about. He's a big one, though. You don't very often see them that big."

Andrew shivered. His teeth were rattling. "He's bigger than I am, for Christ's sake!"

The captain looked. "I guess he is. But they never attack."

"Never?"

"Well, if they're hungry, I suppose. Or if they feel cornered. They can be dangerous if they feel cornered. Probably this fellow was just curious. Wanted to know who this guy was in the water. He followed you home. Hey, where are your goggles? Did you go out there without your goggles? You missed the fun. You see a lot more with goggles on."

"My goggles?" Andrew raised his hand to his shoulder, felt for the goggles. "I don't know. I must have lost them."

"Let me get you a drink. We've got some good rum. The second group is out in the launch. We'll eat as soon as they get back. You've got a treat in store."

"Thanks." The captain went into the lounge and came out with his drink, set it down beside him. Andrew reached for a towel and wrapped himself in it, staring at the drink. He got up, walked over to the side, and peered into the water. The fish was not there. He returned to his chair. Everyone must be in the bow. He was just as glad.

"You must have had quite a swim." It was Ann, coming around the side of the boat with a drink in her hand. "But you should have gone out in the boat. The view was fantastic."

"I'm glad you liked it."

"And now I've been sitting in the bow trying to make some plans. Your friend reminded me when he asked about Daisy: are we going to Sharksmouth? We've got to decide. She's got plans to make too."

"What?"

"Sharksmouth. We have to think about that. Are we going, and if so, when? We have to let Daisy know as soon as we get back."

"I've already been there."

"What? Why do you sound so funny? What's wrong?"

"Nothing," he said, picking up his drink, raising it to his lips. He hated the smell of rum. "Nothing." He put it down without tasting it.

The launch pulled up to the stern, and Marika and Michael, David, Jack, and Molly climbed up to the ship, full of enthusiasm for their adventure. None of them, it was generally agreed, had ever seen anything like the wonders they'd beheld in these waters —the variety of fish, the fantastical coral shapes, the gorgeous colors; even an old wreck—and over drinks and while lunch was being prepared and served, they recounted the highlights of the two excursions for one another's benefit. "And a little octopus!" Ruth exclaimed.

"Somehow I missed that," Andrew said.

"Well, you should have gone out in the boat instead of swimming around by yourself."

"I suppose I should have, but I saw some interesting things too."

"Like what?"

"Like a fish," Andrew replied, laughing. "But no Fingerfins."

"What's that?"

"A character in a book I had when I was a child. A tiny Sargasso fish. He lived in the weeds—colored very like the world of weeds he lived in. Interesting. Probably he was there; I just didn't notice him. Too bad. I wanted to spy him."

"Are you still reading children's books, Andrew?"

"Sometimes, Ruth. Sometimes." He laughed: "To keep my fragile innocence intact." He finished his lunch—the captain was right: the fish was delicious—and took one of David's cigarettes when he offered it. "I'm sorry, David, that I can't stay longer. I'm leaving tomorrow." He shaded his eyes from the sun.

"I'm sorry too," David said. "I'll have to see you in New York, then." He climbed to the deck above them and stood motionless, remote, cool as marble, looking out to sea. Andrew sat watching him, wondering what he was contemplating, if statues contemplated anything.

"I've changed my mind," Ann said, seating herself in the chair David had vacated. "You're mesmerized by him." She followed his gaze.

Andrew looked at her, looked away. Haze floated in patches above the water now, smoky, like steam rising. The captain was explaining it: the hot sun beating down on the surface of the sea caused it to evaporate at a greater rate than the air could absorb, and the moisture recondensed and hung there like smoke. "Sea smoke," he said. "Think of the sea as a huge, gently simmering caldron. That's pretty much the effect."

There's always an explanation, Andrew thought. He quietly regarded his cigarette, idly watched its smoke, the smoke on the water. The day was so clear, yet his sight was not. The figure of David stood in a kind of blur on the upper deck, an interesting angle, an interesting composition. Maybe it was the atomized light—or just the sea smoke, and the smoke from his cigarette lazily twining in the vaporous still air, a little veil to soften the images of the world, keep its sharp edges at bay. "I can't help saying it." Ann rested her hand gently on his arm. "I wish you wouldn't do that." Yes, the smoke worked the other way, too, obscuring him from the world's eye, diverting its attention to the slender tube of tobacco in his fingers.

"I do too," he said. His eyes fell on Kevin's glasses again, indiscriminately mirroring everything he faced. He wondered if he could surreptitiously remove them and drop them over the side. Thinking of glasses, he should probably have his eyes examined. He'd worn glasses for a time in college, but then he'd found a doctor who'd given him eye exercises—a crazy doctor, the Messiah of the Eyes, who'd said the exercises he'd give him would change his vision, change his posture, change his life— and he'd made him throw the glasses away. He'd also told him to wear bigger shoes! Dr. Messiah's own posture, Andrew had noted, was fairly bad. Maybe he needed glasses again; sometimes his vision did seem a little out of focus, or at least less sharp than it used to be. He'd have to remember to make an appointment. One more thing to worry about: going blind. Maybe someone would give him a stick to guide him. Still, better than a brain tumor. Of course, it could be both. Unlikely. It didn't concern him much. He flipped the cigarette over the side. The captain was leaving now. Time to start the engines. The crew hoisted the launch from the water, suspending it between the davits. He heard the windlass cranking the anchor up and soon the ship was moving, the wind sweeping briskly across the stern, people anchoring their napkins, whatever was loose, many of them heading into the lounge. David disappeared. The captain came out onto the back of the bridge, where David had been standing. "Hey, there," he called. Andrew looked up. "You wanted to see the sargasso weed? Come on up. We're coming onto a patch." Andrew climbed up to the bridge deck, and farther up to the flying bridge, the captain following him. He looked out to sea. There it was, all right, a large raft of it off the starboard bow. "Think of the life out there!" the captain exclaimed.

"Yes," Andrew said, "amazing."

"Well, that's the Sargasso Sea."

"I've already seen it, I think."

"That's true, you have. You were in it." The captain looked at him. "Gave you a little surprise, too, didn't it?"

Andrew gave a little laugh. "Yes, it did that," he replied, and the captain started below. Andrew stopped him. "Got a cigarette, by any chance?"

"Certainly. Here you are. Some matches in the drawer here. Take another while you're at it."

"Thank you." He took the cigarettes. "I think I'll sit up here for a while. I like the view." When the captain had left, Andrew lay down on the bench, covering his eyes with his arm to protect them from the sun. He'd left his glasses somewhere.

"I see you're smoking again." It was Michael.

"Yes."

"It would be good for you to stop hiding behind that cigarette, but I guess there's nothing I can do about it."

"Probably not."

"It's a convenient little smoke screen, I suppose. Yes, that's what it is. You think it can't be penetrated. But it works better the other way. *You* can't penetrate it, with that smoke around your face."

"Thanks. I think I'll go down now. It looks as if we're heading back." Michael followed him to the stern. "Oh, look! Kevin's left his sunglasses," Andrew said. "That was a mistake." He picked them up, tried them on, and turned to face Michael. "How do you look?" he asked.

"Don't you mean how do *you* look?"

"No. I mean how do *you* look. In the mirrors, stupid."

Ruth came running around the side. "Take off the goggles, boys. We're taking pictures in the bow. It's time to unmask."

Andrew took off the glasses. "I already have."

"Oh, no, you haven't," she said. "You've got a way to go yet. But it's slipping a little."

"Only a little," Michael said.

"Come on. Let's go." She returned to the bow.

"You know, I hate these things," Andrew said, looking at the glasses in his hand. "I think I'll do myself a favor." He looked around to see if anyone was watching, walked to the rail, and dropped them over the side. "There!"

"What a gracious thing to do," Michael said. Suddenly he laughed. "I'm sorry I didn't think of it first."

"You can't think of everything, my friend. You think of more than enough as it is."

Molly came around the side, beckoning to them. "Hurry up, you two. You're holding up the photos."

"The last tragic photos," Michael said with a grimace.

"Broadway Babies Lost at Sea," Andrew said.

"Writing headlines again?"

"The *Daily News* would never pass it." They headed toward the bow.

"Line up, everybody. This adventure's got to be immortalized." Rick was running around with his cameras around his neck, Kevin following with the bag of equipment, everyone falling into place. He sighted through the lens and shot the group. "Okay," he said, "now we do couples." He snapped Molly and Sam, then Ann and Andrew, Michael with Marika and Yasmine —"Still trying to figure out who's the couple there," he said, winking—then Ruth and Kevin and Jack.

"Try to figure that one out, buster," Michael muttered.

"That's been done," Andrew said to him, "only you don't know it."

"We're all family," Rick replied. "No problem there. Happy families are all alike." He bustled about. "Okay, now a group shot of the girls." He arranged the five women against the rail, the sea behind them. "Think of this as your screen test, ladies." They all waved, and he snapped them several times. "Okay, gotta get the boys. Let's get the captain down here." While they were waiting, he took various other clusters: Michael and Andrew and Sam, Kevin and Jack, then Andrew with them and Andrew with Michael, with Ruth, with David: virtually every possible combination, it seemed. When the captain appeared, Rick posed him with Sam in front of the bridge and took the picture, and everyone applauded.

"I want a picture of Andrew and me," Marika said.

Andrew laughed. "You'll see me again," he said, "but thanks. I'd like that," and he posed with her, arm in arm. "Oh, take another while you're at it," and he put his arm over her shoulder and drew her to him, laughing.

"But Rick," Ann said, "you're not in a single picture."

"We'll take care of that now," he said. He began setting it up, arranging the captain and every member of the group in the prow of the ship. "Let's get one of the crew over here to take it." The captain called and a young man appeared. Rick focused the lens, instructing him on the camera, then jumped into the frame and the crewman photographed the laughing voyagers, women in front, men behind them, smiling.

Andrew turned to Michael. "This could be used as evidence, you know."

"Evidence of what?" David asked, from his other side.

"Evidence of a wonderful day at sea, of course. Didn't you enjoy it?"

"Yes, certainly. Who wouldn't?"

"Yes, a wonderful day at sea," Andrew said as the group dispersed, returning to their drinks, their conversation, to recount once again the adventures of the day. Occasionally the captain joined them to point out some sight or other—a hidden wreck, a school of dolphins leaping; once, even, a humpback whale in the distance. Andrew saw a small, sky-blue squid shoot out of the water, and any number of flying fish, and still more dolphins. The sea was full of life; it was hard to think of it as a desert. What could a fertile sea be like? While the light held, Rick busied himself with trying to photograph the fish, but Andrew doubted that he was having much success. The ship, its lights twinkling now, was nearing home. It passed smartly between the two buoys marking the inner reef and headed into the harbor, gleaming whitely in the dusk, toward the dock, quiet now after the revelry of the morning but with a few remnants of the streamers there still, Andrew noticed, on the empty dock.

"You didn't need your knife," Ann said as they were disembarking.

"My knife?"

"Your silver knife. For the waterspouts, remember? We didn't see a waterspout."

"No, I guess we didn't," Andrew said, surprised. "We didn't see a waterspout."

There was a brisk wind at the airport the next day. Strange how there always seemed to be a brisk wind at airports. Andrew was anxious to be home. Sam and Michael had scheduled a late lunch with a lighting designer in the city, and they had all flown together on an earlier plane. Andrew wished he'd been on the earlier flight, too, but Ann preferred to keep the reservations they had. The Walcotts must be sick of seeing their faces, she'd said, and frankly she was tired of seeing theirs as well, not to mention Michael's. As they were waiting to board the plane, Andrew noticed a familiar-looking couple checking in. Of course! It was the honeymoon couple he'd seen at dinner the night they'd arrived, the couple he'd seen at that place they went dancing the next night, and sent the champagne to. He smiled at them, felt an overwhelming urge to say something to them, to wish them well. "Excuse me," he said to Ann, "I'll be right back."

"Where are you going?" she asked.

"I want to say something to that couple over there." He walked over to them. They were still in line. "This may sound crazy," he began—they looked a little startled—"but I wanted to say hello to you, to speak to you. You were in the restaurant the night we arrived and I noticed you because you looked so happy. I wanted to wish you well. I assume you've just gotten married?" He rushed on. "I wanted to wish you a nice life—no, a good life. That's all I wanted." He stopped. They appeared puzzled, perhaps slightly annoyed.

"We're not married," the man said, "but thanks anyway," and he turned back to the girl at his side.

Andrew felt chagrined. How stupid of him! No one got married these days. What was he doing, intruding into their lives, making all these assumptions? "Well, good luck, anyway," he said, rather lamely. "I meant well," and he returned to his seat.

"What was that all about?" Ann asked.

"I saw them at dinner the night we arrived. I just wanted to wish them good luck," he said, taking his book from his bag and opening it.

"They didn't seem too interested," she said, but Andrew was already buried in his book.

In a few minutes, the flight was called. "Back to the real world," he said, rising, picking up his bag. "No more Fantasy Island."

"I thought it was real enough," Ann said. "You should have stayed on. You could have, you know. I wouldn't have minded. I've got a million things to do when I get back."

"Well, I didn't stay."

"If it's any consolation, those who run across the sea change the climate, not their spirit. That's Horace:

"caelum non animum mutant
qui trans mare currunt."

She laughed. "I can quote Latin too."

"There's something to be said for a change in climate. Did you ever read Catullus?"

"No."

"That's funny. You studied a lot more Latin than I did. Well, maybe you wouldn't have. I don't suppose he played well with the Madams of the Sacred Heart."

"You might be surprised."

"No. Too dirty."

As they were boarding, Ann said, "You know, I just thought of something funny. Rick is so superstitious. He told me he wouldn't live in a building with a thirteenth floor."

"Yes, Ruth told me something like that too."

"But in that last photo he took yesterday—the one of the whole group?—there were thirteen people in it."

"There couldn't have been. There were only twelve of us."

"Yes, there were twelve of us—but the captain made thirteen. Rick'll have a fit when he notices that. And I'll bet he will."

"Maybe he'll destroy the negatives."

"Not before I get a look at them. I'll have to call Ruth, tell her to protect them." They'd found their seats now and were stowing their baggage in the compartment above them.

"What's in the little bag?" Andrew asked her.

"It's something for Julia. I found it in the gift shop at the hotel this morning."

"What is it?"

"Just a silly T-shirt." She pulled it out of the bag and held it up for him to look at. It had three small shells printed on it with the word BERMUDA emblazoned across it.

"I thought you already got her that shell."

"She'll like this better, I think. And I decided to keep the shell for myself."

"You did? Why?"

"Because I like it. I wanted it."

"It's more your size, I guess." He returned to his book.

"What's wrong?"

"Nothing. I saw a fish, that's all."

"Sometimes I think you read too much. It affects your imagination."

"That's what my mother used to say."

"I wish you wouldn't read now, anyway. I'd like you to talk to me."

He closed the book, marking his place with his finger. "What would you like to talk about?"

"The trip, whatever. What did you like best about Bermuda?"

"The sea, I guess. There's not much else."

"I liked meeting Ruth and Rick. They're not like the theater people we're usually with. They actually seem interested in something other than themselves."

"Maybe movie people are different."

"He's really a teacher. I think movies are just a sideline."

"He seems pretty serious about them to me." Andrew looked out the window. "The plane's taking off."

"Yes, and you seem to have control of yourself. You're improving. I expected you to demand a parachute when we were flying back from London."

Andrew laughed. "You're wearing that amulet I gave you. That must be it." He put the book aside and touched his finger lightly to the amber pendant hanging from her neck. "My heart. It makes all the difference."

"No, *my* heart, my pretty heart. I didn't realize it was one of your amulets."

"It is. Take good care of it, it's precious. Let me see it. Take it off."

"Why?"

"Just let me have it for a second. I want to show you something."

She handed it to him. It felt warm and resinous. He took a sheet of the tissue paper that Julia's shirt was wrapped in and tore it into pieces. He rubbed the heart vigorously against his trousers. Then he passed it above the bits of paper, watched them tremble and jump fluttering to the small, misshapen heart.

She looked at him and shrugged. "What's the significance of that?"

"Nothing. It just takes an electrical charge, that's all." He handed it back to her. "It's merely interesting, an interesting phenomenon. Like so many other things."

"In your funny, hodge-podge, helter-skelter mind."

"Yes." He looked at her and smiled—a funny, silly kind of smile. Then he turned to the window, stared out for a while, into the mist.

"What are you thinking about now?"

"My story. Julia's story."

"Are you trying to figure out how to get your funny trio back to Australia?"

"Yes, that's what I'm doing. Trying to get them to Australia." He continued gazing out the window.

"Where are they now?"

He looked at her. "Where are they now?"

"That's what I said."

He turned back to the window, looked out into the gauzy silver mist. The light had no visible source but emanated from the mist itself and shrouded them in its luminous cocoon. "Lost in the weeds," he said. "Lost in the weeds, but swimming."